APOTHEOSIS

NICHOLAS CRIVAC

Stark Road Publishing, Michigan

Visit the author's website at www.NicholasCrivac.com.

Cover design by Kristin Cronkright.

Author photo by Dave Harrell of The Crooked Porch Photography.

First Edition January 2020

Format: I

ISBN: 978-1-7332921-0-8

Library of Congress Cataloging-in-Publication Data has been applied for.

For Mom and Dad

APOTHEOSIS

Ca. No. 2432615184
Document 19, REDACTED. Filed 3/16.
Copy: Correspondence between unknown scientist
and Theodore Sullivan, head of EXLI Corp.

———

Mr. Sullivan:

I must reach out one last time because I believe the new procedure is
XXX XXXX XXX XXX XXXXXXXXX. With all due respect, you may
not be thinking clearly about XXX XXXXXXX XXXXXXXXXX XX
XXXX XXXXXXXX XXXXXXX. Please understand I do not wish to
XXXXXXXX XXXX XXX, but do so with the best interests of EXLI XXX
XXXXXXXXX in mind.

Yes, the newest iteration of the procedure has shown unprecedented
advancements XXXX XXXXXX XX XXXXXX XXXXXXX
XXXXXXXXXX in parallel with established effects on acquired immunity and telomere degradation prevention. However, we've still made
no headway in XXXXXXXX XXX XXXXXXX XXXXX XX XXX XXXXX
XXXXX. Test subjects continue to display XXXXXXXXX
XXXXXXXXXX XXXX XXXXX XX XX XXXX XX XXXXXXXXX. Over
time, the resulting XXXXXX XXXXXXX XXXXX XX XXXXXXX
XXXXXXXX XXXXX XXXXXXX in 99% of patients.

I realize the new procedure has the potential to be significantly lucra-
tive for EXLI. But XX XXXXXXXX XXXX XXXXXXXXX XXXX XXXXXX
XXXXXX XXX XXXXXXXX XXXX XXXXX XX XXXXXXXXX XX XXX
XXXXX XXXXXX. XX XXXXX it's been so long since The Decay
XXXX XXX XXXXX XXX XXXXXXXXX Rejuvenation's true purpose.

I am grateful for Rejuvenation, **XXX XX XXXXXX XXXXX XXXX XXX XX XX** this stage of human history. **XX XXX XXX XXXX XXX XXXXXX XXX XXXXX XX XXXX XXX XXXXX XXXX** saved our species. **XX XX XXXXXXX XXXX XXX X XXX XX XXX XXXX XXXX XXX XXXX XXXX XXXXX XXX XX XXXXXX XX XXXXX XXX XXX XXX**.

I am filing paperwork for an additional period of investigation before release. Please consider this request **XXX XXX XXXX XX** EXLI **XXX XXX XXXXX XXXXX XXXX**.

Respectfully,

Dr. **XXXXXXXX XXXXX**
Senior Scientific Advisor, EXLI Advanced Senolytics

PROLOGUE

WHEN SEBASTIAN MARTIN WOKE IN THE MIDDLE OF THE NIGHT, he knew something was wrong. It wasn't the strange dream he'd been having about a familiar forest or sterile hospital hallways that troubled him. It wasn't the lurching of his stomach, which he blamed on the deep-fried food he'd eaten for lunch in the work cafeteria the previous day. It wasn't even the dull aching he felt in every limb and corner of his body. It was his breath, ragged and stressed, each one a struggle, his lungs burning. His entire body was covered in sweat. The shorts and t-shirt he wore were damp as if he'd been sleepwalking outside in a rainstorm.

Was this what sickness felt like? *Real* sickness? Sebastian had no basis for comparison, but this certainly felt like what he'd read about. Maybe he really had come down with something. An illness or even, a disease.

No, he thought. That didn't happen anymore. Not to people like him. It was impossible.

But something was definitely wrong. Even lying still in bed, his body was stiff and weak as if exhausted after a long day of manual labor. The covers of his bed felt like a blanket of bricks and Sebastian labored to peel them away. When he did, the fresh air of the room rushed over his burning body, and he shivered as his skin broke out in gooseflesh. He struggled against the stiffness in his arms and legs, and pulled himself to a sitting position on the edge of the bed, his stomach churning, every inch of his body aching as he moved.

He looked at the clock on the bedside table, but the red, luminescent numbers were unrecognizable—his vision blurry. Sebastian clenched his eyelids tight, rubbed them with creaky knuckles, then opened his eyes again. He still saw only fuzzy shapes where the clear numbers of the clock should have been.

Sebastian steadied his feet on the floor, then grabbed the edge of the bed and, with all his strength, pushed himself to a standing position. Splintering pain coursed through his body and it took all he had to not collapse. His joints cracked as he tried to straighten his spine, but it remained stiff, only able to go so far. Sebastian let out a painful groan and tried to curse, but it came out as a mumble.

He made his way toward the bathroom, the weakness in his hunched body fighting him the entire way. His knees wobbled with each step. He licked at his dry, cracked lips as he staggered through the dark bedroom and into the bathroom. When he turned on the light it was like someone set off a flash-grenade, only there was no loud bang, just a blast of intense light. The brightness radiating from the bulbs above the mirror over the sink burned at his eyes. He reached up to shield them and, after a few moments, slowly opened his eyes again. The light still stung, but he was starting to adjust.

When he pulled his hand away from his face, Sebastian felt a few strands of the hair above his forehead come with it. *Why in the hell was his hair coming out?* He rolled the hair between his fingers. It felt thin and brittle. He lifted the strands closer to get a better look. He turned it this way and that in the bright light and saw the hair was unmistakably gray.

That can't be right, he thought. It must be the light playing tricks. He didn't get gray hairs. No one who went through Rejuvenation at a young age did. But there they were, *gray hairs*. Maybe they'd been there all along and he had just never noticed it until now. Younger people going gray wasn't unheard of, especially those dealing with stressful situations at work or—

His stomach gave a hefty churn. Sebastian dropped the hair and fell to the toilet where he vomited. Each prickling heave strained the muscles in his back and throat. When he had emptied his stomach, Sebastian wiped at his panting mouth and stood. Pain spiked across his knees where they'd hit the hard tile floor. He rubbed at them, finding the skin tender as if deep bruises had already formed, and wondered yet again just what the hell was happening. First weakness in his body and light sensitivity, then the gray hairs and vomiting, and now his knees.

He ran the sink faucet, leaned over, and began to scoop handfuls of cold water into his mouth in the hopes of removing that acidic taste of vomit from his tongue. One gulp, spit. Another, now drinking the water as he brought each handful to his mouth. It was then, this close to his eyes where his vision wasn't so blurry, that Sebastian finally took notice of the hand he'd been using to scoop up the water. He could see it clearly but it didn't look like his hand at all. The palm he saw was wrinkled, the skin sagging slightly. He turned the hand over and looked at the back where he saw even more wrinkles and dark spots in the skin.

He pushed himself up from the sink and squinted at his reflection in the mirror. Even with his blurred vision at this distance, the reflection Sebastian saw was unfamiliar. A trick of the light or his hazy vision, perhaps? But he'd seen his hand clearly, hadn't he? And it was different. He raised and lowered an arm, watching it in the mirror. When he moved, so did the blurred figure. But it couldn't be him. He knew his shape, and that . . . *that* was not him. Sebastian leaned over the sink more, as close as he could, almost pressing his nose to the glass. His back ached, but what Sebastian saw held him rooted in place.

The entirety of his once dark hair was gone, replaced by thin strands of gray and white where it had not already fallen out. The smooth, healthy skin of his face had been replaced by flesh wrinkled even more than his hands and with a few of the same dark, age spots. He looked down his arms and saw they too had changed, now boney, the creased skin sagging off. Sebastian *felt* the same, his mind clear, but his body had grown old.

He stumbled away from the mirror. His back rammed into the empty towel rack on the wall behind him, sending a new jolt of shooting pain up his back.

No. That reflection. The figure in the mirror. That weak, aged body, it couldn't be his. But even as he denied it, he saw his reflection move with him again and thought: *this isn't possible.* He'd only been asleep for five, maybe six hours. It must be a dream. There's no way this could be happening to him.

Sebastian backed out of the bathroom, disoriented. He stumbled around his dark bedroom, trying to understand what was happening. His body throbbed with pain, creaked, felt tired and frail. His breathing grew even more ragged.

Help. He needed help. Whatever was happening to him, he couldn't handle it on his own. He needed help—fast.

Sebastian staggered to the window, looking across his front yard to the quiet street below, where the world glistened with moonlight. He stared across the street and, through his blurry vision, thought he saw a tiny glow in the distance, a hazy yellow circle—a light on in the main level of his neighbor's house.

He pounded on the window, screaming, but Sebastian saw no movement across the street. He thrashed at the window again, screamed with every breath of air in his lungs until he felt his weakened body sink, heavy on his knees. And still, he stared forward, sure his neighbor, *someone*, might hear or see him . . .

but there was no one. He pressed his forehead against the window, felt the coolness of the glass even as his breath fogged it up. He was exhausted, defeated.

His phone!

Sebastian spun away from the window, stumbling toward his phone on the bedside table, but tripped in the darkness and, this time, couldn't stop his descent.

He extended his right hand instinctively to break the fall, and felt bones in his hand and wrist snap. Sebastian howled, the pain excruciating. But his injured arm almost instantly became an afterthought as his right leg and hip crashed into the hard floor and broke as well. The pain that emanated from these larger broken bones shot through his body in every direction. Tears filled Sebastian's eyes as his body throbbed, his head swam and he was sure the agony and shock would overwhelm him. He was going to pass out—

The sound of the front door opening downstairs brought him back from the brink. Sebastian lay on the floor, tears running down his cheeks, moaning out in pain from his broken body, but he was sure he heard the loud click of the doorknob's mechanism closing. He stifled his sobs, listened closely. More noise: this time shuffling in the entranceway, like someone removing their coat.

It must be his neighbor, Sebastian thought. Somehow, someway, his neighbor *had* been awake and heard him from across the street. *He was saved!*

"Hello?" a voice called from downstairs . . . though it wasn't the voice of the man across the street.

But it *was* a voice Sebastian knew.

What was *he* doing here? He never visited anyone. You visited him, but only when summoned. That was how it worked. That was how it had always worked.

So why was *he* here? And in the middle of the night, no less.

It made no sense. The pain in Sebastian's stomach, the rapid aging. And now the man downstairs. None of it made any—

And then it all clicked into place—like a rediscovered memory. Sebastian finally understood. All of it connected, even the strange dreams he'd been having the last few days, all leading to his unexpected midnight caller—he realized the unbelievable circumstances of what was happening and why.

He didn't have long. Sebastian gathered what strength he had left in his newly aged, broken body and began to pull himself across the bedroom floor with his remaining good hand. His broken bones ground and shifted under the skin each time he reached forward, each time he dragged himself another few inches. His head went light again, hazy, but Sebastian gritted his teeth to stave off the sensation. No! He would not pass out! He had to fight through it!

He pulled himself onward, and each time he paused, Sebastian listened for the mysterious visitor downstairs. Had he heard Sebastian's moans, his movements? No, the footsteps were in the living room . . . then the kitchen . . . slow, searching footsteps around the lower level of the house. The dining room . . . the pantry . . . the bathroom . . .

The visitor had covered most of the first floor already. Soon he'd head upstairs. There wasn't much time.

Sebastian tried to move faster, but the *agony*, the white-hot searing of his muscles, the crunch of his broken bones was too much. He couldn't—

But he had to. Sebastian held his shortened breath and bit his lower lip to stifle his moans, reaching forward again, dragging. And again. Faster, ignoring the pain. The thick, coppery taste of blood on his tongue as it dripped from his lip where his teeth sank in. He crawled on, across the floor, and finally reached his bedside table. Sebastian collapsed, breathing fast as if he'd just finished a set of sprints. But there was no time to rest.

He looked back and saw the door to his room was wide open. He would be seen instantly by anyone who climbed up the stairs.

Sebastian listened for the visitor's footsteps again, but the house had gone quiet. He waited in silence, his body still but for the quick rise and fall of his chest. His breath and the throbbing in his head the only sounds he could hear. Perhaps it was—

But there were the footsteps again, making their way back through the downstairs level. The visitor's movements were casual. No rush. No panic. As though he were enjoying a slow tour of Sebastian's house. Only this time, they did not linger in each room. The footsteps passed through the rooms, doubling back for one last check as they moved on, deliberate—toward the stairs.

Sebastian reached his good arm up, stretching as high as he could and placed his old palm on the bedside table. He pulled his phone down to the floor, touched the screen, and opened the recent contacts. He saw his neighbor's number near the top of the short list, thought of the light on across the street. Maybe, Sebastian thought. *Maybe there was still time.* He dialed, lifted the phone to his ear, and heard it begin to ring.

Below, the visitor reached the bottom of the stairs and paused, listening. The stairwell light came on.

The phone continued ringing.

"Come on. Come—" Sebastian choked out, words faint and raspy in his dry throat. A cough stopped him for a moment. He cleared his throat then added, "Come on, pick up damn it."

The footsteps were on the stairs now, still slow, but getting closer.

The phone rang twice more, then went to voicemail. Sebastian's heart sank. As the greeting began to play out in his ear, Sebastian knew he'd been mistaken. There was no time. He wouldn't be able to call anyone else before the visitor found him. Even if Sebastian redialed, and his neighbor picked up, there would not be enough time. His neighbor would not be able to save him.

No one would.

Above all the unrelenting pain in his body, Sebastian felt this sick realization hit him. No one could save him. *This was it.* It was a strange thought. After so many years. It wasn't the way he had imagined it would happen. Certainly not after undergoing the procedure. Like it or not, the time had come. This was his end.

But he still had one more thing to do. The voicemail greeting playing in his ear ended with a soft beep and Sebastian left his message. As soon as he had finished, he heard the suave voice of his visitor again coming from the stairs.

"Drop that, would you?" the visitor said. His head was just above the landing, floating in the soft light of the stairwell and shadows of the upstairs hallway. He looked directly into Sebastian's bedroom, saw him lying on the floor with the phone pressed to his ear.

Sebastian ended the call. He froze as he watched the blurred image of the visitor climb the last few stairs, reach the second floor, and walk straight into the bedroom. The visitor stopped just inside the door, bathed in the moonlight streaking in from the window, looking down at Sebastian.

"Give that to me," he said, taking a single step toward the crippled form on the floor.

Sebastian narrowed his eyes at the man and raised the phone high in his wrinkled fist. With all the effort he had left in his tired, broken body, he slammed the phone down onto the floor. Once. Twice. Three times. He felt bones in his good hand snap each time he brought his hand down, but he also heard and felt the phone crack and then shatter.

The man near the door sneered.

"Clever," he said. "You clever *old* man."

The visitor stepped away from the door, slid over the chair

from underneath the side desk, and placed it a few feet away from Sebastian lying exhausted and broken on the floor, clenching his jaw from the pain. The man sat in the chair and looked down at Sebastian.

"It's . . . too . . . late," Sebastian said.

"For you. Me, well, I have my reasons for being here. Not that it's any of your concern right now," the man said. "But you *were* chosen. I hope it's some comfort to know that what is happening to you will have meaning. You see, Dr. Martin, you are going to help us, help our cause. The world even. You will aid us in the fight against those who, for misguided reasons, choose to oppose us."

The visitor leaned closer.

"Now, do not lie to me," he said. "What did he tell you?"

For the first time since he had woken up, Sebastian felt like he had a tiny shred of the upper hand. He forced a smirk. "Who?"

"You know who. What did he tell you? Who did you tell?"

"I don't . . . know what—"

"Damn it! Who did you call?"

Sebastian didn't answer, just looked up at the man with the same narrowed eyes.

"Please tell me who you called so you can at least die with a clear conscience, my friend."

Sebastian chuckled. He hadn't thought he had a laugh left in his busted body, but there it was, and he paid for it. The rumble of his stomach felt like knives stabbing at his torso.

"I am clear," Sebastian said. "So go . . . go fuck yourself. I'm not saying . . . anything."

The visitor paused, considered Sebastian for a moment.

"Very well. I hoped you would just tell me, but no matter. We have our ways of finding out anyway."

The two men looked at one another, silent. Sebastian expectant, and the visitor casual.

"So?" Sebastian said.

"So, what?"

"Aren't you going to . . . to kill me?"

The man in the chair grinned. "No, no, no. I'm afraid not." He paused, then leaned in closer. "But I *am* going to sit here and watch. Even if it takes the rest of the night. I am going to sit here and watch you continue to grow old, Sebastian Martin. I'm going to sit here and watch you die."

1

———

The alert pulsed bright red.

One Missed Call.

A call Simon would've gotten if he hadn't forgotten his phone last night.

He tapped the alert and saw, in addition to the call, there was a voicemail. Both were from his neighbor. The only one Simon had ever really become friends with, actually. A friendship born of shared circumstances. Lone bachelors in a neighborhood of long-together couples and growing families. But over time, Simon had got to know the guy pretty well thanks to their conversations over beers, barbecues, and Sentinels games. He was all right, that—

"Hey, isn't that your street?" Will said, putting down his cup, pointing to the TV mounted on the coffee shop wall over Simon's shoulder.

Simon looked up from his phone. Will was right. It *was* Simon's street.

"What the hell?" Simon said. The street on the TV, while recognizable to him, was anything but the quiet suburban neighborhood he knew: row after row of similar houses built on land plots wide enough to give each family room to enjoy their yard but still close enough to allow kids to shout from porch to porch about setting up the next game of street hockey. But what Simon saw when he looked at the TV screen was a street crowded with news vans, camera crews, police squad cars, and police officers trying to restrain a mob of onlookers.

Simon stood, still clutching his phone, and turned up the volume on the TV. He and Will stared at the news reporter on screen.

". . . haven't heard much more since we arrived on scene. The only new information we can report is that the body has been moved from the residence and is now on its way to the county medical examiner for a full autopsy, time permitting."

Simon stared at the screen in shock, but his eyes weren't on the reporter, or the chyron beneath her, which read: EXLI SCIEN-TIST FOUND DEAD IN HOME. Simon missed all that. It was what stood in the background beyond the reporter that caught his attention.

"I recognize that house," Simon said.

"Of course you do," Will said, trying for a bit of calm. "All the houses in your neighborhood look exactly the same."

"Sure, but . . . I recognize the lawn, the trees."

Will leaned forward in his chair, absentmindedly rubbing his clean-shaven, slender cheeks, and looked a little closer.

"You're right. I recognize them too. Isn't it—"

Simon nodded, his eyes growing wider. "Yeah," he said, glancing down at his phone then back up at the TV, finally reading the headline on the screen. "It's across the street from me. It's *Sebastian's* house."

Simon's gaze flashed between the phone in his hand and the news broadcast. With each sentence spoken by the reporter, each new detail shared, his unease grew. *Mysterious circumstances. No signs of a break-in. A rare disorder. Scientists handling harmful compounds. The possibility of exposure.* And Sebastian . . . his neighbor . . . his friend . . . dead.

It all sounded so impossible. Life had been so normal—just minutes before, when Simon had walked into the coffee shop feeling like it was any other weekday morning. He had just been meeting his friend for coffee before work, that's all. He'd agreed to grab the drinks while Will found a table and started reading the newspaper.

Simon had sat, sipped his coffee, and listened to the news according to Will. Whatever the current events might be, they always took on a unique spin when filtered through Will's perspective. After all, Simon knew his friend to be a man of many years, though you wouldn't know it to look at him. That day's topics included a recap of the latest Sentinels game, car recharge prices on the rise, and special coverage of a well-known activist named Darrow, speaking out against Rejuvenation. "Riling people up at some talk in Los Angeles a few days ago. And would ya look at that, says here she'll be downtown tomorrow speaking at the Rightland Center. Wanna go?" He'd said the last bit with a quick wink.

Simon had responded with a roll of his eyes and Will laughed in agreement. Their morning had been off to its usual, normal start. That was until Will had returned Simon's phone.

"It was wedged between the cushions of my couch. Must have slipped out of your pocket when you and Mags were over."

"How'd you find it then?"

"Because the damn thing started ringing in the middle of the night. Shoulda seen me, stumbling downstairs, half-asleep." He had paused, then added, "Who in the hell is calling you so late? You and Mags arguing again? Wait, it's not another . . . you're not—"

Simon had looked up at Will with a serious gaze and said,

"No. Definitely not. I'd never do that." Will raised his eyebrows and Simon added, "Especially not to your sister."

"Good answer, lover boy."

The missing phone notwithstanding, it had been a standard morning. But now, as Simon stood clutching his phone, watching the news on the TV in front of him with Will sitting and watching a few feet behind, everything seemed to turn upside down.

The report was the usual mix of information put forth by live broadcasts and developing stories: rumors, vague interpretations, a little information gathered by the reporter from actual statements. Simon tried to make sense of it all.

Sebastian, who worked the early shift, had been late to the lab, the reporter said. After calling and getting no answer from Sebastian, one of his colleagues had stopped by the house and found him upstairs. Simon wondered when that had happened. He had only left his own house a half-hour ago. He must have just missed Sebastian's coworker arriving and the ensuing madness.

They were saying it was medically induced second-degree progeria—accidental rapid aging. How could that be? Simon wondered. It seemed impossible, but there it was; the reporter had confirmed it.

"Medical examiners were on-scene soon after the discovery of Dr. Martin," the reporter said, "They refused to comment further before departing with what was left of his body."

What was left of his body. Simon's stomach sunk. As the reporter explained, in situations of death by rapid aging, there often wasn't much left of the body, especially if the deceased wasn't found immediately. Body tissue continued to deteriorate post-mortem. Simon shuddered at the thought of it happening to anyone, let alone one of his friends.

Accidental rapid aging. But how? Such a thing was unheard of, at least in—

The reporter said it herself. "There have been no official,

recorded accounts of death from this sort of rapid aging occurring for over 90 years. And then another 50 before that."

From personal research back when it had been his time to decide, Simon knew that during the earliest years of Rejuvenation there had been plenty of rapid aging cases. It was a known side effect in some, which is why, in modern use, EXLI instituted mandatory preliminary screening for all Rejuvenation candidates. It helped identify potential problems, such as natural immunity to the procedure or high susceptibility to medical anomalies such as rapid aging or the inverse.

But why now? Why Sebastian? Simon knew his friend was part of a Rejuvenation research team that handled a variety of dangerous chemicals every day in the EXLI labs. He didn't need the reporter to tell him, though she did, that EXLI had strict safeguards in place to prevent exposure to those chemicals. What she did mention that Simon found interesting was that, when asked to comment, EXLI merely said they were taking the necessary precautions and would "implement lockdown procedures if necessary" should they discover any "potential integrity issues with their laboratories." Beyond that, they deferred to the official police statement that was due later that day.

Despite everything the reporter said, so much still seemed in question. Yet, the official word was that of "an unfortunate accident caused by an unconfirmed exposure to lethal chemicals." Simon wondered if that was even possible. Could a person simply be exposed to chemicals that would cause rapid aging, and not immediately succumb? Could they go about their day and not see any of the side effects until hours later? Or days even? Now that he thought about it, Sebastian *had* seemed off lately. Hadn't he? Tired. Jumpy. Simon had chalked it up to long hours in the lab, but what if it had been some kind of chemical exposure taking effect in Sebastian?

"Even with these initial reports of accidental death, the circumstances around Dr. Martin's death are admittedly strange."

Simon knew this last sentence by the reporter was flimsy journalism. She wanted to keep the story intriguing, keep the fire burning so viewers would keep watching, wanting more information despite the reports of Sebastian's death being deemed an accident.

But it worked because he kept wondering. The situation *was* odd. How exactly could this have happened? Accidental exposure to dangerous chemical compounds didn't happen. Not at EXLI.

But if Sebastian's death wasn't an accident, that left only one other possibility—it was *intentional*. Simon struggled with the idea at first. Intentional? As in . . . murder? No. It couldn't be. The thought seemed too crazy, too much of a leap to even consider given how little he knew at that point. But still . . . Sebastian *had* seemed off lately and accidents didn't happen ·at EXLI. Could it really be true then? Murder? If so, why? Surely there were plenty of more senior scientists at EXLI with valuable, proprietary information. So why Sebastian? What could he have known that others didn't?

And then another thought hit Simon. One which sent a shiver through his body. After all the time Simon had spent with Sebastian, all the conversations they'd shared over the years about work and life in general, what could Sebastian know that would make someone want him dead? And if Sebastian knew something, did Simon unwittingly know it too?

2

———

"Si . . . Simon."

It was Sebastian's voice. Strained. Painful. Exhausted. But more than anything, the voice was ghostly. It was enough to send a chill across Simon's skin. Sebastian's voice called out to him from the small speaker of Simon's phone, called out to him from a dead past.

As he heard his name spoken, Simon thought again about what Sebastian might have known. Had it been enough to get him killed? And if he'd used his last moments of life to call Simon, did that mean Simon might know too? Willingly or not. Why else would Sebastian call him as he lay dying?

"Si . . . Simon. You need to . . . go . . . find . . . illbroo . . . told me."

With each word, each new bit of information, Simon found his thoughts churning, his head filling with new questions.

Sebastian *had* called Simon. Why? He wanted to tell him something. No, Simon thought. That wasn't it. Sebastian wanted him to *do* something. To *go* somewhere.

You need to . . . go . . . find . . .

It sounded as if Sebastian had tried to tell him outright, but couldn't. Not because he didn't want to, but because he couldn't physically speak the words.

Simon's thoughts flashed to past summer days spent in his backyard with Sebastian, throwing horseshoes, drinking beers, and chatting about everyday things. Even after an afternoon spent drinking, Sebastian had always been able to speak clearly. Sure, there were a few slurred words on very rare occasions, but he usually held it together quite well. Now, Sebastian's speech was anything but eloquent. Simon could hear the anguish in his friend's voice. Every syllable sounded spoken through a mouth that was failing, like it pained Sebastian to move his lips and tongue to form simple words. So much so that when he tried to tell Simon where he wanted him to go, all that came out was "ill-broo" and even that single word was unrecognizable.

"That's where . . . at. He's there . . . 1 . . . 20 . . . 120 . . . keeping him . . ."

The message continued, but Simon only found himself more and more confused. That's where . . . what? He couldn't understand what Sebastian was talking about. Who was this *he* Sebastian referred to? And what did the number *120* have to do with any of it?

Simon understood none of it. Then again, for all he knew, Sebastian could have just been confused. Perhaps he had been begging for help, for his neighbor to come to his aid as he struggled to stay alive. The thought sank Simon's heart deeper. His eyes began to well with tears at the thought of Sebastian—this smart, scientist of a man—losing the simple ability to form words or a coherent call for help.

"Find . . . her . . . can help."

Again, all Simon had was questions. Who was this *her* Sebastian referred to? What could she help with? She certainly couldn't help save Sebastian; that was for sure. That time had sadly passed.

Had he not been so broken by the thought of his friend's death and apparent delirium at the end of his life, Simon would have been frustrated. Nothing in Sebastian's message made any sense. None that Simon could glean anyway. But maybe that was the point. Maybe Sebastian's words weren't supposed to make sense. Maybe they were just a collection of nonsense produced by randomly firing synapses in the brain, spoken by a dying man who'd lost his ability to speak or think rationally.

Simon had almost convinced himself the message *was* just the gibberish of a man taking his last breaths. But then Sebastian's voice cleared as if he had been consciously fortifying himself, mustering all of his remaining strength to speak each syllable clearly. And with that effort, Sebastian uttered one final word.

"Hillbrook."

And that was it. The entirety of Sebastian's last short message. Perhaps his final words altogether.

Sebastian's final words.

But what did they mean?

3

———————

THE MESSAGE FROM SEBASTIAN WAS SO BRIEF AND RAMBLING that had it been any other day, Simon might have thought much less of it at first. Extremely odd, yes, but he could have written the message off as a strange pocket dial, perhaps even an out-of-character drunken call from his friend. Either way, he likely would've laughed it off and asked Sebastian about it later.

But not today—the day of Sebastian's death. With everything Simon had heard on the news that morning, everything he thought he might be caught up in, he was convinced the short message his neighbor had left him, no matter how confusing and incoherent, held some sort of importance. If Sebastian's death wasn't a simple delayed work accident as the news had reported, if someone had killed him, then the message could be vital to figuring out who had done the deed and why.

Simon joined Will back at their table, handed his phone over, and watched his friend listen to Sebastian's voicemail. The only sounds around them came from idle chatter of other coffee shop patrons and the continuing news broadcast on the nearby TV.

"In related news, the highly anticipated upcoming press conference to be held by EXLI Chief Executive Officer Theodore

Sullivan is still on schedule for this Friday at their global head-quarters downtown. The general public has been encouraged to attend and . . ."

Simon's mind drifted as he watched Will's eyebrows contract while listening to the message again. Not to more questions about Sebastian's death or the mysterious message left behind on his phone. No, as Simon sat there in silence, watching his good friend across the table listening to a cryptic voicemail left by a dying friend, Simon found himself thinking about Death. It had become such a . . . strange thing. People didn't just die anymore, he thought. Not of traditional advanced age anyway, and rarely from the health concerns of old age. Those were fears of the world long ago, before The Decay. Before the advent of Rejuvenation. Thanks to that breakthrough in medical science, and short of the odd, freak accident, most people lived long, healthy lives until—

A memory flashed in Simon's head. The squeak of his sneakers as he walked down a white hallway . . . a blue stripe on the wall . . . following his parents into a small room . . . beeping machines . . .

He shook it off and continued his previous train of thought, how one day, all who underwent Rejuvenation were sent off to live out their remaining days in a retirement facility. After that . . . well, those retirees did die, *eventually*. But that happened years and years later. A new end that no one really liked to talk about. That was how life went for the vast majority of the world's popu-lation. People endured. Those who chose to undergo the Rejuve-nation procedure, anyway.

Hell, Simon thought, here was a prime example right in front of him. Will. There he sat, phone pressed to his ear, dressed in the collared shirt and dark pants of a young professional. Stylish sunglasses propped atop his short brown hair. Sure, Will might be a little pudgy around the midsection, but for the most part, he was the picture of youth. But Simon knew better. He knew Will was one of the many who had undergone the procedure. A Rejuvenite. It wasn't a secret; most people did it. Though admittedly, Simon didn't know Will's exact, *true* age, but figured he had to be at least double his own—60 at minimum, maybe even 70. But there Will sat, looking like a fresh college graduate, ready to head out into the world on his own for the first time. That was the benefit afforded by Rejuvenation: years passed, but the appearance of physical youth remained.

Will handed the phone back across the table. "You all right, man?" he said.

Simon nodded and said, "I guess. I mean . . . it's just . . . damn. Sebastian."

"Yeah, I know what—I mean, I know I only met him a few times. Your Fourth of July party last year, cards that one time. You two were good friends, huh?"

"Yeah. It's only been a few years, but yeah, we just clicked when he moved in across the street. Us both being around the same *true* age and all. No offense."

Will waved this mention of actual ages away with a quick flip of his hand—as if the very thought of Rejuvenation-caused age disputes and all the usual tensions that came with them were preposterous—and said, "But you knew him pretty well then? I mean, given what we just heard on the news and, damn, that downright spooky voicemail . . . was he all right?"

Simon thought again about the last interaction he'd had with his neighbor. How Sebastian had looked haggard. Not sickly, just tired. And tense. "Actually, he did seem a bit off the last couple days. Kind of nervous. I thought it was just work, but—"

"Did he have any enemies that you know of?"

"Enemies? You think—"

"I don't mean anything by it," Will said quickly, and then said what Simon had been thinking. "I only ask because of, well, everything going on here. I know the news said there was no suspicion of foul play, but, come on. You just said that Sebastian had been off recently. And even if we didn't both just listen to that voicemail, everything about this sounds fishy to me. For Christ's sake, they said he died of rapid aging. *Rejuvs don't* die from that anymore. We're more likely to get hit by a bus or struck by lightning. Boom. No retirement for you, bud. But rapid aging? That doesn't happen."

"I did think about that," Simon said. He leaned toward Will and lowered his voice. "But Sebastian worked for EXLI. There's at least a *chance* he could have been accidentally exposed to something like what they're saying on the news. Right?"

"Maybe. Did he ever mention what he was doing there? Anything about his work?"

Simon shook his head. "Not really. Just normal stuff," he said and saw Will give a small sigh of relief. All the conversations he and Sebastian had had over the last few years rushed back into Simon's mind in fragments. Most of what he could recall was the usual stuff: mundane job talk of overwork and underpayment. Nothing out of the ordinary. Though, Simon thought, whenever Sebastian *did* actually venture into specifics about anything he did at EXLI, Simon had just tuned out. Not because he didn't find his neighbor's work interesting; he just didn't understand it. He couldn't grasp the basics of it, let alone the more technical areas into which Sebastian sometimes meandered. "I guess he mentioned it from time to time, but he was always so busy with everything they were doing that as soon as I thought I was getting a grasp on the latest project they were working on, he was already on to the next one."

The relief disappeared from Will's face. "So he *was* telling you about their projects then?"

Simon nodded. "So what? Talking about it didn't seem like anything out of the ordinary."

"It might not have been a huge deal to him, but do you think the bigwigs at EXLI would have liked to hear he was talking about proprietary, high-security matters outside of work? In case you aren't aware, Simon, EXLI is one of, no, *the* largest corporation in the world. I think ol' Teddy Sullivan and his band of cranky EXLI board members would be plenty pissed to find out one of their scientists was spreading confidential information or project secrets."

"But he didn't tell me anything!" Simon wasn't shouting, but his voice did get louder. He looked around, but no one in the coffee shop seemed to be listening to them. He calmed his paranoia, brought his voice back down to a normal level, and continued. "He didn't tell me any secrets, Will. At least, nothing that I understood. It was all way over my head. I don't know anything."

"But EXLI doesn't know that. For all they know, you're a spy for one of their competitors, or a member of some whack-job Anti-Rejuvenation group like Life Liberation or something. Or worse, they might think you're a black market Rejuvenist. Those creeps would do *anything* to get their hands on new information about EXLI projects to help their shady practices. If my work caused as many deaths as those back alley nuts, I'd want to improve my offerings too."

Simon wondered if Will might be right. He also realized that he'd been so busy trying to figure out whether he knew the same information that could've gotten Sebastian killed, he hadn't stopped to think about *who* might have actually pulled the trigger. That was, if a trigger *had* been pulled. Could it really have been EXLI? It still seemed like a crazy idea to Simon. It was no secret that he wasn't the biggest fan of the massive corporation. They might have a history of being linked to dubious deals and a reputation for intimidating competitors (all denied by their well-paid lawyers, of course), but Simon thought murdering one of their own employees was a step too far, even for EXLI.

"Did Sebastian tell you anything that sounded particularly

significant lately?" Will asked. "Anything about work or just in general?" Simon shook his head. "Well, when was the last time you talked to him?"

"I don't know. A couple days ago, I think."

"About anything related to what he said in that voicemail?"

"No. We talked about finding tickets to the Sentinels playoff game. That was it."

"You're positive?"

"Absolutely. It was just everyday stuff. Not even work-related. Just a quick hey-how-you-doing and sports talk." *That last conversation.* That's what that small exchange a few days prior had been; the last conversation he'd ever have with Sebastian.

"Do you think anything in that voicemail really means anything?" Will said.

"I do," Simon said with a firm nod. "There has to be some-thing important there. Why else would he try to tell me? Not the police. Not his family. He specifically called *me*. He was trying to warn me or tell me something."

Will shrugged. "I don't know. Maybe . . . well, have you considered that maybe Sebastian was just, I don't know, confused, pushing buttons at random, sorta losing his mind toward the end?"

"I had thought of that, yes. But still, why call *me* for help? Sure, I'm right across the street, but what could I have done? Why not just dial 911? There has to be a reason."

"But, that's just it," Will said, his face wrinkling as if the words to come caused him pain. "You heard him. That message. He was . . . out of it. Just wanted help."

"I agree, he didn't sound good, but . . ."

"What is it?"

"His voice at the end, it sounded different, like he was making a clear effort to say that name. *Hillbrook.* And if he did make a deliberate effort, then his choice of who to call was too. So again, *why me?*"

"Because you were friends," Will said in a matter-of-fact tone. "Maybe you were his *only* friend. Busy, scientist-type like him. Who knows? But I know if I was in trouble, I'd call you for help."

"Well, thanks."

"Don't mention it," Will said with a wink, "but as your friend, I feel like the smartest thing to do right now is go to the police. Tell them about losing your phone, the voicemail, everything."

Simon nodded and said. "Do you want me to tell them you heard the message?"

"Yeah," Will said. "It'll help your case. I can corroborate your story."

"You watch too many cop shows, you know that?"

"It's how I stay one step ahead of them."

But even as Will smirked at his comment, Simon's mind continued to connect the dots. Those police shows. Didn't they always run checks on everyone close to victims? Even if Simon didn't go to the police, they'd still likely track him down for questioning. Especially if they checked who Sebastian was friends with, who he might have called. They'd be wondering why—

"Oh shit," Simon said, pushing his chair back from the table, putting on his coat. "The voicemail. Sebastian's phone."

"What is it?" Will's eyes were large, round as he watched Simon's frantic movements.

"The police. They're investigating everything right now. Starting to, anyway. Of course they'll look at Sebastian's phone, to see if he called anyone before he died. And—"

"If they see he called you, they might suspect you."

This thought stopped Simon in his tracks. "Suspect me? I just figured they'd know he called me. Not—"

"If they know he called you, they could think it's a clue, not a warning."

"A clue? That's not—I'd never—"

"*I* know that, but they don't." Will cleared his throat and shifted in his chair. "But probably not, right? Too many cop shows, like you said."

Simon found it hard to forget the thought now that it had burrowed into his head. The police may have already checked Sebastian's phone records. They might be trying to track Simon down right now, perhaps waiting at his home or work. No. That's silly. They couldn't possibly think—

But if they did . . .

Simon quickly pocketed his phone from the table and said, "I'll catch up with you at the office." He gave Will a serious look and then hurried toward the doors of the coffee shop.

4

———

SIMON TRIED TO CATCH A TAXI TO THE POLICE STATION AND EVEN
saw one headed his direction as soon as he left the coffee shop.
He hailed the faded yellow car, listening to the familiar electric
whir of the car's engine winding down as it approached, but it
never reached a full stop. The young face of the driver looked at
Simon through the passenger window with a studying glance, and
as soon as Simon reached out to take the door handle, the taxi's
engine spun up again and it blew by him, heading off down the
road.

"Hey!" Simon blared after the taxi. He could have sworn he
saw the driver's eyes narrow and flash in the rearview mirror
through the back window, glaring once more at the fare he'd just
passed up before the taxi turned a corner up ahead and was gone.

Simon wished he could say it was the first time this sort of
refusal had happened to him, but he knew better. Memories of
being turned away at job interviews, denied service at restaurants,
and rejected by women, flashed in his head. The downsides of
forgoing Rejuvenation were many and had sadly become part of
his daily life since making the decision. This thought persisted as
Simon searched up and down the street for another taxi, seeing

only a steadily increasing flow of young-looking people heading to work on either side, some wrinkling their noses or shooting nasty glances his way as they passed by. He flipped the collar of his coat up higher and hunched his shoulders, feigning an attempt at keeping his face out of the harsh wind that sometimes blew through the city. He gave a frustrated huff, zipped his coat up, and set off in a fast walk toward the police station.

Simon marched down the sidewalk, surrounded not only by people, but the diverse high rises that made up the city's canyon-like streets. Many were old buildings, built more than two centuries ago, in the time before The Decay, still standing thanks to the architectural advances of that time. Even when humanity was crumbling, those magnificent skyscrapers had endured, more than earning their designation as the pinnacle of modern, urban architecture. Of course, they'd all been through renovations since. At least the buildings in this part of the city had. (The disregarded boroughs across the river were a different story altogether.) Most of the repairs had been to maintain and update interiors with new world décor. But the exterior of those long-standing buildings still held an aura of the old world, the time before. Their weathered brick facades showing the occasional crack here and there, reflecting the hints of wrinkles that had only recently started to show up on Simon's forehead, the flecks of gray at his temples. Among these structural relics of the past were newer, cleaner buildings that towered high above the rest and would have normally cast long shadows upon the street Simon now walked had the sky not been filled with clouds. Wind swept between buildings young and old, flapping the hems of coats, occasionally blowing off hats, and biting at Simon's face as he pressed on.

Simon kept his head down, both to combat the wind as well as to avoid eye contact with people walking the other way. At that moment, he wanted nothing more than to be at the police station, despite the fear of what might happen when he got there. At least at the station there'd be no more taxi drivers or commuters giving him odd looks. He usually brushed those kinds of stares off as best he could, but today of all days, he just didn't want to see any of it. But he wasn't at the station yet, and so couldn't ignore the people around him completely. That sea of good-looking, young in appearance professionals making their way to work. Sure, there was the odd resister like him amongst the crowd. Abstainers. Deniers. Whatever name people used, it all meant the same thing —Non-Rejuvenites. Despite their similar choices, looks of solidarity between those others were a rarity as most of them kept their heads bowed like Simon, against the wind and looks of oppression. Some of the passersby did smile, though most did not. Others ignored everyone, wearing blank expressions as they typed away at phones with one hand while keeping half an eye on the oncoming stream of people. But all it took was a brief look up for Simon to catch a glare or wide-eyed stare. *What were they looking at?* It's not as if he was a gray-haired old man staggering down the sidewalk with the help of a walker. Even so, Simon knew he still stuck out amongst these people. Those momentary, offended, and sometimes glaring glances were enough to make anyone feel out of place.

That strange, unwelcome feeling that had become such a part of his everyday life as an adult hadn't always been there though, not until after his decision to forgo the procedure. Family and friends were direct about it; most had given him the usual questioning look or talk at one point. Thanks to the anti-discrimination policies in place at the Odeon Plence Agency, he rarely heard anything outright negative from his coworkers, but Simon knew how they felt. He could see it in their judging eyes across conference room tables, read it in the words they chose to use in emails, sense it in their apprehension to work with him on client pitches.

Not that his world was completely devoid of support. There were the looks from other Non-Rejuvenites, few though they may be, and flyers for advocate groups seemed to be more prevalent in recent years as well. Sometimes there was even support from the other side. Like Will and Maggie. They were the exceptions. Simon doubted he would have lasted more than a few days in the life of an office drone had it not been for Will taking him under his wing that first week. And without that kindness, he would have never met Maggie, dragged along as she had been to that company holiday party by her brother. But Will *had* been friendly and Simon *had* met Maggie. They'd accepted him, even if the vocal majority didn't, or couldn't, understand the decision of people like Simon.

But as he trudged along down that busy city sidewalk, seeing mostly young faces go by, Simon knew: he'd been like them at one point, hadn't he? Or at least, *thought* like them. He'd wanted those Rejuvenation drugs pumped into his system. He'd thought he needed the supercharged immune system and the incredible anti-aging effects that came with it. Even if he didn't fully understand the finer details at the time, he'd *believed* in Rejuvenation. Back before he'd reached the minimum age for the procedure, when he'd wanted nothing more than to be like his parents, his grandparents, like everyone else. To his young mind, it was the only way he would ever be *fully* protected against the deadly diseases he'd learned about in school, the ones his mother had constantly reminded him had nearly killed off everyone during The Decay. It was the expected, accepted path. A rite of passage. And so, Simon had been steadfast in his determination of how his life would go.

But life, as it often did, hadn't worked out the way Simon envisioned it as a young child. It didn't even take him to decision time or even to adulthood to change his thinking. His mind was made up when Simon finally came face to face with what lies at the end of the Rejuvenation path.

SIMON HAD HEARD his mother and father talking in hushed voices for a few days by then, catching scraps of their conversation and hearing his Grandpa Crowe and the phrase "it's just his time" mentioned again and again. He wondered what was going on at first, but only as much as an 11-year-old would before his attention was drawn to something else. He had almost forgotten all about it until his father and mother woke him up early the next Saturday morning, telling him to get showered and dressed. They were going to see Grandpa Crowe at his new home, they told him. So that was it, he thought. His grandfather had just moved to a new house!

He quickly got ready and was in the backseat of his parent's car in no time, anxious for the visit. Why wouldn't he be? Simon adored his Grandpa Crowe more than anyone. The man was as exuberant as they come, even for all his years. Though Abraham Crowe, as he was known to his friends, had no reason to slow down thanks to Rejuvenation. His slim face and mousey blond hair showed no signs of his advanced age. He looked as young and spry as the day, all those many years ago, when he had chosen to undergo the procedure. The benefits of which allowed him to play with Simon for hours whenever they went to visit. Grandpa Crowe, Simon thought, acted more like a kid than even Simon did most of the time. Were it not for the name Grandpa, Simon would have almost thought of the man as more like a brother than his father's father.

And so, as they pulled out of their driveway, Simon wondered what Grandpa Crowe had in store for him. What would they do? What was his new house like? Had he moved to one of the old houses on the hill? Maybe. His grandpa had to be wealthy enough by that point to afford one of those, he thought. Or maybe, dare he think, his grandpa's new home was in Westgate! That would have truly been special. But then he wondered, why had Grandpa Crowe moved in the first place? Simon felt his grandfather's old house was more than adequate, so he was curious why he'd suddenly moved. All these questions and thoughts raced through young Simon's mind as he stared out the car window that day. It wasn't long before Simon's more extravagant hopes were dashed as he saw they were heading in the opposite direction he had hoped; away from the luxury apartments in heart of the city, the old houses on the hill, and the tall reaches of Westgate. They were headed out of the city altogether; out toward the rural areas beyond the suburbs. Where he and his dad had gone camping along the beaches or in one of the campgrounds at the edge of the forests. As far as Simon knew, there was nothing out that way but trees upon trees until the coastline and the cliffs. His interest piqued, Simon sat up in his seat and gazed intently out the window as they continued to drive further and further away from the city. After some time, his father turned the car down a side road, just before a large, bright white sign posted at the side of the road with the letters E-X-L-I plastered across it.

EXLI? Of course, Simon knew what that meant. *Everyone* did. But why would his Grandpa Crowe's new home be out this way? And what did EXLI have to do with it?

"Has grandpa got a job with EXLI? Why? What is—" Simon asked, but received a raised hand from his father. Not a threatening hand, just a signal to silence his questions.

With eyes still on the road ahead, not looking back at Simon, his father said, "You ah, you ever hear of PCMP, Simon?" Simon shook his head. "It means Post-Cerebrational Mobility Phase. It's —" But his father's words cut short when he looked in the rearview mirror and saw Simon's confused expression. "I guess that's a bit too technical for your age. It means re—"

"No," Simon's mother said, shaking her head at her husband. "We can't."

"He should know what's—"

"Just . . . not yet." Simon's mother turned around to look at him, a forced grin on her face. "Don't worry, honey."

"But, what did Dad mean? Grandpa, he's—" Simon said, still confused.

"Your Grandpa . . . h-he's . . . just . . . he'll be f-fine." Simon's mother's eyes had welled up and she spun back around in her seat, looking at the road again.

"Mom?"

But she raised a silencing hand of her own, sniffling, not looking back again. Simon got the hint and was left to his thoughts, wondering what his parents were talking about but unable to understand any of it. PCMP? Post-Cere—what had his Dad said? It all sounded like grown-up stuff to him, so Simon went back to looking out the window, waiting in the backseat of the car until they finally reached their destination.

The building was tall and gray. It didn't look like a house, Simon thought. It didn't even look like an apartment building. It reminded him of those old places on the dirty side of the city, across the river. It looked like . . . nothing at all; just a plain, boring structure built in the middle of nowhere, surrounded by parking lots. They quickly parked, got out, and made their way inside with the other people Simon saw filtering into the building in groups large and small.

Inside, the white walls and sterile atmosphere reminded Simon instantly of a hospital, but the place didn't feel like a hospital. Not completely anyway. It was almost like an amusement park, with long strings of people lined up, waiting to go through gates of some kind up ahead. Beyond that, he saw only elevators.

"Is Grandpa okay?" Simon asked and again received the silencing hand motion from his father. So Simon just walked with his parents. He waited in line with them and soon they were beyond the gates and into the elevators. After a short ride up, the elevator doors opened onto the 4th floor, and they exited into more sterile hallways. It seemed the further and further they went inside the building, the more like a hospital it became. Simon felt a steady unease growing in his stomach at this thought, and that feeling continued to grow as he saw men and women walking by in white coats, and then started to see gurneys of people at intervals along the hallway and spied even more through open doors. And each time he looked up at his parents and started to ask a question, they only gave him a silencing look or told him to wait.

They turned right down a hallway, then left down another. Simon wondered how his parents knew where to go in such a place. It was like a great big maze to him, so he only followed along, wondering when they would finally see Grandpa Crowe. And even more so, why his grandfather would be in a place like this. A minute later, Simon's father stopped them outside a nondescript room, whispered something to Simon's mother, and then led the two of them inside.

The tiny room was lined with silver countertops on all sides and white cabinets above that. There were two men, doctors, Simon could tell because of their coats, standing at the center of the room in front of a small hospital bed surrounded by flashing medical devices on stands. A steady Beep . . . Beep . . . Beep . . . echoed out in the small room, emanating from those machines. The doctors looked up when Simon and his parents entered and stepped forward to greet them. As they did, Simon got his first clear glimpse at the person laying on the bed at the center of the room.

It was his Grandpa Crowe.

Abraham Crowe lay motionless on the bed. His machine-assisted breathing would have been imperceptible were it not for the slow rise and fall of his chest beneath the thin, light blue hospital gown he wore. At various points on his body, electrodes and clamps connected Abraham via bunches of gray and white wires to the other machines that surrounded the bed. His face was still, expressionless. His eyes open, staring blankly up at the ceiling.

At first, Simon had thought his grandfather was merely playing a joke on him. He must be faking that trance-like state to put one over on his grandson. And so young Simon broke away from his parents, past the doctors, and scampered right up to his grandfather's bedside, calling to him. "Grandpa! I know you're faking. Grandpa!" But his Grandpa Crowe did not move, did not blink. After a tug at his grandfather's arm was only answered with continued silence and lack of reaction, Simon finally realized Abraham Crowe wasn't faking. He realized what had happened to his grandfather and where he was.

Retirement.

This place, this sterile, hospital-like building, was a Rejuvenation retirement community. And his Grandpa Crowe, well . . . he was still there, but not like before. The once-lively man was lively no more.

He was there, but he was gone.

———

IT WAS that ghostly image of his grandfather that had stayed with Simon ever since. He always remembered, even after his grandfather's eventual death. The sight of Abraham Crowe, still looking as young as ever, but lying motionless in a retirement facility bed, attached to machines that kept his body alive while his brain stayed active. The thought sent a shiver through Simon, more so than any of the chilly gusts he fought against as he continued his quickened pace along that city street, headed toward the police station he knew was just around the corner.

Had Simon been tempted to reconsider, even with that image

of his grandfather's retirement ever-present in his mind? Of course he had, especially after meeting someone like Maggie, even after she'd accepted him and the decision he'd made. But his second-guessing his decision, well . . . every couple argued. Every relationship went through rough patches, right?

Simon supposed moments of reconsideration were natural. Second-guessing oneself was a normal occurrence in all things; from choosing which shirt to wear to work and what to have for lunch, to where to go on vacation and yes, even Rejuvenation. He was experiencing just such an occurrence at that moment as he turned from the main avenue and down a side street. The strong wind of moments before suddenly diminished and Simon lifted his head to see his intended destination.

Was it truly the right decision to come here, he wondered. He was almost sure it was, but still, there was a lingering doubt in his mind. It was always there, questioning everything. Would the police already be looking for him as he had suspected? If so, did they know about the existence of Sebastian's message already? Would they know what to make of it?

Despite his questions, Simon kept moving forward and eventually found himself standing in front of the police station. He looked up at the red brick face of the building and windows that lined every one of its six stories. It was one of the old buildings of the city. Most of the police and fire department buildings were Pre-Decay, he thought. At least on the outside. He figured it had to do with tradition. There was something about that which Simon respected; the celebration and remembrance of the old ways. He stood there for a moment more, then pulled his gaze away from the building, and quickly made his way inside.

———

IT TOOK ONLY the mention of Sebastian's name to get Simon into an interrogation room. There, he waited for two hours—sweating, wondering yet again whether his decision to go to the police had been the right one, his mind alternating between rational thought and paranoia.

They'd confiscated Simon's phone, but had at least allowed him to call his office first. And so he'd waited, until just after eleven o'clock, when, finally, the door opened and a man stepped into the room. He was tall, wore jeans and a black leather coat too large for his narrow shoulders, wrinkling the collared shirt underneath. Around his neck, dangling from a silver chain, was a badge.

"Mr. Crowe?" the man said, his voice deep and strong like the metallic thud of the door as it closed behind him. "I'm Detective Milo Banks, lead on the Martin case." He walked straight to the table and shook Simon's hand, which crumpled under the firm grip of the detective. Banks gave a weak smile, more of a grimace, which showed the bottom row of his teeth stained yellow. The minty smell of chewing tobacco on his breath. If Simon hadn't been sure of Bank's choice when the detective first stepped in the room, he was now; the sagging skin around his eyes, the thinning black hair that stuck up on the back of his head, the general sense of weariness—the mileage of this man's life showed through, unaided by the advancement of medical science. That vague sense of kinship lessened the tension in Simon's shoulders. Bank released his hand and said, "Good to meet'cha. They keep you waitin' long? Sorry about that. Need anything? Coffee? Piss break?"

Simon said no, he was fine. Detective Banks pulled an empty chair out from the table, sat opposite Simon, and pulled a small, digital recorder from the pocket of his worn coat. He pointed at it and said, "Ya don't mind, do ya?"

Simon shook his head as Detective Banks was already pushing the Record button, setting the recorder on the table between them. Banks sat up tall in his chair, his sharp, gray eyes pointed at Simon, and said, "You have additional information about Dr. Martin's death. That right?"

Simon nodded and, comfortable or not the second before with the notion of a fellow Non-Rejuvenite sitting across from him, his palms began to sweat. His fingers fidgeted beneath the table. "I know that what happened looks like an accident, and it probably is," he said. "Don't get me wrong, I think it's an accident just like the news says, but I got a call from Sebastian last night. He left a message and I thought you guys would want to hear it."

"What was your relationship to the deceased?"

"He was a friend. My neighbor, across the street."

Banks nodded. He let Simon speak, but his follow up questions came fast. "And when did he call you?"

"The middle of the night, when . . . well, it sounds like he called right when . . . whatever happened to him, was happening. His voice, on the message, it sounds like . . . like he's in pain, mumbling. I don't know what he was trying to say exactly or what it means."

"Why didn't you go over to help him?" Banks asked with a raised brow, eyes narrowed.

"I didn't have my phone. I was at a friend's house for dinner and forgot it there. My friend didn't answer the call, but he brought the phone to me this morning. That's when I heard the message."

"And your, ah, friend, he can confirm this story?"

"Yes."

Detective Banks nodded, reached into his pocket, and pulled out Simon's phone. He laid it on the table and said, "Go ahead. Let's hear it."

Simon played the message, Sebastian's voice echoing hollowly off the gray walls of the interrogation room.

"Si . . . Simon. You need to . . . go . . . find . . . illbroo . . . told me . . . That's where . . . at. He's there . . . 1 . . . 20 . . . 120 . . . keeping him. Find . . . her . . . can help. Hillbrook."

Simon watched as Banks listened to the recording for the first time. The detective's eyes were unmoving, concentrating on the phone throughout the entire message, but his chin moved up and down as he bit at the inside of his lower lip. As soon as it ended, he looked up at Simon. "We're gonna need to listen to that again."

They listened three more times before the detective said it was enough. He remained silent at first, shooting a crooked eye Simon's way, studying him, then leaned forward and said, "None of that makes sense to you, Mr. Crowe?"

Simon shook his head and before he could stop himself, said, "Do you think there's anything there? Anything that could . . . I don't know, help . . . anything useful I guess?"

"If there is, that's for my partner and me to decide." At this, Banks leaned back, pulled a phone from his pocket, checked the screen, then put it back. "Can't tell you, not now anyway. But we'll definitely collect a copy of that message for our investigation." Did he see Simon fidgeting again? The beads of new sweat on his forehead? Whatever the reason, Banks then tapped the recorder on the table and said, "These things can be tricky. Strange death. Now this voicemail. Maybe it was a random dial. All this *could* be an unfortunate accident." A sense of relief started to grow in Simon, and then the detective finished, "Though, bad luck for him, wouldn't you say? You happen to misplace your phone, miss the call, and can't come to his aid."

Any shred of relief in Simon evaporated immediately, his shoulders tightening again as two distinct thoughts battled inside his head. Did the police honestly suspect Simon of having something to do with Sebastian's death? It sure as hell sounded like it to him based on what the detective was saying. But those last few words also struck Simon deep. He stared at the floor, his face going long, his stomach sinking . . . *bad luck for him . . . You happen to misplace your phone, miss the call* . . . A reminder that Simon had, by chance, not had his phone on him during the previous night and therefore was unable to help Sebastian when he needed it most.

But then, Detective Banks's hand was on his shoulder, like the comforting gesture of a sitcom dad. But that couldn't be, Simon thought, not this man who'd been grilling him for the last few minutes. Simon looked up and a strong waft of the detective's tobacco breath stung his nostrils.

"I'll say this," Banks said. "Just because you didn't have your phone on you—you wouldn't have been able to do anything anyway. By the time he made that call, Dr. Martin was already beyond saving."

The detective's words made sense. Even if Simon *had* been there to answer the phone and rush to Sebastian's side, he would have had no idea what to do besides call for more help. He had no medical knowledge beyond some office first aid training and what he'd gleaned from the hospital shows Maggie liked to watch on TV. From the sound of that message, and Bank's oddly comforting words, Sebastian's death had already been inevitable when he'd called.

Simon swallowed hard, looked at Detective Banks, and said, "Thanks."

Banks nodded, released Simon's shoulder, and sat up straight in his chair again. "Is there anything else you want to tell me, Mr. Crowe?" he said, his voice softer.

Simon opened his mouth, stopped himself, hesitated for a moment, then said, "No. That's . . . that's everything."

It was a brief hesitation, but Detective Banks noticed it. He did not, however, let on. Not yet. Instead, he stood, picked up the phone and the recorder from the table, and said, "For what it's worth, I'm sorry about your friend." Simon thanked him and the two men shook hands again. "Thanks for your cooperation, Mr.

Crowe. We'll have you out of here shortly." But Detective Banks didn't let go; not at first. He gripped Simon's hand, unmoving, like stone. Banks locked his stare with Simon's for the briefest of moments, as if he could look through Simon's eyes, behind them, and see whatever secret thoughts might hide there. "Are you *sure* you don't have anything else you want to tell me?"

Simon's mind swirled with all the thoughts of that morning. His conversation with Will, the conspiracy theories the two had cooked up, everything. Was Detective Banks's sudden caring tone genuine? What harm could it do to share with the detective what he thought about Sebastian's death? He'd probably feel better once he put his fears into the hands of the police. But he was so close to being out of there. Out of this small, cold room that felt like a prison cell.

He sat up in his chair and said, "I—"

Detective Banks's phone rang from his coat pocket, piercing and hollow in that bare interrogation room, stopping Simon before he could finish. Banks growled, kept his eyes on Simon for a second longer, then said, "Let me just," and pulled the slim phone from his pocket. He glared down at the screen, ready to dismiss the interrupting call, but when he saw the screen his eyes changed. "Hold that thought, wouldja? I need to take this."

Simon nodded and sat back in his chair. Detective Banks tapped his phone, brought it up to his ear, and headed for the door. Simon caught only a brief snippet of the call before Banks exited the room.

"Go for . . . Yeah? What have you got? . . . Really? That's odd . . ."

Simon sat still, waiting for a minute or two. He heard only the creaking of the metal chair underneath him as he adjusted his position and the muffled sounds of Banks talking on the other side of the wall, though he couldn't make any of it out. He tried to keep himself from wondering about the call, but heard Banks's voice in his head. *That's odd.* What was odd? Before his mind drifted too far into paranoia again, he heard the familiar crunch of the door's lock sliding, opening. Detective Banks reentered, biting at the inside of his lower lip with his chin drawn up. He looked at Simon, but didn't say anything.

"What is it?" Simon asked.

A frown grew on Banks's face and he said, "What *it* is, I can't say. But I'm afraid we can't let you leave just yet."

WHAT TO KNOW...

AGE RESTRICTION

A minimum age restriction of 22 years has been instituted to ensure patients reach the body's natural developmental peak.

SPECIAL CASES

Only in very rare instances are people between 12 -22 allowed to undergo the procedure.

ONCE ADMINISTERED REJUVENATION WILL...

HALT BIOLOGICAL AGING

Allowing patients to remain young and attractive, and live longer lives.

PROTECT AGAINST ALL DISEASE

The amazing side effect of advanced immunity saves lives and affords patients the ability to maintain a healthy lifestyle.

SAVE PATIENT MONEY

By preventing unnecessary costs associated with insurance and medical treatments.

MAKE COSTLY RESEARCH OBSOLETE

Eliminate taxes and grant expenditures that would have gone to medical research into individual cures that are no longer needed.

5

———

As Maggie Buchanan pulled her gray sedan into the driveway of her two-story townhouse, she spotted a package she wasn't expecting on the front porch. She parked her car, grabbed her purse, and exited as the soft electric hum of the engine silenced. Maggie made her way up the short strip of sidewalk connecting the drive to her porch, her eyes lingering on the small brown cube sitting on the doorstep as she tried to remember if she'd ordered anything.

Stepping onto the tiny porch, Maggie was about to reach down to inspect the package when she heard a sudden buzz emanating from inside her purse. Her heart leapt and she burrowed her hand inside the bag, searching, feeling her phone give another short buzz, enough to locate it.

This better be Simon, she thought. After calling him a half-dozen times throughout the day, leaving two voicemails, and a string of unanswered texts, it better be him.

But when she pulled the phone into view, Maggie's heart sank as she saw a text, but not from Simon. It was just a coworker. A nice enough woman, Maggie thought, but sometimes her work friends just couldn't take a hint. She read the text and responded

45

quickly that her answer was still the same as when she left the office twenty minutes ago. No, she would not be joining the rest of the team for the weekly post-work happy hour. Not today. She had other things to attend to, like making sure Simon was okay after everything she'd heard had happened earlier from Will. And, presently, figuring out what this package was and who had sent it.

Maggie scooped up the brown box, surprised by the lightness of it, and quickly checked the machine-printed return address. Harborside. Did she know anyone in Harborside? She knew the place, it was up north, but couldn't think of anyone there she knew. Maggie tucked the package under her arm, unlocked the door, and stepped inside.

She kicked off her kitten heels in the entryway that connected the front door to the main living space of the townhouse. Her toes felt instantly better, relieved from their cramped, daylong imprisonment of business wear. She set the package, her purse, and keys down on the narrow table near the front door, and trudged up the nearby stairs.

As she entered the second-story master bedroom, Maggie thought of calling or texting Simon again. Instead, she tossed her phone onto the soft down comforter of the bed in the center of the room, sitting clean and peaceful and made, white sheets tucked in and a mountain of various-shaped pillows near the dark fabric headboard. Simon would see all her calls and texts from before. If he didn't realize she'd been trying to reach him by now, she didn't know what else to do.

As she began her post-work ritual of shedding professional attire for the more comfortable confines of lounging-around-the-house clothes, Maggie couldn't stop her mind from wandering. It wasn't as if Simon didn't have his phone on him, she thought as she peeled off her open-front blazer, hanging it in the closet. She knew he'd gotten it back. Will told her that and most of what had happened between them that morning, ending with Simon's decision to go to the police station. But after that—nothing. Maggie untucked and unbuttoned her dress shirt as she wondered if Simon was still at the station answering questions. Perhaps there'd been some confusion and the police thought Simon was to blame for his neighbor's death. He could be locked up in a jail cell at that very second, metal cuffs digging into his wrists. She imagined him dressed in an orange jumpsuit with a number printed across the back, his new identification because that's how he'd be seen now, just another murderer in the system. It'd been a simple case after he'd walked right into the police station and handed over the evidence that convicted him. No no no, that's crazy talk. It was all just an *accident*. But then, could Simon just be at home ignoring her? Again, no, she thought, he was more thoughtful than that. He would have responded if he could, tell her he was busy or that he'd call back when possible. But as she shimmied out of her long skirt, Maggie stopped and thought: why hadn't he? Why hadn't Simon contacted her if he truly was okay? In their nearly two years of dating, daily communication had never been an issue. They traded countless texts throughout the day discussing how work was going. They chatted frequently about weekend plans and Will always wanting to double date with them whenever he met someone new. Simon called just to check that she'd made it home okay that time she went upstate to visit friends. He called most Mondays to ask whether she'd locked the door when leaving his place in the morning. That one time he even called to ask whether he left his socks in her backyard after the surprise birthday party she'd thrown for him. The truth was, Simon regularly called her to talk about all the everyday, little things in their lives . . . but now, when it seemed to matter most, when his life might be in danger, there were no calls, no texts. Nothing. The only explanation Maggie could think of was that Simon must still be with the police and, for whatever reason, wasn't able to answer her. Not because he didn't want to, because he *couldn't* or wasn't allowed. If he could just respond, at least then she'd know he was safe and not—

Maggie stopped, closed her eyes, and said, "Damn it. Just stop. He'll be fine." She hurled her shirt and skirt into the small wicker hamper in the corner near a faded chest of drawers. She stomped over to her closet and looked inside, searching for a specific piece of clothing; one of Simon's old, hooded sweatshirts from university. She grabbed the sweatshirt from where it sat wadded up on one of the closet shelves and felt the worn, comfortable fabric against her skin as she pulled it on. Despite her average height and stature, Maggie almost swam in the shirt, as it had stretched out even on Simon from repeated wearing over time. Though she had pretty much claimed that particular article of clothing as her own long ago, and had washed it many times since, she still thought it smelled of Simon. Not some pungent odor of man-sweat or even a fragrant scent of cologne, but just a faint, natural aroma unique to him. Eau de Simon. The feel and hint of smell combined for the perfect level of coziness to her. And at that moment, a sense of cozy comfort was exactly what Maggie needed. She completed her lounging ensemble with a pair of what she affectionately referred to as stretchy pants, and felt instantly more at ease. One article of clothing hiding her figure, the other accentuating it, not that she was concerned at all then how she looked in the clothes, only how she felt. Satisfied with the change, Maggie pocketed her phone in the large kangaroo pouch of the sweatshirt and headed back downstairs, tying her dark brown hair up into a ponytail as she went.

When she rounded the corner of the stairs, Maggie was almost surprised to see the package on the entry table, having nearly forgotten about it as she changed. But there it sat, small and mysterious, just enough to take her mind off Simon's unresponsiveness. She dropped the package on the coffee table in the living room before heading into the kitchen to grab a knife. When she returned, Maggie sank into the soft cushions of the couch and slid her phone onto the table next to the package.

She turned on the television mounted to the wall across the room. The thin screen lit up instantly, and Maggie flipped through the channels until stopping on one of the more bearable round-the-clock news stations. The anchor onscreen was currently talking monotonously about an overseas election, but Maggie had a feeling they'd soon be back around to the Martin death. Maggie paused briefly, just as she'd done earlier that day while watching the coverage in the lunchroom at work, thinking about the few times she'd met Sebastian while visiting Simon. They'd mostly only been fleeting encounters, introductions and small talk. But still, she'd known the man too. Not as much as Simon, sure, but she'd spent time with him. He was nice, she thought. It was a simple way of thinking about Sebastian, but she felt it summed him up. He'd usually been quiet around her, except for that day last winter when he'd hunkered down at Simon's house with her, Simon, and Will for an afternoon of hot toddies and euchre as a snowstorm raged outside. She pictured Sebastian, red-faced from drink, finally cracking out of his usual silent demeanor and pounding the table with laughter after one of Will's lame jokes. Any other day the memory would have made Maggie smile, but instead, her heart dropped as she realized he'd never join them again for another snowy afternoon of cards.

She busied herself with inspecting the package's label and fidgeting with the tape holding the cardboard flaps together. As she did, Maggie saw several headlines about the death of Simon's neighbor crawl across the ticker at the bottom of the screen.

TOP STORY: EXLI SCIENTIST, DR. SEBASTIAN MARTIN, FOUND DEAD IN HOME AT TRUE AGE 36 . . .

ACCIDENTAL DEATH DUE TO CHEMICAL EXPOSURE, ADVANCED SECOND DEGREE PROGERIA RULED AS CAUSE BY ONGOING INVESTIGATION . . .

EXLI CEO THEODORE SULLIVAN EXPECTED TO HONOR MARTIN AT UPCOMING PRESS CONFERENCE . . .

Maggie watched as the last few words scrolled off the left side of the screen, followed quickly by another line further detailing EXLI's anticipated press conference and speculation about what would be announced.

She pulled her eyes away from the screen and down to the package. Thankful for the distraction, she bent open the top flaps to see a mass of bubble wrap surrounding something she couldn't quite make out yet. Maggie spotted a small white envelope to the side in the box and plucked it out, ripping her finger along the seam to find a single sheet of paper inside. Maggie recognized the bubbly handwriting of the note instantly as it was so much like her own, though it looked messier than usual, written in haste.

As soon as she saw that handwriting, before even reading the actual message or looking at the signature at the bottom, it all made sense. The package. The lightweight contents. The message. The reasons for both.

At the service you said you wanted this from Aunt Jeanie's storage if it was still available, so I sent it along while we were up there. Please take care of it and please reconsider what we discussed.

— Mom

Maggie read the note only once, glaring at the last line. *Reconsider what they discussed?* She felt her cheeks warm with color and crumpled the note in her fist, tossing it onto the table. She stared narrow eyes at the little ball of paper as it tumbled across the glass, coming to rest near a short stack of coasters. How *dare* her mother try to sneak that little ongoing jab in under the guise of delivering something sentimental?

Dismissing all pretense of the note, Maggie reached into the box and pulled out what was inside, carefully unrolling the contents from the surrounding bubble wrap. When she was finished, Maggie set the packing material aside and studied the blue and white, porcelain bear in her hands as it stared happily back at her despite the crack in the left side of its face that'd been glued together ages ago. She smiled and felt tears well in her eyes, unable to stop a few from spilling down her cheeks. She quickly wiped them away as memories flooded her mind—happy memories, for what seemed like the first time in a long time. She grabbed the bear's head and lifted it off, tipping the body to peek in, as if she'd see the candy—not cookies—that Great Aunt Jeanie used to keep inside.

She wondered if Will had gotten something similar. Not another cookie jar. No, this was the only one Maggie could remember their great aunt keeping in her house. But maybe Will had gotten something else after Jeanie had . . . well, after she'd died. Even thinking it sounded strange. It had been two months since the funeral service, but even now, remembering Great Aunt Jeanie's youthful body in that coffin, it still seemed odd that she was really gone. After undergoing the procedure so many years ago. After avoiding life-threatening accidents her whole life. After spending the last 19 years at that small retirement facility in Harborside. After all that time . . . Jeanie had finally died. Though she'd certainly taken the long road to the end. It was the lengthy future most Rejuvenites expected, but not everyone was so lucky. Rejuvenation had that effect on the world, it gave death variation. But no one, not even the latest generations to undergo the procedure, could escape what would eventually happen. Sooner or later, they'd all face an end. But that was a long later for most of the people Maggie knew.

Her gaze remained on the bear-shaped cookie jar she'd always sought out as a young child and Maggie thought again about Will receiving something in the mail, and if he had, did their mother send an equally passive-aggressive note to him as well? Surely not. What did she have to complain about with Will? He was doing well for himself, their mother would say. Will had just been promoted to Associate Director at the agency, overseeing advertising for multiple high-profile clients. Sure, he hadn't started a family of his own or even found himself a long-term partner yet, but at least when he did date Will had followed the "normal" life. He wasn't doing something as embarrassing as—Maggie stopped herself, and heard Will's voice in her head, what he'd told her the first time she'd had the now all-too-familiar argument with their mother. "Don't listen to her. Mom hasn't even met Simon."

Will was good like that, Maggie thought. Supportive. Always eager to offer advice, whether someone wanted to hear it or not. The real truth was, Will had a knack for sticking his nose into matters where it didn't belong. But when times came when Maggie really wanted someone to talk to, when she needed an attentive ear and only brotherly advice would do, Will had always been there. Even with the 20 plus years he had on her, he was forever her big brother.

It had been no different when she spoke to him earlier that very day . . .

"He'll be okay, Mags. He *is* okay," Will had said. "He's —damn it!"

"What is it?"

"Well I *was* headed to Muldoons, but, shit, instead I'll be sitting in traffic for lunch. They're putting up some kind of roadblocks downtown. I—"

"Will?"

"Oh, yeah, sorry. Look, Simon's fine. Trust me."

"But how do you know that?" Maggie had said, her gaze flipping from the salad in front of her to the small television hanging in the office lunchroom. The story of Sebastian's death was being recapped for the hundredth time. Maggie watched the report and felt herself getting anxious again as she held the phone to her ear. "You said you haven't talked to him since this morning."

"Yeah, well, he was okay then too. A little stressed, sure, but can you blame the guy? He just found out his friend died. He was in shock, reacting how you do when anyone . . . well, when *that* type of person dies." Will's voice had paused at this statement. Car horns blared in the background on the other end of the call. Maggie had known why her brother stopped talking suddenly, because she had been thinking the same thing. Great Aunt Jeanie. It was a different circumstance, sure, but . . . Maggie had remained silent, absently stabbing at several shreds of romaine until Will spoke again. "Then, ya know, on top of that, Simon finds that voicemail on his phone. It was creepy."

"But you really think there's nothing to it?"

"Yup. It was only creepy because we knew it was from a dead guy. That's all. The message was gibberish."

"Yeah, but—"

"Listen, Mags. Simon's smart. He just wanted to do the right thing. To help. I'm sure he's fine."

Maggie dropped her lettuce-speared fork in the plastic bowl, appetite gone, looking up at the report on TV again. "Then why can't we reach him?"

"I don't know. He's probably still talking to the police." Maggie had given an unconvincing Hm-mm of agreement then and their conversation petered out soon after. She'd been frustrated with Will's words, but in the hours since had realized he was only trying to reassure her, because that's what brothers do.

But the worry always seemed to creep back somehow. Even now, as she stood from the couch, cookie jar in hand, and headed to the kitchen, she tried to reassure herself, just as Will might do if he'd been there. Simon was probably fine. He's just caught up helping the police, that's all.

She set the cookie jar down on the counter near the stove. No. Not there.

The police certainly didn't have any reason to hold him there indefinitely, did they? No.

Maggie turned, and placed the blue and white bear on the island counter near a small bunch of hanging bananas. That didn't look right either.

They wouldn't actually *arrest* him. They *couldn't*. Simon didn't *do* anything. No one had. It was an unfortunate mishap.

She grabbed the cookie jar and walked it over to the dining room table opposite the kitchen. She stepped back, gazing at the ever-staring eyes of the bear, and shook her head, wondering if the empty reminder of her great aunt belonged anywhere.

What happened to Simon's neighbor was all just an accident. Contamination of some sort at his job. Will and the news had said exactly that.

But then Maggie registered the sound coming from the TV again, a loud chime and then, familiar words and names catching her ear—Sebastian Martin and unexpected death and EXLI. Initially she thought it was just another round of the same coverage, and kept her eyes on the homeless cookie jar, but then she heard a different voice, a new reporter.

She stepped back into the living room, to the TV, and saw a field correspondent standing on a street—*Simon's street*. Maggie recognized the house behind the man holding the microphone. She'd passed it many times when visiting Simon. She stepped closer to the TV as the reporter went on.

". . . EXLI. Initial reports from officials had ruled Dr. Martin's death an accident, however, we've been told just minutes ago by reliable sources inside the investigation that new developments may refute that claim."

Maggie's mouth went slightly agape as she stood listening. Refute? But that would mean . . .

As if a response to her thoughts, a new chyron appeared across the bottom of the screen: BREAKING: DEVELOP-MENTS IN MARTIN DEATH POINT TO POSSIBLE HOMICIDE.

Homicide?

New evidence.

Maggie instantly thought of Simon. The voicemail. Will had said it was nothing, just the gibberish of a dying man, but . . . it *had* to be the new evidence. That would explain why Simon had been unreachable all day. They'd kept him at the police station, perhaps continued to question him. Maggie felt her concern starting to rise again as she paced in front of the television, watching, thinking, again picturing Simon in a bright orange jumpsuit, chains around his ankles—she caught herself. It would be okay, she thought. Simon had willingly gone to the police to give them the message. How could they suspect him? They couldn't. It was—

Her phone gave a long, hollow buzz against the glass of the coffee table. Maggie ripped her gaze away from the news report and almost leaped toward her phone, picking it up just as it gave another steady buzz. She eyed the caller ID readout on the screen.

It was Simon. Or at least, someone calling from his phone.

Maggie pressed the phone to her ear. "Simon?"

"Hi," Simon said. Maggie heaved a sigh of relief upon hearing his voice, but started pacing all the same. "You okay?"

"Am *I* okay?" She laughed and shook her head. "Yeah, I'm fine, now that'd I've heard from you. How are you? What happened? I've been calling and texting and—"

"I'm fine, Maggie. Sorry for not responding. The police took my phone."

"Are you still there now?"

"No, they finally let me go a little while ago. I'm . . . on my way home now. It was . . ."

"What?" Maggie asked, sensing the hesitance in his voice. She stopped her pacing halfway to the kitchen. The cookie jar bear stared back at her with unblinking eyes.

"Well . . . it's just, it was weird. Again, no need to worry. They told me I'm not in any trouble and were about to let me go after a couple hours, but then, they changed their minds. The guy who questioned me left suddenly, but he never came back. They just kept me locked in this interrogation room all day, gave me some food and coffee from time to time, but whenever I asked what was going on, they said they couldn't tell me."

"They kept you there and gave you no reason?"

"Yeah. I was sitting there all that time and then, about a half-hour ago, some guy I'd never seen before walked in and told me I was free to go. I guess they confirmed there was nothing fishy going on with me and Sebastian's voicemail and—"

"Simon!" Maggie exclaimed, realization hitting her. "They just—there was a breaking report on the news just now. They're considering your neighbor's death a homicide now."

"What?" Simon said, his tone higher, incredulous.

"They said there's some sort of new evidence." Maggie whirled around and headed back to the TV. The headline on-screen that once said "POSSIBLE HOMICIDE" now read just "HOMICIDE."

"But that . . . I don't see . . . that doesn't make any sense," Simon stuttered out. Maggie could hear the confusion in his voice as he tried to work things out. "Why would they let me go right when this is happening? Did the news say what the evidence is?"

"No. At first I thought it could be your voicemail, but they let you go so that doesn't add up, right?"

"Yeah, I guess. I just don't . . . damn, Sebastian, *murdered*? Will and I talked about it, wondered if maybe . . . and after the cops . . . but they let me . . . and now . . ."

There was a pause in the conversation as they both considered new information. Simon hearing of the homicide investigation, Maggie's ears perking up at the mention of his earlier discussion with Will and how it didn't match up with what her brother had told her. She almost asked what he meant but held back.

"Simon," Maggie said in her most serious tone. "Are you okay? I know you're out and safe, but I mean, are you *okay*? Your friend, dying . . . and now, this . . ."

Another pause in the conversation, though Maggie knew it was only Simon collecting his thoughts. When he spoke, his tone sounded calmer, but sad.

"I guess I am. It just feels sorta strange, you know? One day he's here, the next he's not. I suppose the same thing happens anytime someone dies. That feeling like they can't possibly be gone because you just talked to them, even if it's been a while since you *actually* talked to them. And then the voicemail and the police station, and now all this new stuff. It's . . . ah, I don't know."

But Maggie understood what he was going through. More than most people who'd undergone Rejuvenation at least. She wasn't as used to losing people, as Rejuvenites rarely dealt with death in the traditional sense, but she still had some experience. She looked back into the dining room, spying the cookie jar on the table there.

"You want to come over?" It was all Maggie felt like she could offer. A sympathetic ear and company.

"Thanks, but, I don't think so. I'd love to, really, but . . . I think I should just go home. I'm about to my exit anyway and, I'm just . . . tired. Sorry."

"No need to be sorry. You've had a rough day. I'll be here if—"

BEEP. BEEP.

Maggie heard the echo of the interrupting sound coming from Simon's side of the call.

"Hey," Simon said. "I got another call. Can you hold on a second?"

"Yeah. Sure."

Silence followed as Maggie waited with the phone still pressed tightly against her ear. She wondered who the other call was from and wished she'd asked. Will? Simon's work? The police? The moments stretched by and though Maggie was sure it was perhaps only around 30 seconds before she heard Simon's voice return, it felt much longer.

"Still there?" His voice was slightly higher again, confused.

"Yes. Everything okay? Who was it?"

"The detective from this morning."

"Was it about the new evidence?"

"Didn't say. Just said he wants to talk to me again, in person."

"Ugh, so you have to drive back out there?"

"No, actually he's coming out here. He said . . ."

Again, that hesitance in his voice.

"What is it, Simon?"

"Nothing, probably. He said . . . it sounded like it wasn't his decision to let me go in the first place. He seemed kinda mad about it, to be honest."

"Well why would they let you go then?"

"I don't know. I offered to go back, but he told me—he said no. Told me to stay put at my house."

"Jesus, it sounds serious." Maggie's voice wavered. "I'm . . . I'm scared, Simon."

"Me too."

EXLI LIES!

Rejuvenation was invented to stop disease.
Halted aging is the **REAL** side effect.

THE PLANET WILL DIE AND US WITH IT!
Livable space and resources are dwindling as the population of Persisters and Husks rises every year.
Overpopulation will lead to our destruction!

NEVER FORGET the early days of Rejuv experimentation when trials were performed on young children with horrific results.
These experiments continue in secret!

Abstainers Army will strike back!

ABSTAIN OR PERISH!

6

———

Two hours later, Simon was in the middle of yet another failed attempt at remaining comfortable while he waited. He'd tried to keep his mind busy when he initially returned home by preparing some dinner, which worked during cooking, but when it came to eating, his food sat largely untouched and cold on the edge of the coffee table. The few sips of coffee he'd had after only made him jittery. Which didn't make it any easier for him to resist the urge to stand and pace the room. Instead, Simon sat back, sunk into the couch, his feet propped on the table, eyes forward. He stared across the room, beyond the smaller love seat and out the bay window in the opposite wall.

There had been no movement outside since he had returned home and saw a handful of news vans parked on the curb near Sebastian's house. Simon had left the curtains drawn at first. Having heard what Maggie told him about the news report, and seeing numerous reports himself after turning his TV on, he had expected the street to fill up with obnoxious journalists trying to bleed comments out of those who lived on the street. But since he'd been home, all the news vans had left. It had only been in the last 15 minutes that Simon felt it safe to open his curtains again.

He ignored the large TV sitting in the corner to his left. It was tuned to a 24-hour news channel, providing continuous coverage of the case around Sebastian's death. The volume had purposely been set at a lower level, but even that Simon just tuned out for his staring contest with the street. The anchors were just repeating themselves now anyway. There had been no new developments since the follow-up reports of almost an hour ago. Those, at least, had been more informative than anything he'd gotten out of Detective Banks on the phone.

But there had been something in that phone call, hadn't there? Something that had stuck with Simon ever since . . .

"Detective Banks! I just heard there's new evidence to make you think Sebastian's death wasn't just an accident. Was it the voicemail? Does that have anything to do with it?"

"I can't say. But your message is certainly being looked at closer now with the, ah, new developments in the investigation."

"What's the new evidence then?"

"Sorry, Mr. Crowe. I can't say anything more about that right now. We do, however, need to speak with you again about that message you brought us earlier today. Are you at home?"

"You want to talk tonight?"

"Time is of the essence with these types of things, Mr. Crowe. And to be honest, releasing you earlier, well, that wasn't my call."

"Then who—"

"I don't know, but I'm damned sure gonna find out."

"But why shouldn't I have been released? Am I a suspect?"

"Well, n—I can't say. It's . . ." Here, Banks paused for a fraction of a second and then, "I believe you may be in danger, Mr. Crowe."

"Danger? But what—"

"Just do me a favor. Stay put. Don't come to the city. We'll come to you. Don't go outside. Don't talk to anyone. It may be a few hours until we can get to you, so just stay where you are."

"But why do you—"

"Stay put, Mr. Crowe. We'll talk soon."

There certainly hadn't been much to the call, Simon thought. Yes, not much, but there was something, and it kept his body tense.

I believe you may be in danger, Mr. Crowe.

Those words kept Simon alert more than any coffee ever could.

Detective Banks had hung up without another word, refusing to say anything else, leaving Simon now sat back on his couch unable to get comfortable as he peered out at the street, looking for any suspicious behavior around his house. He rubbed his temples, trying to fight off the throbbing that had grown there, stronger with every question and possibility that continued to flash through his mind.

But, as he waited, Simon was offered a slight respite to at least one of the unanswered questions that troubled him. By the time he'd gotten home, locked every door and window, changed into a more comfortable pair of jeans and t-shirt, and attempted to eat dinner, Simon caught the tail end of one of the newest reports about the investigation surrounding Sebastian's death. He flipped to another channel just as the anchor there was starting a new round of the story, sitting above a headline across the screen that read: MARTIN DEATH RULED HOMICIDE. And, as the report progressed, it seemed that whatever Detective Banks had been unwilling to say over the phone related to the new evidence had since been leaked to the press.

According to the news, the city coroner's office had received an anonymous call with two very distinct pieces of information. The first was a tip to check Sebastian's body for a certain type of chemical compound. In the time since, the coroner had looked and indeed found trace elements in what was left of the stomach lining and intestines. The anchor went into great detail about the compound, finally explaining that it had to be ingested orally.

What it all boiled down to, the anchor had said, is that Sebastian must've eaten the chemical that killed him. It was tasteless and odorless, so he wouldn't have even known he was eating it. Given the strict no-food policy inside EXLI labs and the painstaking decontamination procedures when exiting, the theory was that someone must have slipped the chemical into his lunch while at work, or perhaps laced his food at home. The poisoning at work was currently the leading theory since most channels were now quoting an EXLI parking garage attendant saying that Sebastian had left early the day before due to an upset stomach.

That still left the question of who had poisoned Sebastian and why? Apparently, that mystery had been answered by the anonymous caller, who had claimed full responsibility for Sebastian's death and done so as an unnamed member of one of the most influential Anti-Rejuvenation groups. Though the tipster did not say with which group they were affiliated, the latest news reports had whittled the list down to the Sapiens Against Persisters, Life Liberation, and Abstainers Army.

Simon had heard of Anti-Rejuvenation groups taking drastic actions in their cause, but murdering an EXLI scientist was extreme, even for them. The news ran with the story nonetheless, touting a growing war against EXLI by the Anti-Rejuv movement. A weaponization of Rejuvenation side effects against Rejuvenation.

With every new bit of evidence, every interview with a colleague of Sebastian's, every new theory, the story had been growing and growing. It seemed too large now, too important to Simon for him to be actually involved, even as a simple source of information.

But still . . .

I believe you may be in danger, Mr. Crowe.

At about five minutes to 9 P.M., he saw headlights appear outside, followed moments later by a dark-colored car, which slowed in front of his house and pulled into the driveway.

Simon jumped up from the couch and to the window. He peered outside, careful to hide as much of himself as he could. The car had pulled up right to the garage door, just far enough that Simon couldn't see the occupants from his position at the window.

And then, as if in response to their arrival, another set of headlights lit up from out on the street. In the dark, Simon hadn't even noticed the car parked there. It was unrecognizable to him, a nondescript vehicle, but he saw two figures, shadows, inside as the car pulled away down the street.

Two car doors opened, then closed. A moment later there was a knock on the front door.

His nerves still on edge about the car on the street, Simon crept closer to the door until he was standing right in front of it. He leaned toward the peephole, but before his eyes reached it there was another loud knock. Simon jumped back; his breath was rapid, shallow. He stood silent for a moment, forcing himself to calm down, then leaned in and placed an eye close to the door's peephole. The instant he saw the face on the other side, relief spread through his body. He twisted the lock above the doorknob and opened the door.

"Hello, Mr. Crowe," Detective Banks said with a half-nod. He stepped forward without asking. "Let's get inside."

Simon moved aside. "Yeah, um, sure," he said.

Banks moved fully into the entrance. A second man stood on the doorstep behind him. He had a badge like Banks, only clipped to his belt near a service pistol. In every other way, this second man was the complete opposite of his partner; the young face, perfectly manicured blond hair, crisp street clothes, and square teeth that were blindingly white when he bared them in a tiger grin.

He stepped inside the house, shook Simon's hand. It wasn't as firm a handshake as Banks, not even close.

"My partner, Detective Gantry," Banks grumbled as he closed and locked the door.

"Thanks for meeting with us. Simon, right?" Detective Gantry said, his words spilling out fast. "We appreciate your cooperation. This is really just a formality. We'll be out of your hair in no time." He shot a sideways glance at his partner, then looked back at Simon. "Dr. Martin was a friend of yours, yes?"

"He was," Simon answered, turning to Banks. "Did you see that car on the street just now?"

"Oh, yes," Banks said quickly. "Not to worry. Just a surveillance unit I had sent out until we could get here."

I believe you may be in danger, Mr. Crowe. Simon heard the words echo in his head again as the three men stood in the small entranceway for a moment. Detectives Banks moved his head from side to side casually, searching all the areas of the house they could while Gantry watched, tapping the toes of his left foot.

"Are you alone tonight, Mr. Crowe?" Banks said, looking back at Simon.

"Yes," Simon said. "Why—"

"Just a safety precaution." Banks paused, then seeing the look on Simon's face said, "It's a policeman's thing. Maybe it's just a *me* thing. I just like to know as much as I can about the environment I'm in, especially when I'm on the job and in unfamiliar territory."

"But you said on the phone, I might be in—"

"Just a precaution," Banks said, interrupting and giving Simon the slightest of winks. "Let's get down to business."

Simon looked questioningly at Banks for a moment and then

nodded. He led both men into the living room, wondering more and more about Banks's earlier warning on the phone. But Simon played along, even as he kept that warning at the forefront of his mind.

Banks thought, for Detective Gantry's benefit, they should start by going over everything Simon had said at the police station earlier in the day. Gantry had already listened to the recording of the message Detective Banks had taken, so he urged Simon to just tell him anything else. After getting them all fresh cups of coffee, Simon launched into his explanation of the events of the last 24 hours; why he hadn't gotten Sebastian's message until that morning, his reasons for wanting to share the message—everything.

When Simon finished his story, he sat in silence for a moment as Gantry scribbled a few short notes on a pad of paper that sat in his lap. Banks just sipped his coffee, eyes continuing to look around the living room, the nearby dining room, back to the entranceway. Simon looked at both detectives, sitting side by side on the smaller couch across from him with their backs to the window. The men might be partners, Simon thought, but outside of that, they looked like they were from two completely different worlds.

Gantry finished what little he was writing and then glanced over at his partner who remained silent. Simon thought he saw Gantry roll his eyes before he looked back and said, "Have you thought of anything new about that message Dr. Martin left for you since you spoke with my partner? Anything come to mind as far as what it could mean?"

"Nothing," Simon said. "I must have listened to that thing a hundred times by now too and I still have no clue what any of it actually means."

"Well, that's a shame," Gantry said, flipping his notepad closed and standing from the couch. "I was hoping you could help us out, Simon. Thanks for the Joe. I guess we can get—"

"What about the name Hillbrook?" Banks asked, his voice

finally booming to life again. Gantry gave a small sigh and sat back down.

"No idea."

"And the number?" Banks went on. "120?"

Simon shook his head. "Again, no idea."

"And the two people Dr. Martin refers to, what about them?"

"He never mentioned any specific—" Simon said.

"Not specifically, no. Not clearly anyway, but Dr. Martin did make the distinction of at least two separate people. A male and a female. He said 'he' and 'her,' so there are at least two of them."

"Okay," Simon said. "You think one of them is Hillbrook?"

Detective Banks shrugged, looked at his partner, and back at Simon. "We look into all possibilities. Do you know anybody named Hillbrook?"

"Nope. If I did, I would have thought of them immediately when I heard the message. I don't think I've ever heard the name before today. Are you guys searching the city to see if there are any Hillbrooks in the area?"

"Afraid we can't share that information, Mr. Crowe," Banks said.

Simon gave an exasperated huff, shook his head, and said, "Seems this whole thing would go a lot better if you could ever share *any* information. Like, if you're looking for Hillbrooks, are you searching EXLI employees?"

Banks looked curiously at Simon when he heard this last question. "Think we should?"

"Well, yeah. It's where I'd start. I mean, the first reports of Sebastian's death said it was all an accident at EXLI. Some sort of leak. Then these new reports come out about some anonymous caller saying he was poisoned with some super-specific chemical that can only activate when eaten. They're pinning it on the Anti-Rejuv groups, but that kind of thing seems like something only the scientists at EXLI would be able to pull off. That or scientists at a competing company."

"You're a smart man, Simon," Gantry said, his wide, toothy grin resurfacing. "You may not be fully convinced, but we're following all leads as they pertain to the AR groups. That's where the blame lies if you ask me. You know if Sebastian ever had any run-ins with the AR crowd?" Simon shook his head. "Well, if you remember anything, let us know. Like I said, just following up on leads. We also ran a crosscheck through the EXLI employee database, specifically those who work at the labs in their headquarters downtown. No AR connections and no one there by the name of Hillbrook."

Banks gave Gantry an annoyed look.

"What about their other facilities around the country and the world?" Simon asked. "Did you check those?"

"Not every one of them yet, but they're on the to-do list."

"And their competitors?"

Detective Gantry leaned forward but Banks waved a hand in the air.

"No decisions have been made, Mr. Crowe," Banks said. "We don't have the evidence to put anyone behind bars. Not yet. Just unsubstantiated claims like this suspicious anonymous caller. We're still investigating all avenues, but rest assured, Mr. Crowe, you cooperate and we'll do our best to sort everything out, make sure the scumbag who did this to your friend is locked up."

"Yes, of course," Simon said. He'd been steadily inching forward during the last part of their conversation and now sat anxiously on the edge of the couch. He took a deep breath as he sank back into the couch. "I'll do whatever I can to help."

"Good," Detective Banks said. He reached forward, picked up his coffee mug, and tipped it toward Simon as if in a toast. "We appreciate it."

Gantry stood again, watching as Banks took a large sip of his coffee in the same casual manner he'd acted in since arriving. Banks's eyes closed briefly as if focusing his attention on savoring the coffee in his mouth. When he opened them again, he looked up.

At first, Simon thought Banks was looking directly at him, but then noticed the suddenly intense gaze of the detective went over his head, beyond the couch.

"Mr. Crowe? I thought you said it was just you here?"

"It is. What—"

Simon began to turn his head, but before he could see the figure standing in the shadows of the dining room behind him, he heard what sounded to him like a pneumatic nail gun being fired behind his head. Two explosive cracks followed by a short release of pressurized air, all in quick succession.

CRACK! Hissssss. CRACK! Hissssss.

But it wasn't a nail gun at all. The faint ringing in Simon's ears and the sound of ejected shells clattering to the hardwood floor told him that, even before he saw the intruder holding a suppressed 9mm pistol step completely into view. Simon could swear he heard the bullets whip by him as they made their way to the two men seated opposite him.

"Wait. Not—" Gantry started to say as he turned, dropping his coffee mug as he raised his hands to shield himself. The mug smashed against the table sending ceramic shrapnel across the living room. His hands offered no protection as the first bullet penetrated Gantry's temple, a bright red circle forming against his blond hair. Gantry's body jolted from the impact of the shot, then trembled, before he slumped to the floor, his head thudding against the leg of the wooden coffee table.

Detective Banks was faster and luckier. He had just set his coffee mug back down on the table when the figure appeared and fired. Banks immediately went for the service pistol tucked into his shoulder holster. As he did, his body turned slightly and the bullet intended for him caught his shoulder. As the bullet buried itself into his flesh, the burn of it spreading down his arm and into his chest, Banks dropped to the floor between the couch and the table, reaching out to Simon, beckoning him.

"Get down!" Banks yelled as he popped back up, raising his gun with him, and firing. The shots from his pistol sounded similar to those fired from the gun of the figure in the shadows, just infinitely louder, echoing off the walls. CRACK! CRACK! CRACK!

Simon's ears rang louder from the new, unsuppressed gunshots as he dropped to the floor, just in time. As he slid down the couch he heard the faint blast of the intruder's 9mm again and saw one of the cushions on the opposite couch take the impact— one . . . two . . . three rips appearing in the fabric, white cotton bulging out of these wounds instead of blood.

Through the legs of the coffee table, Simon saw Detective Banks drop back down, lying on his side with both hands wrapped around his pistol. Blood poured from his right shoulder, staining the rug and the foot of the couch a deep crimson.

Then Banks was up on his knees again, firing at the intruder. The shots of his pistol boomed, echoed inside that confined space. The ringing in Simon's ears intensified.

Banks flopped back down on the floor as more return fire filled the room.

"Those fuckers!" Banks's voice was like a whisper amidst the ringing in Simon's ears, but he could still tell it was hoarse. Unlike anything Simon had heard from the man that day. "I knew it! We never should have left the station. Crooked bastards!"

Detective Banks looked directly at Simon now, his eyes narrow and focused. "Simon!" Again, that hoarse whisper of a voice.

Simon pointed at his ears and Banks yelled louder.

"When I open fire again I want you to crawl as fast as you can out of here into the next room. Get out of here. Run. Got it?"

Simon nodded quickly.

"Good. Take this."

The detective slid something across the floor toward Simon. The object coasted between the legs of the coffee table and for a brief moment Simon thought it was a small gun. When it hit his extended hand, he knew immediately what it was—his cell phone.

Simon nodded at Banks and slid the phone into his jeans pocket. He tensed his muscles in preparation and was surprised to find that he was ready. If someone had asked him how he might react before the shooting started, Simon would have expected himself to be frozen in fear, but instead, his body yearned to be used. To run. To be active. He figured it was the adrenaline pumping through his system. Before he could think any more on it—

The intruder's gunfire stopped.

Detective Banks sprang to his knees once more.

What followed took only a few seconds, but Simon felt as if time slowed. Banks rose from the floor and fired two shots. CRACK! CRACK! After the second, Simon heard a loud grunt come from the shadows behind the couch. The intruder had been hit! Simon looked up at Detective Banks just in time to hear another gunshot, this one suppressed, coming from the intruder. The bullet hit its mark, piercing Detective Milo Banks square in the chest. He tried to raise the service pistol, but his arm only made it halfway before falling again as he slumped onto his side, unmoving.

Simon had started crawling, then jumped to his feet. He turned, looked back at where the intruder had been shooting from and saw that the man had stumbled back a few paces into the dining room. The final shot of Detective Banks had been a good one, causing enough damage to the intruder that he had dropped the gun he held in one hand to his side, clutching at his stomach with the other. Simon couldn't see the man's face, but he did see a gush of blood spilling from his stomach, out through the fingers pressed to the wound.

The man raised his head from staring down at the wound in his stomach when he heard Simon's hurried footsteps.

Simon turned his gaze back to the front door where he scrambled to twist the deadbolt. Once he heard the click of the lock, he grabbed the doorknob and swung the door open. He darted outside, slamming the door behind him just as he heard two more gunshots from inside the house and felt the door rattle as they hit its other side.

Simon looked out into the street and saw no activity. Nothing like when he had arrived home. No media vans, no news crews, no police. Only Sebastian's house across the street and the bright yellow police line tape that surrounded it. A few of the houses on his street had porch lights on. Some even had interior lights on as well. Had they heard the shots? Were they calling for help? Perhaps he should—no, he couldn't seek shelter with his neighbors. The intruder would simply follow Simon there, killing him and them.

He had to think quickly. He had to get out of there.

Now.

That's when Simon's eyes locked onto the car in his driveway—Detective Banks's car. Or was it Gantry's? But then surely Gantry wouldn't have driven a—he shook the thought away. It didn't matter whose it was, only if they had left the keys in it.

Simon leaped from his doorstep, to the driver's side of the car. He grabbed the handle, pulled, and found it was unlocked. Opening the door, he looked inside to the ignition, but saw no keys hanging from it.

"Damn it!" Simon was in full panic now. He knew he had

only seconds before the intruder was able to stumble his way out of the house and take aim at him from the doorstep.

Simon looked back inside the car. The cup-holders were empty except for an empty paper coffee cup, stained brown around the rim. He hopped into the car, his legs still sticking out, and pulled down the driver and passenger visors. There was nothing there. He looked at where the glove compartment should have been but found the car did not have one, only a rectangular outline to show where the airbag was located. The clock was ticking, he thought. He needed to find some keys or start running. He unlatched the center console and lifted it. Sitting there in the console's storage compartment, on top of a spare notepad and collection of pens, was a set of keys. There were a few standard looking keys, perhaps to a house or locker. Along with these was one with a longer stem and a rounded black cover on its bow.

Simon knew he wasn't out of danger yet. He plucked the keys out of the storage compartment, and when he turned it in the ignition, the car roared to life. Simon couldn't help but smile.

He swung his legs into the car, slammed the door shut. He put the car in gear and started backing down the driveway. Simon saw the front door to his house open out of the corner of his eye.

The intruder stumbled out onto the front step, still clutching his stomach. He raised the gun he held in the other hand, pointing it toward Simon. He then paused just as Simon had finished backing the car out onto the street.

As Simon changed gears from reverse to drive, he turned his head and saw the intruder standing on his doorstep, watching him. Though Simon couldn't see the man's face behind the tight, full-head mask, he caught a glimpse of his eyes. They stared at each other for only a second, but it felt much longer.

A moment later Simon stomped on the car's gas pedal. The engine roared. Its tires screeched and smoked slightly, and the car tore off down the street.

7

Simon took large, gulping, rapid breaths as he barreled the detective's car onto the highway, narrowly missing an SUV turning towards the onramp from the opposite direction. The SUV honked at him from the middle of the road, but Simon barely registered the sound. He continued, his breathing growing more rapid, head still fuzzy.

Images that felt unreal flashed through his thoughts over and over as he pushed the car faster, the internal combustion engine roaring with a power he wasn't used to, pulling him along.

Detective Banks asking questions. Detective Gantry taking notes. That quizzical look on Banks's face and then—the crack of gunshots from the shadows. A coffee cup shattering. Banks yelling for Simon to take cover, returning fire, and then telling Simon to *run*.

It was real all right. Too real.

And now, where was he going? He did not know exactly. A singular idea overshadowed everything else: he needed to get the hell away from his house. Away from the city, from everyone. He needed to get as far away from danger as possible and fast.

The other cars on the highway were streaks of black and gray.

Then burning red taillights, flashes of headlights in his rearview mirror. He kept his foot on the gas, pushing the car faster and faster.

Just go. Run.

A sign on the roadside showed he was heading north. *Good,* he thought. *That's good.* North was away from his house, away from the city.

Run.

Get away from . . .

That man back there. The one who had appeared out of the shadows of Simon's home so suddenly, intent on killing . . .

an assassin . . .

and then the shooting began. Just like that.

Whoever the man was, whatever his reason for being there—he hadn't finished the job.

Run. Get away. Before he catches up to you . . .

Simon whipped his head around, searching for a car speeding along, too close to him, tailing him.

There was nothing there.

Back around to the front, a car coming up fast. The steering wheel squirrely under Simon's sweating palms. The car honking as he swerved around it, back in his lane, then looking around once more, sure he was being followed.

But again, there was nothing. Just the car he'd passed shrinking in the distance.

Desperate for air, hoping it'd calm him, clear his thoughts, Simon pressed the button for the window on the driver's side door.

Nothing happened. Broken.

He banged on the steering wheel with his palm. The thoughts kept coming, swirling. But one above all else: *Why?*

Why was he running? Why were Detective Banks and Gantry

murdered in his home? And, most importantly, why had Simon been targeted to begin with?

The answer was obvious: the assassin had come to the house to *silence* Simon.

It was Sebastian's message. That was the key, the reason the assassin had shown up, to prevent Simon and the detectives from talking any more about Sebastian's message and the information it contained.

Simon was certain now: Sebastian *had* been trying to tell him something before he died, something he chose to entrust only to a friend. He must've had his reasons for not trusting the police. And Simon had taken Sebastian's message right to them.

Detective Banks's words: *I knew it! We never should have left the station. Crooked bastards!*

Simon checked his rearview mirror again. Still nothing.

Maybe it was over.

But, Simon realized immediately, it couldn't be. This wasn't over. Because if the assassin knew so much about Simon, the existence of the message, he also must've known about—

"Will," Simon said. "Maggie." He yanked the steering wheel to his left, crossing two empty lanes until he reached the shoulder of the highway. He did not stop. The car bounced as he crossed the median, over the grass there, tires spinning. He pushed the car through it, back up and onto the road. Heading south, back the way he'd come. Back toward the city. Toward Will. Toward Maggie.

He prayed he wasn't already too late.

Simon pulled his phone from his pocket and dialed Maggie.

The ringing seemed to go on for an eternity, as Simon imagined only horrible things. Maggie dead. Will dead. The assassin waiting to finish him off too.

But it was only three rings before Maggie picked up.

"Hello?"

Simon's body relaxed, if only slightly, the instant he heard her voice.

"Maggie!" he said. "Thank God you answered. You okay?"

"Yeah, I'm good," she said. "Fell asleep for a bit there, but Will just called from home to ask about you and—"

"Will's all right, too?"

"Yes. Simon, yes. We're both fine. What's going on?" She paused. "Wait. What? Why wouldn't I be okay? What's wrong?"

"They're dead! Maggie, they're dead!"

"What are you talking about? Who's dead?"

"The detectives! The ones who came to visit me. Someone showed up, killed them!"

"Oh God, Simon, are *you* okay?"

"I'm all right. I got away."

"What hap—"

"Maggie, I'm coming over right now! Can you please just make sure the house is locked up—windows, doors, everything— and then get somewhere safe? We have to leave as soon as possible."

"Simon, tell me what's going on!"

"It's . . . I can't . . . I'll explain when I get there. I need to call Will. He's closer and—"

"*I'll* call Will," Maggie said, her voice firmer.

"What?"

"I'll call Will. You just focus on getting here safely."

"Okay. Yes, that works. But please, can you—"

"I'll get somewhere safe. You just get here."

"Thanks. Does Will still have that old handgun your father gave him?"

"What? Why?"

"Does he have it?"

"Yes! As far as I know."

"Good. Tell him to bring it. We may need it."

———

THERE WAS a KNOCK on Maggie's front door. Then another. In the split second between those knocks, Maggie's mind reeled. Was it Simon? Will? Someone else?

All she knew was that Simon had scared the living hell out of her. She had heard the panic in his voice, the urgency. And then, he was telling her to hide, to get somewhere safe. She'd called Will and then done as he requested, hunkering down in the small windowless study at the back of the townhouse—had almost calmed herself down when—

KNOCK!

And a second knock, faster and louder this time.

Then a voice. Only a few of the words audible:

". . . up. It's . . . open . . ."

Maggie crept to the door of the study and opened it a few inches. She held her breath as she listened. Her heart pounded in her chest.

More knocking, and the voice again.

"Mags! Open up for fuck's sake!"

Will.

Maggie burst out of the study, racing down the hallway, rounding the corner to the front door where Will's face peered through the side window.

She let him in and then quickly closed the door, latching the deadbolt once more. She turned and was pulled into a hug. It was a short embrace, but the feel of her brother's long arms around her provided a momentary respite from her nerves.

When they parted, Maggie noticed the two large duffle bags Will had dropped on the floor. Before she could ask—

"You hear any more from Simon?" Will said.

"No," she said. "Just that one call, what I told you on the

phone about the detectives being killed and Simon running, headed here.

"Jesus, Mags, what the hell is going on?"

"I don't know, but we should get out of the entranceway."

"Right." Will picked up the bags and nodded at her to lead the way.

"What are those?" Maggie asked.

"Just a precaution. Let's go."

Maggie led her brother down the hallway, around a corner, and into the study. She returned to her spot against the wall in the corner as Will closed the door behind them and dropped the bags again. He knelt and unzipped one. What he pulled out of it was instantly recognizable to Maggie. An old single-action revolver, their father's. Its wooden grip was worn, but the stainless steel cylinder and barrel still gleamed between a few small scuffs. Will zipped the bag then sat next to Maggie in the corner.

"Another precaution?" she asked, eyeing the gun as Will laid it down on the floor in front of them where it nestled into the carpet.

"Better safe than sorry, eh?"

The siblings sat in silence as fear made the minutes creep by. More than once Maggie thought about grabbing the phone in her pocket, dialing Simon, and demanding to know where he was, to know more about what was going on. Instead, she settled for nervous glances with Will as they waited.

Her mind wandered only once, in search of some kind of comfort. It was the sight of Will that did it, sitting there by her side, eyes on the door, *standing watch*. It made her think a summer day long ago when her childhood cat, Cuddles, had run away. Maggie had been convinced the cat was gone forever, crying, even as she was consoled by her big brother. But Will told her that no one, especially Cuddles, would leave Maggie behind. The cat knew its home and loved Maggie too much. After scouring the neighborhood and finding no trace of the feline, Will insisted they wait on the front porch until Cuddles returned. Even if it took all night. Maggie fell asleep eventually, but when she woke again the next morning, Will was still there by her side, still awake, keeping a look out. She'd told him it was no use. But Will refused to relent and shortly thereafter, Cuddles came trotting down the street, black and white fur swaying in the breeze. As the prodigal cat danced up the porch steps and plopped herself down on Maggie's lap, Will had grinned wide, nodded, and said, "Toldja, Mags."

She was thankful to have had Will by her side back then, and many times since. And now. Always standing watch. She kept this in mind as the silence of the room, the night, washed over her again. The unbearable waiting. When she couldn't take the quiet anymore, Maggie said, "I think we should—"

The words suddenly dropped from her lips when she heard— what was it? A slam or clang had sounded—

Outside the room. In the house? Outside?

Maggie couldn't tell. She looked at Will, who nodded and said, "I heard it too." He reached for the revolver.

Maggie and Will both turned, looked at the study door.

Beyond, a few more seconds of silence. Then, faint shuffling.

Maggie's breath caught in her chest. She reached out and clutched her brother's hand. They sat there, waited, and listened for what would come next.

———

Simon turned down Maggie's street, and for the briefest of moments, he imagined the flashing lights of police cars, the screeching of ambulance sirens. He was too late. The assassin had beaten him there, had gotten to Maggie first.

But there were no flashing lights. No sirens. It was only Simon's addled mind imagining the worst of scenarios.

What he actually saw was darkness and the stillness of an undisturbed neighborhood.

The street stretched into the distance. Aside from the mix of cars in the driveways and what additional greenery residents decided to add to small front lawns, each house in the neighborhood was nearly identical.

Simon drove on a little faster than the residential speed limit allowed until finally, Maggie's house rose out of the cookie-cutter surroundings. It was the garden in her front yard that made the house stand out. That rectangle of grass: a young willow tree surrounded by an ankle-high, white wooden fence, and at the base of the tree, flowers bright even in the pale light of the moon.

Anxious at the sight of the house, Simon's foot slipped against the gas and the engine gave a small burst of a roar before easing back. Simon flinched. The neighborhood was silent. He didn't need to raise suspicion by being overly anxious and speeding down the street.

Even still, when he finally reached Maggie's, Simon approached faster than he normally would have on any other day. He was thankful to see Will's truck in the driveway. He pulled close to the curb, moving too fast and too close and suddenly, the car's front tires hit the incline of the curb at the edge of the driveway, jumped onto the lawn and smashed through the little white fence Maggie had built. Simon slammed on the brakes and the car stopped, tilting slightly into the street. Its front right tire on top of shattered pieces of the fence, the back on the side of the driveway.

Simon turned his head side to side, sure the sound of the car smashing through the small fence and the screech of the brakes would rouse some of Maggie's neighbors. He sat silent, waiting, but when he heard no further noise, he figured it was safe.

He stepped out of the car, studying, listening to his surroundings, but heard nothing out of the ordinary. Then, in a lapse of thinking, Simon pushed the car door shut. He flinched again as it gave a loud CLANG. He waited for movement as the sound echoed, faded, but still, heard no reaction. He darted up to the front door of the house, raised his fist to knock, but froze. Instead, Simon pulled out his phone and dialed Maggie.

A moment later he heard the faint sound of ringing from somewhere deep inside the house. Maggie answered after two rings.

"Simon?" she said.

"I'm here," Simon said.

"You scared us! We thought . . . It doesn't matter. I'll be right there."

Simon heard footsteps behind the door, saw the curtain on the small window to the left of the door move aside. Maggie's slender face appeared and smiled thinly when she saw him. A moment later, he heard the locks move and the door opened.

"Simon!" Maggie said, leaping into his arms as he stepped inside and closed the door behind him. He hugged her tightly, then set her down in front of him.

The sight of Maggie calmed Simon more than any of the deep breaths he'd taken that night. Her youthful face, the sweatshirt of his that she wore, the way her ponytail bounced behind her head. And those blue eyes that entranced him so much. She looked like she was finishing up her last year of college, settling in for a long night of finals studying. Seeing her now, feeling the relief her mere presence brought to him, Simon couldn't help but feel lucky. He wondered how a woman like Maggie could ever find a man like him appealing. He was just some mid-thirties, Non-Rejuven-ite. She was beautiful—way out of his league.

Simon's attention was drawn away from Maggie as Will suddenly turned the corner and walked into the front hallway to join them. "There you are. What the hell is going on?" he said.

"Are you both ready to go?" Simon said.

"Yes," Maggie said. "We're ready."

"Good. Then let's get going before—"

"Hold on!" Will said, his voice elevated, strong. "I want some goddamn answers, Simon. Tell us what's going on."

"I can fill you in on the way. As soon as we're safe."

"*No*. Tell me now." Will paused, his gaze fixed on Simon. "Look, Simon. I trust you, but you've gotta tell us what the hell is happening. You call Mags in the middle of the night, scare the hell out of her, then just say we have to go?"

Simon returned Will's fervent stare, saw a similar look on Maggie's face. He understood their concern, their fear and need for answers. He felt it too.

"There's no time." Simon reached out to pull them both along, but the Buchanan siblings stayed rooted in place.

"We're not going anywhere until you tell us what happened," Maggie said.

Simon grimaced, then relented. "Someone showed up out of nowhere and shot them, okay? I told you that. I don't even know how he got into the house. One minute I was talking to the detectives in the living room and the next this man was in the dining room firing at us."

"So it wasn't the cops that tried to kill you?" Will asked. "Neither were on the take?"

"No, of course . . ." Simon's mind flashed back to his conversation with the detectives. Banks's speech slow, methodical. Gantry faster, as if he was in a hurry to be done. And Banks's words: *Crooked bastards!* "Now that I think about it, one of them did feel off."

"Knew it," Will said, snapping his fingers. "You can never be too careful. I swear, some of the shit those higher-ups at EXLI get into without so much as a night in jail, some of the cops have to be looking out for them, on their payroll."

"I take back what I said about you watching too many cop shows," Simon said, shooting Will a nervous smile. "Can we go now?"

"What else happened?" Will said.

"The one went down immediately. The other, the *good* one, helped me escape before being killed himself, but he did mention that he suspected some sort of foul play back at the station. After that, I just ran. The shooter came after me but by that time I was already in the car." Simon shrugged and let the point rest.

"Okay," Maggie said, breaking the moment of silence. "If they're still after you, after us, we need to go."

"You think he might follow you here?" Will said. "Jesus, we *do* need to get the fuck out of here!"

"That's what I've been saying!" Simon said.

"You two get to the car," Will said. "I'll go grab our bags and we can scram."

Will nodded at Simon and Maggie. He then set off in the opposite direction, heading back down the hallway and disappeared around the corner. Simon looked at Maggie, and they turned to the door.

Before Simon's hand reached the doorknob, Maggie stopped him. She grabbed his arm and looked up into Simon's eyes.

"Thanks for coming to get us," she said.

Simon leaned down and planted a firm kiss on Maggie's lips. All the commotion of that night seemed to melt away for the briefest of moments. The next second, their kiss was broken, and the night's urgency flooded back.

Simon opened the front door and peeked outside. All looked quiet. He turned back to Maggie.

"Stay behind me," he said. "If there's any trouble, I want you to run back here. Okay?"

"Simon, I can take care of myself," she said. "You don't have—"

"Just—*please*?" There was pleading in his eyes. His words were not a demand. They were born of fear. She nodded.

Simon pushed the door open wider and stepped out onto the porch. Maggie followed, leaving the door open for Will. If the assassin had caught up and was hiding somewhere close, it was his move. Simon and Maggie were clear targets.

As they made their way the short distance to the car, Simon's nerves felt amplified. He looked up and down the street for any signs of movement. He looked beneath cars, on the roofs of neighboring houses, anywhere he thought the assassin might hide. He saw nothing, and a second later, they passed over the remnants of Maggie's broken fence and were at the car.

Simon opened the door, turned, and ushered Maggie forward with a wave of his hand. She quickly moved past him and climbed over the passenger seat into the back of the car. Simon slid the seat back into place and then leaned in to speak to her.

"Lay down so no one can see you if they pass by," he said.

Maggie lay down. "Hurry. Will you?"

Simon nodded, stood up out of the car, gave the street another scan, then looked back up at the house. He could see through the open door and down the main hallway. There was no movement, no sign of Will.

There was an eerie silence on the street, as if the wind had suddenly died completely. The leaves on the trees no longer moved with their usual autumn shuffle, the breeze dropped silently from his ears. For a moment, Simon thought about heading back into the house to find Will. He didn't want to leave Maggie out here alone, but he had to do something. They were wasting time and exposed if someone did show up. Finally, before Simon had to make a decision, Will appeared.

Will walked down the main hallway of the house carrying two large duffle bags, shifting sideways to get the bags out of the door and then came hobbling down to the car.

"Those'll have to go in the trunk," Simon said.

"All right, can you pop it?"

Simon nodded and slinked around the front of the car, still looking around the street for signs of movement. He opened the driver's door, hopped in, and popped the trunk. When he looked into the rearview mirror, Simon saw the street behind them disappear as the trunk lid rose slowly up to block the street from view.

Simon tilted his head out the open car door and whispered back to Will. "You need some help?"

"I got it. Just be a sec. There's a tire back here that needs to go first."

Simon leaned back inside the car, looking up at the rearview mirror where he could see through just a sliver of the curved bottom of the trunk lid. Through this sliver, Simon saw Will leaning down into the trunk. The car trembled as the tire was freed, dropped onto the street where it caught Simon's eyes as it rolled into a nearby lawn.

When he looked back into the rearview mirror, Simon saw the trunk lid slam shut. The view now unobstructed, he could see Will standing behind them. And about twenty yards behind Will was a black SUV parked on the street and a masked man standing beside it. The man held the same gun he'd used back at Simon's house, pointed directly at them.

"Will! Get down!" Simon screamed.

Will dropped as two gunshots cracked the air behind them. The man by the SUV staggered forward, continuing to fire with one hand while the other clutched his stomach.

"Will!"

"What's happening?" Maggie said, popping her head up from the back seat to look out the window. "Is—"

"Get down!" Simon yelled.

Maggie dropped her head just as the back window shattered, glass raining down over her.

"Where's Will?" Maggie screamed. "Did he get hit? Where is he?"

"Right here," said Will, scrambling into the car, pulling the passenger side door closed. He crouched down in the seat and turned to Simon. "Didn't you hear me? Let's get the hell out of here!"

Simon nodded as he noticed a few lights starting to flicker on in various houses of the surrounding neighborhood in response to the gunfire, the screaming. He grabbed the driver's side door, pulling it shut just as another crack sounded behind them and the window of the door shattered. With his other hand, he reached up and turned the keys still hanging in the ignition. The car rumbled to life.

"Drive!" Will grunted as he reached behind himself and pulled his father's gun into view. With another loud grunt, Will spun around and pointed the old revolver out the space that used to be the back window of the car. He pointed it directly at the assassin, only a few feet away behind the car now, cocked the hammer with a ratcheting click, and said, "Down, Mags. Cover your ears, everyone."

Simon did as Will said, planting his hands firmly against the sides of his head, but even as he did so he kept his eyes locked on the rearview mirror. He saw the assassin's eyes widen through the holes in his mask at the appearance of the revolver in Will's hands, but it was too late. Before the assassin could get off another shot, Will fired. An ear-splitting blast filled the entire car as the first round was fired. Much louder than any round Simon had heard fired that night. The faint sound of the hammer cocking again, the cylinder spinning, then another loud blast. Then another.

Ears ringing from the revolver being fired off in such proximity and such a confined space, Simon peeled his hands from his head, shifted the car into gear, and slammed on the gas pedal—the whole time, his eyes fixed on the assassin in the rearview mirror. The masked man's body jolted back as two of Will's three shots hit him, one in the chest, another in the neck. More lights in the surrounding houses sprang to life, dogs barking, no doubt in response to the booming shots of the revolver. Shadowy outlines of people inside could be seen in the glowing windows, looking down on the street. The last of the assassin that Simon saw before the man became a distant spot in the rearview mirror was of a crumpled form on the pavement that convulsed for a second or two before going completely motionless.

"Simon!" Maggie screamed.

Simon looked away from the mirror and back to the road just in time to see they were heading straight for a car parked on the street ahead. He jerked the wheel to the left and swerved, scraping against the side of the parked car with their own. A moment later he was back in control, rocketing the car down the street.

Will stayed propped up in the passenger seat for a moment longer, a grizzled look on his face and the revolver in his hand still trained out the back window. Once they'd turned off Maggie's street, Will slid back into his seat. He gave another grunt and a long sigh. Will turned to Simon, whose face was still frantic, and gave a nervous chuckle.

"What the hell is so damn funny?" Simon said, his eyes darting between the road ahead and the passenger seat.

Will raised the revolver, faint wisps of smoke trailing from the barrel. His fingers trembled around the gun as he looked at Simon and said in a voice mirroring his hand, "It's . . . n-not like the cop s-shows."

"You did great," Maggie said from the back seat, squeezing Will's shoulder. "Thank you."

"Yeah," Simon said with a nod as he continued maneuvering the car along the street. "Thanks."

Will shifted in his seat again, gave a wheezing cough, and set the gun on the floor. His hand still shook when he pulled it away, wiped his sweaty palm against his pant leg.

"You two all right?" Will said.

"I'm okay," Maggie said.

"Me too," Simon said. "You? For a moment there, I thought he got you."

"Ah, I'll live," Will said as he sank into the passenger seat, exhaling a long, steady breath. "All in a day's w-work for this old man."

"Simon?" Maggie said.

"Yeah?"

"Where do we go now?"

Simon thought for a moment. Where *were* they heading? They couldn't go back to his house. They couldn't go to the police. "I don't know," he said. And then a thought returned: *Run. Get away.* "The best we can do for now is get out of town. As far away from the city as possible until we figure out our next move. Everyone good with that plan?"

They were.

Back to the highway—heading out, away, as far away as they could get before whatever came next. But first—

Run.

8

WITH NO DESTINATION SIMON DROVE THE BATTERED CAR, LOADED now with his friends, onto the highway and headed northbound for the second time that night. He couldn't think of anywhere for them to go. Neither Will nor Maggie offered any ideas. The first hour of the drive was silent, just the occasional sigh from Maggie in the back or a grunt from Will as he tried to get comfortable in the passenger seat. They were all too tired to talk. Too rattled.

Around four o'clock—with Maggie fast asleep, feet pulled up onto the back seat and arms crossed around her middle to fight the cold sweeping in through the broken windows—Will finally broke the silence.

"Simon," he said, voice haggard. "We should get off the highway."

Simon turned to look at his friend and, for a moment, Will's face looked incredibly pale, sickly. Simon almost said something, then noticed his reflection in the rearview mirror and saw he too wore a similar look. It was the moonlight, he realized. It shined through the windshield, bathing them all in a dull, ghostly glow. Instead, Simon simply said, "You think?"

Will coughed and wiped a thin layer of sweat from his forehead. "It'll be light soon. If anyone's looking for us, and I'm sure they are, we'll be spotted too easily from here. We need to get off the highway, onto some back roads with fewer cars."

Simon looked out the windshield as they passed a sign for an exit two miles ahead.

"Warren City all right with you?"

Will nodded.

Simon took the exit ramp and they approached an intersection. He took a right, heading toward a small Re-Station with neon signs in its windows advertising beer, snacks, and other convenience store items. Three large, gray stanchions stood out front with cords hanging off them on either side; car recharging stations. Next to this was a single, yellow gas pump.

"You need anything from else while we're here?" Simon asked as he pulled up next to the lone fuel pump.

Will shifted uncomfortably. "Well . . ." he started, hesitant, then said, "No. Just the gas."

"Will, you sure you're all right?" Simon asked.

Will turned his head, looking at the road behind them, then down at his sleeping sister, before looking back at Simon. "I'm fine. Just get the gas and get us out of here. It's . . . it's not safe yet is all. We're still too close to the city and . . ."

"What?"

"Nothing. I just . . ." It was clear that Will wanted to say something. When he finally spoke again, Simon could see the seriousness in his eyes. "We need to protect her, Simon. You need to keep her safe."

"Who?" His answer was a reflex, but so was his next thought. "Maggie?"

"Yes. She . . . All this, everything that's happened. We were all so close to . . ." Will's eyes were sagging, watery. His nostrils flared as he took a hard breath, as if holding back tears. "I just . . . can't lose her, ya know?"

"Yeah. Of course, yes. Will, I hear you. I understand. I don't want to lose her either. I don't want to lose anyone. All this, it's just . . . crazy. We're lucky just to be alive and, well . . ." Simon looked away.

Now it was Will's turn to shoot an inquiring glance at Simon, whose unfinished words and drooping brow showed something else was weighing on his mind. "What is it?"

Simon turned his gaze back to Will and said, "I'm sorry, Will. I'm *sorry*. It's my fault you and Maggie are here. It's my fault we're all here right now. I dragged you both into this mess. I should have never . . . I don't know, I never should have involved you two. I—"

"Simon. Shut up." Will forced the faintest of smirks onto his face. Simon was taken aback at first, and then Will went on. "This isn't your fault. None of it."

"But *I* got the message. *I* showed it to you. I'm the reason you're here. Why Maggie's here. If I'd have just—"

"What? Not talked to me about it? Come on. You had no way of knowing what kind of message Sebastian left for you. You didn't know we'd end up here; that everything that's happened tonight would happen. You didn't ask for that message and you didn't pull any triggers back at your house. *None* of this is your fault, Simon." Will nodded to punctuate his statement, then sat back in the passenger seat with a groan. He then added, "And anyway, it's like you said; we're lucky to be alive, right? But we *are* alive."

Simon laid a hand on Will's shoulder, felt cold, clammy skin through Will's shirt. "Thanks for having my back. We'll keep her safe. You and me."

Will smiled; Simon was delighted to see his friend's face return to its usual jovial expression.

"Promise?" Will asked.

"Promise."

Will exhaled a long breath and said, "Go on then. Gas us up, and let's get outta here."

Simon smiled and gave Will's shoulder another gentle squeeze. He opened the car door and was closing it just as Will said, "Make it quick."

———

"MAGS."

Maggie's eyes fluttered open to see the backseat of the car as she heard the whisper, felt a hand gently shake her side.

"Hey, Mags. *Wake up*. Don't worry. Everything's okay. We're safe, but—"

"What?" Her mind was groggy, wanting to return to sleep, so much so she couldn't even bring herself to turn over to look at him.

"I just need to talk to you, before Simon gets back. Then you can sleep."

"Back? What—"

"I just need to tell you that, well, it's going to sound weird for me to bring this up now but . . . when you called me tonight, before I picked up the phone, I thought maybe you and Simon had, ya know, another one of your fights."

Even in her foggy, yearning-for-sleep mind, Maggie was shocked to hear her brother's words. She just thought, there goes Will again, sticking his nose where it didn't belong. And *now*?

"Simon and I don't fight."

"Come on."

"We *argue*, but we don't fight."

"Oh, huge difference there."

Maggie felt herself starting to come out of her sleep more, but she still didn't turn around to look at Will. "There *is* a difference.

All couples argue. It's normal. Healthy even. And now is hardly the time to—"

"Call it whatever you want, but you two really need to start communicating better about . . . you know."

"Wait," Maggie said, realization dawning. "Has he talked to—"

"He's said some things to me, yeah," Will said. "As if *I* could possibly know what is going on inside the head of *any* woman. Yeah right." Maggie knew he wanted a laugh for his joke, but she wouldn't dignify one. "Look, Simon . . . He's just trying to understand what's going on with you two and this . . . *issue* you two keep arguing about. He's trying to understand what's going on inside that head of yours."

Maggie flopped onto her back, stared up at the car's ceiling. "Then he should just ask me!"

Will chuckled and said, "Sounds like he's tried, little sis, but communication's a two-way street."

"But we *do* talk." She paused as she thought it through, her mind wandered to their last argument. "We're fine *most* of the time and then . . . whenever we get into anything more, the future . . . and . . ."

"Then what?"

"Then he talks to you instead of me from the sounds of it. Look, I don't want to talk—"

"Come on, Mags. You know it's not like that. Sure, I *want* to help, but hey, at the end of the day, I'm just the friend. Just the brother. It's you two that gotta make it work."

"I know . . ." But Maggie was lost in her thoughts.

"It can, you know?"

"It can what?"

"Work. You two might get in arguments about it, but it's only because you care. Who gets heated over something they don't care about, right?"

"I guess."

"Trust me. *It can work.* You two just have to, ya know . . . communicate."

Maggie finally rolled her head to the side to find Will looking into the back seat at her.

"But what about . . . what others say . . ."

"Ignore 'em. It's *your* life."

"It's not fair to him."

"He says the same thing about you."

Maggie looked sheepishly at her brother, then up at the car's ceiling again, and back to him. "But what about the future?"

"Mags," Will said, raising his eyebrows and looking at his sister matter-of-factly. "What about *now*?"

———

WHEN THEY WERE BACK on the road, they stuck to the country lanes that skirted the highway and wound through the forests and small towns. They chatted for a bit, but silence soon reigned in the car once more as Maggie fell back asleep after Simon had declined her offer to drive.

It was all Will could do to keep his eyes open as well. It felt like everything that'd happened that night was finally catching up with him. The lack of sleep, the call from Maggie, the race to her house, the assassin. Firing the death blows that finally laid out their would-be murderer. The adrenaline had pumped through his body, his finger on the trigger, squeezing it tightly—once, twice, and a third time until their attacker had dropped. And then, they had run. A long night that had taken its toll. He felt it in his body, deep down in his heart. The adrenaline has worn off and he was so very tired.

As Simon drove, Will leaned against the cool glass of the window and stared at the trees that were set back from the road, swallowed in darkness but for where the moon shone down. Cool air flooded the car through the broken windows, producing goose-flesh on his arms and neck, but not enough to keep his eyes from drooping. He wondered how Mags could sleep in such chill, but found himself only smiling at the thought because he knew from watching her grow up that she could sleep almost anywhere.

His mind remained on Maggie, all the years they'd spent together. Good times, bad times, and everything in between. They certainly hadn't had a normal sibling experience, he thought—or had they? Sure, he was 20 plus years older than her, but by the time she could remember him he'd already undergone the procedure, so he had remained unchanged her entire life. She'd always known him as he was now, at least in a physical sense. She'd always seen him the same way. It was their bond that had changed and grown older, stronger. Was that not the normal sibling experience nowadays? It certainly wasn't like it had been long ago, before The Decay, before Rejuvena-tion. That was the old way, the abnormal experience. But, he thought, even if he and Maggie had gone through their lives that way, it wouldn't have changed the fact that he'd been there for her. No matter what. And if he had anything to say about it, he would always be there for her. That was, of course, part of the reason he said what he had to Simon at the Re-Station. And to Maggie.

Because if he ever faltered, Will knew Simon would be there for Maggie. He trusted Simon, not just as a friend, but like a brother. Yes, Will thought, *like a brother*. And Maggie would be there for Simon as well. Both of them, propping each other up.

And together, well, together Maggie and Simon were his favorite people. No doubt about that. Will was damn happy when they got together, which was why he'd been frustrated by all the arguments and nonsense they'd been into lately. He'd seen it all before and so, had done his best to calm the storms, as much as he could anyway. Impart whatever wisdom he thought he had and then let them handle it. They'd see it one day. At least, he hoped.

The passing trees outside the window suddenly blurred as Will felt his eyes close, but he struggled and snapped them open again. No. Not yet. He was tired, yes, but not *that* tired. He fixed his gaze on the trees outside again, focused on them as they flashed by. Tree by tree by tree . . . It was almost hypnotic, which didn't bode well for keeping his eyes open and fending off fatigue. Will knew that. But still, he watched. He studied them, and the darkness behind and around each tree. What was that old saying? *It's always darkest just before the dawn.* That was it. That was now, he told himself. Things certainly seemed dark, but dawn was approaching. He could sense it, almost feel the sun hiding on the other side of night, waiting to peek out from behind the trees and scatter the darkness. Oh, how he wished he could see it, that new dawn. And the next . . . But that sense was overtaking him. The fatigue was overwhelming him. He felt it in the sagging of his eyes, the heaviness of his body, the coldness around him . . . and deep down, way down in his heart. So tired. So very, very tired.

He could fight the feeling no longer. Will's eyes closed, and he drifted off.

Maggie awoke just as the first slivers of dawn were starting to peek over the horizon behind them and filter through the forest that surrounded the road on both sides. It wasn't this new light that roused her however—it was the smell of the trees.

They had been driving through the forest for some time now, ever since they exited the highway and got off the main drag headed out of Warren City. But it was only in the last fifteen minutes or so that the trees around them had started getting really tall, the forest thicker and thicker. Deep green trees stood all around them and as they drove by, the combined smells of each one seemed to swoop into the car through the broken windows. The earthy smell of deciduous trees, recently bare of their leaves, mixed with the sweet, sap-induced aroma of the conifers—a mixture of odors that was pleasant, but stung the nostrils and the senses to life with each inhalation.

Maggie stretched out her arms and legs from the near-fetal position she had slept in, thankful for a smaller frame which allowed her more room to stretch than most. She yawned and let her legs fall back onto the seat as she propped herself up on one elbow and looked between the front two seats of the car.

Will had his head against the window, eyes closed, silent. Simon stared forward, still driving.

"Hey," Maggie said.

Simon flinched, whipped his head around to look at her, and then turned back to the road.

"Jesus, you scared me," he said.

Maggie gave a small laugh and reached a hand forward to stroke the back of Simon's neck.

"Sorry," she said. "I didn't mean to startle you."

"Well you did. Then again, I think just about anything would startle me right now." He paused and looked at Maggie's face in the rearview mirror. "You sleep okay?"

She shrugged.

"As well as can be expected I suppose. I can't believe I was even able to fall back asleep. How long has Will been out?"

"Not sure. Maybe a half-hour, hour, I think," Simon said.

"You've been driving all night. Why don't I take over?"

Simon shook his head. "No. I'm tired, but I don't think I could sleep if I tried."

"If you say so. Did you two decide where we're headed?" She looked out the window at the forest.

"Just to stick to back roads so it's not so easy to spot us. I'm not even really sure where we're at anymore."

Maggie joined Simon in staring out the windshield. The road ahead ran into the distance with no sign of any other approaching vehicles. She turned her head and saw the same thing out the back. Maggie stretched again and swung her feet off the seat. There was a soft squishing sound as her shoes landed on the car floor.

"Yuck," she said. "Did you guys spill something or did it rain on me while I was asleep?"

"What?" Simon said.

"The floor—it's all wet." As Maggie leaned over to get a better look at her feet, the potent scent of the trees was replaced by a different odor. It was strong and coppery. She bent her arm down and touched the floor. The liquid on the floor was tepid, felt slick between her fingers. She knew what it was before she even brought her fingers up in front of her and saw them stained in deep red. "Jesus! It's blood, Simon! Are you—"

"Blood? No, I'm not—"

Simon slammed on the brakes and the car skidded to a stop in the middle of the road. He felt the seat belt dig into his chest as he was thrown forward and saw Maggie hit the back of the passenger seat out of the corner of his eye. Will was thrown forward violently, then back, also held in place by a seat belt, but he did not stir.

"Will?" Maggie said, her voice rising with anxiety. She reached around the seat and grabbed her brother by the shoulders. "Will! Say something!"

Simon threw the car into park and turned to the passenger seat. Will's complexion was as pale and sickly looking as it had been hours before when Simon had discounted the appearance as a simple trick of the moonlight. His cheeks were sunken, his mouth open, but Simon could see Will's chest rising up and down.

"He's breathing!" Simon said. "Will! Can you hear me?" Simon reached over and his hands replaced Maggie's on her brother's shoulders. He gave Will a shake and watched his head wobble from side to side, but his eyes remained closed. "Will! Wake up, buddy. For God's sake, wake up!"

Simon heard sobs coming from the back seat. He turned his head and saw Maggie sitting in the middle, her head in the space between the two front seats. She clutched at her brother, her panicked gaze fixed on him.

Simon's eyes drifted down his friend's limp body until he saw a large, dark splotch on Will's right side. That must have been where the bullet pierced him, Simon thought. Will was hit, but hadn't said a word about it.

Amidst his instant, powerful concern for Will's wellbeing in that moment, Simon also felt an abrupt sinking in his stomach as he took in the scene. It was like a sudden sickness growing within him, but not from any bloody, horrific sight. It infected his mind as much as it soured his stomach. *This is my fault.* The thought had returned. It flashed in his mind and pulsed in his heart. Again and again. *This is happening because of me. It's all my fault.* But then another thought was there, a voice in his head, Will's voice from a few hours before . . . *None of this is your fault, Simon.* Will had known what had happened to him, even then, and still he'd tried to impress upon Simon that none of it had been his fault. Simon had found a shred of comfort in that reassurance last night, but now, he didn't know. His ability for rational deliberation was out of reach, because Will was sitting there, unconscious, with a bleeding hole in his side. Simon tried his best to push the competing thoughts and troubling feelings away to deal with the matter at hand.

Maggie leaned in between the front seats, shook her brother again, and screamed right in his ear. She then hauled a hand back and slapped Will hard across the face.

Will's hands sprang up from his side and his eyes shot open. One hand went instantly to his side and clutched at the wound. The other went to his face and touched the bright red spot on his pale cheek where his sister had slapped him.

"What the fuck, Mags?" Will said in a groggy, pained voice. "Why . . . why'd you do that?"

A nervous laugh escaped Maggie, partly because of her brother's reaction, but more from her joy that he was alive and conscious again. She looked at Will, then at Simon as if to reaffirm what she was seeing, then back at her brother again.

"Will! Thank God you're awake!" she said.

"Yeah, I'm awake. Why'd you hit me?" Will said.

"Will, you're bleeding everywhere!"

"Am I?" He looked down at his side, pulled his blood-soaked hand away for a moment, and then replaced it. "Son of a bitch, I am. Shit. I hoped it would hold up until we reached somewhere safe."

"You knew?" Maggie said, tears now running down her cheeks. "You knew and you didn't tell us?"

"Course I knew! I was *shot*!"

"But why—"

"We needed to get away. There wasn't time to get me help."

"Well there's time now," Simon said, unable to hold back that feeling—that sickness—inside, wanting to do something, to fix what he'd done. He unbuckled his seat belt, ready to act. "You have extra clothes in those duffle bags in the trunk? Something we can use to try and stop the bleeding?"

Will coughed and tensed his face, grabbing at his side.

"Yeah, there're clothes in there, but, oo-boy, I don't think it'll do any good."

"What?" Maggie said. "What do you mean?"

"I mean I've lost too much blood," Will said, looking down at this side. "And from the feel of it, I'm still losing it. That fucker got me good. Feels like Swiss cheese in there."

"No. No, you'll be all right." Maggie turned her head, looking at Simon with wide, frantic eyes. "He'll be all right, won't he? We can stop the bleeding, get him to a hospital."

Simon looked back at Maggie, not entirely sure what to say.

"Even if you could stop the bleeding there's no way you could get me to a hospital in time," Will said.

"You don't know that, Will," Simon said. "There could still be time. You don't know what you're talking about."

Will shook his head and smiled.

"Of course I know what I'm talking about. I don't watch all those cop shows for nothing, remember?" Will laughed, his paunch of a belly jiggling lightly, and then grunted in pain as he clutched at his side tighter. "Besides, you go to a doctor with a gunshot wound, they're going to contact the police and that'll defeat the whole purpose of us leaving town in the first place."

"We can't just let you d-die!" Maggie said, sobbing. "I won't!"

"Sorry, little sis. Looks like that's the way it's gotta be." He looked up at Simon. "Tell her, Simon."

Simon stared back at Will, into his eyes. In all the years he'd known Will, Simon could not remember a single time when he saw the same amount of seriousness he saw at that moment in his friend's eyes. Perhaps the night before, at the Re-Station, when Will had said things that seemed even more important now looking back. Yes, then, but no other time had Will looked that way. His eyes were fixed on Simon, resolute. Simon stared at Will and it was as if that returned gaze washed away his guilt. Not all of it, but enough for him to see, to understand. Simon turned his head to look at Maggie, but couldn't force himself to utter the words. He only nodded.

Maggie could not believe what she was hearing and seeing.

She couldn't believe Simon had seemingly agreed with what Will was saying. Her eyes blazed at Simon the instant after his nod. She burst into tears and dove forward, wrapping her arms around her brother's neck and moaning "No, no, no . . ." Will winced in pain, but hugged Maggie tight, then guided her into the back seat again.

"Help me out of the car, would you?" Will said. "I want to be outside."

Simon looked at Will, then Maggie, before pulling the handle to his left and opening the driver's side door. He climbed out of the car and as he stood up, felt his body crack and stretch from the long hours of driving. The stretch felt good and he stood tall as the trees around him for a moment before jogging around the car and opening the passenger side door.

When he saw the right side of Will's body up close, Simon knew his friend was right. Even if there was a hospital across the street, it was unlikely they would be able to save Will. The right side of his shirt and pants were caked in a mixture of wet and slightly coagulated blood. The seat and side of the door were also smeared in crimson. A pool of blood covered the passenger side floor of the car but for the small island of the gun which still lay between Will's feet.

As Will unbuckled himself and the seat belt drew back into the side of the car, Maggie climbed up into the driver's seat. She grabbed his arm, shook her head, as though if she just held him there, the two men would see reason. They'd agree to get out of here, speed as fast as they could for the nearest hospital even if it was too far away. They'd understand. They'd see. Oh, why couldn't they just see? But when Will took a deep breath and sat forward, Maggie's arm became his crutch, supporting and steadying her brother's position. She surprised herself by not pulling Will back, but helping as he leaned toward the opening of the door.

Simon stepped in and grabbed him around the waist, swung Will's arm over his shoulder and helped him out of the car and to his feet. With his side pressed against Will's, Simon felt the warmth of the wound against him and a trickle of blood ran down his side as he led Will away from the car.

"Where to, good buddy?" Simon said.

Will peered into the forest and said, "Just . . . just put me down over there . . . by that birch tree."

They hobbled together for a few steps until Maggie appeared on the other side of Will, placing his other arm around her neck. The three of them worked their way into the forest until they came upon the tree Will had pointed out from the road. They sat him down, back against the white skin of the birch tree which glowed brightly in the growing rays of dawn.

Once down, Will gave a heavy sigh of relief and looked up at Maggie and Simon with a smile.

"End of the line," he said.

Maggie swooped down to Will's side, wrapping her arms around his neck and sobbing into his shoulder.

"Let's go back to the car, Will. To a hospital," she pleaded. "Let us at least try!"

But Will shook his head once again and patted his sister on the back.

"I told you it's no use, Mags," he said. "Just let me sit here for a while."

"But—*you'll die.*"

Will grabbed his sister's arm and guided her up in front of him so they could see each other clearly.

"Yes," he said. "I will." Will looked up at Simon, then back down at his sister. "But I think . . . I know, I'm okay with that."

Maggie continued to sob, burrowing her face into her brother's shoulder.

"I can't accept it," she said, lifting her head, shaking it. "I just —can't. I'm not as strong as you."

Will looked at his sister with the same serious eyes Simon had seen minutes before in the car.

"You're wrong, Mags. You *are* strong. Stronger than me. You know it. You don't need me to tell you that. But believe me when I say it, because I have a feeling you'll need that strength for a lot more than just . . . ah, just dealing with your stubborn older brother." Will smiled up at them both, chuckled, then winced, and smiled again. "Just . . . can you both just . . . do me a favor?"

Maggie nodded. Her words gone.

"Anything," Simon added.

Will looked at them both, his eyes deep and meaningful. "I meant what I said last night, Mags. And . . . at the station, Simon. Just . . . look after one another, will ya?" The pain seemed to be getting to Will. His words grew more and more broken, his winces more frequent, but he continued. "I know there's . . . always something to . . . to argue about but . . . don't let it win. I've seen a lot . . . and, well, you two . . . I've seen . . . I know . . . it can work."

Maggie broke into a fresh round of tears, now joined with Simon, as they both nodded at Will, smiled at him and listened.

"Will, you—"

"Don't fret about me, little sis. I've . . . had a good run."

Simon knelt on one knee next to Maggie and placed a hand on her shoulder. She flinched slightly at first, and then reached up and grabbed his hand, but her eyes remained on her fading brother.

"But . . . we can't just sit here," Maggie said, repeating her plea yet again, her words more pained than ever. "You can't just . . . die."

Will smiled at his sister again and reached up, placing his hand on hers and Simon's.

"We all . . . have to die sometime, Mags," Will said. And then, almost as if the pain of moments before had suddenly vanished, Will's words flowed together with perfect clarity. "That's life. Not even Rejuvenation can stop that. Better to do it now, having done something to help protect the ones I love than years from now in some government-approved old age home for brainless Rejuvenites."

"But—"

"*Margaret*." Will's voice was clear and strong. "Don't worry about me. It barely even hurts anymore. You two, just, look after each other. Remember: *it can work*. Me, I'll be fine. I'll be just . . . fine."

Will squeezed his sister's hand gently and in turn, she squeezed Simon's. All three shared a look and a warm smile as the sun continued to rise, illuminating the forest around them and making the birch tree at Will's back shine brighter and brighter with each passing second.

Simon looked upon his friend sitting there basking in the morning light. He thought it odd that someone should die at such a young age, then remembered Will wasn't as young as he looked. Simon supposed it was just easier to accept a person dying if they were in an accident or died of natural old age, even if fewer people were participating in the latter than they used to. But Will looked young, even with his pale face he looked in the spring of his life, ready to live on for years and years. It was the strangeness of it all, Simon thought, of seeing someone die who looked so young, but who you knew had lived almost a lifetime by the old standards. At least Will had accepted it, even if he and Maggie hadn't. At least there was that.

Simon leaned in closer to Maggie and Will, forcing himself to smile even as he fought back the tears that always came when losing a dear friend.

The sun shined brightly around them as they waited in the

forest together. The light peeking through the trees illuminated their collective breaths on the chilly morning air. Smoky trails of exhalation swirled and danced together as a soft breeze blew between them. This breathy ballet went on for a few minutes more before they could no longer see Will's breath dancing on the air with theirs and his youthful face went forever still.

9

MAGGIE FELT AS IF HER WORLD WAS CRUMBLING. IN THE SPAN OF just a few hours, she'd been ripped from her home in the dead of night, forced to flee under mysterious circumstances and then— the shooting had started. That man, a stranger, an assassin, had been sent to her house to *kill* her. It didn't seem real. And now . . . this moment. Hunkered in a forest, clutching the corpse of the only constant in her life.

My brother. Will.

The hurt burned inside her chest, deep down in the core of her heart, and Maggie knew it would always remain. She squeezed Will's lifeless hand. It was still warm. She parted his fingers with hers, intertwined them, and held as tight as she could, because to release them was to surrender to the loss. To let go of her brother, and she just couldn't do that. She wouldn't. A part of Maggie knew she couldn't stay there forever, but that's what she wanted to do. In that moment, the last thing on her mind was getting up. She had no thought of moving on. There was only Will—nothing else.

She didn't know how long she stayed that way. When she finally became aware of the world around her again, Maggie felt the skin of her cheeks rough with dried tears even as she wiped away new ones, an ache in the muscles around her eyes. She sniffed and the heavy scent of dirt and leaves caught in her nose, the skin at the back of her neck prickled from the morning chill that clung to the air despite the sunlight slowly breaking through the tree canopy. The remnants of that chill broke upon her face, colder where the tears were still wet, sending a shiver through her body and gooseflesh across her arms underneath the sweatshirt she wore.

As her awareness continued to grow and expand outward from the tiny universe of just her and Will, Maggie suddenly felt another presence: as if Simon had appeared at her side again by some magic spell. She sensed his closeness, crouching down at her side, arm around her shoulder in a consoling embrace as he too stared forward at Will. It was usually comforting to have Simon so close, Maggie thought, and now was no different. She was glad to have him there in that moment and wondered if she would have even half the composure she did had he not been there with her.

But then, amidst the closeness, Maggie sensed . . . something else. It started in the back of her mind—hazy at first, the feeling, out of focus, but it crept closer, became clearer. It was strange, conflicting, something she'd never encountered or expected; a simmering, unusual anger toward the unlikeliest of people.

The anger crept along the shores of her mind, making itself known. She was almost shocked at first, but as the feeling grew stronger, buoyed by her heartache for Will, the resentment made sense. It wasn't even the first burning embers of hatred; she was sure of that. It was almost like, an annoyance. An irritation she couldn't quite shake despite not fully understanding why it was there. But as soon as she let her mind drift away from Will, for that split second of contemplation, the answer presented itself.

Simon.

It was *he* who had fetched them. It was out of concern for their safety, yes, but Simon had been the one to take her and Will away from their homes in the middle of the night. He'd been the reason the assassin wanted them all dead. Because of Simon, and that fucking message he'd received. That was the reason all this had started, the reason they had been shot at by the assassin . . . the reason Will was dead.

Maggie's body shifted closer to her brother, away from Simon. When Simon, his arm still around her shoulder, made to move with Maggie, she squinted back at him. That sharp look was enough. Simon nodded and let her be.

Time passed like this, Maggie closer to Will, inches away from Simon but feeling miles apart. Silence but for the sounds of a breeze through tree branches and the crunch of leaves beneath them. Maggie refused to look at Simon, eyes set instead on her brother.

Broken rays of sunlight fell across Will's face and, for a moment, he almost looked alive again, lost in some deep slumber, but Maggie knew there was no sense in deluding herself. Will may have looked asleep, but he would never wake up, and that thought broke her again. Fresh tears spilled from her eyes, muffled sobs from her mouth. Her mind whirled: what would she do without her brother? How could she go on? What—

"Hey, M-Maggie."

Her stomach sank at Simon's voice. She hated that sick feeling, hated her annoyance at him. She didn't *want* to feel this way about Simon—never, she told herself. More than anything, Maggie wished she could turn and embrace Simon, find comfort in his touch like it was a normal day. But she couldn't push it away, didn't want to, and so she let it in, gritting her teeth at the sound of his voice, hunching away from him.

"Maggie." His voice again and when she turned to peer at

him, Simon said, "We—I, I mean . . . I have . . . I should move the car."

"Go," she said, wanting him to leave so she could be alone, so she could be with Will.

"Maggie? I . . . I don't want to, it's just . . . the car, it's sitting out there, open, and the blood—" He stopped abruptly. "Sorry, I didn't mean . . . It's just, dangerous. If someone drives by—"

"Go," Maggie said again, ending his stuttering attempts at justification for his departure. Maggie tried to soften her face, but found it difficult. "Just go," she said. "D-do what you have t-to do."

Maggie turned her gaze back to Will. She felt Simon's stillness, his indecision. He leaned into Maggie, squeezed her tight, kissed the top of her head, and whispered, "I won't be long." Maggie heard leaves and soil move beneath his shoes, and a moment later, felt the silence left by his absence.

Maggie let out a long, slow breath, relieved to be alone with her brother. With Simon gone, she fell back on old routines and crouched down closer to Will, yearning for his advice.

"Please don't do this, Will," Maggie said in a moaning, strained whisper. "We need you. *I* need you. I don't . . . I can't do this alone." Will was gone and there was only silence, but Maggie kept on, talking to her brother like it was any other day. "I don't want to feel this way, about Simon, about everything. It feels . . . I don't know. I hate it, to be this way, but it feels like I should. I just don't know what to do. Now that you're g-gone I can't . . . *What should I do?*"

Maggie tried to think of what Will might say, advice he'd given her sometime in the past. Something that might provide guidance, as he'd always done or at least offered. Her mind drifted back to before this moment, miles away when they were still tucked in the car and only Will knew of his fatal injury.

It can work. You two just have to, ya know . . . communicate.

It was simple advice, which was usually the best kind. But Maggie could see no use for it, not now at least. It only made her think of Simon, which brought a sour feeling to her stomach.

She stared at Will's unmoving face, searching her thoughts, not wanting to return to those woods, but no matter how much she fought it, she couldn't stop Will's voice from sounding in her head.

We all die. That's life. Not even Rejuvenation can stop that.

More appropriate words, yes. Some of her brother's last. They were accurate too, she thought as she wiped another bout of tears from her eyes. Profound even. But they were still no help to her. Maggie didn't know if any words could ever help. No advice could soothe her in that moment. Not even the special brand of advice her brother usually saved especially for her.

Maggie moved in closer to Will as he sat motionless against the white skin of the birch tree. She took a deep breath, felt the air fill her lungs, and then exhaled as she leaned her head against her brother's shoulder. Her tears had stopped, but the ache had not ceased. Would it ever? Not likely, she thought. It would be there —in her face, in her eyes, and in her heart—from this day forward. She gripped Will's hands again, held them tight in hers, and sat in silence.

Just Maggie and her big brother.

———

SIMON TRUDGED through the forest in a daze, stumbling over roots and small sticks, almost falling to the ground more than once but managing to keep his feet. Alone now, everything he'd been trying to keep out of his mind to stay strong for Maggie suddenly came flooding back. He couldn't fully comprehend his thoughts. *Will had been shot. Will was gone. Will was dead.* Simon wiped tears off his cheeks even as he thought, *it can't be true.* Will had been by his side for years, at work, as a friend. All those mornings listening to Will comment on the daily news, the jokes, the friendship. Simon could still picture his friend, smiling wide, laughing . . . but then the truth walloped him again and Simon knew better. He knew all that was gone. He'd seen what happened. Will was behind him, leaning up against a birch tree, lifeless. And his sister was there, sobbing at his side.

Maggie. Simon felt a pang of shame. How could he be thinking of his time with Will, their friendship, when Maggie was sitting back there crying? Sure, Simon has lost a good friend. But Maggie, she'd lost a *brother*. That was something wholly different. He had seen it in Maggie's eyes, her flailing movements as she protested Will's death. He'd heard it in her cries and sobs before and after Will had spent his final breath. Of course she would want to be alone with him, Simon thought as he continued toward the road.

Simon knew what he was feeling now was nothing compared to Maggie's agony, but he was still struggling nonetheless. He'd sensed it as the two of them sat crouched with Will, felt that mix of pain for the loss of his friend and for the effect it was having on the woman he loved. That hurt on top of hurt had been almost too much to bear, and so Simon had distracted himself, denied the pain, and forced his mind to drift back to their situation. That's when he had thought about their stolen, blood-filled car still sitting in the middle of the road, doors open, motor running. He had suddenly felt the urge to move it, because even if the road had been vacant during the last 20 minutes or so of their drive, there was no telling when someone else might come along and find their car suspiciously sitting there.

He hadn't wanted to leave Maggie, but when the thought of the car potentially being discovered rooted itself in his mind, when the chance to distract from the pain presented itself, he hadn't been able to shake it.

But then, Maggie pulling away and . . . the *look* she had given him. The way she had simply said, "Go." He didn't fault her. He couldn't. It made sense, that she would blame him for what'd happened. Hadn't he been the one to bring Will and Maggie into all this? There was the guilt again, the weight of it, heavier than before. Because now, they weren't simply on the run and frightened. Will wasn't just hurt. Will was dead.

Simon lingered on these thoughts until he passed beyond the edge of the forest and reached the car, in the middle of the northbound lane, still in park, idling. He looked back into the forest and could just see Maggie's form hunkered down next to her dead brother. Simon took a few steps one way, then a few the other, trying to see Maggie's face. When he found it, he thought he saw Maggie's lips moving, as if she were talking to her brother or saying some silent prayer.

Simon turned and, as he stepped up to the road, noticed the trail of blood Will had left from the car to the tree line. The streaks and drops of blood were already dried and dark. If someone had driven by at that moment, they would've seen the blood on the road, as well as the splotches still drying on Simon's shirt and pants, and they would've thought Simon had just murdered someone and hidden the body in the forest.

But that was true, wasn't it? In a way.

The weight in his chest grew heavier and Simon forced his thoughts to the task at hand, shutting out that shame as best he could for the time being. He needed to get the car off the road as quickly as possible.

Twenty yards down, he found a two-track path cutting into the forest. It was obscured by a large clump of trees and Simon would have missed it had it not been for the remains of months or years of tire tracks in the opening of the path.

Simon kicked gravel, dirt, and leaves over the blood that trailed from the road to the forest, then turned the car carefully onto the two-track. He drove until he could barely make out the main road in the rearview mirror, feeling confident he had provided sufficient cover from any potential passing vehicles.

Simon got out, popped the trunk, and looked inside to find the two large duffel bags Will had deposited during their flight from Maggie's house. In the bags, he found spare clothes in both men's and women's sizes, bathroom necessities, and towels; all things one might need should they find themselves on the run. The preparedness of Will made Simon smile, if only briefly.

He pulled two sets of jeans and shirts from the bags, one for him and another for Maggie, and set them on the hood of the car for later. Next, he grabbed the towels and set to work cleaning the car.

He started in the passenger seat, where most of Will's blood had pooled, the revolver lying there like a tiny island in a sea of blood. Simon cleaned the gun as best he could. He didn't know if it would be able to fire again, but once clean, he tucked it under one of the duffels in the trunk. Then he returned to the passenger side to finish the worst of the work: cleaning up Will's blood.

He knelt and began sopping up what he could with a towel, then wrung it out a few paces into the forest. Soak, wring out, repeat. Over and over. The work wasn't cathartic like he'd hoped, but it felt owed to Will, and to Maggie. Like Simon *had* to do it, a morbid penance for what he'd gotten them into, and for his role in what had happened to Will.

The radio was on low while he worked—contemporary music and commercials and just once, a short news segment that reported Sebastian's death, but made no mention of the detective's deaths or Simon.

Once he'd done the best he could with the car, Simon wiped himself off and changed into the spare pair of jeans and shirt he'd set out for himself. After discarding the bloodied towels and dirty clothes in the woods, Simon surveyed his work. He knew he'd never be able to remove all traces of blood from the car. Dark brown spots and the thick, coppery smell would remain, so the inside of the car was by no means spotless, but given the amount of blood there'd been, Simon felt the scene was considerably less horrific now than it had been a short while ago. Which, he knew, was ultimately for Maggie's sake. Whatever their next move, wherever they'd go, they'd have to use the car for at least a little while longer. And there would have been no way of getting Maggie back inside had the car been left in its previous, blood-smeared state. So he'd done what he could and it would have to do, at least until they could ditch this car for another.

He turned the radio off and was just about to head into the forest when he saw Maggie walking slowly through the trees toward him, heard the crunch of dry leaves under her footsteps. Maggie's face was colorless but for the redness that surrounded her eyes. He walked into the forest to greet her and they met up a few paces in. He gave her a weak smile that was not returned.

"You found me," he said. "I was worried that—"

"I saw the car moving through the trees," Maggie replied. She looked at Simon, pain still etched on her face. Simon took a step forward, wanting to embrace her, to comfort her, but she recoiled.

"Sorry, I—"

"You changed," she said, looking down at his clothes. Anything to avoid looking directly at him. "I'm still—I don't want to get you all dirty again."

"I put a change of clothes for you on the hood of the car."

"Oh." It was all she could say. She couldn't bring herself to thank him, not with that feeling still simmering in her. She looked down at herself, at the mess of drying blood soaking into her clothes, at Simon's old sweatshirt, at all of it smudged with dirt and dead leaves. "I guess I should . . ." Then she stopped and looked back into the trees behind her. "But maybe . . . until after. I mean . . . we n-need to . . . to b-bury him." And with those words, she looked back at Simon, her eyes damp and red.

Simon was determined to embrace her now, not caring about his new clothes, but again, she stepped away. He drew a sharp breath through his nose and then said, "Don't worry. I'll do it. I'll —" He choked on the word that would come next and then tried again. "I'll . . . dig. You go change."

"But how . . . what will you—?" she started to say.

"A stick. My hands, if I have to."

It was then that Maggie finally looked fully at Simon. She didn't smile. She didn't say another word. Her expression didn't change in any significant way, but Simon thought he saw the smallest hint of her face softening. Just a little. Perhaps he imagined it, but then again, perhaps not.

Simon nodded as Maggie moved past him, back toward the car. He watched her go for a moment, and then turned and headed for the large birch tree standing tall in the distance.

———

THE SOIL of the forest was much harder than Simon had anticipated; digging a grave with a shovel made of a tree branch or with his bare hands would take hours. Even so, he still intended to do it and got to work. A short while later, he heard movement in the forest and looked up to see Maggie walking toward him. The sight of her dressed in clean clothes, her brother's blood gone from her, buoyed Simon's efforts. When Maggie arrived, she started to say something, then stopped and instead crouched near the birch tree again, looking at her brother. Simon looked at her for a moment more and then continued; scraping at the dirt, pulling out rocks, and clawing at roots with fingers that had long since turned a dark shade of brown. He kept at it until he was left with a suitable, albeit shallow, grave.

They laid Will down in the hole and surrounded him with large branches they had found strewn across the forest floor. The twisted sticks and tree limbs encircled Will on all sides, and made him look like the focal point of some mythological forest painting framed by nature itself. Will the sleeping faun, finally resting after a long day trotting through the wood. Simon held onto this image for a moment, not wanting to disturb that supposed slumber, but knowing they couldn't remain this way forever. He sank to his knees and slowly began to cover the lower half of Will's body with the soil he had dug out and handfuls of freshly fallen leaves. He looked up at Maggie and denial took full hold. He wished Maggie would interject, yell for him to stop. It'd all been a mistake! Will wasn't gone! Stop covering him up! But Simon saw no such thing, only a silent figure, standing at the edge of the grave, watching and sniffling. Her eyes did not return Simon's stare and so he continued the improvised ritual, laying more sticks across the larger logs and branches, making a sort of log-cabin-style mausoleum. With all but Will's face covered now, Simon stood and they prepared to say their goodbyes.

When Simon tried once more to put his arm around Maggie, she moved away and so they stood apart, looking down on Will in silence, but for the sound of stuttering breaths, the sniffling of tears. They stood this way for what seemed like hours, lost in their private thoughts and remembrances, before Maggie crouched down close to Will, whispered something Simon did not hear, and then started grabbing handfuls of dirt and leaves, slowly covering Will's face.

"Let me—" Simon started to say, but Maggie pushed him away and continued grabbing fistfuls of dirt and leaves, dropping them one after another onto her dead brother until his face was covered and she could see him no more. Maggie stood and marched a few paces away, wiping her dirty hands on her fresh pair of jeans. She sobbed, but could not turn back around.

Simon finished covering Will with what remained of the loose dirt and several more branches, taking one last look at his best friend's resting place. He knew it did not do Will justice, but also that it was the best they could offer right now. Simon vowed to return—no matter what happened, if he survived this ordeal, he was determined to come back and give his friend a proper burial. He'd do it for Will and for Maggie.

He moved away from the grave, toward Maggie. As if sensing his presence, Maggie started to head back toward the car. Simon followed her. They had just stepped out of the trees and onto the two-track path near the car when Maggie collapsed. At first, Simon thought she'd fainted, but when he caught her in his arms he could feel her sides trembling with ragged breaths as she once again sobbed.

Simon made no effort to stand her up, instead helping her down to the ground, sitting with his back against the closed passenger door of the car, finally holding her in his arms. He squeezed her tight, wanting her to really feel his presence, to know he was there for her and only her. Maggie leaned in to him, her face on his chest.

"What . . . what are we going to . . . to do?" she stuttered.

Simon remained still, felt his steady breathing against Maggie's ragged breaths. He shook his head slightly.

"I don't know, Maggie. I don't know."

The pair remained sitting against the car as the sun rose over the trees and the chill of the early hours faded completely. The only time Simon moved from his seat was when Maggie asked him to turn on the radio. She wanted to hear something, to feel surrounded by anything but silence. Once the radio was on, it took only three full songs for her to drift off to sleep in Simon's arms.

Simon fought to remain awake, to watch over Maggie. He had been up for a solid day at least, though it felt much longer. Just yesterday morning, he'd been at the coffee shop with Will. It might as well have been years ago. After that, the police station, the detectives showing up at his home—they'd been on the run ever since.

Simon fought his eyes from closing again. He stared into the forest. The trees swayed in the wind, leaves fell swirling to the ground. The scene felt strange, because how could anything look so peaceful at a moment like this? But nature had almost always been like that to him. Serene. Hypnotic. His eyes drifted lower, then closed.

The radio played a slow tune as Simon fell deeper and deeper into a drowsy haze, arms still wrapped tightly around Maggie. The last thing he could remember thinking was that repeated mantra that continued to plague his mind even as he finally fell into sleep.

What would they do now? Where could they go?

What now?

(CONT'D)

ANNOUNCER: . . . reactions from the Rightland Center crowd were harsh in the morning session. During the break, some attendees said they didn't even plan on going back for the second session, citing the lecture's content as "incomprehensible, politically-charged nonsense" and Miss Darrow as an "unfortunate victim of circumstance" whose condition and situation in life have left her "addled-minded and astoundingly ignorant to the ways of the world." Whether in support of Darrow's views or not, attendees all had the chance to hear some of her usual points of interest. Let's listen in.

AUDIO SEGMENT (Darrow): The world is changing. The real question is whether or not it is actually changing for the better.

AUDIO SEGMENT (Darrow): The Rejuvenation procedure--the one we all know today--was not initially developed in any way, shape, or form to be a soldier of vanity. Something that's sadly been forgotten by many, and ignored by others, in the two hundred plus years since the procedure's discovery. The popularized *benefit* of Rejuvenation was nothing more than an unintended side effect of much more important research being done to cure the vast array of diseases ravaging the earth during the period we now refer to as The Decay. Dr. Rodderick Price, whom we all know as the discoverer of Rejuvenation, was trying to find a solution to cure, or at the very least stop or contain the spread of, the diseases that threatened humankind's existence. The very same outbreaks that led to the loss of more than half the world's population. And he did it. Dr. Price found the key in a special mixture of growth hormones and senolytic drugs. Once administered, this Rejuvenation cocktail restored the body's thymus gland, producing a new kind of T cell that drastically improved patient immunity while also eradicating senescent cells associated with the cultivation of disease and progression of biological aging within the body. Though he soon discovered the effects were compartmentalized, stopping every part of the body from aging except, oddly, the mind.

(CONT'D ON NEXT PAGE)

Page 3 of 6

(CONT'D)

ANNOUNCER: Darrow went on to more controversial topics.

AUDIO SEGMENT (Darrow): For even though we can now prevent the physical deterioration of our bodies over time and live beyond any age we ever dreamed about before Dr. Price's discovery, this is what awaits those who undergo the procedure at the end of life's path. Encased in a body of preserved youth, our brains will continue to age and fall victim to a natural death. Granted, the bodily protection from disease afforded by Rejuvenation means the brain remains functioning for much longer than ever before, but it *does* continue to age until a day when the subject reaches the Post-Cerebrational Mobility Phase and can no longer function on their own. Never forget: Without a healthy brain, a youthful body is meaningless.

AUDIO SEGMENT (Darrow): Presently, however, the repercussions of the procedure's continued use and evolution into common practice have, in many ways, far surpassed its initial benefits. The average chronological age achieved by Rejuvenites has now reached 150 years-- that's nearly twice as long as before The Decay. And that's not even taking into consideration those who've entered PCMP and been admitted to retirement facilities. We're long past the decades following The Decay when much of the population was still too scared to move on from the great losses they'd suffered. The

earth's population continued to decline even
after those early forms of Rejuvenation became
available, because people were still too
frightened to even attempt to repopulate. They
lived in constant fear that disease would
return to claim any children they dared
produce. And those early trials of Rejuvenation were still sometimes causing horrific
side effects in some, like rapid aging, and
even death. The world was broken then.
Everyone had lost so much. It's a testament to
our species that we were ever able to overcome
The Decay and those long, fearful years after
. . . but we did. Eventually, the babies did
start to come again. And now, we continue to
add to our numbers, but the existing population isn't going anywhere. The resources of
earth cannot support a continually growing
population for much longer unless some sort of
equilibrium is achieved. Most . . .

(CONT'D ON NEXT PAGE)

Page 4 of 6

(CONT'D)

AUDIO SEGMENT (Darrow): . . . of the diseases
that once ravaged our planet during The Decay
have since gone dormant or disappeared,
leaving us to question the true purpose of
the procedure's continued use. Therefore, it
is my belief, and that of my colleagues, that

Rejuvenation be discontinued as a standard
medical practice. I think that despite going
through the procedure himself, were Rodderick
Price still alive today and able to see what
has become of his work through the prism of
time, he would be a strong advocate for our
cause.

ANNOUNCER: Stirring words, indeed. Though
mentions of others sympathetic to her cause
drew heated responses from the crowd, which
Darrow addressed directly.

AUDIO SEGMENT (Darrow): It is true. I
frequently communicate and work with law-abid-
ing, reasonable groups within the Anti-Rejuvenation movement. Groups like the Humans for a
Natural Existence, who want only candid
discussions and peaceful resolutions, as I do.
But I have never, and will never, work with
radical factions such as Life Liberation and
Abstainers Army. I abhor the violent tactics
and messages of such groups, and vehemently
deny any association or communications with
them.

ANNOUNCER: We've just gotten word that
protesters are preventing those members of the
audience who do wish to return from getting
back inside the Rightland Center. Police are
on scene, but the afternoon's session has
already been pushed back by an hour. We will
hear more from Darrow as she is expected to

remain in town for the big EXLI announcement
scheduled for tomorrow.

ANNOUNCER: In financial news, the EXLI Corporation will hold a shareholders meeting next
Wednesday to discuss the recent . . .

                                          (BREAK)

ANNOUNCER: Ladies and gentlemen, I've just
been handed some breaking news related to our
top story. Two detectives from the 23rd
Precinct investigating yesterday's murder of
EXLI scientist Dr. Sebastian Martin have been
found dead at the home of a man said to have
been providing information about the case.

ANNOUNCER: I'm told the man they were questioning, one Simon Crowe, is now wanted . . .

                              (CONT'D ON NEXT PAGE)

10

SIMON WASN'T SURE HOW LONG HE HAD SLEPT, BUT FIGURED IT had to have been at least an hour or two. When he awoke, his body was stiff, but his mind felt clearer, refreshed. Maggie was still asleep in his arms, her breathing steady now. He thought she looked peaceful, even as her eyelids trembled. He hoped her dreams were comforting, but suspected Maggie's mind was playing out the last night and morning again and again. Simon stroked her hair gently and leaned his head back against the car door.

Inside the car, the radio played the noon news report at low volume. Simon's stare had once again been caught by the hypnotic sway of the trees around him and he only half-listened to the broadcast, catching brief snippets of the report while he shook off the last remnants of sleep.

A radio announcer was introducing the story and then another voice, what sounded like a recording: . . . *The Rejuvenation procedure . . . unintended side effect of much more important research . . . eradicating senescent cells . . . progression of biological aging . . . retirement facilities . . . continue to add to our numbers . . .*

What little of the broadcast he did register didn't interest Simon, though he recognized the recorded voice now and remembered Will mentioning the lecture. His heart sank again. He closed his eyes as the report played on. It wasn't until the announcer trailed off, then came back with added fervor in his voice that Simon's attention was truly caught by the broadcast.

. . . breaking news related to our top story. Two detectives from the 23rd Precinct investigating yesterday's murder of EXLI scientist Dr. Sebastian Martin have been found dead at the home of a man said to have been providing information about the case.

I'm told the man they were questioning, one Simon Crowe, is now wanted for the murders of the detectives as well as the prime suspect in the death of Dr. Martin. Crowe fled the scene and police are now organizing a city-wide manhunt to find him.

Crowe is described as 6'1", 180 pounds. 33 years old, Non-Rejuvenite. I repeat, Crowe has not undergone Rejuvenation, so it should be easier to spot him. Crowe stole the detective's car, a gas-powered, black Freemont. If you spot Crowe or the car, please call authorities immediately. Do not approach Crowe. He is likely armed and dangerous.

Crowe is suspected to have significant ties with the underground Anti-Rejuvenation movement. Unconfirmed reports say he spent the last few years under heavy cover, posing as Dr. Martin's neighbor to get information that could be used against the EXLI Corporation. Sources say that once his mission was complete, Crowe killed Dr. Martin and attempted to flee. When questioned by the detectives, he murdered them as well and escaped to areas unknown. It is speculated he has rejoined whatever group he is affiliated with, suspicions being one of the two largest AR groups —Life Liberation or Abstainers Army.

Again, breaking news from our top story, Simon Crowe is now being sought in connection with . . .

The radio announcer's voice faded away in Simon's ears.

"Son of a bitch!" he whispered sharply. They thought *he* did it! Whether the police were corrupt and supplying false information to the press, or were straight and simply going on the evidence at hand—it didn't matter. Every officer in the city was looking for him.

Simon's head swam. They thought *he* killed the detectives. They thought *he* murdered Sebastian. It was outrageous!

But the police and the news saw otherwise. They, and now everyone listening, thought he was a murderer. Not only that, but he was being made out to be some sort of ranking member of the movement to do away with Rejuvenation.

Simon took a deep breath, soothed by the forest air which held a hint of Maggie's natural, sweet smell. He looked down at her on instinct, hoping for the usual feeling of comfort her appearance had, but found none. Memories of the previous night flashed in his mind, Will dying, that distant look Maggie had given him since, that coldness. No comfort, only the thought that he was in deep, deep trouble.

But at least, for the time being, he was the only one. From the sound of the news report, the police had yet to discover the assassin at Maggie's house. It seemed impossible given how much noise they'd made when leaving—the gunshots ringing out from Will's revolver, the body of the assassin left lying in plain view in the middle of the street. But the report had said nothing about that ordeal, and Simon wondered if the scene had not been discovered yet, or if it was being kept quiet on purpose. Whatever the reason, he at least found solace in the fact that Maggie and Will had yet to be dragged into all this, at least as far as the news was concerned.

But that too was inevitable, he thought. Simon had told the police that Will knew about the message. They would eventually go to Will's house to question him about Simon's disappearance. When they discovered Will, and finally Maggie, gone, they might suspect Simon had kidnapped them both or even that they were part of his underground group of rebels.

The radio announcer was half-way through another round of the breaking news report when Maggie began to stir. As she finally sat up, Simon tried to stand and turn the radio down quickly, but Maggie grabbed his arm before he could reach the volume knob inside the car.

"Wait," she said. "Did I just hear your name on the radio?"

"It's nothing," he said. "Just—"

"Like hell it is!" Maggie listened for a second, then said, "They're talking about you! Simon, do you . . . do you hear what they're saying?"

"Yeah, I heard all right."

Maggie stood up and leaned closer to the open window of the car, listening to the report issuing from the radio. Her eyes grew wider with each sentence spoken by the radio announcer, with each accusation leveled at Simon. "They think all of it, everything, was all you." Simon just nodded. "We should . . . I don't know, talk to them," she said. "Call the police and tell them you . . . tell them what happened."

"We can't, Maggie."

Maggie's brow contracted, her nostrils flared.

"And why the hell not?"

"Because I think the police are in on it."

Her face relaxed again as she tilted her head in question.

"But I don't understand. Those two detectives at your house were . . ." she tried to say, struggling with the last word and then, forcing it out, "murdered. How could they—"

"I don't think Detective Banks was in on it. The other guy, Gantry . . . I don't know. He was odd. But regardless, they were both killed. Someone else is pulling strings—someone who found out that I talked to Banks and leaked that information to whoever sent the assassin."

"But how do you know that?"

"Banks basically said it himself when he was at my house."

Simon remembered the detective's shouts when the assassin had first started firing: *I knew it! We never should have left the station. Crooked bastards!*

"Also," Simon went on, "how else could it have happened? I'm no threat to anyone, then one day I get a message from my neighbor right before he's murdered. I tell the cops and the next thing I know my living room's a shooting range. That's the only thing that makes sense. That's why they, whoever *they* are, tried to have me killed. That message. They killed Sebastian because he knew something and when they thought I knew, they came after me too. They came after all of us."

Maggie's face grew pale. Her eyes darted beyond him, into the forest. When she looked back at him a moment later, her gaze had hardened.

"I'm sorry, I—"

Maggie turned away from Simon. He heard her breathe deeply. She didn't turn around when she spoke. "You said that message was gibberish." She said this hopefully, as if wanting him to agree. As if she wanted the message to truly be nothing, but knew better.

"I did," Simon said, "initially, but after last night, I have to be wrong about that. It has to mean something, but I sure as hell don't know what."

"Well . . . what did it say? Maybe we can . . . you know, figure something out you didn't see before."

"Does that matter right now, Maggie?" Simon said and instantly regretted his words. He had been more preoccupied with their next move, with safety, not decoding Sebastian's nonsensical message. But that's not how it'd sounded to Maggie.

She whipped around, face no longer pale, but red with fury.

"Don't you dare tell me what does and doesn't matter right

now! All of this matters! You say we can't go to the police for help, so who the hell are we supposed to go to then? Huh? We can't help ourselves, but we have to do *something*. We can't just sit here in the woods forever. You said you think there's something in that message, then it sure as hell matters! It matters because it's the reason we were shot at and chased from our homes. It matters because it's the reason we're in this godforsaken forest. *It matters because Will is dead!* Because of that message! Because you—"

And then she halted. Her yelling voice cut short, but her face still pulsed red. Her chest rising and falling rapidly. Her eyes still as fierce and angry as ever. Maggie chose not to finish her last sentence and instead turned back around, staring into the forest once again.

Simon stood still, speechless. He'd had an inkling before that things might go this way, that Maggie would find fault with him for what happened to Will. Hell, he thought, he blamed himself for it as well. He couldn't blame her one bit. Simon didn't make a sound. He didn't move a muscle. He didn't know what to do.

The two of them stood like that for a while before either said a word or moved. It was Maggie who slowly stepped toward Simon, who had remained frozen, face to the ground. When she moved in close, he looked up timidly and said, "I'm sorry."

"I'm sorry too," Maggie said, but wasn't sure she meant it. She felt that someday she would, but not yet. Not fully. Her voice was measured when she went on. "I just . . . we have to do *something*, Simon. We're out of options. You're wanted by the police and chances are I might be too soon. You say they're compromised, so okay, we can't trust the police. Who *can* we trust?"

"You think Sebastian's message will help with that?"

"The damn thing started all this, didn't it? Then I want to hear it because it better help us with something. What else can we do? Maybe, if we can figure out what Sebastian was talking about, what he was trying to tell you, then we can figure out who to take the message to—who can help us."

Simon considered Maggie's reasoning, then nodded. She was right, after all. What else could they do? He reached into the car and grabbed his phone from the center console. He thumbed through the menus, found the message, and set the phone to speaker on the roof of the car.

"Si . . . Simon. You need to . . . go . . . find . . . illbroo . . . told me . . . That's where . . . at. He's there . . . 1 . . . 20 . . . 120 . . . keeping him. Find . . . her . . . can help. Hillbrook."

The message sounded just as confusing to Simon as the last time he'd heard it and was curious if Maggie felt the same as she listened to it for the first time. What struck him during this listen, however, was the sound of Sebastian's strained voice, how it reminded Simon of Will's voice as he was dying. He wondered if Maggie had made the connection as well. When he looked at her, he saw her face pale again, but determined. As the message played, she looked not at Simon but at his phone lying on the roof of the car.

"None of that makes sense to you?" Maggie asked.

"Not really," he said. "I went over it with the detectives last night. We had some ideas, but nothing definitive. It was mostly speculation."

"What about Hillbrook? Or that number, 120?"

"We thought Hillbrook might have to do with EXLI, or a competitor. But again, nothing for sure. We just sort of went around in circles and then . . ." Simon remembered his conversation the night before. "Wait. There was one thing Detective Banks said. That Sebastian was talking about two people in the message, a man and a woman. He figured one of them might be Hillbrook."

"A person, huh?"

"Yeah. You don't think so?"

"It's a possibility. For some reason it doesn't sound right though. I don't know . . . maybe . . . Can you play it again?"

Simon hit play and the message started again.

"Si . . . Simon. You need to . . . go . . . find . . . illbroo . . ."

"Right there!" Maggie interjected, speaking over the remainder of the short message. "He said, 'You need to *go find* Hillbrook.'"

"But you can go find a person just as well as a place," Simon said.

"Play it again."

Simon hit the play button on his phone once more.

"Si . . . Simon. You need to . . . go . . . find . . . illbroo . . . told me . . . That's where . . ."

Again, Maggie spoke before the message finished.

"Right there! Right after he said go find Hillbrook, he said that's *where* something's at. I have no idea what that something might be, but it sounds to me like Hillbrook is definitely a place."

"You're right," Simon said, chancing a small smile at Maggie; it went unreturned. "But, ah, damn it, that just means we're back where we started. If Hillbrook isn't the name of a person, then we're no closer to figuring out who the people Sebastian was talking about are."

Maggie pursed her lips as she hit a button on the phone and listened to the message once more. There was intense concentration in her eyes. Simon could almost see the gears turning in her head as she listened to the message again and again. He admired Maggie as she combed over every word, every detail of the message. He might have even called her determination downright enthusiasm, had it not been for the events of the previous night. Yes, she cared about their current situation, wanted to find answers as much as Simon, but he knew she was really just busying herself. She was grasping at anything to keep her mind busy, so she didn't go back to thinking of her brother.

Maggie's next words weren't directed toward Simon; she was thinking aloud. "Hillbrook is a place, but we don't know where it is, what it is, or what goes on there. But it must be important because Sebastian put it in the message. He wanted us to know. There's a man and a woman. From the sounds of it one of them, the man, is at Hillbrook. He lives there or—wait, it said 'keeping him' so whoever this man is, he's being held there for some reason."

"Like a prisoner?" Simon asked.

"EXLI isn't in the business of keeping prisoners."

Simon couldn't help his mind as it flashed to his grandfather, to the countless others he knew lay motionless in EXLI retirement facilities around the world. Those people were like prisoners, weren't they? Willing prisoners, though, which did not fit.

"But what if this man knows something they don't want others to know. Do you think they'd hold someone hostage for something like that?"

"Not likely," Maggie said.

"Why not?"

"Because if they killed Sebastian for what he knew, then why not kill this other man? Why hold him?" She paused, her mind working. Maggie rocked her head back and forth as she pondered the questions, as if swaying to a beat. Simon remained silent thinking right alongside her, but when the silence broke, it was Maggie who spoke. "Maybe he knows something they don't and that's *why* they're keeping him. They can't simply kill him because then they'd lose whatever information he has. So they're holding him hostage until he gives it up."

"But what could one man know that's so important?"

"That's the big question," Maggie said. "But we're talking about EXLI, right? So it's probably something related to Rejuvenation."

"But EXLI *is* Rejuvenation. They know everything there is to know about it already. They are the ones who've continued to develop it ever since The Decay. Could there really be a man out there who knows something they don't? Something that would actually threaten them?" Everything Simon was saying swirled around in his head. The Decay. Disease. Rejuvenation. EXLI. They were like puzzle pieces he couldn't quite fit together. But one stuck out more than the others. "What if what this man knows has got something to do with a disease? Or, what if they're not keeping him hostage, they're *treating* him. What if he's being kept at this Hillbrook place because it's some sort of quarantine?"

Maggie considered the question for a moment and then said, "I suppose it could be, but it's hard to think that's the case since Rejuvenation protects against all diseases. You know as well as I do there hasn't been a severe outbreak of any known disease for at least a century."

"Yeah, but . . . could all this be about some kind of *new* disease? An *unknown* disease." Simon's mind raced as fresh, horrible ideas sprang into his head. "It's not unheard of. New diseases popped up all the time during The Decay, ones they hadn't even imagined before. If we're dealing with a brand new outbreak, maybe EXLI's involvement is the real telling part. It might mean the new disease affects everyone, maybe even Rejuvenites."

Maggie finally looked squarely at Simon; she frowned.

"Let's hope not." She played Sebastian's message once more. Again, she went over everything aloud, as if speaking to herself or no one in particular. They didn't know where Hillbrook was. They didn't know who the man was and, if he was at Hillbrook, couldn't say for sure why he was being kept there. It could be any number of things. He might be a hostage with information or some sort of patient zero, a carrier for a new disease. In the end, they agreed that if this man was indeed being kept somewhere, it was most likely because his captors didn't want everyone to know about him. Simon and Maggie could sit there and speculate about this mystery man for days, and still never actually stumble across the right answer.

"Then there's the number 120," Maggie said. "Maybe it's a room or floor number at Hillbrook where the man is kept. Again, it's hard to speculate without knowing more. It's only a number."

"Right," Simon said, and no more, letting her work.

"That leaves us with the woman. Sebastian mentions this woman, tells you to find her, and says something about help. Could it be that simple? That Sebastian wanted you to find this woman because he thinks she can help you."

"That's it," Simon exclaimed. "Maggie, that's got to be it. This woman, whoever she is. That's who we need to find—she's the one who will believe us."

"But who is she? We don't exactly have a lot to go on besides the fact that we know she's female. That's *half the world*. More than half."

"We just have to think about everything we know about our situation—what's connected to Sebastian's murder."

"Did the detectives mention if they had any leads?"

Simon explained how Detective Banks had insinuated that he thought Hillbrook might be a person, how he told Simon the police were running checks for EXLI employees with that name. It had all stemmed from the method of killing, that weird chemical that had made Sebastian age faster than normal. Because of that, the whole thing reeked of EXLI, or one of their competitors —someone who had extensive knowledge of the Rejuvenation procedure. At the time, Simon thought it had to be one of them.

"If all this ties back to EXLI or Rejuvenation," Maggie said, "Sebastian had to be targeted because of it. He must have had dirt on something going on with the procedure, something they didn't want the public knowing."

"But what?"

"No clue. We can ask this woman he mentioned, if we ever find her."

"I just . . . I don't know," Simon said. "Could she work with Rejuvenation? Is that why Sebastian trusted her to help us? Maybe another scientist at EXLI that he knew?"

It seemed like the most obvious place to start to Simon, but Maggie was already course-correcting.

"Maybe we're looking at this in the wrong way," Maggie said. Her eyes lit up with a new idea. "Sebastian said that whoever this woman is, she would help us. If EXLI or one of their competitors is behind all this, I don't think anyone within their ranks would be willing to help us. We should be looking for someone on the opposite side, someone who *opposes* Rejuvenation."

Almost as soon as Maggie spoke the words "opposes Rejuvenation," the image of the woman popped into Simon's mind. How could it not? Whenever Simon heard reports of a group like Life Liberation causing problems at a Rejuvenation center or coverage of a piece of new legislation that was trying to limit companies like EXLI, he thought of the woman's face. Her name was synonymous with the more civilized Anti-Rejuvenation counter-culture.

"Darrow," he said.

"What?" Maggie said.

"Lydia Darrow. It's her, right? It has to be."

"Oh my God. Do you think so? I mean, she fits but . . ."

Though Maggie and Simon both thought they were right, that Lydia Darrow was the woman from which Sebastian had meant for them to seek help, they couldn't be sure.

"Simon, what are we going to do? Let's say for a second she is the one, how are we going to reach her? She lives in England, doesn't she? And she travels all the time for her lectures and events. She could be anywhere."

Simon raised his eyebrows, surprised by his knowledge.

"Actually," he said, "She's already here. She's in the city right now giving a lecture at the Rightland Center."

Maggie's mouth fell open. "Are you serious?"

"Yeah. They were just talking about it on the radio before the news story that mentioned me. Said there were the usual protests. So it has to be her, right? I mean, what are the chances she's in town at the exact time we get a message telling us to find a woman who opposes Rejuvenation? And they said she's not heading home right away, that she's sticking around for that big EXLI announcement. It all fits. I should have seen it before. There was even an article in the paper about her yesterday. Will pointed it out when—" He stopped when he saw Maggie flinch at the mention of her brother's name. "I'm sorry, I didn't mean—"

"It's . . . you . . . just, don't . . ." Maggie said, and she pulled away from him again. He could hear her trying to stifle tears. Silence fell between them again. Maggie quickly composed herself and returned to Lydia Darrow.

"So what do we do?" she said. "We find her? Talk to her?"

Something in the back of Simon's mind stopped him from agreeing immediately. He bit his lip, then said, "I know it seems like Sebastian meant her, but . . . well, you know . . ."

"What?"

"Darrow. Do you actually think she'd help us? I mean . . . she's kind of, I don't know, *crazy*, right?"

"Is she?" It was a simple question, but one which, coming from Maggie, sounded strange. Defending Lydia Darrow sounded odd coming from someone who'd undergone the Rejuvenation procedure.

"You don't think so?" Simon said. "The woman is only interested in furthering her agenda. She's trying to get the most significant discovery in human history repealed as if it was prohibition. She's trying to diminish a choice you made, a choice billions have made. Even if Sebastian meant her, do you think she'd stop her whole crusade to help us?"

"Don't be so obtuse, Simon," Maggie said with a heavy sigh. "I'm not saying Darrow is the patron saint of Rejuvenation. I just don't think she's certifiably insane like you say she is. She's been around a long time. She's educated and does make *some* good points on occasion. I can respect that, in a certain light."

"But you really think she'd help us?" he said. "You think, if we can even get to her, she'd be able, or willing, to help us figure out what's going on?"

"She better," Maggie said. Her voice stony and determined. "Because figuring out that message and who's behind all this is the only way to clear your name. And mine once I'm dragged into this." She paused as her face grew red again and then said, "*And Will's.*"

Simon nodded, trying to be encouraging. "All right. We go and see her then."

Maggie snagged Simon's phone off the top of the car and walked around to the other side. She stopped at the passenger door, looked down at it, and then back into the forest in the direction of Will's grave. Simon could see anguish on her face again, the pain that would never leave. She turned, saw him watching her, and said, "If we're going to make it back to town by tonight we better get going. We still need to figure out where Darrow's staying and how the hell we're going to get to her without being spotted. The radio said the police are coordinating a city-wide manhunt. They'll be looking for you everywhere."

11

———

MAGGIE SAT CROSS-LEGGED IN THE BACKSEAT—UNWILLING, AS she was, to sit where her brother had died, or even put her feet where his blood has once pooled on the floor. They hit the road, headed southeast, back the way they'd come, toward a little three-stoplight village called Ferrington. As they drove, they discussed options for getting back into the city unnoticed. Maggie did most of the talking, anything to keep her mind off the thought of being in that car again and the dark brown stains of dried blood peeking out around the edges of the towels Simon had laid down.

They chanced a single, quick drive down Ferrington's main street to ease Simon's fear that the town wasn't populated enough to warrant the one building they sought, and were happy to find it near the opposite edge of town: a small, red-bricked bus station. As they drove by, they saw two electric buses parked near the curb and several waiting passengers milling about and sitting on the sidewalk benches. The Ferrington Bus Station was quiet, innocuous. It was perfect.

He and Maggie knew they couldn't drive the detective's car back into the city, as its description was now part of the radio reports, and they couldn't very well walk back. Therefore, when

Maggie suggested they take the bus—with its frequent departures and ease of buying tickets with untraceable cash—Simon agreed that it was their best option, though the prospect did raise more questions.

"Won't they be searching buses when we get to the city?" he had asked.

"I'm not so sure," Maggie had said. "*Out* of the city, of course, but I don't think they'll search the ones coming *in*. Think about it. Someone fleeing wouldn't be going back to the scene of the crime. And with as many buses as there are traveling in and out of the city every day, the police don't have the resources to check every single one. They'll probably focus on the outgoing buses."

"It's risky." Simon had then added, "But what about once we get back to the city? All buses unload at Penburg Station. The cops'll definitely be patrolling there."

"That . . . is a good question," Maggie had said. Simon had seen her eyes flicker in the mirror, her mind working. "We'll have to find a way to either sneak out of Penburg undetected or get off the bus earlier. But we also need to figure out where Darrow is staying. Without that, the whole trip is pointless."

When Simon had suggested they try to look up Darrow's location using their phones, Maggie shot the idea down fast. They were on the run and their phones could be traced if used, she told him. Were it not for the need to preserve Sebastian's message, Simon might have agreed to smash their phones just to be safe, but instead opted for turning off each phone's cellular and location services in the hopes it would be enough to keep them off the grid.

Satisfied that they'd gone unnoticed during their short scouting trip through Ferrington, Simon drove them out of town, past the village limits, until they came upon a dirt path that led into the surrounding woods. He turned in, driving deep enough into the forest to provide coverage from the road, tucking the car behind a large clump of trees, just to be safe.

They pulled both duffle bags from the trunk of the car, laid them on the ground, and made a quick inspection. They consolidated things into one bag, taking only a pair of clothes each, jackets, two of the remaining towels, a couple bottles of water, the emergency wads of rubber-banded cash they discovered at the bottom of each bag, and lastly, Will's revolver. Their progress was only stifled for a short while when they found a few cans of mixed fruit, which they peeled open quickly and devoured before discarding the cans in the forest. When Simon zipped up the one bag they intended to take with them and threw it over his shoulder, he instantly noticed it was considerably lighter.

"Ready?" Simon said and then took a swig off a water bottle he had kept out of the bag.

"Ready," Maggie returned.

Simon pulled the car keys from his pocket, tossed them deep into the woods, and they started walking back down the dirt path toward the main road that would lead them back into Ferrington.

———

THEY BOTH AGREED THAT MAGGIE, as of yet unmentioned in radio reports, was their safest bet to buy tickets without drawing attention. She'd set off for the station without saying much other than agreeing to meet Simon in a small park a few blocks away.

They were in the thick of it now, Simon had thought as he watched her go, and every step, every mile they moved back toward the city would only get more dangerous. He didn't exactly know what they were up against, and neither did Maggie. He just hoped that Lydia Darrow would be able to help, if they could even find her and then get to her without capture.

But all of that was later. One step at a time, he told himself.

Simon tried to distract his mind as best he could, taking in his surroundings. The park's many trees and benches, the nearby playground, the pavilion in which he sat and the bulletin board hanging to his right, cluttered with park notices, neighborhood announcements, sports team schedules, and various other local news. Given everything that had happened over the last two days, seeing these everyday, quaint things made Simon feel at ease for the first time in what seemed like a long time. He was grateful for that small relief, that fleeting luxury, because before long, his mind began to run wild again.

Ride the bus back to the city. Hope they weren't delayed along the way. Once they got to the city, find a way of getting off the bus earlier than the scheduled destination. Then, back in the city by nightfall, find and contact Darrow. It was simple enough.

But that was if nothing went wrong: if they weren't stopped by the police. If no one recognized them on the bus. If they managed to get off the bus before Penburg Station. If they could find Darrow and, finally, if she agreed to see them. *If.*

And then there was figuring out where Darrow was staying. They'd assumed she had a place in the city, that with her frequent visits and the kind of fame she possessed, she'd have a mansion in the northern suburbs or an expensive apartment downtown.

Almost instantly, Simon thought of one place that fit the expensive, high society scenario he had in his head: Westgate. It was a space of about three square blocks downtown that stood on the western bank of the Tamm River; made even more extravagant alongside the public housing and industrial districts in the forgotten part of the city on the eastern side of the river. But Westgate was a collection of the tallest, most expensive high rises in town that included exactly what Simon had pictured for Darrow: gates, guards, surveillance, everything a person of Darrow's stature, and infamy to many, might want to feel secure.

But there were also celebrities in Westgate, which didn't quite fit Simon's assumption of the woman. And they weren't just celebrities of the movie star variety, but others of renown like high-ranking government officials, influential citizens of the city, and corporate heads. Theodore Sullivan, the head of EXLI, even lived there. Why would Lydia Darrow, leader of the public resistance against Rejuvenation, choose to live in the same building as Sullivan?

"You look deep in thought."

Simon looked up at the familiar voice and saw Maggie had returned.

"Oh, hey," he said. "Sorry, I didn't see—"

"No worries," she said. "I found you. This place is nice." Her tone was almost casual, which surprised Simon.

"Did you have any trouble with the tickets?"

Maggie shook her head. She reached into the small paper bag she'd brought back from town and extracted two bus tickets.

"It was just like I thought, they didn't even card me—just took my name and the name of my traveling partner, I gave them the money, they gave me the tickets. We leave in 40 minutes." She handed Simon his ticket.

Simon looked at the ticket and then back up at Maggie.

"Mr. Chambers?"

"Well I couldn't very well use your real name. So I chose an alias." She then pulled a blue ball cap from the bag and tossed it on the table in front of Simon. "And this."

Simon picked up the hat, ran his fingers across the large, slanted S stitched in gray thread across the front. He looked up at Maggie and said, "Nice Sentinels cap. But why—"

"To disguise that wanted face of yours." When Simon gave her an unbelieving, quizzical look, she shrugged and added, "Hey, it works in the movies."

It was such a Will thing to say, Simon thought. To think something that worked in the movies or on television would work equally well in real life. The sudden memory of his friend sent a pang into Simon's heart. But there was a strange warmth there too; an amusement at the siblings sharing the same thought process. A family connection. Simon didn't mention this feeling to Maggie, for fear of upsetting her. He just smiled, pulled the hat snugly on his head, and nodded.

Maggie sat at the table next to Simon and sighed, as if finally relaxing after the completion of a huge task. "So what were you thinking about? Just now, when I walked up on you."

"Oh, just trying to figure out where Darrow could be staying," Simon said, discouraged. "I had some ideas, maybe Westgate, but . . . ah, I don't know. She could be anywhere. We need to find some other way of figuring it out, because we could guess all year and come up with nothing."

"Maybe we can find somewhere to do more research once we get to the city?"

"If we can even get off the bus without being caught."

"Well, I was thinking on my walk back here and may have figured that one out. A way for us to get off the bus early."

"That's great!" And then Simon saw the look on Maggie's face, a concerned frown. "What? What is it?"

"You're just going to have to trust me," she said, and told him the plan.

WWW.EXLICORP.COM
LIVE
YOUR
BEST LIFE
REJUVENATION
WWW.EXLICORP.COM

12

————

To Simon's relief, there were no problems with their departure from Ferrington and they were on the highway headed back to the city by mid-afternoon.

The bus was only half-full. Though Simon did his best to keep his head down, eyes covered by the cap he wore low over his face, he still made a point to check everyone who boarded, on the watch for anything suspicious. There were a few couples, young and Rejuvenation-young, as well as some solo riders. No one who looked like trouble. It was only after they were on the road that Simon realized he and Maggie were probably the most suspicious of anyone on the bus, the way they'd quickly made their way to the rear-most seats, talking to no one.

But Simon's relief faded as he began to consider Maggie's plan for getting them off the bus early. The plan seemed solid, and on any other day would surely get them off the bus, but with everything that was going on, he wasn't sure it would go as smoothly as they hoped. While no one on the bus seemed to notice, or care, who he and Maggie were, attention would be drawn to at least Maggie when she put her plan into action. If Maggie's face had been in the news since they last heard a report and anyone on the bus or the driver realized who she was, they might not let them off. They might immediately switch their destination from Penburg to the nearest police station, and turn her and Simon over to the authorities.

All this anxiety was why, when Maggie suddenly stood up from her seat a half-hour into their journey, Simon tried to stop her. Maggie waved away his whispered protests as she stepped forward and started chatting with a young woman two rows up. A moment later, Simon saw her thank the woman as a phone changed hands. Maggie repeated her thanks, said she'd return very soon, and settled back down next to Simon.

"What are you—"

"Quiet, Mr. Chambers. I'm doing research like we said."

Simon watched as Maggie's thumbs moved quickly around the tiny keyboard that lit up at the bottom of the phone's screen. He saw her typing search terms into a mobile browser, clicking headlines listed out on a search results page, and scrolling through article after article until . . .

"Look!" Maggie said in a whisper. "Here. This article, it's an interview with Darrow. It's a lot of the usual stuff, questions about her position against the procedure and what she's done over the years, but here, right here. The journalist makes a comment on their surroundings, where the interview took place, saying all the appearances Darrow makes must pay well to afford her . . . *apartment*." Maggie looked up from the phone, her eyes without the disdain Simon had nearly grown used to. Instead, they were bright with discovery. Maggie went back to the phone. "Yes, here, the writer made a point, pretty critical if you ask me, to comment about her 'home overlooking the river' and how, when asked, Darrow said she retained the place to 'keep an eye on Sullivan and EXLI.' It all fits. It sounds like Westgate." Maggie's eyes darted back to Simon when she finished reading.

"It does."

Maggie nodded, tapped the screen a few more times, then returned the phone to the young woman a few seats up. Next to Simon again, she said, "Nice to have a bit of luck."

"Yeah . . ."

"What is it?"

"I just . . . Westgate, it makes sense on the surface, yeah, but . . . doesn't it seem odd that she'd be in the same building as Sullivan? I know Darrow said she wants to keep an eye on him, but . . . it seems strange that either of them would tolerate being in the same building."

"You have a point, but you heard what the article said. All that talk about Darrow being well paid and having a place by the river. It fits Westgate to a tee. It's *something*, anyway."

"You're right," Simon said, searching Maggie's eyes for understanding. "It's all we got. It's something." Simon sank back in his chair, turned to look out the window, and then back at Maggie. He moved from side to side slightly, fidgety, unable to stop his mind from going over what they had just learned and the troublesome prospect of having to infiltrate Westgate. He thought of their entire plan, echoes of Sebastian's message, Will, everything . . . And then, an unexpected whisper from Maggie.

"You need to try and relax."

Simon shot her an incredulous look. "I don't—"

"*Relax*, Chambers."

Alias notwithstanding, the intensified sound of Maggie's voice suddenly offered relief to Simon. She almost sounded like she would have if they'd been back at Simon's house, watching late-night TV, unwinding together after the workweek.

"I wish I could," he said.

"I think it's safe," she said in a whisper, careful not to let her voice travel. "We have a few hours before we reach the city. I think it'll be okay if you try to get some rest. We both should."

Simon rubbed his eyes with one hand, suddenly aware of his

exhaustion. "Rest. That's funny. I don't think I could sleep if I tried."

"Well I want you to try."

Simon shook his head and almost laughed.

"Close your eyes," she said softly and then, to Simon's surprise, reached under his hat and touched his brow, slowly running her fingers downward, over his eyes, lightly pulling the eyelids down as she went. It was something she often did in their regular life. Back before mysterious messages, before assassins, before they were on the run, and before Will . . . Those times seemed so distant, but with Maggie's fingertips dancing across his skin, Simon felt his body relax. Her voice and her touch as she continued to run her fingers down his face, over his nose, cheeks, lips, and his chin . . . And then they were gone.

"Just keep your eyes closed and try to block it all out. You don't hear the bus. You don't hear the chatter. Block it all out. Just listen to my voice."

Simon felt an odd, lightheaded sensation, like a smile in his mind, for it sounded like Maggie was trying to hypnotize him, not lull him to sleep. But whatever she was doing, it worked. With each word he grew more and more relaxed. Her hand found his, she intertwined their fingers, and gave a light squeeze. It was a simple gesture, but after the last 24 hours, it was everything.

"Relax. Get some rest. We're fine for now. Safe. Just relax and get some rest."

The last thing Simon remembered was the feel of Maggie's warm hand parting from his, but the comforting sensation still lingered. After that he was asleep.

———

MAGGIE WOKE to a sudden feeling that everything was wrong. She sat up, trying to break free of the bus's fug, and turned her gaze across a still sleeping Simon to the window on his left. Beyond the misty glass she saw a dark, night sky and the bright yellow glow of artificial lights. The lights of the city.

"Oh shit!" she said, louder than she should have, drawing stares from the passengers a few rows up. She forced an everything-is-normal smile and the noticing passengers looked away.

"Wake up!" Maggie said in a tense whisper after leaning toward Simon and shaking his body slightly. He stirred, but did not open his eyes. "Wake up, Simon!" She had said it without thinking, forgetting the aliases printed on their bus tickets. The name felt strange coming off her lips, saying it for the first time since they had set foot on the bus. She regretted using it immediately, and quickly flicked her gaze back across the bus to see if anyone had heard. There were no turned heads or stares this time. She breathed a small sigh of relief, looked back at Simon, and shook him a little harder this time until finally, he opened his eyes.

"Wha . . . what is it?" he said, groggy, turning to look at Maggie, lifting the brim of his cap to see her eyes round with panic.

"We're here! In the city already. We need to get ready!"

Simon looked past her and Maggie followed his gaze out the window to see the city streets and buildings pass by. She saw office windows lit up, storefronts illuminated brightly to draw customers in, and yellow lamps sending cones of light on the sidewalks over the crowds of people walking there. She darted her eyes up and could just make out the night sky beyond the topmost point of the skyscraper they were currently passing. She saw no clouds, only a thin haze of dark pollution, enough to blot out any stars that might be shining down.

"I fell asleep," Maggie said. "Damn it, I'm sorry. When I woke up we were already—we're nearly to Penburg Station!"

"No use in worrying about it now," Simon said, face shifting from the shock of the suddenly-awoken to a more matter-of-fact expression. He didn't seem angry or annoyed that Maggie hadn't woken him on time. She could not have faulted him if he had been, and was grateful when he made no further mention of her error, and instead said, "We'll just have to do it here."

"Here? But, aren't there too many people?" Maggie asked. "We could be spotted."

Simon shrugged. She didn't need any more than that. They'd missed their window. Now was all they had. They had to chance it. She looked at Simon once more. He gave her a trusting nod and then pulled his hat down over his eyes again.

Maggie stood up into the aisle, pulled their single duffle bag from the open overhead storage compartment, and handed it to Simon. "Here we go," she said in a whisper to herself.

Maggie took a few steps toward the front of the bus, positioning herself near the middle doors. As a few of the bus's other occupants again turned toward her, wondering why this woman was suddenly getting up when they were so close to their destination, Maggie's mind began to race. Her breath came short and quick; her palms were damp. Her pulse quickened, her heart in overdrive. Her awareness of these things only made them worse, she knew that, so she did her best to push them away, to steady herself. She searched her mind for something that would provide comfort and her thoughts instantly went to Will, as they might have on a normal day. But today wasn't normal . . . and Will was gone. Forever. She felt the pain of that fact return, the sadness, and then the simmering resentment toward the man seated a few rows back. Her only remaining confidante and she was angry with him for something which—for involving them with the mysterious message he'd received, thereby making Will and her targets too.

That damn message! It was at the root of all of this, she thought. As much to blame as anything. It was why they'd been forced to go on the run, why Will was gone, and why she now stood in the middle of a half-full bus, the eyes of strangers slowly rising to meet her, feeling as if she were all alone despite Simon sitting a few feet behind her. But she wouldn't let that loneliness consume her. She wouldn't let her anger at Simon or his neighbor's fucking message control her actions. She dug in, stood tall, and took a deep breath.

And then, she began.

"Ladies and Gentlemen! May I have your attention?" Maggie said as loudly as she could, a tinge of nervousness still in her voice. Every person on the bus, aside from the few still sleeping and the driver, turned now and looked at her. "Can everyone hear me?"

"Hey, lady!" the driver called from the front of the bus. The large mirror mounted to his side showed that he was switching his gaze between the street ahead and the middle of the bus where Maggie stood. "Will you please sit down? We'll be at Penburg in about 10 minutes."

"Sorry," she said, looking at the driver in the mirror. "I can't sit down because I have incredibly important information that must be shared with everyone." Maggie turned back to the passengers. "Everyone here is familiar with Rejuvenation, I suppose?"

There were laughs from around the bus and Maggie watched a few people preemptively sneer up at her.

"Of course you all are," she said, "but I bet few to none of you know the extreme danger it poses to yourself and the world. I want to tell you all about the evils of Rejuvenation and why it needs to be stopped!"

More laughter, accompanied by some boos and derisive remarks.

"Lady! Sit down right now!" the driver yelled.

"I can't do that," Maggie said. "Do you all know that thanks to Rejuvenation, at the rate the human population is growing on earth we will be unable to sustain ourselves within another 50 years? Sooner than you think, the world will become uninhabitable. When that happens, the fighting will start again. The wars. Rejuvenation may give you immunity from disease, from aging, but it cannot protect you from a bullet or a knife. When resources run out and desperation sets in, no one will care who's a Rejuvenite and who isn't. We will fall into the old ways again, causing a second Decay and inevitably our own downfall. We are sowing the seeds of our own extinction, people! I implore you to listen to me. Rejuvenation must be stopped!"

Maggie continued to look around the bus as she spoke. The passengers were getting more riled up with each sentence. Even in the dim light of the streetlights and illuminated storefronts outside, Maggie saw color rising in some of the passenger's faces while those who had been sleeping awoke uncomfortably to her shouts.

"You Deniers can all go fuck off!" barked a lone man at the front of the bus.

"You should be ashamed of yourself young lady!" shouted a woman sitting a few rows ahead of them next to who Maggie assumed was her husband. That man, much less cordial than his wife, added, "Go back to the fuckin' barrens with the rest of the Anti-Rejuvenite crazies!"

"Lady! If you don't sit down right now I'm going to *make* you sit down," the driver shouted, his stare threatening in the mirror.

Maggie's eyes lit up and she kept on.

"Listen to what I say. I will help you all see the true evil of Rejuvenation. We don't need their wicked science to live our *best lives*! We can have full, long lives without dooming future generations to a struggling existence or no existence at all! Many of you likely call yourselves Prevailers, but you're anything but. You are dooming our children and their children. You must abstain!

"Rejuvenation is a curse! It makes us live beyond the years God has allotted! What do you think happens to you when your brain grows old? EXLI calls it Retirement Day. Lies! They ship you off to one of their old age homes where there are hundreds, thousands of people just lying there day after day. Their bodies are able, but their minds are too tired to carry on! Mere *husks* of humanity! That is what your future holds if you continue to support this devil's work!"

Part of Maggie thought she was laying it on a little thick, but it seemed to be working. She'd been nervous starting, but now, she felt a surge, as if just hitting her stride, suddenly comfortable with the nonsense she was spouting. Because it wasn't like she believed what she was saying. It was all just recycled propaganda pulled from posters tacked up around the city, soapbox lectures given out on street corners; words they'd all heard or read before from those on the opposing side. No, these words were not her own; it was all just part of the plan. The bus's passengers were trying to yell over her now, shouting obscenities and throwing trash and food at her. The projectiles took Maggie by surprise at first, but she soon used it to fuel her fire. She could see in the mirror that the bus driver was still yelling at her to sit down, but his cries were drowned out by the shouts of the passengers.

"You two! Right there," Maggie shouted as loud as she could, pointing at the couple from whom she'd borrowed a phone earlier in the trip. "You two are still pure, aren't you? You've come to the city to undergo the procedure, correct?"

The couple, a young man and woman, nodded timidly.

"I implore you to change your decision! Abstain!" Maggie shouted at them. "Do not join these *Persisters* who sit around you. Do not undergo Rejuvenation because it's the *popular* thing to do. You won't be living your *best life* as they'd have you believe. Return to your homes because it's the *right* thing to do.

You have a choice! Abstain! Abstain or perish! Damn Rejuvenation!"

As she scanned the faces on the bus, Maggie chanced a look back at Simon, and saw a hint of reassurance on his face. Not enough to give him away or draw attention, but just enough to let her know he thought she was doing well. Was she though? she wondered. Maggie had really tried to drive home her supposed position with that last declaration to 'Damn Rejuvenation!' and hoped that it would seem like she was truly a member of one of the more radical Anti-Rejuvenation groups. Seconds later, she got her answer.

"Shut the fuck up lady!" said a man in the middle seats who, like everyone else on board the bus, looked to be in his mid-20s, but was likely very much older.

"I'm free to say whatever I want!" Maggie shouted back at him. "You can't stop me!"

"Oh yeah?" the man cried. He sprang from his seat and into the aisle, stomping toward Maggie. She kept her face frozen, hard, willing herself to show no fear even as the large man charged toward her. Right on cue, Simon sprang to his feet. He kept his head down, but stepped in front of Maggie just before the man reached her.

"Everyone sit down right now!" the driver barked back into the bus.

"Make me!" Maggie yelled, and from around Simon's body, thrust her middle finger in the air.

"Oh, I intend to, you filthy Denier!" the man from the middle seats snarled out, giving Simon a hard shove in the chest. "Just as soon as your boyfriend gets out of the way. I'm gonna teach your girl here some fuckin' manners!"

"That's it!" the driver yelled. He turned the wheel sharply and the bus swerved, tossing Simon, Maggie, and the angry man into the backrest of the seats to their side. "You two are getting the hell off my bus!" The driver shot a glare at the man from the middle seats and added, "You too, buddy, if you don't sit down right now!"

Simon, Maggie, and the angry passenger regained their footing and stood back up. No one said a word as the bus screeched to a halt, the electric whir of the engine winding down to a low, steady hum.

The doors at the front and middle of the bus opened onto a sidewalk swarming with youthful-looking people in professional attire. The driver got up and began lumbering his way back to them.

Simon turned and looked at Maggie. She nodded, then darted back to grab their bag. Simon had just turned around to look back at the angry man when a fist struck him square in the side of the face. The man's knuckles crashed into Simon's cheek and sent him into the seatback to his right. As Simon straightened again, his hat askew, Maggie watched him shake his head then spin around as if to retaliate. Simon might have been hit again had the driver not held the angry man back.

"Off, you two!" the driver shouted, jerking his head toward the open bus doors. "Before you cause any more trouble. You're lucky I'm holding this guy back for you! Scram!"

Simon rubbed the side of his face as he glared at the man being held back. The angry man returned the sneer, baring his teeth like a dog ready to attack. A moment later, the sneer was gone, replaced by a look of comprehension.

Shit, Maggie thought. She understood that look and grabbed Simon, pulling him down the bus's steps.

"Hey!" the angry man barked. "Hey! You're—"

But they were already through the door, swallowed by the crowd outside.

13

―――――

SIMON AND MAGGIE CAUGHT A FEW MORE GARBLED WORDS FROM the man on the bus, and did their best to ignore them. They kept their heads down. Simon readjusted his hat snugly over his eyes again as they walked through the throngs of people filing by, hoping none of them would take notice. Even a few yards away, Maggie thought she could still hear the man from the bus shouting. But she knew that even if people on the sidewalk around the bus heard the man's words, they wouldn't be able to pick the pair out of the crowd. A moment later Maggie heard the faint screech of the bus's tires as they turned away from the curb and the bus rejoined the traffic on the busy street.

Simon and Maggie didn't talk as they walked. They both understood their predicament. Their first concern was to get as far away from where they'd left the bus as possible. After that, they'd find a quiet spot to hide, and then figure out their next move. So they walked, on and on, block after block for at least 15 minutes until they turned down a side street and the crowd of young-looking walkers around them began to thin out.

Once there were only a few others on the street, Maggie and Simon felt comfortable enough to stop and try to get their bearings. The shops nearest them that lined the unfamiliar street—a convenience store, dry cleaners, hair salon, a used bookstore—all looked like they'd seen better days. Looking skyward, Maggie spotted a few recognizable high-rises in the distance. Chief and tallest among them was EXLI Corporate Headquarters—a series of five gray cylindrical buildings that rose in pyramidal succession from the outside in, the top floor of the middle building emblazoned with a bright red EXLI sign.

"Hard to miss that," Simon whispered, tilting his hat back and pointing up.

Maggie nodded. They had a heading and a long walk to go. She pictured the buildings of downtown stretching out from EXLI, all the way to Westgate, the river, and the old parts of the city on the opposite bank. Something about that image stuck in her mind, something related to their bus ride. But what—

"Simon!" she said aloud, then caught herself and changed her voice to a whisper, "I think I know where we can find Darrow. I mean, *really know*."

Simon gave a questioning, high-eyebrowed look as a couple walked by, giving them both an odd glance. He turned himself and Maggie away from the couple and said, "That's great—"

"It's—" Maggie continued, but stopped when Simon shook his head.

"Not here. We need to find some cover first," Simon said. She nodded. "That guy on the bus recognized me and, these people . . ." Simon looked around the street again.

Maggie understood. Without another thought, she grabbed Simon's hand and directed him toward the nearest crosswalk. She nodded forward, across the street and said, "That should do."

"Where—" Simon started, but then stopped his initial question when he looked across the street to where they were headed. "In there?"

"It's as good an asylum as anywhere else," Maggie said, matter-of-factly.

They crossed the street to the small, rundown church on the other side.

———

As soon as they were inside the church, Maggie knew she'd made the right choice. While the bookstore next door would likely have been just as empty as the church was, she suspected the dim atmosphere, the shadows and alcoves, inside the church would provide them with a little more concealment as they waited out any searches for them near the bus station.

The old church, lit only by the soft orange glow of candles, was nearly silent except for the whispered prayers of the few parishioners present. Maggie and Simon sat in a pew near a darkened back corner, staring forward at the large crucifix made of cut gray stone that hung behind the altar as they feigned prayers. They allowed several minutes to pass like this, watching as a pair of elderly women stood, crossed themselves, and toddled down the aisle toward the exit. When the creak and thud of the heavy double doors closing had passed, and silence returned, Simon and Maggie relaxed, chancing conversation again.

"Okay," Simon whispered, removing his hat and rubbing gently at the spot on his face where the man on the bus had hit him. "What's this about you knowing where to find Darrow?"

"She's in *Oldtown.*"

Simon raised an open palm as if to ask, *What*? "I don't understand," he said. "How do you—"

"It's still sort of a hunch, but it's a confident one," Maggie explained. "We know she has a place in the city, the article I found confirmed that. But it also said she had a place on the river, where she could keep an eye on Sullivan and EXLI, right?"

Simon nodded. "It sounds like Westgate, but you were right, Darrow wouldn't be caught dead living in the same place as Sullivan."

"But how'd you land on Oldtown?"

"It was back on the bus," Maggie said, forgetting to keep her voice down for a moment, clamping a hand to her mouth and looking around, then continuing. "You heard those people."

"I heard them all right."

"Yeah, most of it was just nasty insults, but one of them said something that caught my attention. He told me to 'go back to the barrens with the rest of the anti-Rejuvenite crazies.'"

Maggie, and now Simon, pictured it: the fenced-off blocks of Westgate, high-rises gleaming in the sunlight, and beyond . . . across the flowing waters of the Tamm River—*Oldtown*. At least, that was the most common name for that forgotten part of the city. The Barrens, Hinterlands, Boondocks, Wastelands—it had garnered plenty of names since The Decay. But no matter what it was called, there were still people there. Not all of them were Anti-Rejuvenites. In truth, most weren't. But facts rarely stopped rumors and, like the names, its reputation had grown over time.

Maggie could see understanding in Simon's widening eyes, the orange candlelight around them reflecting, making them sparkle as he said, "Good catch. I didn't hear that, but . . . Oldtown's a big place, Maggie. How are we—"

"But the article said her apartment was *overlooking the river*. There're only a few places in Oldtown tall enough and close enough to overlook the river near Westgate."

Again, Simon pictured Oldtown in his head, saw the small group of towers near the riverside. Before The Decay, the towers were some of the most popular residential spaces available, but like everything in Oldtown, they were now rundown, falling apart. Their upkeep forgotten, ignored by a city obsessed with the new and young. But they'd been made to last and people did still live there. Could that be where Lydia Darrow chose to spend her days while visiting the city? It certainly fit the clues they had.

"I know it's a long shot," Maggie said.

"I feel like all we really have at this point are long shots," Simon said, and grinned as he rubbed at his face again.

Somehow, Maggie didn't know why, that grin cut into her. She didn't want to see it, because she didn't feel like smiling about anything. She'd played nice during the bus ride because they'd had a job to do, but now that they were safe, though in hiding, she felt that now-familiar simmering inside her grow to a boil at the sight of Simon's grin. She heard Sebastian's message repeating inside her head like a chanting harbinger. Her mind filled with images and sounds of what they'd been through over the last 24 hours: an assassin shooting at them, Will firing back, Will bleeding out, Will *dying* . . .

And then that grin. How could he? *How dare he?*

"Just stop, will you?" Maggie said, her voice loud again, echoing up and out, but this time she didn't try to stop herself.

Someone at the far front of the nave made a shushing sound in their direction.

"Stop . . . what?" Simon asked, looking around, ducking his head slightly. "What do you—"

"You know damn well what I mean!"

Another shush came from the shadows near the front of the church, this time followed by a polite request that they keep their voices down.

"Maggie, honestly I—"

It felt like an explosion ignited in her mind. Everything she'd been struggling with, everything she'd felt since Will died against that tree in the forest—all that had built up inside her and she couldn't bear it anymore.

"You're sitting there smiling and it's all your fault! We're ripped from our houses in the middle of the night because you got some damn message from your neighbor. Suddenly we're all targets and have to run. And then . . . m-my . . . Will! My brother is *dead* because . . . because we had to run. Because of that message. That m-man was after you, Simon! He was after y-you and Will died because of it! *Will is dead because of you!*"

It was one thing to feel such things, to think them in the privacy of one's mind, but to say them out loud was completely different. Maggie hadn't wanted to say them, but knew she would have to at some point, knew they'd burst out eventually. Now, a part of her felt relieved, but a larger part felt immediate regret. And an even greater part felt hurt, both from the words she spoke and from the look on Simon's face as he stared back at her, blank, unable to respond. His hand fell away from where he'd been rubbing his cheek as if that pain no longer mattered. His face a picture of guilt.

There was a commotion near the front of the church, more shushing and steps sounding across the scuffed floor. It was a distraction, a momentary respite from the hurtful realities Simon and Maggie were facing. They heard more footsteps walking along the far edge of the nave, and knew their time there was limited.

"I . . ." Simon tried to speak quickly, but struggled with the words, any words.

"Simon, I didn't—" Maggie began, but stopped, unsure what to say next. She hadn't meant what she said? That was a lie. She *had* meant it, harsh though it was. But still, a part of her *did* want to take it all back.

"I'm sorry, Maggie," Simon said, finally finding his voice, though it was a voice spoken through tears. "I'm so, so sorry. You're right. It *is* all my fault. I can't . . . I don't know what else to say. I didn't mean for any of this to happen. I just . . . did what I thought . . . I don't know. I thought you two were in danger. I'm sorry. I . . ."

Simon shook his head, looking down at his hands now clasped in his lap, and Maggie's heart broke for the second time in a single day. First Will, now this. What have I done? she asked herself. How could she say such things to the man she loved? How could she blame him? Simon had just been trying to protect them! He hadn't called them in the middle of the night to invite them on an adventure. He hadn't asked them to leave their homes for a joy ride. They were being hunted. All of them.

The footsteps from the far side of the church were getting closer now, louder.

"Simon, I—" Maggie began, reaching out to grab Simon's hands, but he recoiled. His face seemed to grow darker, even in that dimly lit corner of the old church. But the truth was, Maggie didn't know what she had been about to say. Despite everything she'd just realized, something inside her still fought back. She just couldn't let go of that simmering anger buried inside her. Not yet. "I—"

But whatever she would have said was cut short by footsteps and a new voice.

"*Please!* This is a place of worship. You *must* keep your voices down." Maggie and Simon looked up to see that the voice belonged, not to a priest, but a woman in her mid-60s, true aged, and with the scowl of the fiercest librarian. Standing over them both, looking down, she scanned their faces to see what sort of people would make such a scene in as holy a place as that. "I'm sorry, but I'm afraid I'm going to have to ask you two to leave. We just can't have—"

And then a look appeared on her face that Maggie and Simon both knew. They had seen it an hour before on the bus as the angry man stared them down. They'd been recognized.

———

WHEN THEY BURST forth from the heavy, ornate doors of the church, Simon and Maggie found the dark sidewalks and street outside even emptier than they had been before. A few couples and cars were making their way up and down the street, but it was mostly quiet. That was, except for the elderly church volunteer who'd chased them outside, squawking for help and how she'd spotted the criminals from the news. The few passersby there scoffed at the Non-Rejuvenite woman and ignored her.

Simon grabbed Maggie's wrist and led her quickly down the first alleyway they saw, out onto another vacant street, and then into another alley. He was thankful for the darkness of side streets and alleyways, of the night, as he'd accidentally left his hat behind when they'd fled the church. They continued this way until the voice of the churchwoman faded and they felt safe enough to return to the main roads. They used the large EXLI buildings, still looming over them with that bright red sign burning high in the sky, like a guiding star. They walked on, keeping their heads down when passing others on the street.

It's all your fault.

Simon couldn't stop Maggie's words from the church from repeating inside his head as they walked.

Will is dead because of you!

The stinging words reaffirmed the feelings Simon had been battling inside himself since the forest, his guilt for what had happened. To Maggie. To Will. Their entire ordeal. But to hear those same feelings spoken aloud, to see that look of revulsion on Maggie's face, directed at him, was almost too much for Simon to bear. On top of that, he saw no defense. He couldn't blame Maggie or argue with her, because he had been the one to get them involved. He *was* to blame, he thought, and it burned at his heart, which grew heavier with each step they took.

But then someone else's words echoed in his mind.

This isn't your fault. None of it.

Will. What seemed like ages ago, back when they'd been fleeing the city. After he'd been shot, but before—

Even then, with a bullet in his belly, bleeding out, certainly knowing his time was limited, Will had tried to reassure Simon. He'd tried to impart his usual supportive wisdom as Simon struggled with the responsibility of it all. But the guilt was so much greater now. And Will wasn't around anymore to convince Simon of anything.

Only Will's words remained. They fought against Maggie's.

It's all your fault. Will is dead because of you!

This isn't your fault. None of it.

Out of pure instinct, Simon grabbed Maggie's hand as he led them around a street corner, cutting over to another, larger avenue. He felt her skin against his, and for a brief moment, that touch sent him back to the way things used to be. Back before all this business with a mysterious message from Sebastian, being driven from their homes, pursued, Will's death. But the next moment, their hands parted, and it all came flooding back. Simon wondered if things would ever be the same again, or even close to it. He didn't think so. Not with everything that had happened. Not with the guilt he felt. Not with the way Maggie thought of him now.

But Simon resolved to go on anyway. Even if they could never go back to any semblance of what they'd had before. Even if Maggie blamed him. Even if she *hated* him from this day forward, he'd force himself to accept it. He'd live with that loss if it meant Maggie would be safe.

We need to protect her, Simon. You need to keep her safe.

More words from Will, echoing in his head. Will had been right, Simon told himself. Simon's mind was fully made up. He'd honor his friend's wishes. He'd do whatever he had to do to keep Maggie safe, to protect her. Even if she never forgave Simon. He'd continue to lead them on, down those city streets, to Darrow, to the answer to Sebastian's mysterious message, to clear their names. Because that was the only way Maggie would be safe again. Truly safe.

The battle of sibling words inside Simon's head was over. Won by them both. Simon would expend no more thoughts, no more words to try to wash himself of the responsibility for what had happened, for their current situation. He would own it. He'd do whatever he had to do to find justice for Will, to follow his guidance, to protect Maggie. He would lead them on, no matter the consequences.

The trek toward what they hoped was Lydia Darrow's apartment should have been easy. It should've taken them no time at all to cross downtown. But early in their journey, they found many of the side streets blocked by police barricades and, in some instances, police cars. At first, Simon suspected the obstructions were part of the manhunt to find him, but quickly dismissed the idea; there were too many barricades too close together. He considered backtracking, but knew it would take too long and so they pressed on and chanced the route that would lead them straight into the heart of the city.

It wasn't until they got closer to EXLI Headquarters and saw barricades surrounding the main building's front entrance, circling the mountain of steps leading up to it, that they understood what was happening. In the center at the top of the EXLI steps was a small, elevated platform with a covered podium set in the middle.

They stopped and studied the scene for a moment.

"The announcement tomorrow," Maggie said. "It must be something big. If they are going through all this trouble. They've cordoned off the streets for blocks. They must be expecting a lot of people."

"Well, whatever EXLI has to say," Simon said, "it doesn't concern us right now. Come on. We need to keep moving."

As they walked, the barricades disappeared and the high-rises began to thin out, and ahead, they saw a massive break in the wall of buildings around them. The skyscrapers shrank to mere two and three-story buildings. They soon smelled dampness in the air and heard the rush of water. A block farther and they caught their first glimpse of the Tamm River flowing by.

They crossed a street and, on the other side, saw the river clearly, its depths darkened by the night, but its surface sparkling, reflecting the light of the moon and nearby streetlamps. Across the river, more buildings rose up from the streets, though most of these were in states of disrepair, leftovers and forgotten remnants from before The Decay.

In contrast, on a narrow peninsula of land, was a group of tall buildings separated from the rest of the city by a large fence running around their perimeter. The buildings were spotted up and down with lights turned on inside. Even in the distance, Maggie could see shadows, figures moving behind large, lighted windows. The street below turned into a bridge leading to the other side of the river where a group of much older, but equally tall, buildings stood, mirroring the newer, gated structures on the other side.

"So there's Westgate," Maggie said.

"Yup," Simon said.

"I wonder how many people who own an apartment there actually live there. Probably just the locals, huh?"

Simon nodded. He knew to what Maggie was referring. It was common knowledge how many of the apartments in Westgate, status symbol that it was, were owned by people who didn't have a need for them. Wealthy people who spent most of their time traveling the world, or living in a European villa, but still liked to be able to mention how they owned a place in Westgate. But the local bunch still lived there; politicians like Senator Nolan, CEOs like Christopher Edingham of Founder's National Bank, and yes, Theodore Sullivan.

"Well I guess we're going to get to see the whole thing up close pretty soon," Maggie said.

"Seen it. Not for me." Simon doubled his steps, which Maggie matched. "Come on. Just a little farther now."

The two of them walked silently as they approached Westgate. Closer now, they could see that the fence surrounding the place was lined with barbed wire. Several large spotlights were perched on the fence, spinning slowly, lighting the sidewalk and street beneath. When they finally stopped across the street from Westgate, Simon couldn't help but notice how much the place resembled a maximum-security prison, not a housing complex for the wealthy. He thought it funny that people would want to live in a place like that; he wondered if they really felt they needed to separate themselves from the rest of the city so dramatically. He took one more look at the place, then turned to Maggie.

"It's something, huh?" Maggie said.

"Not really," Simon replied. "Let's go. Almost there."

Simon grabbed Maggie's hand again and the two set off down the sidewalk, past the luxury towers, heading across the bridge.

14

Opposite Westgate on the other side of the river stood several tall, weathered buildings that looked like a strong gust of wind might knock them over. Were it not for the clothes and towels hanging from balcony railings, or the silhouettes of people visible in some of the windows, one might think the buildings were long vacant. But they were, in fact, filled with people. As were many of the surrounding smaller buildings that ran up and down the riverbank because they were all actually apartments—poorly constructed housing facilities that were easy and cheap to lease because of their location. It was like that throughout the entirety of the east side. The whole area had once been part of the main city, with boroughs and neighborhoods populated by all manner of people and cultures. It used to be considered a significant part of downtown, but that was long ago when the city willingly spanned the Tamm River, back before The Decay. First abandoned during the later years of the outbreaks, it had been left to rot after the breakthrough of Rejuvenation. Since those days, the city had been restored and rebuilt, but with a focus on the other side of the river. And over the years, people who could not afford to live in the new city slowly began to move back to the once vibrant and bustling streets of the eastern banks, which was avoided by those fortunate enough to live on the west side or the suburbs that surrounded new downtown. Most averted their eyes from that part of the city, but it was right across the river and sometimes unavoidable. There were countless propositions to have the area bulldozed and rebuilt from the ground up; the people living in Westgate certainly didn't appreciate the eyesore in front of their homes. But no plans ever seemed to stick, and so the area remained, ruins of the time before, a crumbling memory of the past. Many names for it had sprung up over the years, but to most it was known simply as Oldtown.

After Simon and Maggie had reached the other side of the bridge and crossed into Oldtown, they headed toward the tallest of the buildings in that group on the eastern banks of the river.

Unlike its mirror image, the towering apartment building Simon and Maggie approached had no gate and no fence along its perimeter to keep out unwanted visitors. The rectangular building rose high into the air, its age—its weathered, scarred exterior— visible in the moonlight.

Of the people milling around the streets that surrounded the apartment building, Simon and Maggie saw a mixture of Rejuvenites and Non-Rejuvenites. They seemed to have no issue coexisting, an idea that Simon appreciated as he and Maggie strode toward the building's entrance. When they reached the bottom of the steps, Simon stopped and turned to Maggie.

"You can stay down here if you want," he said.

"Simon, I—"

"I'm serious. I'll go take care of it. You can stay. You'd be safer."

"I'm going with you," Maggie said flatly. "I'm not walking away now that we're here. I know you're just looking out for me, but I'm going. I'm part of this." She led them up the steps.

Simon nodded his agreement.

"Besides," Maggie went on. "We don't even know if this is the right place. We could be searching these buildings all night. But if this is it, what are you expecting?"

"I don't know." That was the truth. Simon didn't know what they might encounter if this was Lydia Darrow's apartment building. "Think she'd have some sort of *protection* with her?"

"No idea," Maggie said, "but she's a scientist, Simon. A teacher. A lecturer. I doubt she has an arsenal or a full guard of secret service men staged outside her door." Maggie looked around at the dirty streets of Oldtown, then added, "You still have the gun, right?"

"Yeah, but—"

"I don't want to use it any more than you."

"Good, because I'm not sure it'd even work," Simon said, remembering the gun sitting in that pool of blood on the passenger seat floor. He scanned the surrounding street to make sure they weren't being watched. Then he knelt behind Maggie, pulled the revolver from the depths of his duffle bag, and slid it into the back waistband of his pants, making sure his shirt covered the gun.

"All right," Simon said as he stood again. "Let's go."

Simon pulled one of the doors open on its rusty hinges, and they stepped inside, into a lobby where, like the street outside, people were scarce. Across the room, a round-faced man in a dark gray suit was checking one of the small, metal mailboxes that lined the right side of the lobby. He looked up at them when he heard the front door creak open, but quickly went back to his mail.

"We need to figure out what floor she's on first," Simon said. "I'm assuming one at the top, if she's truly overlooking the river."

Maggie nodded toward the silver mailboxes and Simon understood. They made their way over near where the round-faced man still stood, but he paid them no notice as he closed his mailbox and headed to the elevators. When they were close enough to read the small plaques on the front of each mailbox, Simon's heart sank. There were no names, only apartment numbers. But near the end of the wall where the numbers were higher Simon spied one box that looked different than the rest. In addition to the everyday scratches and wear from repeated use over time, the mailbox Simon now looked at was much worse. It was covered with additional markings, words, harsh epithets and short phrases of contempt. There were signs of previous attempts to scrub and sand off these words, but to no avail it seemed, as it looked like for every word removed, more were etched in the metal overtop of them. Simon and Maggie peered down at the mailbox and could easily make out the inscriptions:

Go home you freak bitch!

Rejuvenation for all!

Traitor.

They didn't bother to read them all.

"I suppose that's hers?" Maggie said, a frown on her face as she read the mailbox front.

"It has to be," Simon said. "Apartment 1632."

They turned and headed towards the elevators, seeing the doors closing. They quickened their steps and then saw a hand reach out between the doors, stopping them. When they reached the elevator, Simon saw the hand belonged to the round-faced man they'd spotted earlier. He smiled and Simon saw wrinkles bunched up around the man's eyes, across his forehead and cheeks.

"Going up?" the man said with a chuckle.

"Ah, yeah, but, we can get the next one," Simon replied.

"Nonsense. I already stopped the door for you. Besides, you don't wanna ride that other elevator. Been making strange noises for a week. Come on."

Simon looked at Maggie, but she only gave a weak shrug and smiled at the man. "Thank you." And they stepped inside.

Simon had hoped he and Maggie would be able to ride up alone, maybe talk out their plan in the short seconds it would take for the elevator to reach the top floor, but the friendly, round-faced man had put an end to that.

"Floor?" the man asked.

"Oh, um . . ."

"Sixteen, please," Maggie said, quickly.

"You got it." The man pushed the round, faded 16 button on the panel of numbers, split into two columns, next to the inside of the elevator doors. After, he pushed the button for floor 15.

As they ascended, Simon was amazed at how long the elevator ride felt. He knew his mind was just playing tricks with him. He looked at Maggie who gave a forced smile. When he glanced at the elevator's third inhabitant, he saw the round-faced man still wore a wide grin, which accentuated the wrinkles on his face from this close up. Simon began to wonder how old the man was, how old he *truly* was—maybe late 40s, perhaps even 50.

"New to the building?" the man asked.

"Yes," Simon said, trying to gather a suitable answer in his mind. "Well, ah, actually, we're hoping to move in soon. Just taking a look around."

"Looking for a place of your own, eh? You newlyweds?"

The question caught both Simon and Maggie off guard. After everything they'd been through, everything Maggie had said back at the church, the thought of being newlyweds seemed downright bizarre. Simon began to worry their hesitation was clear on their faces, obvious, uncomfortable. But then—

"Yes," Maggie said. She grabbed Simon's arm, tilting her head to his shoulder. The affection, even feigned, felt both odd and right to Simon. "Been married just two weeks. We're hoping it works out here."

The round-faced man chuckled. "Oh, that's great. Always nice to have a new couple in the building. Most people around here are nice enough. Very accommodating."

The elevator made a soft dinging noise, slowed, and came to stop.

"This is my stop," the cheerful man said, extending a hand to Simon. "It's been a fun ride, Mr.?"

But Simon was ready this time. "Chambers. Ed Chambers."

"Nice to meet ya, Ed." He turned to Maggie. "And you, miss." Maggie didn't bother with a name, but just nodded and smiled. "Hope everything works out for you two. If it does, I suppose I'll be seeing you around." He gave them a wink, which Simon and Maggie returned with forced grins as the man exited the elevator.

As soon as the doors closed, the pair stepped apart and released a sigh of relief. No words necessary.

One more floor to go.

Almost there, Simon thought. If the elevator would indeed lead them to Lydia Darrow. Maybe not. Perhaps this was the wrong building and they'd have to start again in one of the others. But he didn't think so. That mailbox downstairs, it had to be right. And if that were true, they could be seconds away from Darrow. Or seconds away from arriving at the floor only to find an apartment heavily guarded by men with far bigger guns than the one Simon had tucked in his waistband. He felt his hands begin to tremble slightly as the elevator climbed again. A light sweat broke out on Simon's forehead and palms. He wiped his hands on his pants, hoping Maggie didn't see his sudden nervousness.

The elevator dinged again and came to a clanky stop. Simon breathed deep, expecting the worst. He stepped forward in front of Maggie to shield her as best he could in case the elevator doors opened and there was a barrage of gunfire upon them. He reached behind his back and grasped the handle of the gun tucked there. A second later, the silver doors in front of him slid apart and revealed the hallway beyond . . .

Nothing. No armed security guard pointing an automatic weapon at them, no suited sunglasses-wearing men with coms in their ears, not even a camera mounted on the wall pointed into the elevator to spot would-be visitors. Just a wall covered in flower-print wallpaper of dingy, faded yellow and a small sign marking the room numbers in both directions.

Simon stuck his head out of the elevator and looked both ways down the hallway. Again, he saw nothing—only apartment door after apartment door. He expelled the breath he'd been holding and let his hand fall from around the handle of the gun. Simon then motioned for Maggie to follow him.

They turned toward apartment 1632 and started down the hallway.

"There's no one here," Maggie said.

"You were right," he said.

"Seems kind of dangerous now that I think about it. I mean, you saw what people wrote on that mailbox downstairs."

Simon shrugged.

"Could be bravery, maybe naivety. Not sure, but she doesn't seem like the most scared woman, if you ask me."

They reached 1632 and stood for a moment, silent, looking at the door. It bore no words of hate like the mailbox downstairs, but was scuffed and faded like the rest of the hallway. They looked at each other.

"Ready?" Simon said.

Maggie nodded and took a deep breath.

Simon reached up and knocked on the door. He watched for movement through the small, round peephole. A moment passed before they heard footsteps behind the door. They were soft, light.

"Yes? Who is it?" a voice said. The West-Midlands English accent was apparent immediately, though muffled slightly through the door. But there was something else, something odd about the voice, a high-pitched nature and strange youthfulness to it.

"Miss Darrow?" Simon said.

"This is she. May I help you?"

Simon and Maggie looked at each other in confirmation. They'd found her.

"Um, well, yes. I hope so."

"Who is this?"

"Oh, sorry. My name is—" Simon paused for a moment, wondering if he should give his real name. Darrow would certainly have been keeping up on the news. She would know his name. If he used it now, she might immediately refuse to talk to him and even call the police. Then again, if he used an alias, she might not trust him when she did find out who he was. It was risky, he thought, but he decided it was best not to lie to the woman from whom he was trying to get help. "My name is Simon Crowe. I need your help, Miss Darrow, if you're willing. I need to speak with you."

The silence that followed made Simon's mind race, wondering if Darrow had retreated upon hearing his name and was at that moment calling the police. He then heard something hard hit the other side of the door at its bottom. There was a brief sound of creaking, like footsteps on old wooden steps, then the high voice returned.

"Mr. Crowe, is it?" Lydia said from the other side of the door. "Yes. I recognize you from the news."

She was watching him, Simon thought, looking at them through the peephole in the door.

"Yes, that's me," he said. "But—"

"I recognize your friend as well."

"You—what?" He looked at Maggie, confused, then back to the door. "Where—"

"The news. First it was just you, then they started talking about her, as your accomplice. And some other man."

It was just as they had feared, Simon thought. His mind flashed back to the squawking woman at the church. She had recognized them *both*. This was why.

"Well, whatever the news is saying, it's wrong," Simon said. "Maggie and I haven't done anything. We—"

"Your friend," Lydia interrupted again. "She looks . . . unnaturally young."

Perhaps the news had mentioned Maggie's Rejuvenite status, perhaps not. Maybe after all these years, all it took Darrow was one glance. She just *knew*.

"That's right. But it doesn't matter. She—we mean you no harm, Miss Darrow. We just need to speak with you."

"Sorry, but I'm afraid it's too late for me to be taking visitors."

"Please! We really need to talk to you. You recognize us. You know how desperate our situation is. Please, I—"

"Listen here, young man," Lydia interjected, her voice more forceful now but still unusually high-pitched. "It's late. I've had a long day and already said no. Now I know you're in a pretty pickle of a situation, and I'm sorry about that. You may be innocent, but I don't see how I can possibly help you in any way besides one. I promise not to call the police on you. You can go on your way and we'll pretend you were never here. I only hope I'm not making a mistake."

"But you *can* help!" Simon said. "Please just hear what we have to say. We think that whatever we're mixed up in has to do with more than just a couple deaths. We think that Sebastian Martin was murdered because he knew something he shouldn't have. Something about EXLI—something *bad*. Please just hear us out. You can help, I'm sure of it."

"You're wearing out my patience, Mr. Crowe." And then,

through the door, they heard Darrow's voice, but more muffled this time, as if she were talking to someone else, or . . . on the phone.

"What's that? We can't . . . Please don't call the police. I'm sorry we disturbed you. Please. Just allow me to explain. Sebastian . . . Dr. Martin, the EXLI scientist who was murdered, he was a friend of mine. He left me a message. I think you—"

Lydia's voice was back in full, clear.

"I've had quite enough of this. I didn't know this Dr. Martin fellow. He might have been a friend to you, but he was no friend of mine. Whatever he had to say, I'm sure there are more qualified people out there to help than I. Now please leave or I will have no choice but to call the authorities. Good night, Mr. Crowe."

Simon knocked on the door again, a little more forcefully this time. He felt the heat of anger in his face. He couldn't understand why she wouldn't at least hear what they had to say.

"Please!" he pleaded. "We have nowhere else to go. You can help us, I know it. The message Sebastian left me, he mentioned a woman and I think he meant you. I know he meant you!"

The creaking noise came from behind the door again, then another small slam at the bottom of it. Footsteps again, this time heading away from the door.

"Miss Darrow asked you to leave."

The voice came from behind them. Maggie and Simon turned to see—the round-faced man. His once cheerful face was absent of the smile they'd seen before, in its place a hard expression and sharp-angled eyebrows.

"You? But I don't under—"

"The lady asked you to go, so go," the man said.

Simon didn't have time for this, whatever it was. He didn't care about this Good Samaritan. They needed to speak with Darrow. He turned back to the door, pounded on it again and said,

"Please! Sebastian's message also mentioned someone else, a man. We don't know who he is, but we think he's being held somewhere against his will. Some place called Hillbrook. I don't know—"

There was a rush of footsteps again from inside the apartment, this time headed back toward the door. Simon heard a shriek from Maggie and turned to see the round-faced man had pulled a pistol on them.

Then, the door swung open.

Standing in the doorway was Lydia Darrow. Even after seeing her on TV and in the newspapers countless times, it still seemed odd to see Darrow in person. She was a small woman, though due to her condition she looked like no woman at all. To the uninitiated, Lydia Darrow looked like just another average 12-year-old girl waiting for the day when she could join the rest of the crowd in the mock-eternal youth provided by Rejuvenation. But she was already one of them and had been for some time. As she stepped out into the hallway, Simon noticed how tiny Darrow truly was, the top of her brown hair reaching only the middle of his chest. Her arms were thin, almost underdeveloped. If one knew the unique circumstances of her life, she was a sight to behold, for though Lydia Darrow stood before them a pubescent girl, she was in reality older than Simon and Maggie combined.

Simon stood frozen, shocked at the sudden reversal and heightened tension of the situation: the round-faced man drawing on them, the sudden opening of the door, the emergence of Darrow. Maggie leaned closer to Simon and gripped his hand tightly as their eyes darted between the man with the gun and the tiny woman standing in the doorway.

"What did you just say?" Lydia said.

"Which part?" Simon said, hesitating for a moment. His eyes continued shifting between Darrow and the gun pointed at them. I don't know . . . can we . . ."

Lydia gave a flip of her hand and said, "At ease, Derrick." Derrick hesitated for a moment, then holstered his weapon. Lydia's attention never left Simon. "Now tell me, what did you just say?"

"I'm not sure . . . You mean the message Sebastian left for me?"

"You said—"

"Hillbrook?"

Lydia's eyes lit up.

"*Yes*. That's it. Hillbrook. You're sure about that name?" Lydia said quietly, looking around the hallway suspiciously.

"Ye . . . Yes," Simon said. "But we don't know—"

"Of course you don't know. How could you unless you were a member?"

Simon stole a glance at Maggie and saw that she wore the same confused expression he could feel on his face. He turned back to Lydia. She nodded at the man named Derrick, who immediately turned and marched back down the hallway. Next, Lydia stepped aside, looked at Simon and Maggie, and extended her slender arm in welcome.

"Right. I suppose you two should come in," Lydia said. "It appears we have something to discuss tonight after all."

EXCERPTS: DARROW, LYDIA. "A CHOICE DENIED." MY LIFE, LIVED: AN AUTOBIOGRAPHY. COLEMAN PRESS. 41-49. PRINT.

———

. . . in my younger years, I . . . foolishly thought achieving some level of acclaim and wealth would fix the problems in my past. . . . I discovered that a large bank account and notoriety are not a panacea. In the end, there's no such thing.

. . . I made the choice to change . . . I would champion my cause, not in an effort to fix childhood woes, but so that my strife would never again be another's. My work would be . . . for all humanity. For our future as a species. . . . I planted my stance firmly in the ground like a well-rooted tree . . .

. . . My drive comes from a choice denied.

Leading up to my tenth birthday . . . I had developed an advanced case of Ewing's sarcoma. . . . the cancer had already spread from my bones to the surrounding and distant tissue and muscles . . . The survival rate of such cases is low, and since I was still too young to even consider Rejuvenation as a last resort, my parents opted for the treatments that were available.

I underwent repeated rounds of radiation therapy, chemotherapy, and operations . . . My father said I was a fighter, even then, and for two years, this was my life. . . . Had research continued and advanced post-Decay, who's to say what sort of cures medical science may have found, including one for my own illness?

. . . I had reached the minimum chronological age for special cases, my parents, desperate to save the life of their only child, decided that I would undergo Rejuvenation at the age of twelve. Ironic as it sounds, I have never been afraid to admit I was terrified then. What child wouldn't be? . . . doctors tried to ease my anxiety by doing their best to explain . . . How the growth hormones and senolytic drugs would ultimately upgrade my body's acquired immunity, its ability to recognize and fight antigens . . . destroying my cancer from within . . . How the advanced T cells now produced by my body would also target my own cells . . . instead of causing an autoimmune disorder . . . would start healing my body at the cellular level—manipulating and upgrading my DNA . . . preventing the telomeres at the end of my chromosomes from degrading, from shortening, which in conjunction with the destruction of senescent cells in my body, would halt biological aging, even in someone so young as I was.

My mind was foggy back then and I can't say I understood much of it. But enough sank in, eased my mind, and before long, I was set to go under the needle, so to speak. My memory of the actual day of the procedure has faded somewhat with age, but I distinctly remember looking out the window that morning, seeing large, fluffy snow falling outside, and wondering if I had missed Christmas. It is a rather childish thought, but ironically, one that has stayed with me every day since.

That decision by my parents has also stayed with me my entire life, not merely because of my perpetual physical youth, but because I was never given the chance to decide for myself.

. . . I am not angry with my parents for their decision. I wouldn't be alive today if they hadn't chosen Rejuvenation for me. The ineffectiveness of my earlier treatments and the illness itself forced their hand. . . . In reality, it was no choice at all. That's what I find myself often cross about, that's what drives me, the fact that neither I, nor my parents, were really allowed to decide our fate for ourselves.

Because as it turned out, it truly was *our* fate.

We coexisted at first, evening football matches in the back garden with my father, hours spent baking in the kitchen with Mum. These were the things a young girl often did . . . as the years went by, and I began to mature mentally while my body remained unimpeded by adolescence . . . Arguments between my parents started to become frequent, about what was best for me, how I should be cared for. It was almost as if I were sick again. . . . My poor father was never able to fully grasp the concept, what I had become. . . . When he wasn't busying himself in the garage by building a replica of some old car, he found other ways to actively avoid me . . . barely even acknowledged when I walked into a room . . . This coldness bled into his relationship with Mum, and they inevitably split. I never saw him again.

. . . Mum had always been there for me . . . as I prepared to take my final year of secondary school, the cracks in her started to show. . . . They were little mentions, slip-ups, and I tried to laugh them off. . . . near the end of my undergraduate studies, Mum too . . . could not reconcile the divergence of my appearance and mind. . . . I used to see her from time to time, but the meetings were difficult . . . until the day she was retired to The Kingsley Centre of Birmingham.

I continued . . . on my own. It was not easy, but living your personal truth rarely is. I learned a great many things in that time . . . sadly, not everyone who's on your side stays that way. Some develop doubts in the cause, but come around eventually. Others lose hope completely. And sometimes, those who seem the most promising are seduced by the opposition. Those departures hurt the most . . . But I found my calling and, ultimately, those who shared my vision of the world, those who look on me . . . as an equal. Some, even, as a leader.

And so, I stand before this world, a model of contradiction, a young appearance coupled with my many years. The very thing that saved me has become my adversary. . . . Though, I've always found it's more about what happens along the way than the duration of the journey.

15

LYDIA LED HER TWO VISITORS INTO THE LIVING ROOM. SHE walked lightly, as if trying to avoid squeaky floorboards that hid underneath the thin, gray carpet running wall-to-wall.

The room was filled with the smell of fresh, mixed herbs. Basil and thyme. In the small kitchen on the other side of a half-wall separating the rooms, Simon saw steam coiling over a pot simmering on the stove. His nose caught other smells too, cooking carrots, broccoli, and something rich baking in the oven. A small cutting board and wet knife lay on the counter next to the stove.

While Lydia darted into the kitchen to turn off the stove, Simon and Maggie stood in the living room, taking stock of their surroundings. The room looked like a hundred other living rooms and also, upon closer inspection, like a hundred people might have lived there before Lydia. It wasn't in a total state of disrepair, but the lighting fixtures and paint job could use a revamp, full of cracks and scuffs. The furniture looked newer, as if Lydia were perfectly content to stay in a rundown apartment, but drew the line at her seating arrangements. Against one wall sat a long couch that could easily seat four people. Next to this, a leather armchair with two small tables on either side, each holding a small stack of books. The lamps in two of the corners shed soft, white light across the entire living room and a long, rectangular coffee table sat in the middle of the room topped with a clay bowl full of plums.

Directly across from the couch, set in the exterior wall was a pair of sliding glass doors with long, plastic shades drawn to the side. Outside, Simon could see a small balcony, and in the distance, across the river clearly visible from that high perch, the brightly lit towers that made up Westgate.

There was a clock and a small TV mounted onto the wall near the hallway. Besides that, the walls of Lydia's apartment were bare. Though Simon did spy a small picture hanging in the kitchen. From the living room, he could only make out one tall and one short figure in the photo, no faces. Though he suspected one of them was Lydia.

Their host came out of the kitchen, abandoning her dinner, and stood in front of the coffee table. She motioned them to the couch.

Simon and Maggie sat next to each other in the center of the large couch and looked up at Lydia. Her small form was made more striking outlined by the moonlight through the glass doors behind her. They had expected her to sit down, but she remained standing as she questioned them.

"So," Lydia said. "Tell me everything. Your side of the story about why you are wanted for murder, about this message your EXLI friend sent you, why you think I can help you. Everything that led you here tonight."

Simon cleared his throat and then told Lydia Darrow their story, talking for nearly a half-hour, and praying the whole time that she might be able to help them.

"That's quite a tale, Mr. Crowe," Lydia said after she'd listened to Sebastian's voice mail for the third time.

"You don't believe me?" he said.

"Oh, I believe you. It's really too fantastic to be anything but true."

"So what now?"

Lydia was silent for a moment.

"Patience, Mr. Crowe. I need to be sure I understand all the information available."

"You can help us, can't you?" Maggie said. "You let us in because Simon said *Hillbrook*. That means something to you."

"It most certainly does," Lydia said with a nod. She paused, studying them closely before she began again. "Now, I do have some information which may help you and perhaps even me. The only hesitance I have is that some of it is very important, very secret information. Why should I put my trust in you?"

"After everything I've just told you?" Simon said. "You still don't trust us?"

"You story notwithstanding, I do not know you, Mr. Crowe. Aside from what I've gleaned from the television."

"But that's just it. You know our situation. You know we're wanted. And we came to you for help. What else would we have to gain by coming to you?"

She studied Simon for a moment, then said, "Fair enough, I suppose. If I were to go on, you must swear to me that you will not divulge anything you hear tonight to anyone else, ever again. Even if you are caught by the authorities and they try to force the information from you, whatever they promise or threaten, you must not tell a soul what I am about to say. Doing so could compromise years of plans and efforts by some of my . . . associates." Lydia moved her thoughtful gaze to Maggie. Her eyes narrowed. "Miss, I have to be honest and say that I am still having some misgivings about you."

"Me?" Maggie said. "Why me?"

"Because of your condition, dear. You are like me. You have

undergone the procedure and, though I am constantly reminded by my opposition of how hypocritical it is, I cannot say that I altogether trust our kind."

Maggie sat stunned for a moment as she processed what she'd just heard.

"*Our kind?*" Maggie said. "What—listen, you don't have to worry about me. I'm not some uppity Prevailer. When it comes to Rejuvenation, I don't try to convince anyone of anything. Rejuvenation is each person's personal choice. Besides, I'm wanted by the police now just like Simon. You said it yourself."

Lydia looked from Maggie to Simon in question. Simon nodded.

"You can trust her, Miss Darrow," Simon said. "I promise."

Lydia raised her eyebrows. "Well, that means an awful lot coming from someone I just met."

"Of course you can trust me!" Maggie said, red rising in her cheeks. "I'm here, aren't I? Just because I've undergone Rejuvenation doesn't mean you should trust me less!"

"My dear, I—"

"No!" Maggie exclaimed, standing from the couch, pointing at Darrow. "I've been through all this with Simon. I was with him when we were shot at outside my home. I was there when my brother *died* in front of me! So don't you dare tell me about your *misgivings*! Are you going to help us or not?"

A small smile appeared on Lydia's face. "I am."

"Good!" Maggie sat with a huff, then looked up at Lydia a little sheepishly and added, almost as an afterthought, "And I'm sorry for yelling."

"Not to worry, young lady," Lydia said. "Your passion gives you credibility." Lydia looked at them both now. "So we are clear, then? If I tell you about Hillbrook, you won't tell anyone else. Agreed?"

They both nodded.

"If you don't mind, I'd like you to say it out loud."

They did.

"Thank you," Lydia said and began pacing. Though she lived in the body of a twelve-year-old girl, Lydia's thoughtful face, her hands clutched behind her back, the straight posture, all her mannerisms and carriage showed her maturity. This was as evident as ever when she stopped, turned to them, and began talking like she was giving one of her lectures.

"Now," Lydia said, "I know you, dear, are familiar with the Rejuvenation procedure, but I want to make sure we're all on the same page. Mr. Crowe?"

"Yes, I am," Simon said. "Very much so, in fact. I studied it quite a bit before I made my decision."

Lydia beamed.

"That is excellent to hear, Mr. Crowe. I admire those who educate themselves instead of simply jumping into it." Lydia looked at Maggie. "No offense. It is just a somewhat sore subject for me given my . . . Well, would it be too presumptuous on my part to assume you are both already aware of my unique history?"

Like most people in the world, Simon and Maggie were aware. Regardless of which way a person leaned with regards to Rejuvenation, it seemed that everyone knew the story of Lydia Darrow. They nodded.

"Excellent. Given that, and your familiarity with Rejuvenation, I assume you also know what happens at the end. By that I mean PCM Induction: the day a person who has undergone Rejuvenation reaches a certain, advanced age and can no longer function despite the health of the rest of their body."

Simon thought of his grandfather, lying on that bed, motionless . . .

"PCM?" he said. "You're talking about the deterioration of the brain."

"Correct, Mr. Crowe," she said. "Commonly called Retirement Day, but, if you'll allow me to be scientifically accurate, the correct term is Post-Cerebrational Mobility. When the divergence of the mind finally catches up to Rejuvenites."

The basics of what Lydia was talking about was another topic most people were familiar with, even if they didn't know the technical terms. Those who did their research before deciding on Rejuvenation, like Simon, often knew a little more. Ever since the modern Rejuvenation procedure became a permanent, rather than temporary, solution, and reached a point where a person's body could essentially live unimpeded by time, there had always been one caveat to that supposed immortality. The body remained the same, but the *mind* continued to age. And the real kicker was, no one knew why. After all the years, all the research, it was still a mystery. Before Rejuvenation, the brain had been thought of as part of the body, and it still was from a biological standpoint. But since the procedure, the idea of body and mind had diverged because that mysterious problem with Rejuvenation remained.

"Even today," Lydia continued, "when a person undergoes Rejuvenation, their brain deteriorates and, inevitably, becomes so aged that it is no longer able to function efficiently. They are post-cerebration, beyond thought, unable to use their minds properly to control their bodies. The person is still fundamentally alive; they are just no longer able to function as they once could. It starts slow, but eventually the person loses all mobility. PCM Induction. They become motionless beings that—"

"Husks." The term popped into his head and Simon said it aloud before he could think otherwise. "Sorry, I—"

"Don't bother. Yes, that's the name some have chosen to use. A little too brash for my taste. But yes, that is what I mean: those who can no longer move and who spend their remaining days lying frozen at home under the care of loved ones, or at one of the many *luxurious* retirement facilities graciously set up by the EXLI Corporation.

"You want to know what Hillbrook is, Mr. Crowe? Hillbrook is one of those retirement facilities—the original and largest one, in fact."

Simon shook his head, confused.

"No, that can't be," he said, as memories flooded his mind. "I've been—I've read about those places before and I've seen reports about them on TV. The largest one is outside the city, isn't it? A fair way out, in a whole other county, I thought, up by the bluffs. My father and I used to go camping at a state park near there when I was a kid."

"The Shepherd's Institute," Lydia said.

"That's it! The Shepherd's Institute. I always thought that was such a weird name, but then again, it is a place housing a bunch of brain dead people who—"

"Not brain dead, Mr. Crowe. Their brains are very much alive and active, they've just lost the ability to control basic motor functions, to control the youthful bodies they so desired to maintain."

"Okay. Sorry, you're right. That was—so, you're saying The Shepherd's Institute is Hillbrook?"

"Yes."

"I've never heard it called that before."

"No, you wouldn't have," Lydia said as she continued pacing. "Not unless you were a longtime member of one of the larger, more influential groups. You see, Hillbrook is a *code name* given to this particular retirement facility, used only in the innermost circles of what you know as Anti-Rejuvenation groups, people like Life Liberation."

"You mean those whack-jobs who spend their time bombing Rejuvenation centers?" Maggie asked. "Is that who we're talking about?"

Lydia stopped and looked fiercely at Maggie and Simon.

"Life Liberation is a very misunderstood group of like-minded people. They have, to the best of my knowledge, *never* been involved in any of the bombings or violent protests you have seen on the news, radical in their ways though some of them are. Unfortunately for them, being a well-known supporter of the Anti-Rejuvenation movement often makes them guilty by association."

"Okay. Okay. So Life Lib doesn't bomb anyone," Maggie said. "But you're saying this name, Hillbrook, is their code word for The Shepherd's Institute? Why use a code name if you aren't planning illegal acts of protest or worse?"

"Well," Lydia said, "along with being associated with the more radical groups, another reason Life Liberation is often thought to play a part in the more violent protests is because known members used to be overheard speaking about such facilities, whether it was actually secretive talk or just casual conversation. To combat the accusations and prejudice caused by eavesdroppers, Life Liberation's leader developed a set of code names for, among other things, all Rejuvenation-related facilities around the world. From the centers where the procedure is administered, to the headquarters of EXLI and other providers, to the retirement facilities set up for retirees."

"Does that mean Sebastian was a member of Life Liberation? Because he used the name Hillbrook?" Simon said.

Lydia shrugged her tiny shoulders and held up her hands.

"I don't know," she said. "He could have been, but I don't think so. Still, he did know that code name, which means he had to be involved in some way with a group like Life Liberation. He certainly would have been useful to the group, given his position at EXLI. Whether he was a member of Life Lib or another group or not, we know that he was trying to tell you about The Shepherd's Institute. The fact that he used the code name means that he was trying to keep others—the police, EXLI, the media—from knowing what he was talking about should his message fall into their hands."

Simon glanced at Maggie and found her looking beyond their host through the glass doors, out over the city, deep in thought. Lydia resumed pacing.

"All right," Simon said. "Maybe Sebastian was an AR spy; maybe he wasn't. What's important is that he wanted us to know about the facility. He was directing us there. We don't know the specific reason, but it must have to do with the man he mentioned in the message, where they're keeping him."

"If what you are thinking turns out to be correct," Lydia said, "and there is a person being held prisoner for some unknown reason, then yes, that does all sound like a very likely explanation."

"So we go there then." It was Maggie who said it. Lydia and Simon stared at her.

"Excuse me?" Lydia said.

"We go there," Maggie repeated. "We go to The Shepherd's Institute and see what we can dig up about this mystery guy. We ask questions until they tell us what we want to know."

Lydia frowned. "And just how do you expect to do that, my dear? You're both wanted by the police. Do you expect to simply walk in and roam the halls unimpeded, searching patient after patient, asking the staff if they know of any secrets hidden there? Highly improbable. Of course, it *could* be possible to get in unnoticed, falsify identification, if you know the right people, but even that—"

"We have to try!" Maggie was adamant. "We have to do *something*. We have to figure all this out so we can clear our names. And right now, all signs point to Hillbrook. That's where we'll find the source of all this. It's not Simon. It's not even Sebastian and his message. It's that man, whoever he is. He's to blame for all this and he better have some fucking answers! So we go."

Lydia and Simon were, for a moment, speechless. They saw the fury in Maggie's eyes and considered their next words carefully.

"I don't think we should be idle by any means," Lydia said, looking directly at Maggie. "But, my—Maggie, may I? Simply waltzing into the largest retirement facility in the world, questioning EXLI's practices, and asking questions about a person you're not even certain is actually there will only lead you to a jail cell. Besides, if EXLI and the people at that facility are doing something illegal, if they're holding someone prisoner, do you really think you'd discover their wrongdoings out in the open by roaming the halls?"

Maggie considered Lydia's words, then shook her head.

"I don't mean to discourage or insult. I simply think it wise to consider matters carefully before rushing into something drastic that will land you in the hands of the authorities you have, until this point, been able to avoid."

"So what *can* we do?" Simon pleaded. "If we can't go to The Shepherd's Institute, what are our options? Maggie's right. We need to figure this out. We found you. We know what Hillbrook is, but there's still the man. How do we find out who he is without going where Sebastian wanted us to go?"

Lydia stopped pacing and looked at the clock on the wall.

"You wait," she said.

"We—what?"

"Mr. Crowe, ever since you said the word Hillbrook on my doorstep and then came into my apartment and started telling me your story, something hasn't felt quite right to me."

Simon sat back against the couch, wondering if he'd somehow been intimidating or suspicious to Lydia since arriving. "I'm sorry. I didn't mean—"

"No," Lydia said. "It's not you that's felt off, it's the entire situation. All the events that I now know transpired over the last two or three days, the last week actually."

"You mean even *before* Sebastian's death?"

"Yes." Lydia held one of her small hands out, ticking off her fingers as she spoke. "We have your friend the EXLI scientist and his sudden, mysterious death. Then there's the strange message he sent you just before he died. Since receiving that message, you've been chased and almost killed, all seemingly in the name of this message your friend left. Everything you've experienced hinges on that message and its true meaning. You think everything depends on figuring out that message, and it very well might, but I think there are other forces at work here, certain happenings that may shed new light on the message and what's really going on.

"The first happened last week when I learned of the upcoming EXLI announcement—the one scheduled for tomorrow in this very city. EXLI's press conferences have always been erratic in their timing, but this one seemed different. From the very beginning, it has been touted as a major announcement. You've been through downtown tonight. You must've seen the fanfare, all the preparations for tomorrow's event. Whatever Theodore Sullivan and EXLI have to say, I suspect it is somehow related to your friend Sebastian's death."

"You think they had him killed because he knew about tomorrow's announcement?" Simon said. "Why him rather than any of the other scientists who probably worked on whatever EXLI is announcing?"

"Perhaps he knew *too* much. Perhaps he knew something he was not supposed to know."

"But how do you know there *is* information out there," Maggie asked. "How do you know there's something that'd be that damning to EXLI and whatever they are announcing?"

Again, Lydia smiled.

"Good question, my dear," Lydia said. "I know that such information exists, because I am in town to collect it."

"I thought you were in town to give a lecture and hear Sullivan's announcement," Simon said.

"The lecture was scheduled so that my presence won't look suspicious. The real reason I am here is to collect information about whatever this new announcement is. I have known that something large was looming on the horizon with EXLI for some time now—six months, at least. And now, here it is."

"But where are you getting this information?" Maggie said.

"I know certain people, certain contacts within EXLI who are sympathetic to the cause."

"You mean spies?" Simon said.

Lydia laughed her high-pitched, girlish laugh and shook her head.

"Well, I guess some might call them that, but I certainly don't," Lydia said. "They are just like-minded people who have, through past experience, found themselves working for EXLI and who want to help the movement in any way they can."

"So these spies—these moles, if that's a more appropriate word—you're meeting with them soon?" Simon said.

"Yes, but only one of them. He is the highest-ranking of the contacts we have inside EXLI, which is the reason he has access to the information he does. He's been working with us for at least ten years now and we've been very fortunate that he has not been discovered. There have been close calls in the past. We had to be extremely careful this time. He could not risk simply leaking information to us during the development of this latest project. Something about enhanced security protocols by EXLI. Instead, he promised to collect everything he could and deliver it in one package once the announcement goes public."

Tomorrow, Simon thought. Would the information Lydia came

to collect be able to help them? Could all their running be over by this time tomorrow?

"And you think the information he has is the same information that Sebastian tried to communicate?" Simon said.

"That I do not know," Lydia said. "It seems very likely that the two mysteries are linked at least. Your friend Sebastian could have stumbled across the information that my contact intends to provide. Then EXLI found out, perhaps thought him the mole, and they killed him to prevent him from leaking what he knew.

"We'll obviously know more once I've taken the meeting, but my source has never steered me wrong, difficult though he may be at times.

"The truth is, we can sit here and speculate all night. I have countless theories myself, each more horrifying than the last. But until we hear what Sullivan has to say tomorrow and then get the information from my contact, we just won't know."

"So we wait then," Simon said. He looked at Maggie, silently begging her approval. She looked as unhappy as he was, but she nodded.

"We wait," Lydia said. "It's the safest thing right now." Lydia saw her visitors trade another look, knew exactly what they were thinking, and spoke before either said another word. "You are, of course, welcome to stay."

"If we're caught here," Simon said, "you'd be considered an accessory."

Lydia waved off the idea.

"I've been called worse. Much worse. Don't you worry about me. Stay. I want you to. I'm expecting no other visitors tonight or tomorrow, besides my driver, Derrick."

Simon motioned a thumb toward the door to the apartment. "You mean that man with the gun from the hallway? He's your *driver*?"

16

———

Simon awoke to crackling, the sound of something tossed into a frying pan. The smell of cooking sausage filled his nostrils. He sat up in the leather armchair where he'd spent the night, turned to look into the kitchen, and saw Lydia standing in front of the stove. There were multiple pans warming and packages of food on the counter. Eggs, a loaf of bread with a crispy crust next to the toaster, a can of Heinz beans, and a cutting board with sliced mushrooms and tomatoes. After the last two days, it looked like a feast to Simon.

He glanced at Maggie still asleep on the couch, thought briefly of the awkward goodnight they'd shared the previous evening, then stood. He felt the miles of the previous days on his feet, in his muscles as he stretched and heard his joints crack. Simon yawned wide-mouthed and felt the tender bruise that had formed on his cheek from the punch taken on the bus. He rubbed at the spot as he smacked his dry lips and breathed in the smell of breakfast.

Simon walked into the kitchen and whispered to Lydia, "You sure do like to spend time in the kitchen."

Lydia turned around, a spatula in her small hand. She wagged it at him.

"Good morning to you too," she whispered. She stole a look into the living room, saw Maggie still asleep, and kept her voice down. "I do enjoy cooking; have since I was little." Lydia smirked and pointed the spatula behind her, at the photo on the wall Simon had spotted the previous night. Up close, he could now clearly see the smaller figure in the photo was Lydia, the other a young-looking blond woman who shared the same square face and small nose as Lydia. Her mother, he assumed. "But don't go getting any misconceptions about your male superiority, Mr. Crowe." She punctuated her last sentence with an incredulous pff sound. "The only reason I made you dinner last night and am now cooking for you again is because it is my duty as host."

"You sound like my grandmother, you know that?"

"Is that so?" Lydia raised a single eyebrow at him.

"Yeah. That's not bad, it's just . . . well, it's your comments, kidding or not. That whole defense against male oppression sort of thing. My dad said she got a lot of that after she and my grand-father split up."

"I assure you I feel no oppression from any man, Mr. Crowe. It was indeed a simple joke."

"Still, whenever we'd visit my grandmother when I was growing up, she'd make similar jokes. At first I didn't understand, because I didn't really see or hear as much of that sort of thing in my daily life."

"Yes, you wouldn't, would you?" Lydia said, turning back to the stove to flip the sausages that sizzled in their pan. "You're a Rejuvenation baby."

Simon nodded. As a child born after Rejuvenation had become standard practice, he knew his concept of discrimination hadn't been like his grandmother's. The prevalent, modern experi-ence was a direct response to the procedure and those who chose to forgo it. Though, not like the ageism of the old world. It was a new form, based solely on physical appearance rather than the number of years a person had lived. Discrimination, it seemed, was a never-ending spectrum. Everyone experienced it at some point. Some more than others, and in unique ways. "Different times, I guess."

"Different, yes, but in many ways the same," Lydia said, frowning. "It's the way of the world, I'm afraid. Humanity has a lamentable habit of falling back into old ways. We cling to the familiar, you see. The everyday things that make up our modern culture. The names of our cities and streets; our phones and newspapers; right down to our retail stores and the products we buy. We had the chance to move on from all that, to forge new, better ways of doing things in a society reborn post-Decay. But instead, we fell back on what we knew because it was convenient and familiar. That's not inherently bad. We have societal structure again. An organization to daily life. General civility. But we also have division. Overpopulation. Pollution. Toxic relics of the old world, carried forward into the new despite our advances. Like those replicas of old petrol cars some people still drive around despite the modern prevalence of electric vehicles. Old, familiar things have a way of lingering around, even after all these many years, because they make us feel secure. And when we're comfortable, we don't want to let go.

"Sadly, this also applies to perceptions, to beliefs. Even outdated ones that are hundreds and hundreds of years old. Like the discrimination of which your dear grandmother spoke. Immediately post-Decay, the modern sense of intolerance, of nearly all forms of discrimination, of oppression, were almost forgotten ideas, purposely left behind by most for the sake of saving our species. It was one of the few positives to come out of all those long years of waiting, as humanity cowered in fear that the diseases would return. Then slowly but surely, we came to our senses and back from the brink. We began re-populating, taking back the world we'd lost . . . but we didn't learn. We started falling into the old ways, quarreling amongst ourselves, pitting people against people again. Those familiar intolerances of the past returned. Alternative forms, yes, but the same ugly concepts. Only influenced by a world built on Rejuvenation. So, different times, yes, but very much still the same."

Simon felt as if he knew what it was like to be one of Lydia's students, listening to an early morning lecture. Like he'd made it to class while he was still waking up, but felt his mind almost fully alert now as Lydia's words sank in. The thought of familiar ideas in different forms. Once lost, then brought back. The habitual ways of the world. She was right. Simon had certainly never seen the same level of blatant sexual discrimination about which his grandmother had joked. But it was still in the world, as Lydia said, as were other forms of intolerance seated on race, religion, sexual preference, you name it. Prejudices like that could never truly be eradicated. Just diminished or replaced with new ones.

"The procedure's changed a lot of things like that. Including how we all view age," Lydia said, then smirked. "I mean, look at me."

They shared a small smile as Simon turned, looked out the glass doors of the balcony, to the city beyond. The river running silently below, a barrier between Oldtown and the rest of the city. He turned back to the kitchen, dragging his gaze over the half-wall, at Maggie, still sound asleep on the couch, breathing softly.

"How do you like your eggs?" Lydia asked.

"Oh, whatever's easiest. Scrambled?" he said.

"Right. I'll add a touch of my secret seasoning. You'll like it." Lydia grabbed a small, collapsible step-stool leaning against the kitchen wall. She unfolded it, set it in front of the stove, and climbed both steps to retrieve a large, unlabeled spice jar from the cabinet overhead. She returned the step-stool to its home against the wall and held the jar up to Simon, whose attention was drawn back to Maggie.

"Your experience with newer forms of intolerance is unique, Mr. Crowe."

Simon turned back to Lydia and said, "What's that?"

"How old is she?"

Simon hesitated, his gaze shifting between Maggie and Lydia.

"I don't really know," he said, and laughed, then added, "Does it matter?"

"I suppose not," she said with a shrug. "I was just curious— not really whether she had told you, but whether you actually cared."

"Well I don't. If she doesn't, why should I?"

Lydia's eyes brightened. "Spoken like a true member of today's intelligent, tolerant generation." Lydia began mixing the eggs she'd just cracked in a bowl, then dumped the contents into a new pan. "You're not like the majority of the crowd, thus your relationship is . . . different."

"Why? Because she chose to undergo the procedure and I didn't?"

"Precisely."

"I told you, I don't care if she doesn't."

"Does she though?"

"What?"

"Not care?"

"She—" but Simon stopped. The last haze of sleep left him and everything that had happened between Maggie and him over the last day came rushing back. The frustration. The yelling. The coldness. His resolve to accept her blame, if only to keep her safe. Simon tried to think back, before all that. "We've talked about it, yes, the attention we draw sometimes. I like to think it doesn't bother either of us." But did it? he wondered. "We're not that far apart in appearance anyway."

"No, you aren't now—but you will be. One day. Have you thought about that? Have you thought about what you will do ten years from now, or 30? What will you do when your age *does* change your physical appearance?"

Simon had thought about it. He'd heard the stories of what happened when a naturally-aging person and one who had undergone Rejuvenation engaged in a relationship. He'd thought about it a lot before deciding to forgo the procedure. He knew those types of pairings usually didn't last, or lasted only until the Non-Rejuvenite began to show signs of aging. After that, well, most of the breakups were ugly. That history had been the main source of strife between him and Maggie in recent months. They both knew what lay ahead in their future—if they even had a future now, he thought—and it scared them. They'd tried to talk about it, but it always led to . . .

Looking back now, those arguments all seemed so trivial. Given the last two days, what happened in the woods, in the church. In those moments, it had seemed like they were fractured beyond repair. And yet . . .

"What will I do?" Simon said. "Whatever I can."

"You mean . . . Rejuvenation?"

"No." Simon hesitated. The image of his grandfather flashed in his head. "Well, I don't—I mean, I've made my decision about the procedure. I have my reasons and Maggie is okay with it. She wouldn't be with me now if she weren't."

But was she even still *with* him, he wondered.

"But what if?"

"I guess anything's possible." Simon couldn't believe what he was saying, but he knew it was true. He felt the realization hit him as if it was the first time. It washed over him like a warm bath, cleansing away at least some of the hurt from the night before. For Maggie, he'd consider just about anything. For Maggie, he'd consider Rejuvenation. "I suppose it's not out of the question. I'd do whatever I have to for her, to keep her, but I'm not just talking about Rejuvenation. I'd work at it, you know? You have to work at it—love, I mean. Regardless of age."

Lydia's eyes danced. She smiled.

"You love her?" she asked.

"With all my heart," Simon said.

"Even if you grow old and she ends up casting you aside for a younger model?"

"Yes." There was no hesitation in his voice. Despite everything they'd been through, everything that had been said the previous day, Simon's feelings for Maggie remained as resolute as they'd always been. "I hope that doesn't happen, but even if it does, it won't change that I love her."

Lydia's grin grew wider.

"What are you—" Simon said, then stopped and followed Lydia's gaze, turning to see Maggie sitting up on the couch, eyes open, watery. His face turned red instantly. "Oh, hey," he said. "Morning."

And finally, for the first time in what felt like forever, a *real* smile spread across Maggie's face as she locked eyes with Simon. She beckoned him over with a look and he obliged, skirting the half-wall into the living room and sitting beside Maggie on the couch. She wrapped her arms around him, and he felt her squeeze tight.

"S-Simon," she said. When they pulled apart, tears were running down her cheeks. "I'm sorry. I—"

"Oh, hey, no, you don't need to be sorry," Simon said. "You've been right about every—"

But Maggie was having none of it.

"No! *You're* the one who's right." Maggie held his hands

tight. "Listen to me, Simon. What I said back there, in the church, it was terrible. *Terrible.*"

"You had every right to say those things, Maggie. Will's . . . he's gone, and I—" Simon was crying now as well.

"You tried to save him. And me. That's what you did. If you hadn't warned us, if you hadn't come to the house, we would have . . . You shouldn't feel guilty because Will got caught in the cross-fire. And I shouldn't blame you. It's not your fault, Simon." She squeezed his hands tight and stared into his eyes. "Listen to me. *It's not your fault.*"

Simon could see the honesty in her eyes, how she was saying these things for his benefit, but also to drive home the point in her mind. He reached up and wiped the tears away from her eyes. Before he knew it, or expected it, Maggie planted a kiss on his lips.

Reconciled, they looked back into the kitchen to see Lydia busying herself at the stove, softly humming a happy tune as she cooked.

———

THEY ATE the breakfast Lydia had prepared for them at the table next to the kitchen. The seasoning on the eggs was indeed wonderful, as she had promised Simon. Along with the food, she also offered some good news.

"I've decided to take you with me tonight when I meet my EXLI contact."

"Won't he be angry with you?" Simon said.

"I expect him to be furious, actually," Lydia said, "but once the three of us are there he won't just turn us away. We have a deal he wouldn't dare break."

Simon sipped his coffee. He tried to quell his curiosity, but couldn't.

"Who is he?" he asked. "This spy of yours. You speak of him as if he's Sullivan's right-hand man."

Lydia straightened, making herself as tall as she could.

"He's certainly not his right- or left-hand man. That dubious honor is already taken. Purcell's always been Sullivan's closest lapdog. And Samar . . . Dr. Vapula . . . well, he used to have sense, integrity. Something I try to instill in all my students. But that was decades ago. He's beyond reach now. My contact is, however, someone extremely important. I can't tell you his name —for confidentiality reasons, of course. Don't take this as a sign of mistrust. It's just that the less you know, the better."

Simon and Maggie nodded their understanding, but their curiosity was incessant.

"So what *can* you tell us?" Simon said.

"Only that he's a scientist, like your late friend. He's been with them for years and is involved in many of the major projects at EXLI. If he's not too angry to answer tonight, you can ask him any other questions you wish then."

With that, the subject was dropped and breakfast over. They helped Lydia clear the table and wash the dishes. Simon enjoyed this mundane, everyday task; it felt cathartic in the midst of everything that was happening. When they were finished, there wasn't much to do but wait.

Simon and Maggie took turns showering, before taking their places on the couch again next to Lydia, who sat in the armchair, her legs dangling over the edge. They talked about their plans for the meeting that night, and then their conversation turned to more everyday subjects: their jobs, their families, the holiday party where Simon and Maggie first met.

It was around two o'clock when they turned on the TV and found a news broadcast. The EXLI announcement wasn't officially scheduled to start until three, but they wanted to make sure they didn't miss anything if it began earlier.

The image on the screen showed a young-looking, female news reporter in a red dress. She held a microphone in one hand and a handheld tablet computer in the other. Her gaze alternated between the camera and tablet as she gave her report.

Behind the reporter, hundreds of people stood on the steps leading up to EXLI Headquarters, a collection of the general public and members of the press. Reporters were everywhere, all engaged in broadcasts or prepping for the forthcoming announcement. Onlookers loitered around them, talking to each other as they watched the small stage at the top of the steps, surrounded by barricades and several police officers. There was no one on the stage yet, only four chairs near the back and at its middle, a slender, black podium with a bouquet of microphones.

The stage was set, the audience was there, but the showman had yet to arrive.

Simon, Maggie, and Lydia sat in silence as they listened to the reporter on the screen and waited. They were part of the audience now, those standing in the streets of downtown and watching around the world, all waiting for Theodore Sullivan to show his face.

17

———

AS THE ELEVATOR CAME TO A STOP, THEODORE SULLIVAN checked his reflection in the shining silver surface of the doors.

Damn, I look good, he thought as his bright, gray-blue eyes lingered on his reflection.

He wore a deep-navy suit, a white shirt, and a tie that matched his suit. A small handkerchief popped out of his breast pocket. His dark shoes, shined to perfection, were gleaming in the silver walls. He was fully aware his outfit cost more than all the clothes worn by the four people in the elevator with him.

Yes, he thought, *I certainly do look good.*

He knew that, from a distance, his suit looked like nothing more than standard, black attire. But the devil was in the details. He was sure of the saying's validity. A person needed to look closely, think acutely, to truly understand what was happening around them. Sullivan was thankful because he knew most people didn't pay that kind of attention; they didn't look closely enough. But their loss was his gain.

The elevator chimed softly as the silver doors parted and Sullivan, along with the four people behind him, exited.

As the group walked across the lobby, Sullivan looked

through the building's glass doors and saw for the first time the multitude of people gathered outside EXLI Headquarters. His assistant had told Sullivan the crowd was big, but until now, Sullivan hadn't understood just how large the crowd had actually grown. Seeing all those people now, scattered down the steps, across the street, and down the intersecting avenues, made him smirk. All those people, come to see him.

Standing on both sides of the glass doors were two groups of men and women in white lab coats: EXLI scientists. These were the men and women who had made it happen. Sure, Sullivan had introduced the impossible idea and had hammered at them day in and day out until they finally gave him results, but it was their work in the end. Today, however, was Sullivan's day. Today was the day he'd get his credit for all that work.

He walked on as the scientists caught sight of him and those following in his wake. Sullivan didn't look back.

His eyes were drawn, as they always were when he exited this building, to the large painting hanging above the doors, a portrait of a cheerful, round-faced man with electrifying blue eyes, the man who had started all of this: Rodderick Price, the Father of Rejuvenation. Sullivan pushed the sudden throbbing in his mind away. *Not today.* He sneered at the painting and felt Price's piercing eyes follow him as he walked to the exit. He quickly averted his stare and felt the briefest tinge of embarrassment for doing so, for letting the painting—*those eyes*—win again. But the feeling was gone in an instant as Sullivan refocused on the glass doors ahead and the mass of people waiting outside.

The crowd nearest the stage began to notice Sullivan's approach. This news spread quickly and soon even those on the surrounding streets, those who had no direct view of the stage but watched on large screens hung across the roads, began to cheer. By the time Sullivan had left the building and made his way onto the stage the crowd had erupted into hysterical applause.

Sullivan molded his angular face into a smile, waved to the crowd and the TV cameras like a presidential candidate who'd just won the election by a landslide.

Look at them, he thought. *Eating it up already and I haven't said one word. Just wait until they hear.*

The four people who had followed Sullivan to the stage, a couple and two men, sat in the chairs behind the podium.

The EXLI scientists filed through the glass doors and formed a line behind the stage, all of them putting on their best professional faces for the cameras. The entire line was made up of Rejuvenite men and women, but for three people who stood at one end. Two of them were men, one of whom wore glasses and looked to be in his late 40s; the other had bright gray hair and was at least 60. The third aged scientist was a slender woman around 40 years old. It had been no surprise to these three why they'd been asked to join the end of the line. Respected though they were as members of the EXLI team, they showed their true age, still *looked* old. They understood why Sullivan wanted them standing outside the crowd's line of view.

Sullivan spent a few minutes smiling and waving to the crowd, stopping only briefly to give a few hellos and good afternoons into the microphones. As he moved around the stage, his tailored suit never wrinkled. His manicured black hair stayed perfectly in place. That grin of his bright and wide. When Sullivan figured he had milked the crowd's adoration enough for the news crews, he motioned for the sea of people to quiet down and silence fell immediately.

"Hello everyone!" Sullivan said. "Thank you. Thank you. I appreciate the warm welcome.

"Thank you all for coming. I can honestly say that I didn't expect this large of a turnout, but I am grateful to everyone who came down here today to hear what I have to say, and to those watching around the world." Sullivan placed a hand over his heart. His warm rumble of a voice grew more honeyed. "It shows that *you* all care as much about our work as I do, which is saying an awful lot.

"Now, before I get too far, there are a few people to acknowledge. I'd like to thank Mayor Witlock and his lovely wife, Janet, for coming out today. Your support has always been a boon to the work we do here at EXLI."

Sullivan stepped aside so the crowd could see the couple sitting behind him rise to their feet and wave. Like everyone on stage, the couple looked like they were in their mid-20s. The man wore a gray suit and tie, his wife a tight dress that looked as uncomfortable as the matching heels on her feet, though she had no trouble standing in the ensemble and waving to the crowd like a beauty pageant contestant.

The crowd roared their approval for Mayor Witlock and his wife—though not, Sullivan was pleased to hear, as loud as they'd applauded him.

"Next," Sullivan continued. "I want to thank Dr. Samar Vapula, our Chief Medical Officer, and Michael Purcell, EXLI's Head of Project Development. Without their leadership during our research and development, the work behind today's announcement would not have been possible."

Sullivan stepped aside again, allowing the crowd to see the two men on the stage behind him, but knowing most of the watching eyes would remain on him. Always on him. *And why shouldn't they be?*

Purcell and Vapula waved to the crowd. They both wore suits, though Purcell's was darker, which made his red hair stand out and skin look even paler than usual. Vapula, on the other hand, was dressed in light brown that almost matched the tone of his skin. His jet-black hair swayed as he waved his hand.

The crowd cheered, but only half-hearted now. They were

primed and didn't seem to care about all these formalities and introductions. They wanted *him*.

"Last but certainly not least, I want to thank the scientists who made up the majority of the team on this project. Their brilliant minds, countless hours of work, and incredible dedication are certainly at the heart of today's announcement."

Sullivan waved to the line of scientists in lab coats standing behind the stage. Some waved to the crowd, others simply nodded and smiled. Some of the people near the front of the crowd noticed the three elder-looking scientists and shook their heads or looked away, but nothing more beyond that.

"Okay, everyone," Sullivan said, patting the air to silence the crowd. Again, they went quiet almost instantly, obedient as trained dogs. Sullivan forced a solemn expression onto his face and his hand returned to his chest. "I have one last item to address before the announcement. Many of you are aware that EXLI lost one of our own earlier this week, Dr. Sebastian Martin. Dr. Martin was not an active part of the project I am speaking about today, but he was still a valued member of the EXLI family and he will be sorely missed. I want to take this time to remember Dr. Martin. Please join me, if you would, in a moment of silence."

Sullivan bowed his head, as did the others on the stage and the scientists behind them. The crowd was silent. The only sounds were the distant rumbles and honks of cars somewhere deep in the city.

Sullivan counted the seconds in his head. *One . . . two . . . three . . . That's enough.*

Sullivan raised his head.

"All right, folks. On to the main event!"

The crowd roared again, and then silenced quickly, trained and waiting.

"We're here to talk about EXLI's latest development in Rejuvenation. While it is already a safe, effective procedure, we at

EXLI are continually working to improve Rejuvenation. Whether that be researching ways it can be administered to children earlier in life in order to save them from an unfortunate illness, or improve practices around the country to completely eliminate any chance whatsoever of unfortunate mishaps, extremely rare though they may be. The goal of our work is to help everyone in the world lead better, more fulfilling lives. We strive to make all Rejuvenation practices flawless, so that everyone who undergoes the procedure is given the time they desire to live their best life possible.

"We continue with that goal today. The newest iteration of Rejuvenation is perhaps the single greatest advancement we have made since . . . well, since Dr. Rodderick Price first discovered Rejuvenation."

For a split second, Sullivan's eyes narrowed in an almost imperceptible wince. But he'd known it was coming and fought back against it. *Not today.* Then went on.

"Through all our work and advancements, there has always been one part of the individual beyond the procedure's influence. I speak, of course, of the human mind."

A low murmur spread through the crowd. Sullivan raised his voice to speak over it.

"No matter how much we've improved Rejuvenation, there has always been one complication holding us back. A final equation to solve. One last roadblock that's prevented us from transferring its incredible benefits to a person's mind. But that, ladies and gentlemen, is about to change."

Sullivan felt the immensity of his revelation flow through his body, through his voice booming into the crowd. All the people watching him here and on television screens around the world were hanging on his every word as they slowly realized what he was talking about, what his announcement truly meant for them and every member of the human race. He saw that dawning comprehension spread through the faces in the crowd and felt the spark of triumph that lived in his chest burn greater.

"Today I am thrilled to introduce the latest advancement in Rejuvenation technology," Sullivan said. "Not only will our latest iteration of the procedure prevent a person's body from aging, but it will now also prevent the mind from aging as well.

"Rejuvenation was created as a way to fight the plagues of old and has since protected us against all disease so that we may live longer, healthier lives. So that we all may live our *best life*! And now, it will protect us from the greatest disease of all: the disease of death!"

Sullivan was almost yelling now, though his voice retained a friendly, celebratory tone. He pounded his fist on the podium to emphasize his words.

"There will be no Retirement Day for us, my friends. No longer must anyone be afraid of what waits for us at the end of nature's path because we have discovered a way to prevent that end. Once administered, this newest Rejuvenation procedure will freeze the body *and* the mind, allowing anyone who undergoes this amazing advancement to live for as long as they wish.

"Let me assure you that just as Rejuvenation allows your bodies to function normally, this newest procedure will do the same for your minds. Synapses will still fire. Thoughts will still flow freely. Only now, none of it has to end.

"Yes, my friends. The answer is *yes*! Humankind's time of apotheosis is upon us! I speak of undisturbed youth! I speak of everlasting life!

"Even as I stand before you now, our Rejuvenation centers around the world are being informed of this latest advancement. They are being taught how to properly and effectively administer the procedure so that it will be available to you all within a few days.

"If you are worried about not being eligible for this new

procedure because you have already undergone Rejuvenation, fear not. We have developed a method for supplementing you with this latest advancement so that you too may enjoy its benefits. You have my word, no one shall be left out." Sullivan paused, nodding at the crowd as they cheered. He salivated at the words he knew would come next. "And when I say no one shall be left out, my friends. I mean it. I am delighted, no, *honored*, to announce that for the first time in history, this groundbreaking new iteration of Rejuvenation will be available, to *everyone* . . . free of charge."

The roar from the crowd hit Sullivan as if it were a physical wave of adoration. Like a warm wind enveloping his entire body. He basked in the sensation and thought, *So this is what it's like to be worshiped.* And it was that thought that caused Sullivan, for the first time, to grin for real.

"Yes! We all deserve the opportunity to live our best lives! And *I* am here to see that through.

"EXLI will be distributing a report that provides further details on this latest advancement and instructions for scheduling your personal procedure. This report should answer any questions you may have, but should you have any others, your local Rejuvenist will be able to help you."

Sullivan exhaled as if exhausted, as if he'd been wrung out by the work of his announcement. He paused and looked at the crowd, as though he needed to catch his breath from the earth-shattering news he'd shared with them. The crowd knew it was all for them, and he knew they adored him for it. Sullivan looked out over the crowd, eyes stopping and starting as if staring at each person individually. He lowered his voice to a pensive tone.

"We are all lucky to be alive at such a momentous time in human history, my friends. This is a great day, one that you will all remember for a long time, or perhaps . . . forever.

"Thank you and good day," he finished.

The crowd erupted, a mix of applause, cheering, and shouted questions from the news reporters pushing their way toward the stage. Square leaflets colored EXLI-blue and -white started raining down from somewhere high above.

Sullivan stepped back from the podium, gave the crowd a high wave, bowed, then turned and headed back toward the entrance to the main EXLI building. The four others on the stage and the line of scientists followed in his wake as the deafening roar of the crowd continued to sound.

FREE
REJUVENATION
FOR
ALL
SCHEDULE AN
APPOINTMENT
WITH YOUR
REJUVENIST
TODAY.
313.364.9079
info@exlicorp.com
www.exlicorp.com

18

FROM THE MOMENT THEODORE SULLIVAN APPEARED ON STAGE, through his many thanks and the moment of silence he held for Sebastian, and his eventual exit from the stage to the roaring applause of the listening crowd, Lydia remained quiet. She stood, leaning against the half-wall that separated the kitchen and living room, and listened to Sullivan's words.

After the major announcement had been revealed, Simon stole a glance at Lydia, but saw no change on her face. That, or her reaction had been so quick, and so quickly repressed, that he had missed it.

The announcement left Simon open-mouthed and shaking his head. Amazed, but also fearful. They had done it. EXLI had finally done it. They'd figured out a way to transform Rejuvenation from disease prevention to life extension to a cure for natural death.

EXLI had just given the human race *immortality*.

When Sullivan left the stage and television news analysts began discussing their reactions to the announcement, Simon looked at Lydia again. A part of him expected, unfairly, to see a girl throwing a tantrum—stomping around the room, fists clenched, cheeks fiery red, complaining about the unfairness of what Sullivan had done to her cause. The reaction Simon actually saw was different.

Lydia Darrow was silent at first, but she was clearly troubled. She pinched the bridge of her nose and clenched her eyes closed as she breathed out a long sigh of frustration. She looked like an adult when confronted with a great and vexing challenge, in a state of wonder at the situation happening but knowing it would have to be dealt with. When Lydia opened her eyes, Simon saw that they sagged a little, how tired she was, as if she had been up all night worrying.

"Is it even possible?" Maggie said, the first to break the silence. "I know what I just heard, but it doesn't seem like it can be real."

"Apparently it is," Lydia said. "Sullivan is a proper bastard, but I don't think he'd be so bold as to pull some sort of hoax. No. This is very real."

"My God," Simon said.

Lydia gave a scoffed huff.

"For those who believe in such a thing, it would seem *God* has been taken out of the equation, Mr. Crowe. Sullivan and his team of scientists have seen to that. It seems that they're taking everything but themselves out of the equation, in fact." Any hesitation Lydia had of speaking moments before was gone now. Her words vented out. "Even after Rejuvenation, there was always a threshold, a limit to what we could do, a point we couldn't cross, because if you ask me, we weren't *meant* to cross it." Lydia shook her head and began to pace, her breathing rapid, her face darkening. "Honestly, what can they possibly be thinking? Despite the arrogance of Sullivan and his team, and everything I've seen through my many years trying to reason with them, they've always been grounded in science, in cause and effect. How can they not see what this kind of discovery will do when unleashed into the world?"

Maggie and Simon knew she was talking about overpopulation. *Worse* overpopulation. Famine. Energy deficiencies. The whole nine yards.

"Even now, we're at a tipping point. The world's population is nearly as plentiful as it was before The Decay. I've been speaking out about this for some time now, but EXLI just won't acknowledge the facts. Sullivan has always claimed that Rejuvenation has a way of balancing the population out because, as he said, it didn't last forever." Lydia looked out the sliding glass doors, across the city where thousands of people were flooding the streets around the EXLI building. "Those bastards! Using the reasoning that Rejuvenation didn't last forever when they were working to make that very thing true all this time. I can't say I'm surprised by the lies, but still, it's maddening. I suppose it's just our way—humans."

Lydia stopped pacing and turned back to her guests. "I apologize," she said. "I am, I know, misanthropic at times, but it's not without reason. You've seen what they've done, what they are doing. Given what happened before, how The Decay nearly caused our extinction, how can they possibly believe this newest means of Rejuvenation is a good idea? I fear we're doomed to repeat the mistakes of the past.

"Sullivan has spoken before about ending the threat of another Decay once and for all, but he has no control over that. In the end, no one does. It's a limit imposed on us by nature. No matter what we do, we can't stop the world from fighting back when threatened. It did it to us before when endangered by overpopulation and over-consumption. The world couldn't sustain the numbers to which we had grown and it won't be able to do it this time. Sullivan thinks he's found a way to stop catastrophes like The

Decay from happening again, but he's wrong. He's not stopping anything; he's simply quickening its approach."

"But there has to be something that can be done," Maggie said. "EXLI must be able to see reason. How can they ignore such massive and immediate problems?"

"Another trait we humans have, I'm afraid," Lydia said. "Curiosity and imagination; extraordinary attributes when used properly, but they can often make us blind to consequence. We see only what we *want* to see. And in this case—"

"Money?" Simon said, but knew he was wrong as soon as he said it.

"Not money. Not anymore," Lydia said. "You heard him. They're giving this new procedure away for free, which to be honest, confuses and frightens me almost more than the procedure itself. Why simply give it away?"

Simon and Lydia screwed up their faces in thought, pondering the question. But Maggie looked between them as if the answer was obvious, then spoke in a matter-of-fact tone.

"Because then more people will go through with it," Maggie said. "EXLI is going after the fence riders, not the people who are already pro-Rejuvenation."

Of course, Simon thought. It was obvious now that it had been spoken aloud. He gave Maggie a confident nod.

"Yes, I suppose it does make sense, in a way," Lydia said. She cracked her knuckles and started pacing again, her brow lopsided, still in thought. "But EXLI has been going after the undecided for years with all manner of promotions, and they've never given anything away free. In doing so, they may be able to sway more people to undergo the procedure, but they stand to lose billions, if not trillions. And at the end of the day, EXLI is a business. It just doesn't add up."

Lydia pinched her chin as she thought and walked the room.

"Whatever the reason, it's hard to believe Sullivan would give up that kind of cash," Simon said.

"Actually," Lydia said, stopping to look at Simon and Maggie directly. "I believe Sullivan is beyond money. There's something else he's after."

"What's that?"

"Power, Mr. Crowe. He's after *power*," Lydia said. "You see, over the past few years, I've felt I was having an impact on the public opinion of Rejuvenation. Nothing dramatic enough to over-throw EXLI, but enough at least to get the ball rolling, to get people to *think*, to ask questions. I've done my best to play by the rules, to educate people instead of slinging negative rhetoric at Sullivan, EXLI, and all those on the opposite side of the issue. But after today, after what Sullivan has said, I fear that I've completely underestimated my opponent. Perhaps 'underestimate' is the wrong word. I've misunderstood him, what his true goals are."

"But if not money, then what? Immortality?" Simon said. Sullivan's end goal had to be in the new procedure itself, immor-tality. The person who gave that to the world would definitely earn themselves the kind of power Lydia was talking about.

"For the average person, immortality is a worthy enough goal. EXLI is always touting how Rejuvenation gives people the ability to live their best lives. You've seen the advertisements, I'm sure." Simon nodded, but then Lydia said, "Effective marketing, but nonsense. For most people, immortality would only allow them to live their best lives because they'd have eternity to get it right. But not for Theodore Sullivan. He wants more. Did you catch everything that he said today? Everything he *really* said?"

Simon and Maggie both nodded, but weren't sure.

"Did you hear what Sullivan said about everlasting life? He said the time of humankind's *apotheosis* is upon us. Do you realize what that means?

"It means that, even if they were charging double for the procedure, Sullivan would have no concern for the consequence of money. He's interested in power. Obsessed. What he said today, how he *acted*; it's clear his goal is power—at EXLI and over the human race. And he'll do whatever he needs to attain it; that includes ignoring facts and keeping secret anything that would damage his operation."

"But how do you know that?" Simon asked. "What makes you think there's something he's hiding."

"Because Theodore Sullivan is *always* hiding something," she said. "And because your friend the scientist is dead."

Could it all be true? Simon wondered. Is that what Sebastian knew, what Sullivan was hiding? And was that the reason they killed him?

"Dr. Martin may have discovered some dangerous side effect," Lydia said, "or something else along those lines, and they killed him for it. We can't know if Sullivan himself got his hands dirty. I doubt that. But I do know that nothing happens at EXLI without his approval. *Nothing*."

"Couldn't it have been the announcement we just heard?" Maggie said. "Maybe Sebastian found out about the new Rejuvenation procedure and they wanted to shut him up before he said anything. Or maybe he was going to go public about the overpopulation issue with the new procedure. EXLI wouldn't want one of their own scientists speaking out about their practices."

"That is true, but as a whole I don't think so," Lydia said. "I've been speaking out about the overpopulation caused by Rejuvenation for years. It's a simple 2+2=4 problem for people to realize that the issue is going to be compounded by the new procedure. And as for your friend spoiling the announcement early, it's hard to believe they would kill him for that. Threaten him with death if he told, perhaps. Even lock him away until the announcement was made, which seems more likely. No. Whatever it was, I don't think they would actually kill him just to silence him for a couple of days. It has to be something more than that."

"So then what could it be?" Maggie said.

"That is *the* question," Lydia said, placing her fingers in an L-shape against her chin and lips, thinking. "But for the answer, we first need more information."

They all knew what that meant. Not information from the news or the report EXLI was putting out about the new procedure. No, Lydia was talking about her meeting, the one happening that night with her EXLI mole. Whatever information her contact had to give her, it would be more trustworthy than anything accessible to the public and more useful than their never-ending speculations. Real, verified information from within EXLI's operation might just be the key to figuring out Sullivan's strange motivations, and what he was really trying to hide.

———

IT WASN'T long after Sullivan's announcement that Lydia's phone began to ring. It was reporters, call after call with questions about her reaction to Sullivan's announcement. Lydia excused herself to an office down the hall to take the calls, but as soon as one ended and she returned, her phone rang again. She spent most of the day tucked away in her office, leaving Simon and Maggie to sit in the living room watching coverage of the press conference.

Simon tried to keep his mind occupied, but his thoughts inevitably drifted back to the enormity of their situation. Sebastian's murder, his message, running from the police, the implications of the Rejuvenation advancement. It was all so overwhelming. It seemed too large to him, too big of a problem for Maggie and him, or even for Lydia, to do anything about. But they were in it now and in it to the end, whatever that end was.

The day passed and outside the apartment's sliding glass

doors, the sun set behind the tall buildings of Westgate and the city. The bright glow of the sun's last remaining light illuminated the steel and glass of the structures; it reflected off the river and made everything, the entire city, seem as bright and cheerful as the multitude of people still celebrating Rejuvenation in the streets and, likely, around the world. It was nearly eight o'clock before they heard a door open and then the sound of Lydia's light footsteps.

Lydia walked into the living room, exhausted eyes but face still full of color. "Reporters," she croaked, and shrugged. Her voice was hoarse from hours spent talking and she headed to the kitchen for a glass of water.

"So this meeting," Simon said, "When is it?"

"In about an hour," Lydia said. "It'll take us about half that time to get there, so we better start getting ready. Let me eat something and then I'll have the car brought around."

"Do you think it'll be safe? I mean, for us to go out tonight. We're still wanted by the police. They'll still be checking cars."

"Leave that to me."

And with that, Lydia began rooting through the fridge. As she prepared a sandwich, Lydia pulled a phone from her pocket, flipped it open, and hit a single button. "Transport. 20 minutes," she said. "Thank you, Derrick." She slipped the phone back in her pocket and took a ravenous bite of her sandwich. "The car will be here shortly. You two better get ready, though I don't suppose you'll need to bring much more than yourselves."

"What about our bag?" Simon asked.

"It'll be here when you get back. If you want anything from it, best to make it quick, Mr. Crowe," Lydia said as she walked by him. "We're leaving in 10 minutes."

Lydia headed down the hallway and disappeared into the room at the end.

Simon left the bag where it was, but went through it for

cash, which he stuffed into his pockets. He shrugged at Maggie and said, "You never know." Simon turned back to the bag and fumbled through it until he found the one other item he was looking for; the revolver, stashed in the duffle since the previous night. The whole time, he kept his eyes on the hallway.

He took the gun from the bag and quickly tucked it into the back waistband of his pants, flipping his shirt over it. He grabbed a light jacket and put it on to conceal the bulk of the gun a little more. He zipped the bag up, stood, and turned to face Maggie.

He spun around, showing Maggie his back.

"How's it look?" he whispered. "Can you tell it's there?"

"No," Maggie said. "It looks all right. Simon, do you think we should be doing this?"

"I don't necessarily like it, but we need to be protected. What else can we do?"

Maggie nodded, then knelt by the bag and pulled out a jacket of her own. She stood, slid it on, and said, "It's probably best if we both wear them."

Simon planted a small kiss on Maggie's forehead.

Lydia came down the hallway wearing a long, dark coat with large buttons down the front. Her hair was pulled into a bun. She didn't look like she was about to put her life in danger. She looked like she was on her way out to dinner in the city on a chilly autumn night.

"Are we ready?" Lydia said.

Simon and Maggie nodded.

"Off we go, then. Derrick will be waiting."

They rode the elevator most of the way, then stopped on the third floor and took the stairs down the remaining floors. Their footsteps echoed off the concrete walls of the stairwell. Flakes of old paint crunched beneath their feet. Simon felt the gun in his waistband press against his back with each bend of his knees.

When they reached the first floor, Lydia led them out a back door and into an alley.

A black car was waiting for them. The driver's side window slid down to reveal Derrick's round, smiling face beneath a black driver's cap.

When the driver's door began to open, Lydia said, "No need, Derrick. We're in a bit of a hurry. We can manage."

"If you say so, Miss Darrow," Derrick said and closed his door.

Lydia tugged open the side door and they followed her inside the car, Simon taking one last look up and down the alley before closing the door. Thanks to Lydia's small frame, they all fit comfortably in the backseat.

"You know the address?" Lydia said.

"That I do, Miss Darrow," Derrick returned.

"And if you could, see to it we avoid any remaining police checkpoints."

In the rearview mirror, Derrick's eyes flashed to Simon and Maggie. "As you wish. Shall we?"

"Please."

Derrick nodded, then turned his head both ways as he looked down the street at the end of the alley. He turned the car right and they were off.

"We should be there in about half an hour, depending on traffic," Lydia said. "When we get there, please allow me to do the talking."

"Do you think there'll be a problem?" Simon asked.

Lydia's eyes danced from side to side as she considered the question for a moment.

"Well, my partnership with this man is extremely secretive," she said, "so any change in our schedule is quite serious. To tell you the truth, I'm relying on the element of surprise. If I called him and asked if you could come, he would almost certainly say no. But if I just show up on his doorstep . . . well, better to ask forgiveness than permission, you see."

Simon wasn't altogether confident in Lydia's tactics, but knew there wasn't anything they could do about it at this point, and so dropped the subject. He resigned his gaze to the window and watched building after building pass by. They crossed the bridge and, after driving through a vacant warehouse to avoid a police blockade near Westgate, entered back into the newer, more populated part of the city. They skirted the edges of downtown, avoiding the barricades and all the people who were surely, even at this hour, still crowding the EXLI building.

They drove for about 15 minutes until they reached a suburban area on the northern edge of the city. They turned down a four-lane road lined with small buildings—grocery stores and a department store, a barbershop, a couple gas stations, some bars and restaurants. About a mile down the road, they turned left onto a side street which led into a subdivision filled with row after row of identical-looking houses.

"That's where we're going," Lydia said, pointing a skinny finger out the center of the windshield.

Simon and Maggie leaned forward, their eyes following Lydia's finger. At first, all Simon could see were more rows of houses stretching farther and farther down the road. But looking closer, he spotted a row of houses in the distance higher than the ones they were passing now. Most of the houses around them were nearly the same, built together as part of the industrialized housing programs during the rebuilding efforts after The Decay. But the row of houses in the distance was different—they were each unique.

As they got closer, Simon realized that the houses must be leftovers, similar to the Pre-Decay skyscrapers still in use downtown. Once new, state-of-the-art constructions, these homes had been abandoned for medical facilities when the plagues ran rampant around the world. After Rejuvenation was discovered and people began moving back to houses of their own, few wanted to return to their old homes. Despite their education on Rejuvenation, how it would protect them from any disease that might be lurking around the old houses, people were still scared. Houses like the ones on the hill felt haunted. So many of the buildings were bulldozed until, eventually, people realized their folly and switched gears, eager to save such landmarks of the past age. The leftover homes became antique commodities, sought after by many and even now reserved for the very wealthy. People like collectors, doctors, city officials and . . . high-ranking scientists at EXLI.

Despite how fashionable the houses were, they weren't surrounded by large, protective gates or searchlights. They weren't as frequently patrolled by the police as Westgate. Short of their unique appearance, high price, and the mythology that came with them, the leftovers were just another part of the neighborhood.

They began to move up the hill and the houses they passed began to change. Though they had seen leftover houses before, Simon and Maggie couldn't help but stare at the strange buildings, so unlike any of the modern, uniform housing arrangements they'd ever lived in.

Simon saw a tall brown A-frame surrounded by an old, wooden deck that ran around the entire house. Next to this was a two-story white house with bright blue shutters and a small, columned overhang at the front door. Simon saw that Maggie was particularly fascinated with a small, one-story home on a corner they passed. It had a large front window and, were its shades not drawn, he was sure they would have been able to see right inside and spy on whoever lived there.

"Here we are," Lydia said.

The car slowed down and stopped in front of a ranch-style

brick house surrounded by grass and tall trees hanging over the roof, casting it in shadows even under the moonlight. A cracked sidewalk cut through the grass to a mahogany door with a tarnished gold knocker.

"Should we follow you now?" Simon asked. "Or are you going to tell him about us first?"

"Oh no, you are going to go with me right now," Lydia said. "He won't like us simply standing on his doorstep for the entire neighborhood to see. Come." She turned her attention to the driver. "Derrick, as soon as we exit, please take the car away from here. Stay relatively close, but make sure you aren't seen. I don't think it wise to have you sitting out in front of the house waiting for us. I'll call when we are ready."

Derrick touched the brim of his cap and nodded in the rearview mirror.

They got out of the car, which sped away, and Lydia began up the walkway toward the house. Simon and Maggie followed and a few moments later were standing on the half-circle concrete stoop in front of the door. Lydia reached up, stretching her thin arm high, grabbed the knocker, and thumped it against the door twice.

Simon heard footsteps behind the door and the click of a lock. A second later, the door began to open. For a brief moment, Simon saw the figure of the man opening the door. Simon's eyes met the man's and he saw them dart from Simon to Lydia and then to Maggie. Before Simon could get a good look at the man, the door slammed closed.

"What the hell is going on?" the man whispered from behind the door. "It was supposed to be just you! You need to leave right this moment."

"Things have changed," Lydia said. "Let us in or we'll be sitting out here all night."

"You can't just—how do I know I can trust them? Whoever they are."

"Because they want to remain as unseen as you and I. Now let us in before your nosy neighbors get suspicious."

There was silence from behind the door for a moment. All Simon heard was his breathing and the wind rustling the nearby shrubs and leaves of the tall trees hanging over the house.

A second later, they heard sliding locks and the door creaked open. The man had disappeared, hidden behind the door as he opened it for them.

"All right! Get in here quick."

"Thank you," Lydia said and stepped inside.

Simon and Maggie followed. The heavy door gave a loud thud as it closed behind them, making them both jump.

"You've put me in quite a compromising position, Lydia," the man said, ignoring his startled guests as he replaced the locks on the door.

Their host was a short man with a pudgy belly that pressed against his sweater. His gray hair was combed back and he wore a pair of slender spectacles on his nose.

As soon as he got a look at the man's face, Simon knew he recognized him. He wasn't sure where, but he had seen him before.

"Bringing strangers with you like this!" the man continued, "How could you? Suppose I should have known. This is just like when you let those Indian doctors tag along—"

"Indian doctors?" Lydia exclaimed. "You're still on about that? That was six years ago!"

"The fact remains, we're supposed to be keeping all this quiet! I don't know what they'll do to me if they find out, but you sure love to make it difficult, don't you?"

"Settle down," Lydia said. "These two are fine. They won't be going to the authorities any time soon." Lydia gestured toward Simon and Maggie like a game show host introducing a prize. "This is Mr. Simon Crowe and Miss Maggie Buchanan."

The man stared at them. Then his eyes bulged with recognition.

"So this is your idea of keeping things safe and discreet? You bring the most wanted *fugitives* in the city to my house?"

Lydia smiled.

"All a misunderstanding, I assure you," she said, then gestured to their host. "This pleasant gentleman is Mr. Maxwell Lewis."

"*Doctor,*" Maxwell Lewis said.

Simon extended his hand. Maxwell hesitated, then reached out and gave Simon's hand a firm shake. Simon looked directly at the man and realized then how he knew Maxwell.

It was when they were watching the EXLI announcement on TV. Maxwell had been one of the scientists standing behind Theodore Sullivan, one of the three older-looking members shunted to the end of the line.

Maxwell released Simon's hand. He then took Maggie's hand gently and gave her a nod.

"Well," Maxwell said, "I guess I have no choice but to play along. Come to my study then. Lots to discuss, so let's not waste any time. I fear we have less than we might think."

19

Simon, Maggie, and Lydia followed Maxwell into the house. It didn't take long for Simon to realize their host did not care for interior design or had no time for it, likely spending much of his waking life working at the EXLI labs. The walls of the entranceway and living room were a dirtied yellow color that had once been white. The wood paneling of the dining area was faded and splintered in places. No pictures hung on any of the walls. They passed through a kitchen that was clean and bright, its long counter almost touching the door to the backyard that was set in the adjacent wall.

They turned down a short hallway off the kitchen that led to Maxwell's study; a large room with a cluttered desk and numerous bookshelves. In the center there were two short couches and a large armchair arranged in a circle around an old, claw-footed coffee table. Near the front were two sets of windows, each with curtains pulled closed but for a sliver of space at the center which looked out over the front yard.

"Please, make yourselves comfortable while I ready the tea," Maxwell said. He exited the room and a few moments later, Simon heard the faint clanking of a kettle and ceramic drinkware.

Simon and Maggie took a seat together on one of the short couches. As they did, Simon felt the revolver tucked into his back waistband press against his spine. He shifted slightly to lessen the pressure on the gun and wondered again if bringing it had been a good idea.

"Just relax and be yourselves," Lydia said as she sat on the other small couch. She sank back into the cushions, her child's legs dangling over the edge as she struggled briefly like a turtle turned on its shell.

Simon and Maggie couldn't hide their smiles. Part of Simon was glad for the break in the tension. "Do you, ah, need a hand?" he said.

Lydia saw their grins, turned faintly pink, but said, "Enjoying yourselves, are you? I assure you I can manage, thank you very much. I've done so my entire life, even if my stature gets the better of me sometimes." She adjusted herself into a more comfortable position. "Now that we've overcome that little obstacle, back to business. I know Maxwell seems a bit agitated, and he is, but it's all because of me. It'll pass."

Maxwell returned from the kitchen with a tray filled with a teapot, four cups, and a white aluminum tin containing an assortment of sugar cookies. He grimaced when he saw his guests again, but continued, setting the tea tray down on the table.

"Oh, biscuits even," Lydia said. "You spoil us."

"Yes, only the best for you, my dear," Maxwell grumbled. "Help yourselves." He did not sit with them, but instead went to the desk against the wall where he sat in a rolling chair that creaked under his weight. He leaned over and reached to the floor.

What Simon first took for a filing cabinet next to the desk was more. There was indeed a short filing cabinet there, but between it and the floor was a separate box with a small metal keypad at the front of it; a safe. Maxwell punched a finger at the keypad, typing in a code.

There was a soft beep and the little door swung open. Simon couldn't make out exactly what was in the safe but it looked like a small stack of papers, maybe a folder or two, and a few other items that looked like small boxes. Maxwell reached in, grabbed something, and swung the door shut with a faint clicking noise.

Maxwell pocketed something as he rejoined the group and sat in the armchair. He studied his visitors for a moment, then slid what remained in his hand onto the coffee table.

It was a key. About half the size of a normal house key. It had the number 34 engraved on the bow.

Lydia stopped nibbling on the cookie in her hand and stared at Maxwell. He sat back in his chair and clasped his hands in his lap.

"What's this, Maxwell?" Lydia said.

"That is the key to a lockbox at the Regency Bank on Bormello Avenue in Wakefield," he said in a hushed voice. "In that lockbox you will find an encrypted hard drive containing a digital copy of the information I have for you. The password to bypass the encryption is *Methuselah*. Be sure to remember that."

Lydia sat up straighter and grabbed the key, holding it up in front of her like a rock hound examining a gem.

"Is this some kind of joke?" she said. "We've never done anything like this before, even during that ghastly business in Croatia. What's with all the cloak and dagger now?"

"This is nothing like Croatia. It's much worse. Do you know what kind of scrutiny I've been under lately, Lydia?"

Simon didn't know what past business they were referring to, but he could understand Maxwell's need for secrecy. He'd heard stories from Sebastian about the complex security measures at EXLI and figured they must be heightened to the extreme for someone like Maxwell. EXLI was likely watching him and his entire research team at all times while in the labs. Simon wondered if that surveillance extended to the scientists' home lives. Were they being watched right now?

Lydia nodded but still pressed. "I do know, but even still, I wish you would have told me your—" She stopped when Maxwell gave a sudden grunt and an indignant laugh. Her eyes flashed to Maggie and Simon, then back to him. "Okay. I get it. Are we even, then?"

Maxwell nodded.

"If you were just going to send me off to a bank to retrieve everything," Lydia continued, "why risk meeting under such high scrutiny? You could just as easily have mailed me the key, or had it delivered."

"I wanted to meet because I need to impress upon you the enormity of the situation," Maxwell said. "Once you use this information, go public with it, EXLI will know they have been infiltrated at a high level. None of the scientists will be safe, especially the old farts like me.

"But it's worth the risk, my old friend. Everything will change after this, for good or bad. The tricky part is, there's more to it than even I understand. Even with everything I do have, there's something else they're hiding. Something more secretive, and that's saying a lot."

Lydia glanced at Simon and Maggie again, then returned her eyes to Maxwell.

"But then what *do* you have?" Lydia said. "Is it still enough to—"

"Oh, it's enough all right," Maxwell said. "I only pray there's time left to properly explain the ramifications to the masses."

"Then tell us, Maxwell." Lydia raised the key in her hand so they could all see it clearly. "What does this lead to?"

Maxwell hesitated. He licked his teeth, looked sideways at his fugitive visitors.

"Are you sure they are all right, Lydia?" Maxwell said.

"I am," Lydia said.

"But how do you—"

"They knew about Hillbrook."

Maxwell stopped. His eyes broadened at the mention of the name *Hillbrook*. He looked at Simon and Maggie with new interest.

"Did they now?" he said. "So at least some of what the news is saying is accurate then? They're members of one of the groups. The *resistance*."

Lydia shook her head.

"Then how did they know about Hillbrook?" Maxwell said.

"We were left a message by a friend of mine," Simon said, tired of being spoken for.

"Well, I—" Maxwell said.

But Lydia stopped the conversation before it went any further.

"Enough," Lydia said. She'd had enough of being sidetracked. "Maxwell, tell me what's going on."

Maxwell's curious gaze lingered on Simon, then he turned to Lydia and said, "As you wish, my little lady."

Lydia glared at Maxwell, but only for a moment. She pocketed the key and sat up, straightening her coat as if sitting in a conference room, preparing for a business meeting to begin.

Maxwell cleared his throat and said, "After this morning's announcement I suspect you have some guess as to what kind of information I have to share, eh?"

"Of course," Lydia said. "Repercussions of the new procedure, beyond the usual negative impacts of Rejuvenation, which will themselves, be compounded exponentially."

Lydia's words were general, but Simon knew what she was referring to because they'd discussed the issues in her apartment. Overpopulation, lack of food and water to support that population, energy consumption reaching unsustainable levels—the works.

Maxwell smiled and clapped at Lydia.

"You've hit the nail on the head as always," he said. "EXLI continues to refute, among other things, the idea of an unsustainable population even in the face of a population that never dies. It's insanity.

"The whammy though is what they're doing up here." Maxwell knocked a finger against his temple. "They're messing around with our noggins and no good can come of that if you ask me."

As he listened to Maxwell, Simon couldn't help but feel conflicted about the man. Maxwell was clearly on their side. He had been fostering the takedown of EXLI for years, trying to make it happen from the inside. He had invited Lydia to his house that night to share with her important information that would help that cause. But there was still the fact that Maxwell had been part of the team that created the new Rejuvenation procedure. He had helped create the problem they were now fighting. Simon didn't know how the man was able to do it, to distance himself from his work, to be an active part of the problem for the sake of keeping his cover while also working secretly to be a part of the solution. What kind of person could do such a thing? Apparently the kind of person who was sitting right in front of them. A person who, though a bit agitated by their presence, still seemed for the most part at ease with the life he led.

"I *am* asking you," Lydia said. "What the hell have they been doing?"

"Scientifically speaking, the whole thing's quite ingenious, actually. *Horrifying*, but ingenious nonetheless," Maxwell said. "Sullivan told us exactly what they are doing in that speech of his, but people only hear what they want to hear.

"With this newest advancement in Rejuvenation, EXLI is providing the human race with a means of living forever, barring the usual threat of physical damage. They are promoting and explaining it in much the same way as bodily Rejuvenation. Improved acquired immunity, halted immunosenescence, and telomere degradation prevention—all the typical contributors to disease protection, prevention, and the halting of the aging process. But now with the added benefit of stopping cerebral senescence. They're telling the world that, quite simply, it stops the body *and* mind from aging. The mysterious divergence, no more. This is true, but that is not the only thing it stops within the mind. Over time, it also inhibits ambition for and the ability to achieve cognitive advancement."

"Wait, are you saying—"

Maxwell nodded and his face sank. What little cheerfulness he had shown his visitors since they arrived disappeared, replaced by steady, tired eyes and a grave tone of voice.

"I'm saying it's a neurophysiological nightmare. Asynchronous neuronal action potential, synaptic atrophy, long-term synaptic depression. Little to no potentiation. There—" Maxwell stopped when he saw the wide-eyed, blank stares on Simon and Maggie's faces. "Forgive me. It's . . . what I'm talking about is . . . well, it's structural plasticity—it's learning. It occurs mostly in young people, but it does continue into adulthood. When unproductive synapses—pathways for electrical and chemical signals in the brain—are not regularly used, they can be deemed unnecessary and are eventually *pruned* away by the brain. But when this happens, those unproductive connections are replaced by new ones. It's called synaptogenesis. But the new procedure prevents this process, or severely inhibits it. Yes, it keeps the body *and* the mind's biological age young like everyone seems to want, but it disrupts synaptogenesis from occurring even as the brain continues to identify more and more synapses as unproductive. Slowly but surely, synapses get pruned away, but the majority are not replaced as they'd normally be.

"This results in . . . well, I'll put it this way. After undergoing this new iteration of Rejuvenation, a person's capacity to learn and grow will be stunted. Not in such a way that would turn them into mindless drones or, dare I use the word, zombies. It's much more subtle than that, almost surgical in nature. It starts with dull headaches in the back of the skull, just enough to be annoying and easily dismissed as a medicinal side effect. Those last for about two weeks. But then, the confusion starts. Test patients described it as a thin fog in the brain. Over the next four to six months their thought processes become hazy, they have trouble focusing, but eventually . . . well, we can't tell if the mental fog ever completely fades, or if it just becomes normal for them. What's strange is that, when these side effects have completely taken hold, most patients are still able to go about their daily lives. They function just as well as before but there's something *missing*. They become highly suggestible under the right stimulus. And they become complacent, no longer interested in developing beyond their current existence.

"And there's no way around it. We studied these side effects of the procedure for some time, trying to find a way around them. Not that Sullivan cared. He's always been aggressive, but this last year or so, he's grown so . . . agitated. Reckless. Probably why he's not sleeping, or so I've heard. He wanted to go public six months ago, but after some begging from me and my team, he allowed us an extension to do more research. I admit; I was foolish. I thought he had seen reason. But when the new deadline expired and we still hadn't cracked it, Sullivan moved ahead with plans to announce the new procedure. Of course, we objected again. I even filed paperwork and wrote a damn letter to make it as bureaucratically official as possible. But he made it clear in his refusal to us that if word of the side effects ever got out, we—the scientists—would be blamed. He said it wasn't a threat, it was the truth, because *we* had failed to find a solution.

"And now millions . . . *billions* of people around the world right at this very moment are rejoicing in the fact that they can now stop their minds from aging. They can finally overcome the last major roadblock that has plagued Rejuvenation since its inception. They are celebrating what they believe is an amazing discovery. Clamoring for it, which I suspect is all part of Sullivan's plan. And they don't realize the harm it will do to the human race.

"We're talking about the development of our minds, the very evolution of our species. And I'm not referring to that rubbish about humans only using a fraction of their brains. The very thought is insulting. We use it *all* and be thankful we do. What I'm referring to is how this procedure will cause the end of all forward thought. No more advanced thinking. No more creativity. The ability to further ourselves as a people, gone. The loss of our culture and any hope that it will evolve beyond the level it's at now. It means the loss of the spark that makes us human, that yearning for more, *to be more*."

Maxwell let his words rest and stared at the room. They were all thinking it, but Maggie summed up their initial thoughts with one simple sentence.

"This is unbelievable," Maggie said, looking at Maxwell. He stared back and for perhaps the first time, realized he was in the presence of someone who had voluntarily undergone Rejuvenation.

"Is it really?" he said to Maggie. "How long did you spend thinking about Rejuvenation before you underwent the procedure? Did you think about it at all or did you simply go through with it because it has become the norm?"

Everyone, including Maggie, knew Maxwell was right. Living a natural life had become abnormal, Rejuvenation the accepted practice. Most people on the planet didn't think twice about undergoing Rejuvenation. They simply did it because it was a thing one did, like breathing and eating. Rejuvenation had become a part of life and most people jumped at the chance to try any new variation of it without thought of the consequences.

"But anyone who refuses the new procedure will remain unaffected," Simon said. "They won't be immortal, but they'll retain the ability to learn and develop, and they'll do something once they learn of the side effects. They'll fight back."

"Solid thinking," Maxwell said, "Perhaps wishful. But Sullivan has already thought it through. Given the nearly six months it takes for the side effects to truly take hold, he believes that by the time anyone is the wiser, it will be too late. By then, the masses who've undergone the new procedure will effectively be an army under his control, and that having the numbers on his side trumps any strategic thinking of the remaining population that may oppose him."

"But will a few months really be enough time for that many people to undergo the new procedure?"

"Sadly, yes. You heard his announcement. Rejuvenation centers around the world have already been prepped to start administering the procedure in the coming days. And they better be ready, because demand will be high."

"Because he's giving it away for free," Lydia said, putting the pieces together.

They all understood. Sullivan was playing up his handout of the new procedure as some kind of philanthropic gesture for all humankind. But it was really about increasing demand for it. Once the world found out the new procedure would be free, everyone interested would want it as soon as possible. Even those who might have been on the fence in their decision would be clamoring for the new procedure. It was Sullivan's best bet for getting as many people to undergo the procedure in as little time as possible. The prospect of immortality was one thing, but *free* immortality? Everyone would want it.

"But even if all these people go through with it," Simon

asked, "what makes Sullivan think they'll listen to him? They may be highly suggestible, but why would *he* have command over them?"

"That is a question I haven't been able to fully answer myself. I can only assume Sullivan believes the world will look to him as a savior and do his bidding because he is the one who gave them immortality. Even if he isn't immortal himself. Not yet anyway."

Maxwell's words struck a new chord in Simon. What he just said seemed like a flaw in Sullivan's plans. Even if Sullivan got his way and people followed him, the plan only worked for as long as Sullivan remained alive. He had undergone the old Rejuvenation procedure, but they all knew that didn't last forever. And he wouldn't dare go through with the new one, not in its current state, or he'd become stunted like the rest. Sullivan may think the masses under his control will be able to overpower the remaining intelligent population, but he would still want to stay above those masses himself.

"I just can't believe . . ." Lydia said, shaking her head. "I mean, Sullivan has long ignored what is right in front of him. He ignores the growing overpopulation and food shortage issues *every day*. Despite all that, even I didn't think he'd go so far as to stunt the advancement of the human race, just because he holds some sort of massively inflated and twisted sense of superiority. How could he ignore the ramifications of such an act?"

"I don't think he's ignoring anything, Lydia," Maxwell said. "At least not like those other issues. Sullivan knows the limiting effects of the new procedure and yet he's pushing it out to the public. I've worked for the man for years now and, although you won't like me saying this, he *is* extremely intelligent. He's never forced out a procedure advancement like this before. He always knew that if there were ever a flaw in something EXLI provided it would kill them financially. But he's changed. He's obviously not concerned about money anymore. Nor is he concerned about the EXLI reputation. This time, he just *had* to get it out there.

"Sullivan knows by forcing this new procedure into the world and creating such high demand for it, he will be stunting the vast majority of the human race. A majority he hopes to lead. And from what I have deduced, should all go to plan, he believes anyone who's left, any sort of resistance that may spring up once the truth comes out, will be easily dealt with. Whether by his army of followers, or the eventual ravages of time on those who reject immortality. He believes that, ultimately, he'll be in charge with no threat of defiance. Sullivan *wants* those early struggles to play out, be done and over with. He *wants* the world to be stunted. He wants *control*."

They all sat in silence for a few moments as the realization of what was happening, what was at stake, sank in. Everything Maxwell had divulged, all their discussion, it all seemed too unbelievable to be real. But Maxwell had laid it all out for them, and apparently had the evidence to prove it, locked away in a bank for Lydia to collect. The end goal of Sullivan's plan seemed so outlandish to Simon because it was so massive. Some might say EXLI already had control over the world, but what Sullivan had in mind was something wholly different. So many things had to fall into place, had to go just right for it all to come to fruition. Would Sullivan put his reputation, his entire life into such a plan that could fall apart should a rogue scientist like Maxwell or rival like Lydia learn the truth and speak up? There had to be something else they weren't seeing. Something else that gave Sullivan the confidence he needed to follow through.

But then Simon remembered what Maxwell had said before launching into his revelations.

. . . there's more to it than even I understand . . . something else they're hiding. Something more secretive.

"What haven't you told us?" Simon said, unable to keep the

thought from spilling out of his mouth. Maxwell looked at Simon, tilting his head like a curious puppy, the strange gesture so odd-looking in the tense atmosphere of the room.

"Yes, as unfathomable as it seems, there is one final piece of information to share. Something that remains outside my grasp, but that I fear is the key to all this."

Simon, Maggie, and Lydia leaned forward in their seats like children hoping to hear their favorite bedtime story. Lydia's appearance in this respect was eerily realistic, Simon thought, then shook the thought away.

"And before you ask, Lydia, yes, I have included what I am about to tell you in the packet of information waiting for you at the bank."

"Thank you," Lydia said. "You know me too well."

Maxwell snorted. "I've wondered for years now whether that is a good or a bad thing." He took another quick look at the three of them, then started to explain his last bit of information.

Maxwell told them how, a few weeks prior, he'd been deep into smuggling out the information he'd already shared with them, having already been at it for more than a year. Everything about the new procedure's side effects, their failed efforts to find a solution, and Sullivan's threats. He reiterated how the task has been enormously difficult given the high level of security at EXLI—cameras and microphones recording their every move.

Maxwell stood from his chair as he talked, pacing around the room. He stopped from time to time, peeking out the sliver of open space in the window curtains, as if checking for signs of being watched. But each time, apparently satisfied, Maxwell resumed his pacing and his tale.

He told them how, despite the high security at EXLI, there was one room he'd been allowed in that did *not* have the surveillance of the others—a conference room in the center of the top floor of the EXLI building, surrounded by offices reserved for the higher-ups like Sullivan and his inner circle.

"Now I know why," Maxwell said. "With everything I've told you tonight, it's no wonder Sullivan and his closest confidants don't want conversations in that room recorded. But therein lies his mistake, because we and the other senior scientists had weekly progress reports with Sullivan in that very room, which he wanted documented. And so, we'd bring along a mobile recorder, and take it with us when we left."

Simon felt like he could have stood up and taken the next part of the story over from there. During the rush to find a solution to the side effects in the last few weeks before the announcement, when tensions were high and everyone was distracted, the mobile recorder had been mistakenly left in the room. And much to Maxwell's surprise, when he returned the next day to retrieve the recorder, or see if it had been discovered and disposed of, he found the device still there.

"It picked something up," Lydia said. Her face expectant, she licked her lips, hungry for more.

"Oh yes," Maxwell said. He told them how the recording had been running the entire previous day, from the status meeting with the scientists, through hours of silence, and a few shorter, private meetings between Sullivan, Purcell, and Vapula. They had mostly discussed the progress of the project. That was, until one of those meetings had been interrupted. Maxwell paused before saying anymore and bit his lip. He looked at Lydia, then shot a glance at Simon and Maggie. "I've been stupid to keep this here with me. It's . . . *dangerous*, but I felt you needed to hear . . . well—"

Maxwell reached into his pocket and pulled out a rectangular object the size of a lighter.

"I will play this for you only once," Maxwell said. "This is the only incriminating evidence I've kept at home and it's been burning a hole in my pocket all day."

Lydia nodded at Maxwell, as did Simon and Maggie to show their encouragement.

Maxwell returned their nods and said, "Listen closely."

He pressed a button on the side of the object in his hand and set it on the center of the table.

At first, Simon couldn't hear anything, but then, as the recording played out, he heard three distinct voices. One was nasally and high, the other deeper but with a fading Indian accent. The third voice, the one that commanded the conversation, he recognized immediately as Theodore Sullivan.

Ca. No. 2432615184
Audio Recording TSCP 3. Filed 4/15.
PART: Theodore Sullivan, Samar Vapula, Michael
Purcell.

SULLIVAN: . . . flooded with black-market
practitioners. The sooner we release a procedure they can't duplicate, even using their
usual unsafe methods, the sooner they will be
forced out of business.

PURCELL: You don't think they'll be able to
adapt?

SULLIVAN: You're kidding me, right? We can't
even fully adapt yet. The damn scientists
wanted their extra time to try and figure it
all out, but they're no closer now than they
were five months ago. You know as well as I do
that we need to launch soon to protect our
investment. We need to tighten our grip on the
public so we can focus our efforts elsewhere.
Hopefully this time next year I'll--

(A door opens, closes)
(Rushed footsteps)

SULLIVAN: We're in a meeting, Sam.

VAPULA: Sorry sir, but I've just received word from the facility. The subject broke free last night.

SULLIVAN: Him? Ah--

> (A groan)
> (A creak)

PURCELL: Headache again? You oka--

SULLIVAN: I'm fine, damn it! How long was he free?

VAPULA: Only a few moments.

SULLIVAN: How long damn it!

VAPULA: 3.2 seconds.

SULLIVAN: Jesus Christ. How could this happen? All this time. All the interactions I've had with him. There's never been an issue. Now this? They were supposed to keep him contained.

VAPULA: He was, sir. They were prepping for the next round of tests. On the way to 0-800. It happened in transit.

PURCELL: Did the sensors pick up anything significant?

VAPULA: Yes.

SULLIVAN: Tell me someone's already linked up
with him to see if he reached anyone.

VAPULA: They did. He cast a wide net, but
there *was* a focus on one individual. A lower
level scientist.

PURCELL: An *EXLI* scientist?

SULLIVAN: Why him?

VAPULA: They don't know yet. Could've been a
choice, but it could've just as easily been
random.

SULLIVAN: And you're sure he connected with
this man?

VAPULA: Almost positive. I'm headed over there
now to investigate. I'll link up, see if I can
get a confirmation.

SULLIVAN: You better be damn positive.

VAPULA: Yes, sir.

PURCELL: Do we know what the subject said
to him?

VAPULA: Not yet.

SULLIVAN: Then we need this man interrogated! He could have told him everything.

VAPULA: Maybe, maybe not.

SULLIVAN: And what the hell does that mean?

VAPULA: The process, what he was able to do, it's still so beyond our comprehension. We just don't know how it works. This man, the one he connected with, he might not even be aware of what happened.

PURCELL: But you're not sure? He *could* know.

VAPULA: Yes. He might be fully aware now. Then again, their contact might be buried. He might not know at all or never realize what happened. There's just no way--

(Pounding on a table)

SULLIVAN: I want this taken care of! *Now.* Before anything does come of it. They got his name, right? The one he reached.

VAPULA: Martin. Sebastian Martin.

SULLIVAN: Call Avery. Tell him we need to take care of someone.

(Pause)

(Breathing)

VAPULA: Standard protocol, sir?

(Pause)

SULLIVAN: Actually, I think we can use this to our advantage--to send a message about groups like Life Liberation and destabilize them at the same time. Get Avery in my office by the end of the day and we can go over specifics.

VAPULA: Yes, sir.

(Fading footsteps)

20

Maxwell was sitting back in his chair, hands clasped in his lap; he watched his visitors. He raised his eyebrows at Lydia, but it was Simon who spoke first.

"Those sons of bitches!" Simon exclaimed. He rose from his chair and pointed a finger at the recorder. "They killed him. They killed Sebastian! They weren't even sure that he was a threat and they killed him." He looked around the room, eyes falling on Maggie whose face showed rising color. Simon knew what she was thinking. He could see the anger in her contracted eyes, her clenched jaw. "And Will! Their actions—Sullivan's—led to Will's death too!" He tore his eyes away from Maggie, unable to watch the pain in her eyes and stared at the table, shaking his head.

"And they tried to pin it on the Anti-Rejuvenation groups," Maxwell snorted out with disgust. "Typical EXLI fearmongering."

Simon looked up again, focused on Maxwell. "Play it again."

"I'm sorry, Mr. Crowe," Maxwell said, "but I told you I would only play it once." Simon attempted to grab the recorder, but Maxwell snatched the small device off the table first. He pressed his thumb to a button on the bottom and then dropped it on the floor where he smashed it with his foot.

"What the hell did you do that for?" Simon yelled. "That recording could have cleared our names for Sebastian's murder!"

"Keep your voice down, or you'll have to leave." Maxwell fixed Simon with a direct stare. "I sit on a very precarious perch. You don't realize the danger I've put myself in by collecting this information for Miss Darrow and meeting with her tonight. Not to mention allowing the presence of you two. If you don't like the way I do business, then go!"

Simon's nostrils flared. He wanted to leave all right. He'd had enough of Maxwell's theatrics. But Simon knew he needed that recording. He stepped closer to Maxwell.

Lydia leaned forward and raised her hands between the two men.

"Please, both of you settle down," she said, then looked at Maxwell. "Mr. Crowe is upset—"

"You're damn right I am!" Simon said. He locked eyes with Maggie again, saw a fiery look in her eyes that he knew matched his.

"We're *all* upset about this situation!" Maxwell said with a huff. "That doesn't give him the right to—"

But Maxwell's ranting stopped abruptly as his gaze shifted from Lydia to Simon, who stared back, red in the face.

"I'm . . . I'm sorry. Dr. Martin. He was your friend. I . . . I apologize. You must be—" But Maxwell couldn't finish his sentence. No matter. They all knew what he meant.

Simon looked Maxwell square in the eye, gave him the tiniest of nods, though his eyes remained narrowed.

There was a brief, awkward pause before Maxwell found his words again. "I knew him, you know? Dr.—Sebastian. We didn't work directly together, but I knew a bit about him. We had lunch once or twice together in the EXLI cafeteria. He seemed like a nice guy."

"Yeah. He was."

Simon was grateful for the silence that followed, but he still fumed under his breath. He paced behind the couch, thoughts of Sebastian and Will in his mind. Of Maggie and him on the run. And that recording, the one that could set at least some of this right. The recording that Maxwell had just destroyed.

"Wait a minute," Maxwell said, snapping his fingers. "You said you knew about Hillbrook from a message your friend sent you."

Simon nodded.

"That was part of it, yeah," he said.

"And this message was from Dr. Martin?"

Simon stopped his pacing, nodding again. His nods got slower and slower until he stopped, his eyes on Maxwell, but not focused, his face static with thought.

"My God. It's him," Simon said. "The person they were talking about in that recording. The one they called *the subject*. It's the man Sebastian was referring to in his message. It has to be!"

"Dr. Martin mentioned a man?" Maxwell asked.

"How do you know it's him?" Maggie said. "How can you be sure?"

"Yes, Sebastian's message mentioned a man, but until now we didn't—" Simon said. "Well, we still don't know *who* he is, but the subject they mentioned has to be the guy. It makes sense now. You heard them—Sullivan and the other two sounded *very* concerned about this subject getting loose. For whatever reason, whatever happened, they are keeping him locked up. *Contained*, they said. They're keeping him hidden because of what he knows or who he is."

He looked to Maggie for confirmation that the newfound

thoughts spilling from his head were correct. But any agreement she might have shown was tarnished by the mention of Sullivan's name. The sound of it carried venom. Her nose wrinkled and brow contracted when she heard it, as if it pained her to simply hear the name of the man whose actions had set in motion the sequence of events that had led to her brother's death.

"But what could he know?" Lydia said.

It was the next logical question, Simon thought. What could this man, this *subject*, know that would cause EXLI to lock him away like that? And, what could he have possibly told Sebastian that would have got him killed? But then, on that recording they said—

"I don't know, but something else is bothering me. They said the prisoner only escaped for a couple seconds. How could this man contact Sebastian and tell him anything of importance in such a short time?"

"I think," Maxwell said, "the mode of communication isn't nearly as important as the content."

"Could he have told Sebastian about the new procedure?" Maggie asked, her facial expression returning to normal. "And the side effects?"

"It's a possibility," Lydia said, "but I don't think so. The cognitive side effects were common knowledge amongst the scientists working on the new procedure, right?"

"For the most part, yes," Maxwell said.

"Well, if that's true, then why are they keeping this subject and whatever is happening with him secret from you all? Why are Sullivan, Purcell, Vapula, and whoever is working with them at this facility they mentioned the only ones who know about the man they have locked up? There has to be another reason for him contacting Dr. Martin, and for Dr. Martin to contact you, Simon."

Maxwell nodded, looked up at Simon who had begun pacing again.

"Could you tell me more about this message?" he said.

Simon said he could do one better and reached into his pocket, extracting his cell phone. He pressed a few buttons and laid it on the table so they could all hear the message as it played.

The message still sent chills through Simon. At least now, it had more meaning, Sebastian's cryptic words beginning to make sense.

"Hmmm," Maxwell said, rubbing his wrinkled chin, mumbling to himself as he worked out all the details Simon and company had done over the previous days. "It all seems to be pointing to this mystery man, the one we now think is the subject Sullivan and his people have locked up somewhere."

Simon and Lydia nodded, but Maggie raised a questioning eyebrow.

"But we know where they're keeping him," Maggie said, as if every word she said was obvious. "If this man is the same one that Sull—that he and his men talked about in the recording you played for us, then the facility they spoke of has to be Hillbrook. Sebastian's message said that's where they're keeping him."

"My lady, I believe you are correct," Maxwell said and smiled. "And what of this number? 120. What might that mean?"

"No idea," Simon said with a shrug.

He suggested it might be a floor or room number at Hillbrook. Maxwell shot the idea down quickly, explaining how The Shepherd's Institute was comprised of only 20 floors. Nineteen, if you factored out the lobby level, so the number in the message couldn't pertain to a floor. 120 also couldn't be a room because the rooms at The Shepherd's Institute were marked by numbers *and* letters, such as 1A, 2A, 3B, and the numbers only went up to 50.

"But it has to have something to do with where they're keeping him," Maggie said.

"I agree," Simon said. "But something tells me that unless we run across Sullivan and—" He stopped himself, looked at Maggie for a reaction to the name, but only saw her looking at the floor. "Unless we can coax him into spilling his secrets, we won't know what that number means until we're actually there."

Maxwell turned his head sharply at Simon.

"Excuse me?" Maxwell said. "Until *who* is *where*?"

"Us. Hillbrook. Until we go there."

"You still want to go to Hillbrook?" Lydia said.

"Don't you?" Simon said, the color in his face rising yet again. Why did it seem so hard for Lydia and Maxwell to understand? Hillbrook was the key. It's where everything was pointing. Everything they knew, at least. It's where Sebastian was leading them and where Sullivan and his people were keeping this man, this . . . subject. It's where everything ended. If they were going to figure out what was going on, if Simon and Maggie hoped to clear their names, get justice for Sebastian and Will, then they needed to go to Hillbrook.

"You can't possibly think you can just stroll into The Shepherd's Institute, Mr. Crowe," Maxwell said.

"It's a public facility, isn't it? People go in and out every day to see their relatives. Lydia even said with the right—"

"But you're wanted by the police. Your faces are plastered all over the city, especially in EXLI-controlled facilities. There's no way you'll be able to get inside unnoticed. Even with disguises. You'd be discovered and arrested on the spot. Not a chance."

"Well we have to try."

"Do we?" Lydia said.

Simon looked at the small woman, brow contracted.

"Yes! Of course we do," he said.

How could she still not see that all the answers were there, at Hillbrook?

"With the information Maxwell has gathered for us, we can expose EXLI and Sullivan for what they truly are. We can bring them down with evidence about the new procedure. I'm positive that, over time, as they are investigated for the side effects, more information will be exposed about what is going on at Hillbrook. And we will have the recording Maxwell played for us tonight as soon as we go to the bank. As you said, that recording implicates Sullivan, Purcell, and Vapula in Sebastian's murder. There's no way any court would see otherwise given that evidence."

For the first time in the minutes since he'd listened to Maxwell's recording, Simon felt his anger break. He realized that everything Lydia said was correct and rational and, given time, Simon was sure it would all come to fruition. But he still felt the need for instant justice, felt he and Maggie were owed it given their tribulations of the last two days. More important still, Sebastian deserved that justice. Will deserved it. Not just quick revenge, though at that moment Simon felt even that would suffice, but real justice. And not sometime next year. Not in six months. *Now*.

"But if we go there," Simon pleaded, "If we know exactly what they are doing there, then we can stop them even faster."

"Yes, we likely could," Lydia said. "But is it worth the risk to you or Maggie, or any of us? We're so close to this all ending. Once we have the information from the bank, this will all be over. There's no reason to go to Hillbrook and risk being caught, risk our lives. If we do, then none of this might come to light. Sullivan and EXLI might get away with everything."

That did it. The thought of Sullivan and EXLI winning, of getting away with the murder of his friends, and more, broke Simon of his irrationality. The rage, the need for justice had by no means left him completely, but Simon's mind cleared enough for him to understand their best course of action.

"You're right," he said, grabbing his phone from the table. "Let's go to the bank, get the information, and be done with this."

He placed a hand on Maggie's shoulder and looked in her eyes. "Agreed?"

Maggie placed her hand on Simon's, squeezed it tight. She nodded and said, "Agreed. I'm ready for . . . for them to pay for what they've done. I'm ready for this to end. I think we all are."

Lydia reached in her coat pocket and pulled out her phone.

"Then I think we're about done here," she said. "I'll call for Derrick."

"Oh," Maxwell said, and raised a finger. "About that, Lydia. It seems likely that my house is under surveillance at this very moment. I have no proof, but it is likely. It might be a camera or two, rather than a person, but for the sake of safety, I've arranged for another, more *secure*, means of transport."

"I appreciate the thought, Maxwell," Lydia said. "But I'm sure my driver will suffice."

"He may, but please, do me this favor. At the very least, allow them to escort you."

"And just who is this transport?"

"Oh, some friends of mine, and yours too." He paused. "Come to think of it, they should be here by now."

Maxwell pushed himself out of his chair. He walked to his desk and grabbed the small phone on the filing cabinet.

"Maxwell? Is something wrong?" Lydia said.

He shook his head, hitting a button on the phone.

"Probably just running behind. I told them to be here by half past. I'm sure—"

There was a spray of blood behind Maxwell as his head jolted to the side; small shreds of skin, skull fragments, and thick globs of pulverized brain matter stuck in a clump against the wall like wet spaghetti and slowly started to ooze down. Maxwell's hand fell to his side, the phone dropping to the floor as his body tumbled.

Maggie, Simon, and Lydia screamed as Maxwell's body

collapsed over the desk, blood tricking from the bullet entry wound in his temple. Maxwell's limbs spasmed and he slid off the desk, hitting the floor with a wet thump just as two more rounds struck the wall.

Simon pulled Lydia and Maggie to the floor as the sniper's shots cut through the window, small chunks of glass raining down with each successive shot. Simon yanked the revolver from his waistband.

"Go! Go!" he cried, and pointed at the door. "Head to the kitchen! Crawl!" He pushed the women ahead of him and, staying low to the ground, they started crawling. Bullets continued to streak by over their heads. More shots hit the side of the house; Simon wondered if the sniper had given up on accuracy and was just shooting blindly, or if he knew they were on the move and hoped to catch them as they made their way into the next room.

In the hallway, they lay on the floor, unsure of what to do next. Lydia's eyes were frozen on the wall, her mind back in the study, on the scene they'd just witnessed. Maxwell, shot dead. His tumbling, lifeless body. She shivered and then looked up, glaring at the gun in Simon's hand, but said nothing. Maggie's eyes darted around the group, coming to rest on Simon, who kept signaling them to stay low.

Simon held his gun-free hand up to both Maggie and Lydia, indicating that he needed a few moments to catch his breath, to think.

Simon's mind raced as they lay in the hallway. Did they really, he wondered, have any options? They were trapped. What could they do? They obviously couldn't go outside or they'd be picked off by the sniper as soon as he had a clear shot. They could try to sneak out the back door and hope there was a path they could take that the sniper couldn't see. But who knew what or who was out back? For all Simon knew, there could be another sniper waiting for them, or a group of men just biding their time until Maggie,

Lydia, and he tried to sneak out the door. They'd snatch them up or kill them on the spot. They were stuck. His first thought had been right—they had no options at all.

But they had to do *something*.

Simon made up his mind. He had to at least try to get them out of there. If they had no foolproof options that meant their only choice was to attempt escape, whether it meant potentially walking into the crosshairs of a sniper or not.

He looked at both Maggie and Lydia, and saw their faces showing obvious and expected signs of fright. Simon suspected that his face showed no different.

"Listen," he said in a low voice. "I think our best bet is to try and get out of here through the back. I want you both to stay behind me. I'm going to crawl into the kitchen and see if there's a way out."

"Are you sure?" Maggie said. "There could be another shooter out there."

"I know."

"I'll go," Lydia said, her voice now stronger yet still the strange high pitch of a young girl. "I'm smaller. They might not see me. I can do a little recce, then come back here, and let you know if it's safe."

Simon shook his head.

"I understand where you're coming from, Lydia, but I can't let you do that. I'll go on ahead. It has to be me."

"I don't see why—" Lydia began.

"Why does it *have* to be you?" Maggie said.

"It just does," Simon insisted and gave Maggie a deep look. She hesitated, then nodded. Simon placed the gun on the carpet so that he could fully embrace Maggie. He squeezed her tight and they shared a quick kiss. He closed his eyes for a split second, enjoying the closeness of Maggie, wondering if this would be the last time he'd ever hold her.

Simon opened his eyes and pulled away from Maggie. He went to grab the gun again, but found it gone. He looked up to see Lydia, already crawling away up the hallway, the revolver looking massive in her small right hand.

"Lydia!" Simon almost shouted. "Come back! I'm—"

Lydia paused at the sound of his voice, looked back with a steely gaze, and said, "Your chivalry is noted, Mr. Crowe. Now stay down until I come back."

What could they do? Maggie nodded, as did Simon, though with reluctance. They watched as Lydia turned her head back around and started inching toward the kitchen again. The hallway was actually rather short, but looked much longer with Lydia's small form crawling through it. They could hear her ragged breathing, see her thin arm struggle with the weight of the revolver each time she lifted it. A few moments later, she reached the spot where the carpet in the hallway connected to the kitchen's hard floor.

Lydia sat with her back to the wall, using both hands to clutch the gun. She readied herself to face whatever awaited her, when she froze, noticing something peculiar. The sound of gunfire had stopped. She looked back down the hallway and saw Maggie and Simon still lying beside one another, heads up and looking at her.

Simon had noticed the gunfire stoppage as well and looked back into the study that had moments before been a shooting gallery. He could see the circle of chairs they had been sitting in. He saw debris on the floor inside the room from where the bullets had ripped parts of the walls apart after impact. He saw Maxwell's body, unmoving. But the room was quiet from what he could see and hear. There was no movement and no sound of additional shots ringing out.

Had the sniper left? Almost certainly not, he thought. The sniper could be moving positions, closing in on the house to finish them off. That, or circling the house, knowing that they would try to escape out the back.

Lydia arched her neck around the corner and peered into the kitchen. She saw no movement—not in the kitchen, in the adjacent dining room, or out the small window above the sink which looked across the rear yard of the house.

Holding the revolver tight in both hands, Lydia climbed to her feet but remained in a crouched position. She slowly made her way into the kitchen, keeping as low to the ground as possible and holding the gun out in front of her. She scanned everything around her, side to side, repeatedly. She reached the edge of the counter below the sink and paused for a moment, steadying herself and taking a couple of deep breaths. She slowly began to stand upright, extending her neck as far as she could to try to catch a glimpse of whatever was out back.

Her eyes reached level with the windowsill and in the darkness caught one quick glimpse of a small, grassy backyard with a short tool shed in one corner. A moment later, shadows moved across the yard—multiple shadows.

Spooked, Lydia fell back onto the kitchen floor. The gun in her hands slipped from her sweating fingers, dropped to the floor. She flinched.

The gun did not go off as she had feared, but just as Lydia reached down to grab it again, the back door burst open, swinging with a thud against the wall.

A slender man dressed all in black, dark paint streaked across his face, stomped through the door. A compact, scoped sniper rifle was strapped across his back; in his outstretched hand, he held a smaller 9mm pistol. He swung the pistol around toward Lydia, a grimace on his face.

But she had been ready. The hammer was cocked, barrel pointed at the intruder. Lydia clenched the revolver in her small hands, prepared herself as best she could for the forthcoming recoil of the gun. She closed her eyes, squeezed the trigger . . .

There was no blast of gunfire. No shake from a firing gun in her hands. Only an empty click. Lydia's eyes shot open. She cocked the gun again, pulled the trigger, but heard only the metallic click of dry fire.

The revolver was empty. In all the haste and confusion of the last two days, Simon had forgotten to reload it. Much to Lydia's dismay.

The man sneered at her. He took a step closer, his 9mm trained on Lydia. Her instinct was to close her eyes again, to not look at her oncoming death. But Lydia stared back at the man, gritted her teeth.

The blast of a gun sounded. Another shot. Then another. But Lydia felt nothing. Her would-be killer rocked to the side as each shot coming through the open door hit him. He staggered back, slammed into the fridge where he left a red streak of blood as he slid to the floor, dead.

Lydia dropped the empty revolver from her shaking hands and fell to the floor behind a small outcrop of cabinets.

That was when Simon bolted into the kitchen. He kicked the pistol away from the man's hand, just in case there was any life left in him, then went to Lydia's side.

"Are you okay?" he panted. Lydia could only nod in response.

Simon heard a commotion outside. He told Lydia to stay down, hidden, then stood tall. He wished he'd picked up the dead man's gun instead of kicking it.

Three figures dressed in dark pants and jackets, tactical vests, and what looked to Simon like old paintball masks and goggles, marched through the door and into the kitchen. If their black-ops, militaristic appearance wasn't already enough to show their seriousness, the semi-automatic tactical rifles held by the two taller figure was. The shorter, third masked figure in the middle brandished a sleek, stainless steel .45 pistol with a black grip.

Simon froze, knowing immediately that he was done for—they all were. One of the taller figures checked the dead man's pulse, then rejoined his fellows where they'd stopped on the other side of the counter. They did not raise their guns. Simon started for the revolver Lydia had dropped, knowing it was empty, but hoping the threat might—

"Stop!" the shorter figure yelled in a breathy voice Simon could tell belonged to a woman.

But Simon did not stop. He grabbed the revolver and when he raised it again, saw the two taller figures had raised their weapons at Simon. He froze.

"Oh, please. We know it's empty," the masked woman said. "Besides, we're not going to hurt you. We're here to get you out of here."

"What?" Simon said. His head was spinning, but he figured it had to be some kind of ploy to get him to lower his defenses. "Your guns say otherwise."

"You raised a weapon to us first, pal." The woman's voice had an annoyed air to it now.

"You were just trying to kill us!"

"That wasn't us." She motioned her head to the dead man near the fridge. "It was that guy. You're welcome, by the way. Now if you're done, we *are* here to help. Where's Maxwell?"

The name of the house's owner gave Simon pause, but he didn't lower his gun just yet.

"In the study. He—he's dead."

The masked woman took a step back, staggered slightly. She raised her hands at the two figures at her side. They both lowered their rifles.

"See. We're not here to hurt you. Who are you, anyway? Maxwell said it would only be the one."

"We're friends of Lydia's," Simon said.

"Where is she? Is she hurt or—"

Hearing her name, Lydia climbed to her feet. When she popped up into view from behind the cabinets, the woman in the mask released a sigh that was both surprise and relief.

"Lydia!"

"Zoë!" Lydia said, her nervous shaking of moments before now gone. She looked up at Simon. "You can put that thing away, Mr. Crowe. She's telling the truth."

The woman named Zoë holstered her pistol. She reached up and pulled the goggles she was wearing forward and off her head, letting them hang on her wrist. Even in the shining orange light of the kitchen, her eyes, now free of cover, blazed a bright shade of green as they gazed at Simon impatiently. She slid her mask up and off her head, freeing a stream of long, auburn hair. Her face was slightly pale, freckled, but red in the cheeks.

Simon stared, finally lowering the revolver without even realizing it as Lydia rounded the cabinets to hug Zoë.

"We need to go, Lydia," Zoë said. "There could be more on the way."

Lydia nodded, looked at Simon and said, "You heard her."

Simon had questions. So many questions. But his primary thought was Maggie. He slid the empty revolver into his waistband as he turned back to the hallway, but Maggie was already stepping out into the kitchen. Simon rushed to her, wrapped his arms around her.

"Are you okay?" he asked.

"Yes. Who are those people?" Maggie said.

"I don't know, but apparently they're here to help us."

"Come on you two!" Lydia called at them.

Simon led Maggie back to the rest of the group. Zoë wrinkled her nose briefly at the sight of Maggie. The two men standing at Zoë's side turned toward the newcomer as well. Their facial expressions remained a mystery, hidden behind the masks they wore, but they kept their rifles pointed at the floor.

"We seriously need to get out of here," Zoë said, then motioned to Simon. "We wasted enough time trying to talk your friend here down."

"Lead the way," Lydia said.

Zoë nodded to the two men at her side. One of them went into the house toward the front door, the other disappeared out the back. Zoë quickly put her mask and goggles back on, then turned to the group.

"Follow me," Zoë said. "It should be a straight shot to the truck, and we have plenty of men out there to cover us, but in case anything goes down, stay behind me."

Plenty of men? Simon thought. *What kind of operation was this?* "What do you mean by—who *are* you people?"

Zoë shushed him and motioned for them to follow as she stepped toward the back door, craning her neck around the edge of the door to look outside. She grabbed her silver pistol, pointed it in front of her, and then disappeared outside.

Simon reached forward and tugged on Lydia's coat sleeve. She turned, shooting him a frustrated look.

"What?" she whispered.

"Who is that woman?" Simon said.

"There'll be time to explain later."

"But—"

Lydia shushed Simon and he relinquished the line of questioning, following her and Maggie out the door.

The back of Maxwell Lewis's house was not unlike the front. There was a small patch of grass that extended toward a waist-high fence marking the end of Maxwell's property and the beginning of his neighbor's. There were a few trees sprinkled throughout the yard and a small flower garden near the back porch. In one corner, atop a small tool shed, was a figure dressed similar to Zoë watching over the yard with a rifle set on a small tripod.

The taller masked man who had left out the back door earlier was now standing to one side, motioning Zoë and the rest of the group toward him. They all marched as quietly as they could over grass that Simon could feel through his shoes was wet with night-time dew. When they reached the tall man, he motioned for them to continue down the edge of the yard toward the back fence.

Simon followed the group as they walked toward the fence, looking around the yard and back up toward the house every few seconds, searching for anything suspicious.

When they reached the fence, Simon saw another masked man waiting on the other side. It was hard to miss him, given his hulking size. He lifted Lydia's tiny body entirely over the fence as Zoë hopped across in one swift motion. The man offered a helping hand to Simon and Maggie as they followed.

They made their way up the side of the rear neighbor's yard to a black SUV parked on the street ahead. The tall figure leading the way opened the back door and Lydia climbed inside.

Simon stopped and looked into the vehicle, not sure, even after following them all this way, whether climbing inside was a good idea. Zoë saw this hesitation but would have none of it.

"Get in," she demanded.

"Why should we go with you?" Simon said. "Why can't we go in Lydia's car?"

"Because her driver's dead." Zoë looked inside the car at Lydia. "Sorry to tell you, Lydia. The sniper must have recognized Derrick and tagged him while he was waiting down the street."

"Thank you for relaying the news," Lydia said, her eyes suddenly heavy.

Zoë turned back to Simon, flashing stern eyes at him through her goggles.

"Now get in the car," she said, jerking her thumb toward the open door. "Or I may use my gun on you yet tonight."

Simon understood. He helped Maggie into the back of the SUV and scrambled in after her. Zoë climbed into the passenger side. The other masked figure sat his large frame behind the driver's seat and removed his mask. Underneath, the face of a bald, dark-skinned man with large, kind eyes. A moment later they were on the road, speeding away from Maxwell's neighborhood.

As best he could, Simon had held his tongue while they escaped the house. But now that they were safely on the road, he wanted answers.

"All right," he said. "Someone tell me what the hell is going on here! Who are you people? Where are we going?"

Zoë removed her goggles and mask, again releasing her flowing auburn hair, though it looked black under only the light from passing streetlamps.

"Yes, Lydia," Zoë said, raising an eyebrow in Lydia's direction, then glancing at Simon and Maggie, "I'd like to know some things as well. For starters, who's the Persister? And this other one, he's quite mouthy. What's his deal?"

Lydia sat up in her seat, straightening her coat in a dignified manner, and looked around the car.

"Zoë," she said, "This is Simon Crowe and Maggie Buchanan. You probably recognize them from the news reports of the last few days."

Zoë's eyebrows seemed to raise even more with recognition, so much so that Simon expected them to run right up across her forehead and into her hair.

"Mr. Crowe, Miss Buchanan, this is Zoë Drake, commander of Life Liberation."

LIVE YOUR B~~E~~ST LIFE

SAY NO!
TO
REJUVENATION

LEARN THE REAL FACTS THAT PERSISTERS & EXLI DON'T WANT YOU TO KNOW!

Children and young adults below the ages of 22 are STILL VULNERABLE TO DISEASE and many continue to DIE every day!

Regular medical practices have become antiquated or forgotten. Research into treatments and cures for individual diseases are said to be redundant, but that is a LIE!

Abstainers are still susceptible to disease, simply because they choose to forgo the procedure. UNFAIR!

LL

21

———————

Though he had only met Lydia Darrow in person a little
more than a day ago, Simon had known plenty about the woman
before that time. He'd first heard her name as a young child and
had grown accustomed in the years since to seeing her on TV,
reading about her in the newspaper, and hearing excerpts of her
voice on the morning news radio. He knew that, through her
many engagements as the leading spokesperson against Rejuvenation, Lydia had encountered and grown connections around the
world with people from all walks of life. But in all that he'd read
and learned about her over the years, there had always been one
constant about Lydia and the company she kept. That was, Lydia's
adamant stance that she had absolutely no ties to any of the
radical Anti-Rejuvenation groups—particularly Life Liberation,
the one group, more than any other, she repeatedly disavowed.
Which was why, when Simon found himself in the back of a
blacked-out SUV with Lydia and this woman who was apparently
Life Liberation's leader, his mouth fell instantly open in shock.
Not because it was mere minutes after they'd all narrowly
escaped death by sniper. Or because their savior from that deadly
situation had been the leader of the very radical group that Lydia

has so often disavowed. Simon was shocked by how friendly the pair acted toward each other. With introductions out of the way and the danger at Maxwell's house behind them, both women's demeanors quickly changed, softened. They began talking as if they were old college roommates reconnecting and chatting about days gone by. Simon sank back into the seat listening, though a million questions swam into his mind.

Had he been wrong about Lydia all this time? It certainly seemed so. Just two days ago he'd sat in a coffee shop, joking with Will about how crazy Lydia was. He'd thought he knew her and what she stood for, but after what they'd been through since meeting her, and now this interaction in front of him, he knew he'd been mistaken. He'd witnessed her passion first hand when discussing Rejuvenation back in her apartment. He'd seen her intense reaction when discussing the repercussions of the new procedure with Maxwell. But she wasn't just posturing and politics. He'd watched her pick up a gun, ready to use it to defend herself and the fugitives she'd adopted into her cause. He knew now that, despite her public persona, Lydia wasn't what he'd thought she was at all. Not what he expected. She was more. She was better. Despite her size, she was bigger than all of them; more important.

Lydia wasted no time in dispelling the news reports claiming Simon or Maggie were the murderers of Sebastian and the detectives. Zoë pointed out that she had already suspected as much since the reports were connecting Simon to Life Liberation. And as she put it, she "knew everyone in the LL and had never seen Simon's scared mug before." Zoë sneered at Simon as she said this, as if his association with her group tarnished its reputation in some way, more than it already was in the public eye. Lydia gave Zoë a quick overview of the last two days, everything from her lecture downtown to meeting Simon and Maggie, the mysterious message from Sebastian, and ending with the meeting she had arranged with Maxwell.

"I'm surprised Max kept your meeting at all," Zoë said. "He called me as soon as that asshat Sullivan stepped off the stage. Sounded scared as well, to be honest. Must've known he'd need a bit of protection."

The two women stopped. They looked at each other in silence, sharing the same unspoken reaction to Zoë's words. *Maxwell.* They let a long, thoughtful moment of reflection for their departed friend play out before continuing their conversation.

"I suppose I didn't give him much of a choice," Lydia said. "He definitely didn't like it when I showed up on his doorstep with these two. But I had no other option. I . . . it's just different this time. The announcement, the new procedure, people in such grave danger, people being *killed*."

Zoë pointed to the left at the road ahead to tell the driver where to go and then turned back to look Lydia directly in the eyes.

"It certainly feels different," Lydia went on, "EXLI has gone to some great lengths in the past to protect their work, but never to killing—at least, not that I am aware. We're all vulnerable, every one of us. It's—"

"That's enough," Simon interjected, finally broken from his silence by Lydia's last words. "I want to know what's going on."

"I believe you are well aware of what's happening, Mr. Crowe," Lydia said, turning to face him. "Tonight we—"

"I'm not talking about what happened back at the house. I'm talking about now! Where are we going?"

Lydia raised her eyebrows at Zoë.

"Somewhere secure," Zoë said, facing the front of the vehicle again. "One of our safe houses, north end of the city. That's all I can tell you at this point."

Lydia leaned in toward the center of the vehicle between the two front seats.

"I'm sorry, but we need to turn around," Lydia said.

"We know the way to our own safe house."

"I'm sure that you do, but we can't go there. Not yet anyway. We have to make a stop."

Zoë shook her head as she turned to look at Lydia.

"Where?"

Lydia pulled the small key she'd been given by Maxwell from her pocket and held it up.

"Wakefield. The Regency Bank on Bormello Avenue. Maxwell hid information there and we need to retrieve it."

"No can do, Lydia." Zoë's voice turned harder with a tinge of emphasized finality. "Maybe if it was on the way, but Wakefield is on the other side of town. We need to get to the safe house. EXLI obviously wants you all dead, so keeping you safe is priority one."

"But—"

"Look," Zoë said. "You said you need to go to a bank? I'm sure that means whatever Max stashed away for you is locked up, which means it will still be there in the morning. The bank will be closed at this hour anyway. Whatever it is, it can wait."

Lydia sat back in her seat, acknowledging her defeat with a sigh and a mumble. She pocketed the key, crossed her tiny arms, and turned her gaze out the window.

There were a few minutes of quiet as they continued driving. Simon held Maggie's hands tight in his, her head resting on his shoulder. Simon stared past the two front seats and out the windshield. The faded lines of the road and surrounding buildings zipped by on both sides, blurred, barely visible under nothing but the light of the moon and the streetlamps that occasionally dotted the curb. He didn't know exactly what road they were on or where they were, but there was a vague familiarity to it all. Simon supposed that had it been a normal night, he would have recognized where they were, but tonight was anything but normal.

A crackling sound issued from the front of the car. Zoë reached up and pushed a button on the small two-way radio attached to her vest. "Bravo, come in. Status report," she said.

"We're clear," came a gruff voice from the radio's speaker.

"Roger that, Russell. Were you able to pull anything off the sniper?"

"Signaling device," said Russell, "but it looks like he didn't hit send until we started shooting at him. Readout shows only a few minutes were transferred before we stopped it."

"Anything in those minutes?"

"Not much that I can tell. Names and such, then a mention of Wakefield, but it cuts off right after that."

"Shit. Arthur, turn us around." Without a single moment of hesitation, the driver, Arthur, slowed the car briefly, cranked the wheel, and pulled a U-turn, speeding them off in the opposite direction. Zoë looked at Lydia and saw comprehension dawn on her face.

"The bank," Lydia said.

Zoë nodded and then spoke into the radio again. "Russell, I'll send you location details. Meet us there as soon as possible. Do not engage until we arrive unless absolutely necessary. If they show up before we do, let me know. Out." Zoë turned around to look at her three passengers, but focused on Lydia. "Looks like you're going to get your wish after all. That sniper was communicating with someone. I'm guessing his employers. If EXLI knows about Wakefield, we have to assume they heard about the information Max left for you at that bank. If they send goons to retrieve it, we need to be there to head them off. Normally I'd just have my guys stake it out and, if worse comes to worst, have them go in and retrieve the box themselves. But since they'll need that key of yours to do so, well . . ."

"How long will it take us to get there?" Simon asked.

"20 minutes, give or take. We'll have to backtrack a bit. That's also not accounting for any unexpected roadblocks or traffic." Zoë stared at Simon for a moment, and he noticed that her bright green eyes were more alive than ever. It was as if she was glad they weren't going to the safe house, excited by the idea that they wouldn't have a quiet trip to the bank the following morning —like she welcomed any chance of confrontation. Zoë pulled back a little in her seat and then looked at the rest of the group. "If we're lucky, we may just have a nice, discreet stakeout waiting for us when we get there. If not, well, let's just say that Max's house isn't the last place you three are likely to encounter gunfire tonight."

22

Zoë had been correct about the time it would take them to get to the bank. Their trip across the city to Wakefield Township would've been even shorter had they not needed to detour around a makeshift police checkpoint set on one of the main roads. Luckily, they'd spotted the flashing lights of the squad cars parked ahead in time to turn down a side street without being seen. They continued the rest of the way to Wakefield via side roads to avoid any other checkpoints that might have been placed on the main throughways of the city.

When their vehicle turned onto Bormello Avenue, Zoë spun around in her seat to face them. Simon knew what she would say before the words even came out of her mouth.

"Remember," Zoë said, "I want you three to stay in this car and keep your heads down, no matter what."

"We heard you the first thirty times, Zoë," Lydia said, speaking the exact sentiment Simon had been thinking.

"Very funny, but you'll hear me say it as many times as I have to until I'm sure it sinks in. We're taking a big fuckin' chance bringing you here instead of going back to the safe house. But given the circumstances, we needed to act fast. So just sit tight while we survey the situation."

Simon looked past Zoë as she spoke, out the windshield. On the west side of the road ahead he saw a small car dealership. Just beyond this, seemingly hovering in the darkness, was the sign for the Regency Bank. Its rounded logo and letters lit up in white and green near the front of the bank's parking lot.

"Looks calm," Simon said as they slowly approached the bank. Except for the glow of a single security light inside, the bank was dark. There was no sign of anyone in its vicinity except for another black SUV, similar to the one in which they were currently riding, parked in the shadows near one corner of the gray brick building.

Maggie pointed between the seats at the waiting vehicle and said, "Your people?"

Zoë squinted out the windshield and nodded.

"That'll be Russell and his crew," she said. "There *should* be another vehicle. I don't see—damn it. Arthur, where are they?"

Arthur shook his head as he turned the car down a street that ran along one side of the bank. He slowed, brought their vehicle to stop at the curb, and flashed the headlights. A moment later, the SUV parked in the shadows flashed its lights in return. Arthur looked at Zoë, who hit the button on her radio again.

"Bravo team. This is Alpha. Come in."

"Go for Bravo."

"Russell," Zoë said, "What's your status? Any activity?"

"You got me, plus three. Negative on the activity."

"Where's our other backup?"

"Last I heard they were still on the way. Should be here soon."

"They better be," Zoë said. "Let's at least hope they show up before anyone else does. *If* anyone does. We may have lucked out. Seems quiet here. Let's give it a few hours to be safe. Pull back a little ways so we're not as easy to spot. Head up Bormello, but keep in view of the bank. We'll move into the dealership parking lot, try to blend in with the rest of the cars. Out." Zoë turned to Arthur. "You heard me."

The headlights of the SUV parked in the shadows of the Regency Bank parking lot came to life. It turned around and headed up Bormello.

Arthur shifted their vehicle into gear and cranked the wheel hard to the left, turning them around. Then a hard right, up the small driveway leading into the dealership parking lot. Arthur tucked their SUV in a spot that overlooked the bank, snug between a red compact car and a large pickup truck. For a moment, their headlights shined across the side street, up over a small, bordering strip of grass, and into the bank's parking lot. He shut the engine off, and the lights went dark.

Silence fell inside the car, but for the soft sounds of breathing and creaking movements on the seats. It was two full minutes before anyone spoke.

"Do you think they'll show up—someone from EXLI?" Maggie asked.

"I don't know," Zoë said, keeping her face forward, watching the bank instead of looking back in response to Maggie. "If they heard your conversation with Max and know what's hidden at this bank, it'd make sense for them to come straight here. So the fact that they *aren't* here yet bodes well for us. If no one shows up, we'll have Lydia go in there first thing in the morning and snatch up the lockbox."

"Why can't we go in now?" Lydia asked, her voice almost pleading. "We're here. Can't we just . . . you know, break in there and take the lockbox?" Zoë returned her gaze into the back seat, eyebrows rising as she looked at Lydia, who went on. "Not to speak ill of you and your people, Zoë, but we both know you possess the knowledge and experience to infiltrate that bank."

Zoë kept her eyes on Lydia. She nodded, pouted her lips in agreement, before a smile crept on her face.

"By all means, scoot on over there if you want," Zoë said, "but unless you know how to break into the vault *inside* the bank we're shit out of luck. Getting into the building is easy, getting into the vault—where your lockbox is likely stored right now —*that*, we can't do. Not on our own."

"Oh," Lydia said, sitting back in her seat. "I see."

Zoë gave a victorious smirk, but it was short-lived as the radio on Arthur's shoulder crackled to life.

"Alpha Team, this is Charlie! Come in!" the voice on the other end of the radio barked. Whomever it was, they didn't wait for the usual acknowledgment. "We're not gonna make the rendezvous. Turned a corner and ran smack into a police barricade. We turned around but they spotted us and are in pursuit!"

Zoë shook her head, slammed a fist against the dash. Arthur looked at her but she only gave a curt nod and looked back out the window at the bank.

Arthur pressed the button on the side of his radio and said, "Copy that, Charlie Team. Ditch 'em if you can. If not, lead them as far away from us as possible. You hear me? Do *not* lead them here!"

"Copy that."

"Good luck."

The radio gave another crackle and went silent.

"Well," Arthur said, looking at Zoë, "There goes our additional backup."

"We don't have enough men for this," Zoë said, still looking out the window. She ran a hand through her hair.

"We can manage. You and me here. Russell's got, who? Phillips, Hayes, and James as support in his car. That's six. Six is more than enough for a stakeout."

"For a stakeout, yes, but if shit goes south—"

"We'll be fine," Arthur said.

Simon wondered if Arthur believed the words he said. Zoë didn't seem convinced. But the massive man in the driver's seat sounded confident, and that put Simon at ease.

A minute went by. Then two. Then five. Simon stared at the bank, the side of his head leaning against the cool glass of the window. He watched for any signs of activity, but saw none. No movement. No sound. Just stillness and night. His eyelids started to feel heavy, the silence and darkness around him starting to take effect on his tired body. As another minute ticked by, Simon thought that maybe Arthur had been right. Maybe no one would come.

Simon saw a flash of light out the corner of his eye. There was movement on a cross street far ahead. At first, it was just head-lights, flashing in the distance as they passed between other build-ings. Might it be a taxi or some other late-night driver unrelated to their situation? They hoped . . . but the car turned down Bormello, its headlights steady now, growing larger, brighter. The car hardly slowed as it approached, tires screeching as it turned into the bank's parking lot. The four-door, silver luxury car made no effort to hide its intended destination. It drove straight up to the bank, stopping next to the rectangular concrete parking barriers which lay on the ground in front of the glass entrance doors.

"Aw, shit," Zoë said, looking at Arthur with large eyes that questioned his reassuring statements of minutes before. She jerked her head once toward the backseat where Simon, Maggie, and Lydia sat. "We may have to improvise."

They all turned their attention back outside in time to see the doors of the newly arrived car open up and two black-suited, young-looking men with dark hair exit. The driver opened one of the rear doors and reached inside, pulling another man out of the backseat. This man wore a pair of faded jeans and a wrinkled white t-shirt. He stumbled as he was yanked from the car, holding up his hands and nearly falling to the ground. The glasses perched on his nose were askew. They heard an unrecognizable yell as a third suited man, this one with blond hair, exited the backseat holding a small gun trained on the man in the jeans.

"He's not wearing any shoes," Simon said.

"What?" Zoë said.

"That guy, the one who looks like a hostage. He's not wearing shoes." Simon leaned forward in his seat, studied the man being marched from the car. "They must have snatched him right from his house in the middle of the night. I wonder who—"

"I'd say he's the bank manager," Lydia said, climbing up onto her knees in the backseat, her head craned around Arthur so she could view the scene in front of the bank.

It made sense, Simon thought. They knew the sniper had notified his employers, likely EXLI, about what he'd overheard at Maxwell's house. About the bank and the lockbox. Instead of coming straight to the bank as Simon and company had done, these men in the suits had first stopped off to kidnap the person who could get them into the bank and the vault.

Zoë pressed the radio on her shoulder again and said, "Russell. You see them? Get ready to move in one minute." She turned to the backseat. "Change of plans. The goons are obviously here and we need to act. Normally I'd tell you all to stay here with Arthur to look after you, but since we're short on manpower I need anyone who's willing. Except you, Lydia. You're staying here."

The protesting color rising in Lydia's face was visible even in the dimness of the vehicle. "Really, I must object! This is my—"

"We can't risk it, Lydia, so save your breath." Zoë held up a hand and shook her head. "You need to stay here until we've secured the bank. Simon?"

"Yes?" His attention was instantly drawn to Zoë. Her voice commanding.

"You're coming along with Arthur and me to the bank." She looked in Maggie's direction, her nose upturned. "You there, Persister, I—"

"Stop calling her that," Simon said, glaring at Zoë. Then, trying to mimic her take-charge demeanor, he said, "Maggie stays here." He turned to Maggie. "I can't risk you getting hurt."

"Simon," Maggie said, "I'm perfectly capable of—"

"I know you are, but I don't want you to go. Stay here, protect Lydia."

"*Excuse me*?" Lydia said. "Need I remind you all that I'm not a child, though I may look—"

"Enough!" Zoë almost shouted. "Yes, we're all capable of doing lots of things. Blah, blah, blah. Now's not the time to argue. Simon, you're coming with us. Maggie, Lydia, you two stay here. Keep a lookout for us. I'll leave you a radio." Zoë motioned behind the backseat to the storage area in the rear of the vehicle. "Hand me that bag and then suit up, Simon. Once they're inside, we make our move."

Simon reached behind the backseat where he found a large, black duffle bag and a few spare articles of clothing, including a lightweight bulletproof vest. He picked up the duffle, which was surprisingly heavy and gave a metallic rattle as he handed it forward to Zoë. When she opened it, Simon's suspicions were confirmed. Weapons. She pulled out two magazines, already loaded, and handed them to Arthur who was already giving the M4 rifle in his hands a quick inspection.

Turning his attention to the back again, Simon first put on the bulletproof vest over his shirt, helped by Maggie to ensure the straps were clipped properly and the vest fit snugly around his torso. Next, he pulled on a dark jacket similar to the ones worn by the other members of Zoë's group and clipped a spare two-way radio to one shoulder. When it was all on, Simon pulled a mask and goggles from the back as well, but did not put them on just yet. He knew that if he looked in the mirror, he'd bear a striking resemblance to any one of the Life Liberation members he'd seen that night. *Soldiers* was a more accurate term, he thought. Might as well call them what they were. Simon didn't particularly like the idea of joining their ranks, even if only temporarily, but he did feel safer suited up like one of them.

No sooner had he zipped his jacket than Zoë handed him a black, 9mm pistol, which she'd pulled from the duffle. "It's loaded. That, plus the revolver you're still carrying should be enough to cover you for now." Simon checked the safety on the gun, then tucked it into one of the large pockets of his new jacket. He reached behind himself and pulled Will's revolver from his waistband, holding it up.

But Simon didn't need to ask. Zoë was already handing him a small box of .45 shells. He took them and reloaded the revolver before tucking it into his other pocket.

He looked at Maggie, knowing his face showed something far from confidence, and more likely reflected the immense fear Simon saw on her face. But Maggie forced out a weak smile anyway and squeezed his hands.

"They're on the move," Arthur said.

Everyone in the SUV went silent again as they watched the four men in front of the bank, who'd reached the entrance doors. With the muzzle of a pistol dug into his back, the man without shoes fumbled with a ring of keys he'd pulled from his pocket. He flipped through the keyring for a moment or two before finding the one he wanted. He slipped it into the lock, twisted, and then pulled the unlocked door open.

Even from a distance, Simon saw the small flashing light jump to life on the wall just inside the door. The suited men pushed the shoeless manager toward it.

The man punched a code into the security system keypad and the flashing lights stopped. One of the dark-haired, suited men grabbed the bank manager by the arm and pulled him toward the back of the building. They were followed by the other two suited men and a few seconds later all four of them disappeared from view.

"Time to go," Zoë said into her radio, then added, "Remember: We are precise. We are calm. We are in control. Slow is smooth. Smooth is fast." Simon didn't fully understand everything she said, but thought it sounded appropriate; the kind of thing a swat team commander might say before a stealth operation. The LL soldiers in the other vehicle got the message because their acknowledgment came over the radio without question. Arthur too gave Zoë a confident nod. He'd obviously heard this mantra from her many times before.

She looked at Simon. "Ready?" He shrugged as if to say, "What choice do I have?" Zoë seemed to accept this as the best response she'd get and gave a nod. She reached toward her feet and from the car floor pulled up the mask and goggles she had been wearing earlier in the night, sliding them over her head. Arthur followed suit before he and Zoë opened their doors and slipped outside the vehicle with practiced ease. Simon took one last look at Maggie and Lydia, pulled on his mask and goggles, and opened his door.

As soon as he stepped outside, Simon's skin prickled from the chill on the air. He realized just how stuffy and warm the inside of their vehicle had become as the cool, nighttime air enveloped him, sneaking under his collar and up his shirtsleeves. But the chill felt good. It revitalized his drowsy senses of minutes before, helped balance the rush of adrenaline coursing through his body already. He took in large, deep breaths, louder now under his mask. But he felt calmer now. He could do this.

Zoë pulled her silver .45 from the holster on her hip and then motioned for Simon to arm himself. He pulled the gun she'd given him from his pocket, but kept it pointed at the ground, his finger off the trigger. She beckoned him forward to join her and Arthur.

They stalked through the shadows, weapons in hand, moving toward the entrance of the bank. As they made their way across the street, Simon spotted three figures in the distance dressed in dark clothes and masks similar to their own, creeping toward the bank from the other side. Both parties moved as silently as possible, methodical, hopping the low concrete barriers at the front of the bank's parking lot and meeting up near the large, glass entrance doors. They crouched; hoping to remain unseen should anyone inside look out.

Zoë signaled with her hands to the LL soldiers on the other side of the door. They responded with firm nods and similar hand motions.

"Simon," Zoë whispered. "Stay here with Arthur and keep a lookout. If anyone else shows up, do not hesitate to use that thing." She pointed to the gun in his hand. "Safety off." He nodded almost out of instinct, feeling his blood pumping, a thump in his chest. His quickened breath sounded even louder now under his mask. As he clicked the safety off on the pistol, Simon couldn't help but feel that, whether a threat came from inside the bank or some new arrival, he was far from ready for a gunfight.

Zoë turned back around and gave another hand motion to a bulky man on the other side of the entrance, who in turn nodded and sprang forward, grabbed the handle of one of the doors and pulled it open. As he did this, his fellow masked figures jumped to their feet and darted inside the bank, each with pistols drawn. One of a more average build, similar to that of Simon. The other was smaller in stature, but still looked solid, unhesitating. Zoë moved after them. The man who'd been holding the door followed, raising a black SAR similar to Arthur's as he went.

Simon watched all this happen in a matter of seconds, then turned to look at Arthur, who stood tall now, like a watchful statue, rifle pointed out over the parking lot. He must have noticed Simon's attention in his periphery, because he gave a simple reaffirming nod, and then returned to his surveillance of the surrounding area. Simon stayed crouched, felt his skin prickle again, this time with anticipation. His adrenaline surged as countless thoughts of what might soon happen inside the bank ran through his head. He looked back toward the SUV, but it was too far away to see the windows clearly. They'd been tinted anyway. He wondered what would come next and turned his gaze back toward the bank's entrance just in time to hear what did.

A series of shouts issued from inside the bank. There were several quick bursts of different sounding gunfire. Simon cowered down lower in front of the bank at the sound. He didn't know whether the shots he heard came from the guns of the suited men or the members of Life Liberation. He suspected both. More gunfire and yelling. The front door closest to Simon suddenly shattered, the bullet that pierced it zooming out into the night. Broken shards of glass scattered across the sidewalk, sparkling like diamonds as they fell to the ground. After that, the gunfire and shouts ceased.

There was a crackle from the radio on Arthur's right shoulder and the one affixed to the coat Simon wore. A voice issued from both.

"Clear!" It was Zoë, shouting. "James! Bring the truck closer. Prepare the med kit. Russell's been hit in the leg. We're bringing him out now."

The lights of the SUV parked down the street burst to life. The vehicle bolted from its spot, sped the short stretch down the road, and turned into the bank's parking lot. The vehicle screeched to a stop next to the silver luxury car. The driver, James, jumped out, suited up like the rest of the LL soldiers, though he wore no mask or goggle over his buzzed head. James darted to the back of the vehicle, popped open the rear doors. He pulled out a small gray case—the medical kit. He began pulling bandages, various small medical equipment, and tiny bottles from it, laying them out in the back of the vehicle.

"Should we go in and help them?" Simon said, turning to Arthur.

Arthur shook his head, keeping his stare and rifle pointed toward the street. "Zoë's orders were to stay here, so that's exactly what we're going to do," he said, his voice a deep, confident rumble.

"But it sounds like—"

Simon's words were cut short as, to his side, he saw two masked Life Liberation soldiers helping a third exit through what remained of the shattered front door. The two unharmed soldiers supported the third man who hopped on one leg—Russell. Simon couldn't see Russell's face, but could tell by the way he jerked his head at every step that he was in a great deal of pain. As soon as the trio was clear of the door, they started making their way to the SUV that had just been pulled close.

Zoë burst out of the bank next. She spent a brief moment to watch her two soldiers helping the injured Russell, then turned to Simon and Arthur.

"We need Lydia's key!" she demanded.

"We—" Simon began, his mind suddenly blank for a moment before realizing what was going on. "I don't—she's still got it in the car."

"I know!" Zoë said, her voice raised and drenched in frustration. "The damn manager hit the silent alarm. At least Phillips knocked the guy out cold for his troubles. But we only have a few minutes before the cops show up. We need that key now!"

Simon didn't need to be told again. He was up and sprinting toward their vehicle before he knew what was happening. When he reached the SUV, he yanked open the back door of the driver's side, and found Maggie and Lydia crouched together in the backseat.

"I need the key!" Simon yelled into the car, his voice muffled from the mask he'd almost forgotten he was still wearing.

Lydia flinched back against Maggie. Even though she knew the figure in front of her was friendly, Simon's sudden, masked presence and shout had startled Lydia.

"What?" she said a second later.

"The key! To the lockbox! Give it to me."

"I'm not giving you anything," Lydia responded, much to the confusion of everyone listening. The momentary shock in Lydia was gone. She sat forward, raised her chin, and stared directly into Simon's goggles. "If we now have access to the vault, I want to go in and get the lockbox myself."

"We don't have time for this!" Simon panted, his voice louder and more forceful. "Zoë says the alarm's been triggered. The police are on their way, so give me the key!"

"No."

Simon shook his head, not in disallowance, but frustration. He knew he couldn't win the argument. Nor did he have the time to try. He motioned Lydia forward, reaching to grab her hand and help the small woman out of the vehicle.

"Do you want me to go, too?" Maggie said.

"No," Simon said. This was something on which he would not budge. "Stay here. Stay safe. We'll be back as fast as we can and then we're all out of here."

Simon shut the door and, a moment later, was on his way back toward the bank with Lydia in tow. He wished they could move faster, but Lydia, being who she was, could only sprint as fast as her short legs would carry her. He kept motioning for Lydia to move faster, and she did the best she could until they reached the bank. Hayes and Phillips, the masked figures who had carried Russell to the other SUV, had returned and now flanked the entrance. Zoë stood to one side. She held out one hand in question and shook her head. Were she not wearing a mask, Simon was sure her face would be showing utter incredulity.

"What the hell is *she* doing here?" Zoë seethed, pointing at Lydia. "You were supposed to get the key!"

"She wouldn't hand it over," Simon said, "I *improvised*. She's here, so let's just get the lockbox and get the hell out of here."

Zoë growled with disapproval, but knew she could do nothing about Lydia's presence now. She led her into the bank. Simon followed without thinking, leaving Arthur, Hayes, and Phillips outside.

Upon entering the bank Simon took in the carnage of the battle that had occurred there. The floor near the entrance was strewn with fragments of glass from the shattered front door. Bullet holes peppered the walls and counters of the bank. Service brochures, deposit slips, and other papers of various kinds littered the floor as well. Near the back, in the direction Zoë and Lydia headed, Simon spotted four figures splayed out on the floor. The three suited men all had dark bullet holes visible at various points on their bodies. Each lay in a pool of slowly spreading blood. The fourth figure was that of the bank manager. Zoë had been right. The man was still breathing judging from the motion of his chest, but Simon noticed a large welt forming on his head where he had been knocked out by the soldier Phillips.

Simon stood frozen amongst the ruin of the bank. He gripped his unused pistol in his hand. Zoë and Lydia disappeared inside the large vault behind the teller counter. Simon waited. He heard bits of speech coming from the vault, but saw no movement. Moments later, he thought he heard a faint whine coming from outside. Simon turned his attention toward the front doors where he spied Arthur and the other soldiers holding their positions near the entrance, still as gargoyles. He stepped closer to the doors, holding his breath, trying to hear more.

"What is that?" Simon whispered to himself, tilting his head as if trying to listen more closely to a nonexistent speaker on the wall. Before he could make out the sound clearly or saw the car racing down Bormello Avenue, Simon heard Arthur's voice answer his question, shouting into the bank.

"Police!"

"Police!" Simon repeated as he whipped around, shouting toward the vault. "Zoë! Lydia! We need to go. Now! Police are coming!" He watched the back of the bank, the entrance to the vault, but saw no movement. What could be taking them so long? Simon was just about to investigate when Arthur lumbered by, passing Simon and running into the vault. A moment later, he exited with Zoë and Lydia in tow. Lydia carried a long, rectangular metal container that looked quite heavy supported by her child's arms—Maxwell's lockbox.

The group of four reached the entrance of the bank just in time to see flashing red and blue lights streak down the street outside and turn sharply into the parking lot.

"Shit," Simon said.

The police car's tires squealed as it swerved around the parked SUV and silver car, stopping as close as it could get to the now crowded entrance.

Hayes and Phillips, who had remained at the entrance, turned and ran quickly inside, joining Simon's group. Both sides of the police cruiser opened up and two uniformed officers got out with service pistols drawn, using the doors for cover. At the same time, Russell and James climbed into the back of the SUV parked outside, pulling the doors closed. As they did, the officers each fired two shots in their direction. Simon couldn't be absolutely sure, but the last thing he thought he saw as the doors of the SUV closed was a man inside jerking back—as if he'd been hit. Even if he had been, the doors closed securely after him.

The two officers stood rigid behind their car doors. They were shouting toward the bank, demanding that those inside come out with their hands up.

"We need to do something!" Simon said, turning to Zoë and Arthur.

"Is there a back door to this place?" Arthur said.

"Negative," Zoë said. "We'll need to make a break for it out the front."

"No way," Simon said, shaking his head. "The cops'll start firing on us. We'll never make it."

"I agree," Arthur said.

"James and Russell?" Zoë asked. "Think they can swing the truck around close enough for us to hop in if the cops start shooting?"

"No dice. I saw James hit as he was trying to close the back doors. And I'm not sure about Russell, could still be in too much pain. Got no response on the radio."

"Shit. I guess that leaves us with one choice. Arthur, Phillips, Hayes—you cover Lydia, Simon, and me. We'll run for it around the bank and see if we can make it across the street, back to our vehicle. If we can, we should be able to provide suppressing fire to get the rest of you out of here."

"You're not talking about shooting them, are you? The police officers?" Arthur objected. "That's not how we do things."

"I know that, and trust me, we're just going for cover fire. But if push comes to shove . . . I don't like it either, but we need to be ready to do what we have to. I expect more cops to show up any second. We need to act now." A moment passed in silence, broken by another shout from one of the police officers outside. Zoë looked at the group and said, "Everyone ready?" They all nodded. "Good. Let's go!"

Arthur, Hayes, and Phillips stepped out of the front door of the bank, guns raised, and began firing in the vicinity of the police. The officers quickly ducked behind their car doors.

Zoë motioned for Simon and Lydia to follow her as she exited the bank, slipping behind their cover. They jogged along the front of the building, headed for the corner. Lydia, who refused to give up the lockbox to anyone else, struggled with its weight.

Despite the cover fire, one of the police officers chanced a look around his door and began to return fire. Soon after, the other officer did the same. A bullet found the left leg of Hayes, bending her knee awkwardly and sending her crumbling to the ground.

Simon was about to turn back at the sound of the return fire when he saw Zoë suddenly jerk to the side, spin, and collapse. In the shadows around them, he could see her moving from side to side on the ground. She was hit, but still moving at least, Simon thought. That was the good news. The bad news was that Zoë's fall had stopped their progress. He and Lydia were at a standstill.

The police officers spun around behind their car doors to reload. Arthur opened up again, sending measured blasts from his M4 rifle into the hood of the police car while Phillips pelted the surrounding area with his pistol. A moment later, they stopped, in need of a reload themselves.

That was when the police made their move. Both officers rose to their feet, one with his gun pointed toward the two standing men at the entrance of the bank and the other with his gun on Simon's fleeing group.

"Stop right now!" one of the police officers yelled. "Place your weapons on the ground! All of you! And put that box on the ground as well little girl!"

Everyone froze, except for Zoë who still rolled from side to side on the ground, clutching at her chest, gasping for breath. Even Arthur stopped; afraid his movement would cause the officers to open fire once more on him and Phillips, or all of them.

"Do it now! Drop the guns! Drop the box and step away!"

With guns pointed directly at them, caught in a stunned state, they were stuck. Arthur and Phillips hesitated, then tossed their weapons onto the ground ahead of them. Hayes gave a loud grunt of pain from the ground as she pushed her weapon away. Simon dropped his pistol as well and stepped to the side.

"Now you, sweetheart," the officer said. "Drop that and step away."

At first, Simon didn't realize to whom the police officer was talking, but then it clicked. Lydia. The officers obviously hadn't recognized who she was in the shadows around the bank. All they saw was a young girl. Perhaps they figured her a hostage.

"Set that box on the ground, sweetheart, and walk toward us. We'll protect you. Just do what we say and you'll be all right."

Simon knew that in any other situation, Lydia would probably be furious with any person thinking of and speaking to her as a child. However, Lydia kept her cool this time and slowly stepped forward with the box still clutched in her hands.

"Set the box on the ground first. Do you hear me, little girl?"

"Oh, I hear you, gentlemen," Lydia said, her voice surprisingly calm given the situation. "But there's no way in hell I'm going to set this box down. It belongs to me and unless you have the proper warrant you may not part me from my property or search it without my say so."

A strange, confused expression ran across both officers' faces. They stared, considered her as she took a few more steps toward them, as if challenging their authority.

"Okay," the officer said. "I'm not sure exactly what's going on here or who you are, but I want you to—"

There was the rumble of an engine and the squealing of tires. Simon looked out toward Bormello Avenue and saw a dark, four-door car speed into the bank's parking lot, adding to the collection of vehicles that had been growing there ever since the arrival of the silver car.

The dark four-door screeched to a halt behind the police cruiser. Its doors flew open. Four figures exited, dressed in all black. Simon's memory flashed back to his house, the lone sniper who'd appeared out of the shadows of his dining room. But now there were four of them, and they each wore bulletproof vests, 9mm pistols pointed in their hands.

The sound of the car's arrival and opening doors spun the police officers around. In an instant, both officers were down, shot by the new arrivals. With the police officers out of the way, the new set of gunmen turned their attention to Lydia, Simon, and the Life Liberation soldiers, opening fire on them all.

Lydia fell to the ground at once. Simon thought at first that she'd been hit by one of the flying bullets. But she had fallen of her own accord, doing the only thing she could do in hopes of avoiding the gunfire. She was out in the open, with nothing to crawl behind. Lydia dived to the ground, curling around the lockbox she'd been carrying. All she could do then was *hope* not to get hit.

Hayes crawled forward, arms outstretched, attempting to go for the gun she'd thrown to the ground moments before. But the next instant, the top portion of her mask splintered, caved in, and she crumpled to the ground, struck in the head by a bullet from the newcomers' guns. Arthur started sprinting toward Zoë, narrowly escaping the gunfire spraying around him. Phillips turned to find cover back inside the bank, but in doing so, took two shots to the back, knocked to the floor just inside the doors.

Simon couldn't believe what he was seeing, frozen in place. Had it not been for Arthur tackling him to the ground, he would have surely been shot himself. Simon's mind reeled as he crawled behind one of the concrete parking barriers, thankful it was just large enough to provide adequate cover. More gunshots sent fragments of the gray concrete flying into the air. In a few short moments it seemed they had been decimated, brought to their knees with a barrage of gunfire. Simon kept his head down. He couldn't see anything but the sidewalk. He didn't know whether

Lydia was alive or dead. The only person that seemed to have been unaffected by the new flurry of bullets was Zoë, who was still writhing on the ground. Arthur scrambled over to cover and protect her. Simon knew he had to do something or they'd never get out of there.

"Come on!" Simon yelled, finally lifting his head toward Arthur. "We can't stay here. They'll kill us!"

They were about to make a dash for it, back inside the bank, when—

"Wait, Arthur." The voice issued from the radio on Simon's shoulder. Arthur tilted his head toward the radio on his shoulder, listening closely, then reached up to press the talk button.

"Russell?" Arthur said. "Where are you?"

"I'm in the truck in front of the bank."

"You okay?"

"Better than James. He . . . he took one square in the throat. He's gone."

"Russell, we need to get out of here."

"I know. That's why I told you to wait. I was able to crawl myself into the driver's seat over here. In a couple seconds, those guys will be in close range. When I go, you go. Get out of here. Got it?"

"Got it."

Arthur placed his hands on the ground, preparing to spring up when the time was right. Simon chanced a glance over the concrete barrier and saw their attackers walking toward Lydia's crumpled form.

There was a flash of red and then white light as the SUV was thrown into reverse. Its engine roared as it rocketed backward. It struck two of the gunmen before they had a chance to jump out of the way. One man was pulled right under, the truck's bumper slamming into his pelvis and thrusting the top half of his body to the ground. His head whipped to the pavement with a loud, sickening crunch and he disappeared under the truck. The second man was able to make a slight move away, but it was not enough. He too was hit by the bumper, knocked to the ground. The truck's back tire climbed up onto his chest, the weight of the back half of the SUV crushing his torso. If that hadn't finished him off, the front tire did.

The two other gunmen in black were luckier. They dived to the side and avoided the SUV altogether. As it barreled past, one of the men turned on the ground and opened fire, sending 9mm shots through the driver's side window. A moment later, the truck turned haphazardly, out of control and smashed into the police cruiser, where it stopped.

Two men down, two left. Simon knew they had only seconds before their attackers would return to their feet and open fire once more. He saw movement ahead and looked up to see Arthur on his feet, pulling a struggling Zoë to hers. But they wouldn't have enough time. Even if they could get Zoë moving, she wouldn't be able to run fast enough in her condition to get away. The gunmen would catch up. So Simon did the only thing he figured he could do. He reached into his other pocket, which still held Will's revolver, pulled it out, and started firing in the direction of their attackers. The shots blasted from the gun, one after another. Cock the hammer. Pull the trigger. Crack! Repeat. Any doubts Simon once had about the gun's ability to fire after being soaked in his friend's blood quickly faded. As he fired, the blast of each shot brought Simon back to that night a few days earlier. He saw Will's face swim in front of his contracted vision, saw his friend firing from the passenger seat of the detective's car as they fled the assassin. Will had been shot himself, but had continued to fight for his friends. Even after they had escaped, Will had led them out of the city, knowing with each mile they drove he had less and less of a chance of surviving. He had accepted his death. He had expected it to happen. That was what Simon felt at that moment as he emptied the revolver in the direction of the remaining gunmen. One of them fell to the ground, struck in the back, but still able to scramble for cover along with his partner. But Simon continued firing so that his friends could find shelter and get away. He continued firing, knowing his death was imminent. He expected it to happen. Accepted it.

What he didn't expect to happen, however, was to hear yet another roaring engine. As the last shot from the revolver was spent, the tremble of the gun subsided. Simon stood frozen, watching the men in black peek out from behind the doors of the police cruiser. The blast of the revolver was gone, replaced by that rumble of another vehicle breaking through the ringing in Simon's ears, approaching behind him. Simon turned just in time to see the SUV they had arrived in streak across the street and bounce up over the curb, heading straight for where Zoë and Arthur stood. The truck climbed up the short length of grass between the curb and the edge of the bank's parking lot, rocking back and forth as it hopped back onto the pavement. It screeched to a halt in front of Zoë and Arthur, providing a barrier between them and the gunmen. And through the windshield, at this close range, Simon could just make out Maggie's face wracked with concentration, her hands clenched to the steering wheel.

Arthur turned toward Simon and yelled, "Let's go!" Simon wasted no time. He took off, tucking the empty revolver back into his pocket as he sprinted for the truck.

Maggie climbed from behind the steering wheel to help Arthur, who was struggling to hold his leader back. Zoë, her left arm and side smeared red with blood, had regained her feet and breath. She ripped her mask and goggles from her head, screaming "S-stop! Let go . . . of me . . . damn it! Lydia! No!" Her arms flailed as she tried to break free from Arthur, who grabbed at Zoë's arms repeatedly, trying to pull her back toward the SUV.

As Simon approached, more gunfire split the air. He heard

something crack close by, turned and saw bullets pelting the opposite side of SUV. The passenger side window shattered just as he reached the vehicle and attempted to help Maggie and Arthur wrangle Zoë. She seemed to be weakening from blood loss, exhaustion, or a combination of both, and they were finally able to push her into the backseat. Simon and Maggie climbed in after her as Arthur provided new cover fire with an automatic pistol he'd pulled from the driver's side door.

Zoë clutched at her arm and chest, breathing in jagged gulps of air. She was bleeding badly, but up close Simon saw that the blood came from a wound in her arm, not her chest, as he'd feared. Though based on the holes in her jacket, she was lucky she'd been wearing a bulletproof vest underneath. She tried to sit up, but slid down in the seat, her head lolling from side to side, dazed.

"Arth . . . no no . . . need to . . ." Zoë panted out, each syllable sounding like it required great effort.

"Come on, Arthur!" Simon yelled from the backseat, ripping off his mask and goggles. "We're in. Let's go!"

Arthur stood poised near the open driver's side door, gun pointed toward the men in black. His stare remained forward at the call of his name. He dared not take his eyes off the enemy.

"Wait!" It was Zoë yelling, finally able to form complete words. She slid up in her seat, gasping for breath still. "Lydia!"

"She's gone," Arthur said. His usual booming voice suddenly flat, definite.

"But you don't know that! She could still be okay. We have to—"

"No." Arthur finally turned to address the group in the backseat. He removed his mask and goggles, and ducked his head into the SUV, pointing out the windshield. "She's not dead. She's *gone*. They've taken her."

"What?" Simon said, suddenly noticing that all gunfire had

ceased, replaced by the whine of police sirens in the distance. He looked out the window toward the men in black and saw they were retreating. Each man was backing away as quickly as possible, holding their guns out in front of them. One also held the lockbox. The other had Lydia's small body slung over his shoulder. It wasn't clear whether or not Lydia had been wounded in the crossfire, but her flailing arms and legs told them any injuries she may have sustained had not been fatal. Not yet anyway. A moment later, the men tossed the box and Lydia into the back of their car and then climbed into the front seats.

"We can't let them take her!" Zoë said. She leaned forward, attempting to climb over the center console, to get outside. Arthur placed a hand on her shoulder to stop the effort.

"We have no choice," he said. "By the time we all got to the truck they'd already reached Darrow."

"But we're going after her, right?" Maggie said.

"*We* are getting out of here. Zoë's hurt bad and needs a doctor. We all need to get to the safe house. Now sit back and hold on."

Arthur climbed into the driver's seat, slammed his door, and threw the SUV into reverse. He hit the gas and the vehicle bounded backward, up over the curb.

"Arthur, no!" Zoë yelled. "We have to go back! We have to get Lydia! That's an order! We can't let them take her! Not Lydia!"

"Sorry, boss. No can do," Arthur said as he backed them up, the truck bouncing violently until they reached the street between the bank and the car dealership. "More police are on their way. We need to go. Phillips is going to follow the men who took Darrow and report back to us."

"Phillips?" Simon said.

"He's in the bank. Came to when you were firing off that revolver. He radioed in, said he'd stay behind to track them."

"But I didn't—" Simon said, looking down at the radio that

had been attached to his coat, but saw only shards of it left—pierced by a bullet. He'd been *that* close.

Simon looked behind them, saw the car that held the remaining two gunmen, the lockbox, and Lydia Darrow speeding out of the parking lot and down Bormello Avenue. He then spotted Phillips, the last remaining Life Liberation soldier, exiting the bank, heading toward the other SUV.

Arthur shoved their vehicle into drive and they sped off down a side street.

"What about your other men?" Simon said.

Arthur looked into the rearview mirror. Simon didn't know whether he was trying to look at him, or catch the eye of Zoë who had finally started to gain control over her breath, but whose gaze had fallen to the floor as she struggled with pain in her arm and body.

"James and Russell are already in the truck. Philips will grab Hayes on his way out."

"Do you think . . . are they all . . . ?" But Simon couldn't finish the question.

"If they're still alive, Phillips will provide any help he can," Arthur said, maneuvering the SUV onto another street, its tires squawking. "We can't—no sense in worrying about it now."

Simon sat back, pulling Maggie close. She hugged him tightly.

"Where are we going?" Simon asked.

"To a safe house," Arthur said.

"Yeah, but where—"

"You'll find out when we get there," Zoë said, her commanding voice suddenly back, if only for a moment. She had lifted her eyes, which swam with pain, her beleaguered face a mess of tears, perspiration, and smears of blood. Zoë sat up tall in her seat, stretching her midsection with a grimace, pressing a hand against her bleeding arm. Her gaze shifted to the front seat, but Arthur's eyes stayed on the road. She looked back at Simon and Maggie. "We should have gone straight fuckin' there to begin with instead of coming out here. Lot of good it did. Dead people and a kidnapped woman; that's what we ended up with. We didn't even get the one thing we came out here for in the first place. The whole situation was cocked up from the start!"

As he saw the anger and disappointment on Zoë's face, Simon knew she was right. They'd come to the bank to head off EXLI, to prevent them from getting the information Maxwell had stored in the bank. Not only had they failed to obtain the lockbox with the information, but several LL soldiers had died in the process. And they'd lost Lydia, the most important of them all, the leader of the fight against EXLI. Gone. Simon's face dropped with exhaustion, with defeat. He remembered how, earlier, as they departed Lydia's apartment for Maxwell's house he'd thought they were headed toward some kind of conclusion. The culmination of everything they'd been through over the last few days. But now, they were on the run again. They had failed, and the end seemed farther away than it ever had.

23

ARTHUR TURNED THEIR VEHICLE ONTO THE MAIN THROUGHWAY OF Wakefield and they joined the small, but steadily growing stream of early morning traffic. Soon after, they heard more sirens in the distance and saw the traffic ahead start to part for the flashing lights headed their way. Arthur maneuvered the SUV toward the curb, making sure he was on the outside lane, boxed in and obscured by cars on all sides when the police cruisers zoomed past. There were five police cars in all and everyone watched in the rearview mirror as the flashing lights turned down Bormello Avenue and disappeared. The traffic ahead and all around them resumed, and they joined the flow of cars with everyone else.

Despite trying to keep a low profile amongst the other cars, Simon understood why Arthur was now pushing the speed limit a little more than he normally would when trying to be discreet. Though it was still quite dark out, the sun would be rising soon, hampering their ability to blend in with the other cars. The first police officers who had arrived back at the bank were sure to have called in the situation, including the vehicle description of the black SUV. If that weren't enough, the morning light would make the shattered windows and other battle scars of their vehicle easier to see. Whether another police cruiser headed toward the bank spotted them or a concerned citizen who happened to see a truck peppered with bullet holes headed the opposite direction, they were sure to stand out amongst the other cars that *hadn't* just been in a shootout.

In the backseat, Simon and Maggie helped Zoë remove her jacket and the tight bulletproof vest that had undoubtedly saved her life. Once she had, Zoë took several great breaths in a row, the deepness of each apparent from the rising and falling of her chest against the black tank top she wore.

She mumbled a halfhearted thanks before sitting up tall again, continuing to take more deep breaths. Zoë then lifted her bare left arm so they could all see the wound in the upper bicep near her shoulder. She grabbed one sleeve of her jacket and began to wipe away the blood smeared across her shoulder and arm. Despite this effort, the wound continued to bleed. "Arthur? Did we restock the truck's med kit?"

"Ah, shit," Arthur said. "No. Supplies were low so the other truck got the only kit we had left. Sorry."

Zoë grumbled. "We'll just have to do this the old fashioned way." She handed her jacket to Simon. "Here. Cut off that sleeve."

"With what?" he said.

Arthur's hand appeared over his shoulder. There was a folded tactical knife in his palm. Simon grabbed it.

Over the next few minutes, Zoë instructed Simon on how to cut up her jacket and use the material as a makeshift bandage for her wound. He followed her instructions as best he could, though she yelled at him more than once. He would have liked to chalk her outbursts up to the blood loss, but he knew better. When finished, Zoë examined the jacket-bandage, tugged on it with her good arm, and then looked directly at Simon.

"Looks good, soldier," she said, much to the surprise of Simon.

"Will you be all right?" Maggie asked.

Zoë sat back against the seat. A normal person, upon being shot and then bandaged up, might have let out a sigh of relief, relaxed in their seat, and said thanks. But Zoë showed no signs of slowing down or relief, giving Maggie a narrow-eyed glance.

"I'll live. Once we get back to the safe house I'll have our doc take a look—get the bullet out of me, clean it up. Give me some of those good pain meds." At this thought, the smallest of smiles flashed on Zoë's face, though it faded quickly as she stared at the road ahead, wheels always spinning in her mind.

Simon sat back in his seat. He turned his attention to Maggie, gave her a nervous shrug before something caught Simon's eye out the window. At first he saw only the buildings and cars they passed, all of which appeared rosy in color as the sun began to show itself on the horizon. Then he realized—

"We're not headed back the same way we came last night— the direction we were headed when you were first taking us to the safe house. Where are we going?"

"It's another safe house," Zoë said. "You didn't think we only had one, did you?"

"I didn't know."

"We can't head back into the heart of the city. Cops'll be everywhere now." Zoë rolled her eyes at Simon. "So we're headed to a place we have on this side of town. Somewhere we can resupply, sort out next steps before we head out again. Hopefully we can get there before it is full-on daytime. What's our ETA?"

"About 15 minutes," Arthur said without even looking back at them or in the rearview mirror.

A short time later, they broke the Wakefield Township limits and the road they traveled on reduced to a single lane. Fewer and fewer cars littered the road, and those that did were headed back into town, not out of it as they were. The surrounding businesses of minutes before were gone, replaced by housing subdivisions and then industrial parks.

Arthur turned down a side street. Large, square buildings billowing steam and pollution into the air surrounded the road on both sides, separated by tall wire fences. Large boom trucks, cranes, and flatbed semis were stationed or driven between the buildings while men wearing hardhats and tool belts worked at various spots on the ground. As they drove on, one side of the street turned into a collection of trailer lots and tall warehouses. Arthur pointed ahead, but it took Simon a moment to find what he was pointing at—a smaller building on the corner of their current street and a gravel crossroad. Though he'd almost missed it, seeing it now Simon thought it looked out of place between the surrounding structures. He could tell, even from a distance, that the place had probably not been used for its original purpose in many years.

It was a church. Standing above the trailers behind it and about half as high as the warehouses to its side, the church was in a state of immense disrepair. Whatever its original color had been, Simon couldn't tell for the building now showed only the sickly yellow and gray color of decomposition. Many of the stained glass windows that had once adorned the oval frames around the church were now boarded up. There were a few windows left; the images once depicted in the colored glass had long since faded, now covered in a thick layer of dust and grime.

The corners of Simon's mouth twitched at the sight of the building. Thinking of how, despite the unconscious avoidance of churches he'd experienced in his everyday life for years, this would be the second one he and Maggie had visited in just the last couple days.

Arthur pulled the SUV into the driveway of the church and

around the back out of clear view of the street. There were three other cars parked in the back—another black SUV similar to the one in which they rode, a dark blue sedan, and a large box van. Arthur parked next to the van.

"All right," he said. "Let's get you inside and looked at. Can you two help her out?"

"I'm fine, Arthur," Zoë said. "I hurt my arm, not my legs." They exited the car and started to make their way to the back door. Zoë turned to Simon and Maggie. "Don't go wandering off, you two. Out here, or inside."

Simon looked up at the church and saw that as they walked closer, its condition did not appear to improve. He caught a whiff of something pungent—a mix of the oily smell of their industrial surroundings and a musty odor of decay coming off the church. Its color looked even worse up close, black spots of rot added to the yellow and gray he had noticed from a distance.

They made their way up a small flight of rickety steps that led to a door at the back. Arthur knocked. Simon heard a voice say something from the other side, but could not make out what it was. Arthur didn't wait for the voice to finish. He pounded on the door.

"Open up damn it!" he said. "Zoë needs Ben!"

The door swung open and Arthur stepped inside. Zoë, Maggie, and Simon entered as well, following Arthur into a small, dim room on the other side. The room was nearly empty, but for a few boxes and a single metal cabinet in one corner. There was also a door set in the center of each wall.

When they were all inside, a short, round man dressed in a pair of dark pants, boots, and a white t-shirt stained with sweat closed the door. He turned to look at them all with a timid grin and beady eyes. Arthur had already disappeared through a doorway on the other side of the room. A moment later, he returned with a skinny man dressed in faded jeans and a collared shirt.

"What have you gotten yourself into this time, Zoë?" the skinny man said.

"Oh, you know me, doc," she said, stepping forward.

"I do. You playing with explosives again?"

Zoë shook her head. "Bullets."

"Let me take a look."

The doctor pulled back the jacket-wrap Simon had tied around Zoë's arm. Beneath the shredded, blood-soaked jacket, he examined the bullet wound in Zoë's shoulder. A moment later, he let go and looked up at her.

"Well, it could have been worse," he said. "Doesn't appear to have hit any arteries. We'll definitely need to get that bullet out and patch you up right."

"Then let's get to it."

"Is there anyone else I need to take a look at?" The doctor scanned the room, his eyes pausing on the unfamiliar faces of Simon and Maggie.

"Afraid I'm the only lucky one," Zoë said with a grimace. She saw the doctor's stare and added, "Simon, Maggie, this is Doc Doss."

He nodded in their direction and said, "Call me Ben. Never did like the way *Doctor Doss* rolls off the tongue." He gave a weak grin. "Zoë, follow me." He turned to face the short man in the sweat-stained shirt. "Peter, can you please take the others to—"

"Nope," Zoë interjected. "They go where I go."

Ben opened his mouth to say something else, saw the stony look on Zoë's pale face, and stopped himself. He nodded and waved them all along as he opened one of the doors.

Arthur gave Simon a confident nod. Simon grabbed Maggie's hand and they followed.

They entered a long hallway almost as dim as the previous room except for the yellow glow emanating from aged fixtures set in the ceiling. Framed pictures hung every few feet on the walls with images of what Simon figured were various moments in religious history, though he had no knowledge of what they were. A few of the actual frames and pictures were missing, leaving behind rectangular patterns of discoloration on the wall. Doors interspersed the pictures and discolored spots every so often, all closed.

Ben stopped at one of the doors. The doorknob gave a slight crunching sound as he twisted it and the door swung inward. When he took his hand away, his fingers and palm were reddened slightly with rust. He wiped his dirtied hand on the leg of his pants and stepped through the door. The rest of their group followed.

While the entrance room and hallway they'd previously been in had seemed small, cramped, and dusty from non-use, the space they stepped into now was almost the exact opposite. It was a large, sprawling room. Decorative fixtures hung at various points around the vaulted ceilings, bathing everything inside with warm, orange light. Though Simon had limited experiences in churches, he knew this place to be the main place of worship. Most of the space was taken up by the nave, the large seating area filled with row after row of long, wooden pews, some of which had rotted clear to the floor while others still stood, rickety though they looked. The sanctuary in front of the pews sat on a rectangular dais a single step above the floor, complete with a bare altar and presider's chair set off to one side. Long scratches across the floor showed that the small, ornate credence table had been dragged from the other side of the sanctuary to be placed next to the chair. Atop this table sat a black bag, a small cardboard box, and a collection of various sized bottles of clear liquid.

"Over here," Ben said, leading Zoë onto the dais. He pointed at the large chair; the once crimson cushions of its seat and back had long since faded to a dusty brown color. "Sit back so I can get at that injured arm."

Before she sat, Zoë turned, pointed a finger at Simon and Maggie. "You two, take a seat. This shouldn't take long." She looked to Arthur. "And you, get on the horn with Phillips. I want to know where they've taken Lydia."

"I just tried the radio again," Arthur said. "Nothing. I think he's gone dark while—"

"I don't care!" Zoë shouted. "Find him so we can find Lydia!" She said no more, turning on the spot and sitting down in the ancient chair. As she sat back, a puff of dust billowed up into the air from the cushions.

Ben grabbed one of the bottles off the table. He dug into the box, pulling bandages, syringes, forceps, and other various medical items from it, laying them out side by side on a towel he'd spread out on the table, before setting to work on Zoë's arm.

Simon and Maggie made their way down the aisle of the nave, stopping when they found a pew that looked sturdy enough to support them. They paid no mind to the hard wood of the pew, only relished the feeling of finally being able to sit down, to relax in a stationary location, if only for a minute or two. Now that he was off his feet, Simon's legs ached; he felt a dull pain at the center of his back and his knees.

He saw the same mix of exhaustion and relief on Maggie's face. It was the first time since they had left Lydia's apartment the night before that Simon had had the chance to take a good, long look at Maggie in a well-lit environment. She looked exactly how he felt—exhausted. There were dark spots under both her youthful eyes and smudges of dirt and sweat across her face. Her hair was disheveled, but in his eyes, still framed her face beautifully.

Simon could only imagine how he looked to Maggie. They

had both been through the same ordeal, but while Maggie had the aesthetic advantages of Rejuvenation on her side, Simon was confident that his naturalness wasn't helping his tired appearance.

Zoë mumbled something near the front of the church, turning Maggie and Simon's attention back to her for a moment. Ben retorted, telling her to sit still.

Simon's gaze drifted away from them again as the minutes passed by, studying the church with a closer eye. Spotted here and there were the stained glass windows and boarded up empty frames Simon had seen from outside. He saw a few other doors at the sides of the room leading off to unknown areas of the church. To the left, a small room could be seen through a space in the wall that had once held a large window, long since taken out or shattered. Two cabinets hung on the walls near the altar; their doors covered in enough dust to almost hide the golden, swirling designs etched into the glass. And there, about halfway up on the wall of the apse behind the altar, was the faded imprint of a large cross. The cross itself was gone; whether it had been taken down with careful hands or simply fell through the natural course of time, Simon did not know. Despite its absence, the shape of the cross remained, showing on the wall in an eggshell white that stood out when compared to the yellowish walls surrounding it.

There was a mumble behind them. Simon craned his neck around to see Arthur standing near the doors at the back of the church, speaking into the radio on his shoulder. Simon waved at him. Arthur put up a hand at first as he continued to talk into the radio. A few seconds later, he released the button on the side of the radio and walked over.

"We can make space if you want," Maggie said, patting the empty section of the pew at her side.

"Thanks, but I'm good," Arthur said. He motioned to the radio and then added in a lower voice that wouldn't carry over to Zoë, "No time to rest."

"Still nothing?" Simon asked.

Arthur shook his head, ran a hand over it. His brow furrowed with concern. "I'd like to know where our man is, but to be honest, I'm glad for whatever downtime we can get right now. Zoë needs it."

Simon and Maggie nodded. As worried as they both were for Lydia's safety, wherever she may be, part of them was still glad to have at least this minimal respite.

"So, is this your headquarters or something?" Simon said, swirling his hand in the air to indicate the entire building around them.

Again, Arthur shook his head.

"Life Liberation doesn't really have a traditional headquarters. We operate wherever we can. Station people where we need. Whatever we have to do. This is just one place we've claimed."

"And, Peter?" Simon said, referring to the squat man in the stained t-shirt that had opened the door for them.

"He's a . . . caretaker, of sorts. Watches over this place, makes sure it's ready, still secure. There's no telling how long we'll be able to use a particular safe house. When it's compromised, we move on. Peter'll transfer away, watch over the next place."

"I see."

Arthur's radio crackled to life. There was no voice, just a few short bursts of something that sounded like grunting, rasping breaths as if someone had just run a series of sprints. Arthur grabbed the radio, pressed the button on its side. "Phillips? You there? Repeat your transmission. Over." He paused and they all listened.

Nothing.

"Phillips?"

Still nothing.

"Was that him?" Zoë's shout echoed across the room,

followed by a grunting reaction to whatever the doctor was doing. "Arthur! What—"

"It's nothing, Zoë," he said, tilting his head toward her. "Just static."

"I want an update as soon as you hear anything!"

"Aye, aye," Arthur said, moving his gaze back to Simon and Maggie.

"Do your men usually take this long to respond?" Maggie asked.

Arthur shook his head.

"You think they noticed him," Simon said.

"We don't know anything yet," Arthur said, "but our men are highly skilled. We know how to follow people without being seen."

"He better not be dead!" Zoë shouted from the sanctuary. Her loud voice bounced off the walls of the empty church.

Arthur didn't bother to look back at her this time.

"Do you think he could be?" Simon asked.

Arthur waved off the question.

"Hope not. Anything's possible, but I prefer to think it's unlikely."

"Then why hasn't he reported back yet?" Maggie said.

"He could be focused on the task at hand. He might not want to bother with updates until he knows where they're taking her. Could be anything. I think—"

"We should have just followed them ourselves!" Zoë said, pounding the armrest of the chair with her good arm. Ben scolded her, telling her to settle down. But Zoë continued. "We don't know if he's alive. Hell, how do we even know if Lydia is still alive at this point? They could have killed her at any moment since they took her!"

Arthur wheeled around again, this time taking a few steps up the aisle so he could look Zoë in the eyes. "No, Zoë. She's alive," he said. "I know that for a fact."

"How?" Simon said.

"Because they took her," Arthur said. "While we were saving Zoë, those men in the black clothes walked right up and took Lydia, and the lockbox. Why take her with them if they just planned on killing her? They had a clear shot at the bank, but they chose to take her instead."

"But, at Maxwell's house, the sniper was shooting wild," Simon said. "He was trying to kill us all."

"We don't know that for sure. He killed Dr. Lewis, but was he trying to kill all of you, or just you and Maggie?"

Simon realized that Arthur was right. He was right about all of it.

"Think about it," Arthur went on, looking toward Simon again. "Darrow is the ringleader of the entire Anti-Rejuv movement. Not just some public figurehead. She's the *leader*. I'm not saying we don't run a solid operation here, but without her, there'd be no LL. No legitimate AR groups at all. Without Darrow, this whole thing falls apart. She's the glue that holds all this together, makes us stronger than we ever could be on our own. Whether the people that took her know just how crucial she is, I can't say. But they know she's important and that makes her valuable to EXLI, to Sullivan. At least until—"

But Arthur couldn't finish the thought. They didn't need him to. They all knew what he was thinking.

They sat in silence, but for Zoë's moans near the altar as the doctor continued to extract the bullet from her arm and then sew up the wound. Peter the caretaker brought in a large platter of ham sandwiches, which they devoured. After, time seemed to slow, creep by, though Simon knew it had to have only been about 20 minutes. They sat as Ben finished up with Zoë, waiting for word from the man trailing Lydia's captors, anything that would break the dull silence. Simon felt his eyes start to droop, his head nod backward. He'd just slipped into that hazy state of consciousness between waking and slumber when the radio on Arthur's shoulder suddenly squawked to life.

"—in. Repe—. —illips. I've reach—"

Zoë, who had finally settled in the chair and been letting Ben do his work, suddenly sprang to life. She sat up straight, motioning with her good arm at Arthur as she shouted, "What's that? Did I hear Phillips? Arthur! What's is it? What's he saying?"

Arthur waved her words away. He tilted his head closer to the radio as the voice continued to crackle through. Zoë kept shouting for him, desperate for any news. Arthur pressed his ear fully against the radio on his shoulder, trying to hear what the voice was saying. But Zoë continued, waving, trying to get up, while the doctor held her back. Silence mere seconds before, the room was now cacophonous, too much for Arthur to make out what was being said over the radio. He turned, darting up the aisle and out the doors into the quiet confines of the small antechamber that stood as a barrier between the main entrance doors and the rest of the church.

"Damn, it, Arthur!" Zoë said, still struggling to get to her feet. "Get back here!" And then, for a moment, she turned her head to glare at the man who'd been patching up her arm. Her narrowed, piercing eyes said it all. Ben stopped what he was doing, raised his hands in surrender, and took two steps back.

Zoë jumped up from her chair, her arm now in a sling, and wobbled on her legs for a second, lightheaded. She shook the sensation away and marched down the aisle after Arthur.

"I've got your pain meds, ya know, if you still want them," Ben called after her. Zoë raised a hand in acknowledgment before she disappeared out the doors. Ben turned away, grumbling under his breath, and started picking up the bloodied bandages, rags, and medical equipment he'd been using to fix up his patient.

Muffled voices were coming from the antechamber; Zoë and Arthur conversing. Neither Simon nor Maggie could discern specific words. But they knew the topic of conversation. They'd all heard the voice on Arthur's radio. It was Phillips reporting in. Hopefully, with Lydia's whereabouts.

Simon looked at Maggie, but her eyes were fixed on the doors leading out of the church, listening. She was likely wondering, just as he was, what would happen when Zoë and Arthur re-entered the room. What news would they bring? Where would it send them? Was Lydia still alive as Arthur suspected, or would Phillips report the worst? Countless questions swam in Simon's mind as he turned his eyes in the opposite direction, to the discolored pattern on the wall of apse—the absent cross. He stared at it, listening, wondering what was next for them. With the exhaustion Simon felt at that moment, he wondered if he could even physically bear more. Another venture out. More running. Another mission. He didn't know if he had enough left in the tank.

But an image of Sebastian flashed in his mind. Will. Detective Banks. Maxwell. The Life Liberation soldiers at the bank. Everyone who'd given up their lives along the way. And Lydia, whose status remained a mystery, but could easily be gone already like all the rest.

The voices in the antechamber went quiet. One of the doors opened. A cloud of dust and paint chips fell from the walls.

It was Zoë. When she'd left, her arm in a sling, exhaustion growing on her face from her injuries, she had looked as haggard as they all did. But now, when she stepped into the room, she appeared different. Recharged. Determination etched onto her face. Zoë's green eyes blazed as she looked across the room.

"I'll take those pain meds now, doc," she said, striding up the aisle, passing Maggie and Simon as she made her way back up to the sanctuary. "Give me whatever you got. Enough so I can use my arm again."

Ben stopped what he was doing, looked quizzically at Zoë, then gave a sure-why-not shrug and reached for the small black bag on the table. From inside it, he pulled out a medicinal vial full of liquid and a syringe.

Simon stood from the pew and said, "You heard back from your man then?"

Zoë looked up from her arm, where the doc was already injecting her. She gave no flinch as the needle went in.

"Yes," she said. "He had a bit of trouble getting back to us, had to ditch the truck. But Phillips managed to get away, continue on foot."

"What'd he say?" Maggie said, now standing as well. She followed Simon up the aisle. "Did he tell you where they've taken Lydia?"

Zoë nodded and wasted no time with extraneous details. "*Hillbrook.*"

It took a moment for the answer to sink in for Simon. He had assumed her kidnappers would have taken Lydia to EXLI Headquarters, maybe even Sullivan's office. Maybe some sort of secret hideout of their own, like the church in which he now stood. A darkened warehouse where they could interrogate Lydia under a bright lamp until she gave up the information they wanted. Not a Rejuvenation retirement facility.

But then Simon heard a pained voice echo in his mind. A voice muttering words he'd listened to repeatedly over the last three days.

That's where . . . He's there . . . Hillbrook.

Hillbrook.

That place. It'd been a distinct part of the mysterious message that had started this whole ordeal. And no matter where Simon had gone, no matter what he'd done, he always seemed to be drawn back to Hillbrook. The Shepherd's Institute. Whatever name was used, that place kept coming up again and again. Like it was calling to Simon. Pulling him forward, beckoning him to come see what secrets it held. As if Hillbrook was the nexus of everything. The source of all their troubles, and maybe, the solution.

"We should have seen this coming," Simon said. "Everything that's happened, it's all connected. Whatever is going on with Sullivan and EXLI, whatever he's up to, Hillbrook is where it's happening. *That* is their base of operations."

Simon tried to recall the events of the last few days, everything they'd learned. He tried to visualize it all spread out before him like puzzle pieces. He knew it all fit together somehow, but couldn't see the picture on the box. He didn't know what the finished product should look like. There had to be something else. Some other missing piece he was forgetting.

That's where . . . He's there . . . Hillbrook.

He's there . . .

"That's where they're keeping him," Simon said. "The man Sebastian mentioned in his message. That's where *he's* at, so that's where they're holding Lydia."

Zoë studied Simon for a moment, as if she could see into him, watch the wheels turning in his head. She then closed her eyes, let out a long breath. The painkillers the doctor had shot into her arm were taking effect.

"So what do we do?" Maggie asked. "About Lydia."

Zoë opened her eyes. She looked at them with a crazy little smile, a wild, wide-eyed expression on her face. She flexed the hand on her injured arm. Her green eyes sparkled with excitement, determination.

"We go get her."

Ca. No. 2432615184
Text Comm. 613. Filed 4/17.
PART: Samar Vapula, Michael Purcell.

PURCELL:
its being taken care of

VAPULA:
Keep me posted.

8:17 AM

PURCELL:
Team 2 on the way back. Get to the lab

VAPULA:
What about Team 1?

PURCELL:
compromised

VAPULA:
Shit. Did they get it?

PURCELL:
Yes
and her

VAPULA:
Her? You mean Darrow? Alive?

                                                  PURCELL:
                                                  For now.
                        Just get to the lab. I'm headed their now
                He wants to know what she knows. interrogation starts
                                                  asap.

VAPULA:
And after?

                                                  PURCELL:
                        She'll be disposed of. Just get here!!

VAPULA:
On my way.

24

—————

Zoë had wasted no time. Minutes after Phillips radioed in, Simon and Maggie found themselves standing around the altar, listening to Zoë and Arthur explain their plan for infiltrating The Shepherd's Institute. Simon wondered how Zoë did it. How one minute she could be sitting down, exhausted and woozy from blood loss, getting a bullet hole in her arm sewn up . . . and the next, on her feet, wide-eyed, and ready for action. No doubt, the painkillers helped. But Simon had seen Zoë's fervor for the well-being of Lydia and suspected the idea of rescuing her close friend and ally played a larger role in Zoë's motivations. She had quickly pulled together the knowledge they needed to formulate a plan of action, and spelled out in a rapid set of commands that went unchallenged by anyone in their small group.

After, they'd been given 15 minutes to wash up and put on the fresh sets of clothes furnished by Life Liberation. Innocuous jeans and t-shirts for them both. A light jacket for Simon; a sweater for Maggie. When they met back up near the front of the church, Simon had been shocked initially at the sight of Zoë and Arthur in everyday clothes. Zoë, her hair pulled back in a tight ponytail, wore a pair of jeans and a tight-fitting top. Arthur was in jeans as well topped by a gray, collared shirt that fit snuggly around his broad shoulders and large biceps. Both looked strange out of their tactical gear, Zoë uncomfortable.

"Phillips is still holding a lookout position at Hillbrook," Zoë had said. She peered around the altar, eyes stopping on each one of them for a brief moment. She didn't bother asking them if they were ready. They were. They had to be because it was time to go. She pulled her silver pistol from the waistband of her jeans, checking the magazine, the chamber. Arthur did the same with his 9mm. "These should be enough for the car ride. Protection, just in case. No weapons allowed inside the facility. Still got that revolver?"

Simon nodded and reached into his waistband, pulling out Will's revolver. The cold steel of the barrel against the skin of his back suddenly gone. The gun felt different in Simon's hands now, lighter after he'd fired it empty back at the bank. After he'd felt its power in his hand, heard the blast of it each time he'd pulled the trigger. Simon stepped forward and laid the revolver on the bare altar next to two other handguns Zoë and Arthur had pulled from their person. Next to this, he also laid his cell phone. He wouldn't need to carry Sebastian's message with him, not where they were going. Still, when he'd stepped away without the revolver and the phone, a part of Simon felt incomplete, vulnerable.

Zoë must have seen this feeling on his face. She had given them all a nod and said, "We got you. This'll work."

That had been almost half an hour ago. Since then, they had piled in the blue sedan from the safe house, Arthur driving, and hit the road. Simon had watched intently out the window during their entire drive thus far. They had skirted around the city, avoiding most major roads, until they turned onto one Simon recognized. He'd been down this road many times as a child with his father on weekend trips.

The H-20 highway was a four-lane minor thoroughfare that cut through the massive forest growing just west of the city and extended to the sea. The majority of the forest south of H-20 was part of a state park, which encompassed the land all the way to the sandy beaches frequented by families in the summertime. While that part of the forest was mostly flat, slowly declining toward sea level, the northern portion rose in elevation until it peaked into a large hill. The western edge of the hill faced the sea and dropped sharply into bluffs, the bottom of which was a maze of sand and rocks.

Most people who'd accepted Rejuvenation had been to the top of that hill before, because they had relatives living there. Or rather, existing there. High up on the crest of the hill, obscured by the surrounding forest, stood The Shepherd's Institute. EXLI's flagship retirement community, where Rejuvenites from the surrounding metropolitan area lived out their remaining days once they'd entered the Post-Cerebrational Mobility Phase. Retirees. Husks. Whatever they were called, they all shared the same condition: highly aged brains no longer able to control their forever-youthful bodies. Only motionless beings were left, shells of their former selves, waiting for the inevitable.

EXLI had never given a specific reason for why they decided to build the facility so far away from the city, but Simon had a hunch the distance may have been the biggest factor in the decision. People in the city didn't want a place like The Shepherd's Institute so close to their daily lives, so visible. They didn't want a constant reminder that someday, unless something else caused an unforeseen death, they would all eventually end up there or in another facility like it.

But that had all changed in the last few days, Simon thought. Theodore Sullivan had announced EXLI's breakthrough to the world. They had figured out a way to stop the body *and* the mind from aging, making facilities like The Shepherd's Institute a thing of the past, or so Sullivan had claimed. Given what they had learned the night before at Maxwell's house, the new reality Sullivan had proposed—that dream of immortality—was all a lie. The truth was far worse than they had imagined, and they didn't yet know every part of it. There was still something else just out of their reach, a secret that Sullivan and his cohorts at EXLI were hiding at the top of that hill.

"How much farther?" Zoë asked, looking from her watch to the road ahead. But it was not their driver who answered.

"About 10 more miles," Simon said. "There'll be a stoplight and a sign on the right. There's a road that goes off into the forest that way." He motioned out the passenger window. "Bimini Drive. As far as I know, it only leads to one place."

Zoë turned around in the front passenger seat, her eyebrows raised at Simon. "You seem to know an awful lot about this place."

"I used to go camping up here with my Dad, in the state park," he said, pointing out the window toward the south side of the road. "We'd always pass the sign. Kinda hard to miss." Simon's mouth remained open for a moment, more words on his tongue, but he refrained and sealed his lips. The memories swirled in his head. Riding in the passenger seat of his father's car, the backseats loaded with camping gear, fishing rods, a packed cooler. Bright summer days spent building sandcastles at the beach, wading into the blue waters of the sea. But one memory connected to this road always rose above the rest. That day long ago, the long drive out of town, being led down sterile hallways, his grandfather lying motionless on a hospital bed . . .

They drove on. The number of cars joining them on the road increased the closer they got to Bimini Drive. While Simon knew that a large number of people came out to The Shepherd's Institute daily, he hadn't expected to encounter so many when they ventured there. Ahead and behind them, vehicles seemed to surround their small car until there was a convoy of sorts filling both lanes, all headed in the same direction.

"There it is," Arthur said, nodding toward the windshield.

Simon arched his neck around the front seat and looked ahead. A large, white sign stood just beyond an upcoming intersection. *EXLI* was painted on the sign in tall, bright blue letters. Below this was *The Shepherd's Institute – 5 Miles* and an arrow pointing north.

They followed the long snake of vehicles rounding the corner and turned onto Bimini Drive. The road ahead stretched out before them, packed with vehicles all headed to the same destination.

It rose out of the trees like a mountain or great monument. The Shepherd's Institute. The entire facility was comprised of only three buildings, two of which sat off to one side. These smaller, single-story structures were used for power and other utilities. The main building, where the patients were housed, stood 20 stories high. Its exterior was the sterile, gray color of freshly dried concrete. Small windows dotted the sides of the building at equidistant intervals, marking each floor. From a distance, the entire facility looked like a large concrete block had been dropped into the forest from the heavens. Simon couldn't help but think about how much it resembled a common storage unit used to keep excess furniture or boxes of old clothes. But that's what The Shepherd's Institute was, he thought. Wasn't it? A storage unit? Only, this one held people.

A chill ran over Simon's shoulders and down his spine at this thought. His breath caught in his chest as the image of his motionless grandfather flashed in Simon's mind again. He tried to shake the memory, but it lingered in the periphery of his mind as The Shepherd's Institute loomed ahead. He knew the memory was unlikely to go away, not while they moved closer and closer to that place. So he let go. He allowed the memory to sink in, pervade his thoughts. He let his fear take control . . . and it worked. It was only a memory. The moment passed. Simon felt his breath return to normal, his pulse steady, and his mind refocus on the mission at hand.

Back before they had left the safe house, Simon had played out many possible plans in his head that Zoë might come up with for how they would infiltrate The Shepherd's Institute. Given what he'd previously heard from Lydia and Maxwell, he assumed the task would be a difficult one. Most of the scenarios Simon thought of involved things he'd read in thriller novels or seen on television—grand schemes that required days of planning by a rogue team of soldiers, everyday people thrust into compromising circumstances, or deadly mercenaries. These made-up people would go over every detail of the plan again and again until it was etched into their minds. Only then would they head out and attempt to implement their scheme, pulling it off with surgical precision and achieving their end goal, whatever that may be. Simon saw himself, Maggie, and numerous members of Life Liberation tunneling under the facility like prisoners trying to escape the confines of their cells. Maybe they wouldn't need to dig, but instead navigate sewer tunnel systems that ran beneath the facility, only to pop up smack dab in the room where Lydia was being held. They might figure out a way to cut the power to the entire facility and sneak in under the cover of darkness, subduing armed guards with knock-out gas or sleep-darts. Perhaps they would somehow drop in from the sky, parachuting onto the top of the building and fighting their way through wave after wave of armed guards until they discovered where Lydia and the mysterious man from Sebastian's message were being held prisoner. All these scenarios and more had run through Simon's mind, each one more complicated, fantastic, and impossible than the last. But the actual plan Zoë had presented turned out to be much simpler.

As they approached the facility with the other cars, they were directed into one of several large parking lots. Arthur pulled their car into the next empty spot in line and was quickly followed by the car behind him pulling into the spot to their left. He turned off the engine, pocketed the keys, and turned to Zoë.

"Go time," Arthur said. He pulled the pistol he'd been carrying from his pocket, collected Zoë's as well, and put both in the glovebox.

Zoë turned to Simon and Maggie.

"You two ready?" she said.

They both nodded, not saying a word.

"Just remember the plan."

Yes, Simon thought. *The plan.* Zoë had gone over everything before they'd left the church. It seemed easy enough but . . .

"We just walk in?" Maggie had asked upon hearing Zoë's straightforward approach.

Zoë had looked annoyed, sighed, but nodded. She'd then gone on to explain that walking through the front door was actually their best option. The Shepherd's Institute wasn't a military base or some kind of high-security operation; it was a Rejuvenation retirement community—a medical facility. It wasn't the sort of place that'd be guarded by soldiers with automatic weapons. It was a place where the general public could go twenty-four hours a day to visit those who had not died, but were still lost.

But Simon hadn't been convinced. Especially since Lydia and Maxwell had previously both dismissed Simon when he'd broached the idea of going to The Shepherd's Institute.

When he pressed Zoë for more, he learned that her confidence wasn't based solely on her planning. "This isn't our first rodeo," she'd said. "We've been inside before. Not with two fugitives, but hey, we can handle it. Trust me, the facility's openness is our ticket in." She explained how they'd pretend to be like all the rest, pose as siblings going to visit a relative. As it turned out, Arthur's grandmother had been a resident of The Shepherd's Institute for the past 10 years.

Simon had looked at Arthur then, whose brown skin looked even darker standing next to Zoë's paleness and red hair. "Um, not to poke holes in your plan, but, we don't exactly *look* related."

"Fine," Zoë answered, rolling her eyes, "Step-siblings. Or Arthur's my husband, you two are my siblings. It doesn't matter. They'll be more concerned with those of us who're filthy Deniers anyway. If they ask, just say we're family."

Simon had no more questions. It all made sense and sounded like it might just work. But still, it seemed *too* simple. Too easy.

"Just stick to the plan," Zoë said, seeing the look of concern on Simon's face. "Keep your head down. Let Arthur and me do the talking. Once we're past security, I'll take it from there. Got it?"

Maggie and Simon shared a glance, then nodded.

"Good. Let's go. Remember—one big happy family."

They exited the car and joined the walking crowd of people making their way toward the main entrance of the building. A line of frosted glass doors ran across the front of the building like a row of giant white teeth. The Shepherd's Institute chomped away as lines of people filed inside.

Simon had once vowed never to come back to this place. Ever. As a child, he simply didn't want to see his Grandpa Crowe lying motionless in that hospital bed, unable to live the life he once had. But as Simon grew older, he realized the memory of his grandfather was only one of the reasons for his vow. The other was this place. The Shepherd's Institute. Hillbrook. And any of the other countless retirement facilities around the world. It was what they actually were, what they represented. Floor after floor, room after room, and bed after bed filled with people who had reached the limits of what Rejuvenation could offer them. They were all motionless beings like his Grandpa Crowe. Husks. They were still technically alive, but to Simon, none of them were truly living. They were simply clinging on to life, making some flawed effort for one more year, one more day. They couldn't just . . . *let go*. Neither, it seemed, could Simon. His vow had been broken, because here he was. His reason for returning was different from all the rest who filed in around him, but he was here nonetheless. They were all here together, pulled back to this place by some sort of anguished magnetism. Unable to let go like all the people lying in beds on the floors above.

As they moved closer and closer to the doors, Simon saw that their disguises—or lack thereof—helped them blend in quite well with the crowd. Some wore suits and professional-looking dresses, while others were in casual wear like t-shirts and jeans. He even saw a few children and women wearing flip-flops. The only physical characteristic about Simon that might make him stand out was his Non-Rejuvenite appearance. While the mass of people filing into the building all wore various styles of clothing, most of them appeared young in the face—they had all undergone Rejuvenation. While Simon was anything but an old man, he was sure that at least a few of the awkward stares he received from those around him were because his face actually reflected his true age. Arthur, who was at least as old as he was, did not seem to be affected by the distinction, so Simon tried to shrug it off and continue.

They kept with the flow of people and soon passed through the entrance doors into the main lobby of The Shepherd's Institute. The room was cavernous, its walls bright white but for splashes of color brought by various pieces of modern artwork hung at eye level. The ceiling rose high above the large crowd that moved to and fro like a single, large organism, herded toward a honeycomb of rectangular checkpoints near the back of the room. Sitting to the side of each of these checkpoints was a single person dressed in a light blue shirt and pants resembling surgical scrubs, holding a clipboard-sized computer. Beyond the check-point area was a bank of elevators that could be seen rising and descending through a near-transparent, frosted glass wall.

Simon grabbed Maggie's hand so as not to lose her. They each had to push against the swaying crowd from time to time to keep pace with Arthur and Zoë. For one, fleeting moment of panic Simon thought he had completely lost them in the sea of bodies, but then found the pair waiting by a nearby helpdesk kiosk. Zoë gave Simon an impatient look while Arthur busied himself with a pamphlet from the kiosk counter. It wasn't until they got closer that Simon saw the image on the front of the pamphlet, a familiar photograph of Rodderick Price with a super-imposed speech bubble touting the many benefits of his wonderful discovery. Arthur chuckled as he read the inside pages, but quickly replaced the pamphlet when Simon and Maggie rejoined the group.

Soon, they'd face the first true test of Zoë's plan. Had the staff of The Shepherd's Institute paid attention to the news reports of the last few days? Or had they been briefed to look out for Maggie and Simon? Zoë hadn't thought it would matter. She'd stressed to them the enormity of the facility and its operation. Thousands and thousands of people filed through The Shepherd's Institute every day. She'd told them they marched people though the checkpoints as fast as possible, like the constantly rotating turnstiles of an amusement park. They were to keep their heads down, follow instructions, and do as the rest of the herd did. If they did that, Zoë had assured them that everything would be all right.

After a few more minutes of shuffling with the rest of the crowd, they reached one of the checkpoints. With barely a look at them, the man in the blue clothes started into a spiel he no doubt repeated thousands of times a day.

"On behalf of the Extended Life Corporation, welcome to The

Shepherd's Institute. Your loved ones will be happy to see you. Please step forward," the man said.

They all stepped closer, separating themselves from the waiting line of people behind them.

"All four of you?"

They nodded.

"Who are you here to visit?"

"Our grandmother," Arthur said, taking another step forward, putting on a cheerful tone unlike anything Simon or Maggie had heard him speak before. "Lenore Isaacs. We've all been looking forward to spending some quality time with her. We haven't had a chance to see her in—"

"Yeah, okay," the man in the blue clothes said, stopping Arthur's attempt at sounding like a normal visitor. Arthur fell back into the group as the man's fingers danced on the computer in his hand. "Right. Lenore Isaacs. Resident of the 7th floor. Room 15c." Perhaps it was the tricky hands of fate or mere coincidence, but when the man at the checkpoint looked up from his computer again, his eyes locked on Simon. "Please hand me your IDs and then step through the checkpoint one at a time. You first, sir."

Simon was initially struck motionless, caught off guard that he should be singled out. Had the checkpoint man recognized him? He pointed to himself in an unsure manner and, when the man in blue nodded agitatedly back, Simon stepped forward, stumbling slightly over his feet. He reached into his pocket to fish out the phony ID Zoë had given him earlier. The new plastic of the ID card was slick between his fingers as nervous perspiration began to seep from his palms and his forehead. He pulled the card out and handed it to the man in blue before glancing back at the rest of his group. Maggie and Arthur tried to appear encouraging, while Zoë shot him a fierce, thin-lipped look that told Simon he should return his focus to the checkpoint.

The man in blue ran the face of the ID card across the top section of his computer. Simon held his breath, knowing that this was the moment of truth for their fake ID cards. There was a moment's hesitation between when the checkpoint official swiped the card, a moment that seemed much longer to Simon as he felt droplets of sweat continue to collect on his forehead. He squeezed his palms tight, feeling the dampness there as well, wishing he had Maggie's hand to clutch for reassurance. The moment seemed to extend out, far longer than any single moment should. But then, a small green light flashed on one corner of the computer. It gave a high pitched beep. The man in blue glanced back up at Simon and handed him back his ID.

"Step through."

Simon felt a rush of comfort at the sight of the green light and the sound of the beep, but it was fleeting as a new wave of anxiety found him when he stepped up to the hollow, rectangular arch in front of him. He tried to act casual, as if he had made the trip hundreds of times before, but felt his nerves must be showing. He stepped through the checkpoint, expecting sirens to suddenly blare and red lights to flash brightly around them—but nothing happened. He knew the archway was a scanner of some kind, but as he stepped through, he felt nothing and heard no protest. A moment later, Simon was on the other side and the wave of comfort returned. He turned around, trying to keep his smile at a minimum as the rest of his group gave reassuring looks.

"Next."

Zoë stepped up. She appeared much calmer than Simon knew he had. She smiled wide as she handed the man in blue her ID, watched as it was swiped, and then nonchalantly walked through the scanner. When she sidled up next to Simon on the other side, he was sure she would have given him an elbow nudge to the ribs had they not been in a public place.

After seeing two ID cards work flawlessly, Maggie seemed to

have gained the confidence she needed to make it through the checkpoint with nearly the same nonchalance as Zoë. Arthur was the last one through. There was never any doubt that his ID would work, as it was legitimate. When they were all through, the checkpoint official stuck a thumb over his shoulder, pointed back toward the elevators.

"Please proceed to the elevators. Floor 7. Room 15c." He hadn't even looked at them when he said it, his gaze already pointed toward the next group of people in line.

"Shall we, Artie?" Zoë said, the wide smile molded to her face now directed at the towering man next to her.

That expression. That smile. *Artie?* The words she spoke sounded strange, like nothing Simon would have ever expected to come off Zoë's lips. Her tone had changed as well to match the odd words. Her voice was higher, almost lighthearted. The way she carried herself was looser, friendlier. Zoë's whole demeanor seemed . . . off. At least, Simon thought, off for her. But he knew what she was doing. Why she seemed so odd. Zoë was doing her best impression of acting like a *normal person*. She was good, Simon thought. Good enough. Anyone who knew Zoë's real personality, as they did, would be able to tell how uncomfortable she was being *normal* and interacting with everyday people. Simon could sure see the cracks. But he suspected those around them would be none the wiser.

Zoë motioned to the flow of people exiting other checkpoints, all heading toward the elevators. She urged them on with the friendliest of waves.

While the opposite side of the checkpoint was by no means as crowded as the main lobby, it was still a flurry of people all headed in the same direction. Zoë, ever the leader, even when she was feigning normalness, took point of their group and led them through the sea of visitors to the closest elevator.

The doors of the elevator were as white as the walls around

them, but when they shuffled inside Simon saw that the interior was a shiny chrome color. All four walls reflected their faces at them and they kept their eyes down to avoid catching stares from any of the other visitors in this confined space. More people crowded into the spacious elevator, pushing Simon, Maggie, Zoë, and Arthur to the back. Once full, a voice near the doors sounded.

"Floors?"

There was a smattering of requests. Floors 3, 7, 14, and 19 were called.

"20, please," Zoë said. "Thanks!"

When the elevator doors closed, Simon knew their real mission had begun. It was at this point that Zoë's plan became hazy, unpredictable. She'd explained how once they were inside the facility and past the checkpoints, they would be free to roam. All guests were to a certain extent. There were cameras, sure, but she doubted anyone paid too close attention to the live feed. The Shepherd's Institute's patient floors were a maze of hallways and doors leading to wards full of people whose brains had, as Zoë put it, "turned to mush." Each floor was a chaotic swarm of guests, nurses, and doctors moving to and fro. There were simply too many people to keep track of at any given time, should someone be watching. Zoë planned on using that chaos to their advantage, to remain unnoticed.

But even if they could move about, that still left the question of where they needed to go. Where was Lydia being kept? How would they find her?

"Ah, see, that's the tricky part," Zoë had admitted. "We don't know where she's being held, so we'll have to find someone who does."

25

The elevator ascended, stopping with a soft chime at the floors that had been selected. As the crowd inside began to thin, Simon got another clear look at the front of the elevator, specifically the keypad that showed the numbers of each floor. It was arranged in two symmetrical columns, floors 1-10 on the left, 11-20 on the right. Below these were the usual buttons for opening and closing the doors and the emergency call button.

It was a strange thing to focus on. He supposed it caught his eye because the keypad was usually just an ordinary object. But here, it meant so much more. Simon marveled at the thought that each floor represented by one of those numbers on the keypad was filled with room after room of people—Rejuvenation retirees spending their remaining days lying motionless in bed. It made him think of Sebastian. His friend who would never fill one of those beds because he had been murdered, taken before his time. It was Sebastian—his message—that had first mentioned Hillbrook. He had wanted them to come here because he knew EXLI was hiding something at this very location. But what? But *who,* was more accurate.

The elevator chimed again and Simon watched the illuminated

19 on the keypad suddenly go dark. The elevator doors opened onto a long, white hallway and the last person who was not a part of their group exited. The doors closed and the elevator slowly began to rise once more.

"Okay. Stay behind me," Zoë said, her fake bubbly tone disappearing, replaced by her normal hardened voice. "Act natural."

They all nodded in agreement and said nothing more as the elevator continued to rise. Simon wondered if any of them would be able to act natural given the situation. A moment later, the elevator stopped. There was another soft chime and the doors opened.

Simon had to keep reminding himself that they were in a public place frequented by everyday people. While he and those in his group were not there for everyday reasons, as far as the powers that be knew, they *were* just another family on their way to visit a brain-addled relative or friend. Zoë and Arthur stepped out of the elevator first. Seeing their casual manner, Simon altered his stride to appear more at ease, as he had first started to creep as if trying to avoid detection by some watching individual. He grabbed Maggie's hand for a sense of comfort and she squeezed back, acknowledging her own nervousness. They followed along as Zoë and Arthur began to make their way down the hall.

This floor looked like every other one Simon had spied each time the elevator doors had opened during their ascent. They'd been deposited into a wide hallway that ran for as far as he could see. From outside, looking up at The Shepherd's Institute, Simon had only noticed the number of floors and the height and width of the building. He hadn't realized its depth, but now saw that each floor was more massive than he originally thought. The hallway in which they walked stretched out into the distance, bustling with visitors and staff. Stocked medical carts and empty beds lined much of the corridor. The walls on each side of the extensive hallway were painted a bright white, but for a single fat, light-blue line that ran down the middle, broken only by doors and intersecting hallways.

Simon continued walking alongside Maggie, following Zoë and Arthur, trying to appear as unsuspicious as he could but thinking he was doing a piss poor job of it. He didn't know where Zoë was leading them, but the farther and farther they walked the more anxious Simon became. Men, women, and children, along with nurses dressed in pastel colors walked by—all of them, except for the children, looking like they were in their early to mid-20s. Rejuvenites, walking the hallways, while their futures filled the rooms around them. Each time they passed any open doorway, Simon spied what looked like endless rooms lined with human forms lying still in bed after bed after bed. Some were surrounded by visitors, but most were not. The patients simply lay there, unmoving, waiting.

Simon felt like he was in the center of it now, the heart of Rejuvenation. More so than if he had been in one of the medical centers where Rejuvenists performed the procedure. More than if he'd been standing in the labs at EXLI Headquarters where the science of it all was researched and advances were made. Being in this place, walking the halls of The Shepherd's Institute, knowing he was surrounded by people who had already lived the amount of worthwhile life that Rejuvenation could provide them, made Simon's chest tighten. His breath felt short. He felt his heartbeat race and small beads of sweat return to his forehead. More flashes of his grandfather. He was surrounded. They all were. And Zoë was leading them deeper and deeper into it.

"Are you okay?" Maggie whispered.

Simon turned his eyes to Maggie, saw her concerned expression.

"Yeah. Fine," Simon stuttered out.

"You're crushing my hand," she said.

Simon released his grip on Maggie's hand, letting go completely and wiping his sweaty palm on the leg of his pants.

Zoë's pace suddenly quickened. Simon looked ahead and saw what had caught her eye; a doctor, or what looked like one anyway. He was dressed in blue scrubs with a white lab coat over top. His hair was dark and short, his face like everyone else around him, was young. Simon watched as the man said something to a passing nurse, opened a door on the left side of the hallway, and stepped through it.

Zoë reached the door a second after the doctor, followed by the rest of their group. Simon wasn't able to see through the small window in the center of the door because Zoë was peering into it herself, but he assumed she was watching the movements of the doctor who had just entered. A few seconds crept by. Simon gazed around, wondering if anyone had noticed them loitering there. Zoë pulled the door open.

"Come on, he just went into one of the rooms at the end," Zoë said, stepping through the doorway.

They followed and were now in another, smaller hallway, though it had a similar design scheme as the main hallway—complete with blue lines running down the center of each wall, stretching out to where the opposite end of the hall ended in another, smaller elevator. Zoë marched on and they moved in her wake. Simon peeked through the windows of the other doors in the hallway and saw that they were all small offices. He continued with the group until they reached the last door at the end of the hallway.

"He went in here," Zoë said in a whisper. "I'll go first."

Zoë casually pulled opened the door.

"Maybe it's here?" she said, her high, bubbly voice returning, a touch of upward inflection, confusion. Zoë stepped into the room and they all followed.

"Excuse me," the doctor said from behind a desk. "This is a personal office."

"Well! It would appear that we're a bit lost then," Zoë said with a giggle. Simon couldn't see from behind her, but he was almost sure that Zoë was batting her eyelashes at the doctor, showing him the full extent of her large, green eyes. "So sorry, *doctor*."

The doctor's face changed, his furrowed brow loosened and he gave a smile.

"Ah, it's all right. This place can be quite the maze. Why don't I help you find where you're going?"

"Oh! Thank you *so* much," Zoë said.

The doctor got up from behind the desk, a smug look on his face, and walked around to where Zoë stood. He was just about to say something when Zoë grabbed the doctor by one of his wrists and spun it around his back. A small pop sounded from his wrist and Simon hoped she hadn't broken anything. Zoë grabbed his other wrist with her left hand, then sank one of her sharp elbows into the center of the doctor's back, slamming him down onto his desk, narrowly avoiding a cup full of pens and sharpened pencils. The doctor let out a brief Hey!, followed by the thud of his head on the desk and a pained groan. He struggled to break free, but Zoë's hold was firm despite her injured arm.

"Hel—" the doctor started to shout, but his words were muffled by Arthur's strong hand being slapped over his mouth. The doctor continued mumbling, trying to speak. Whether to call for help or shout at his attackers, Simon did not know.

"Just take it easy, doc," Zoë said, her normal voice returning as she leaned down to look the doctor in the eyes. "We just need some information. We don't want to hurt you. Understand? But before my friend here takes his hand away, we need to know you aren't going to scream out. Deal?"

The doctor stared up at Zoë for a moment. His eyes focused

on her as he considered her sudden change of demeanor, her commanding words. Then his body relaxed in her grip and he nodded.

"Thought you'd see it my way." Zoë nodded at Arthur, who slowly lifted his hand off the doctor's mouth. Zoë, however, did not release her hold.

"Will you let me go?" the doctor said.

"Not before we have a little chat," Zoë said.

Simon, who had all this time stood frozen near the door with Maggie, watched Zoë as she appeared to tighten her grip on the man bent across the desk. From the moment Simon met Zoë, she had never seemed quite as intimidating as the Life Liberation soldiers with which she surrounded herself. Even that first time he'd seen her at Maxwell's house—she had been masked and dressed in dark clothes like the rest of them, but when she stepped into the kitchen, she'd been flanked by two larger men. She led the charge into the bank to try and retrieve the lockbox, but even then she had others around her. And she had been shot. She wasn't indestructible by any means, Simon thought. Although, this was hard to believe after watching her actions of the last-minute. She had switched effortlessly between a calm demeanor as they walked into the building to flirtatiousness as she *accidentally* stumbled into the doctor's office. And moments later, immediately changed to the hardened face Simon now saw staring down at the doctor. For the first time, she appeared truly intimidating in her own right, despite the hurt she must still be feeling in an arm that had taken a bullet mere hours ago, painkillers notwithstanding.

"What do you want?" the doctor said with another grunt of pain.

"Tell me where they're keeping her," Zoë said.

"Who?"

"Lydia Darrow. We know she's here. Where are they keeping her?"

The doctor's eyes contracted from the pain of Zoë's hold, but his brow furrowed further into confusion.

"Lydia . . . what?" the doctor said.

"*Lydia Darrow*!"

"Lydia Darrow? That crazy Anti-Rejuvenation hypocrite?"

"She's *not* crazy, or a hyp—you know what? None of that matters right now. Just tell me where she is!"

"I have no idea what you're talking about. Why would she be here?"

Zoë leaned in closer, as if to whisper in the man's ear, but kept the hardness in her voice.

"That's where you're wrong, doc. My man saw her brought to this facility. She's here somewhere."

"Well if she is, I have no idea where. I was never told a thing."

Zoë glared down at the man she held in her vise-like grip. She dug her elbow into his back a little harder, forcing another small, painful moan from the doctor.

"You better not be lying to me," she said.

"Stop! I'm not lying. I don't know anything!"

"He doesn't know anything," Simon croaked out in an unsteady voice, taking a step forward.

Zoë turned her head to look at Simon, her eyes bulging. She didn't like being interrupted and he knew it. Though Simon wondered if Zoë had actually crossed the line from intimidating the poor doctor to being downright mean to him. If he didn't know, he didn't know.

"He doesn't know anything," Simon repeated, more confidence in his voice, saying the words with emphasis.

"Maybe," Zoë said. She eased up, lifting her elbow from the doctor's back but keeping her hands wrapped tightly around his wrists. He gave a sigh of relief when the pressure released. "Time for plan B."

"What does *that* mean?" the doctor said, his voice trembling with fright.

"It means that, while *you* may not know where Lydia is being held, you probably know someone who does."

"But—"

"What's your name, doc?" Zoë interrupted.

He hesitated a moment, still obviously unsure about the role he'd play going forward.

"J-Jackson," the doctor said. "Dr. Jackson Wiley."

"Okay, Dr. Jack. I'm going to release you. When I do, don't try anything. Got it?"

Dr. Jack nodded without hesitation. Zoë let go of his hands and took a half-step back to allow him a little space. The doctor pushed himself off the desk and into a standing position. He turned around, rubbing at his wrists, gazing at the entire group of intruders in his office. He wasn't just looking at them, he was studying their faces so he could identify them all later should he be able to break free. His eyes lingered on Simon and Maggie.

"Now, who do you report to?" Zoë asked, drawing the doctor's attention back to her.

"There are several administrators here, I—"

"Yeah, yeah, but who's the main one? The head honcho?"

"Well, there really isn't one particu—" Zoë slapped Dr. Jack across the face, leaving a faint, pink mark on his cheek. "Ow! Hey, you said—"

"Stop stalling. Who's the one in charge of this place?"

"Dr. Ellis." Dr. Jack shrank back against his desk, as if expecting another strike from Zoë.

"And where is Dr. Ellis's office?"

"21st floor."

Zoë looked at the rest of her group, her eyes rolling in disbelief, and raised her hand again. But Arthur stepped forward, and her hand was stayed.

"I thought this place only had 20 floors," Arthur said, looking to Zoë then back at the doctor.

"Most people do," Dr. Jack said, his eyes darting between Arthur and Zoë's hand. "All the main treatment areas are on floors 2-20. The 21st floor isn't really a floor at all. Not a full one. It's just made up of a conference room that gets used once a month and the head administrator's office. You can't see the 21st floor from the ground because it sits at the center of the top of the building."

"Thanks for the architecture lesson," Zoë said, lowering her hand. "Now take us up there."

"No one sees Dr. Ellis without an appointment."

Zoë leaned toward Dr. Jack, her nose and brow more pointed than ever.

"Does it look like I care about appointments?" she said. "How do we get up there? That other elevator outside?"

The doctor's eyes flashed around the room again. He paused, then nodded.

That seemed to be enough for Zoë. She stepped behind Dr. Jack and placed a hand on his shoulder, pushing him toward the door. Simon and Maggie stepped aside. "Arthur, you head out first with the doctor. Make sure the coast is clear and call the elevator. Once it's here, we'll join you."

Arthur nodded and ushered the doctor out of the office. A few seconds passed and there was a knock on the door. Zoë slid by Simon and Maggie, looked out the window. She jerked her head in a motion that said to follow her before slipping through the door and into the hallway. Simon grabbed Maggie's hand, gave it a quick squeeze and the two headed out to join the rest of their group.

The secondary elevator was much smaller than the elevator

they'd taken up to the 20th floor. Likely because only doctors and other qualified personnel were supposed to ride in it, Simon thought. As the elevator doors slid closed, Simon looked to his right and saw a keypad similar to the one in the main elevator. The only difference in this keypad was that in between the floor numbers and the additional buttons, there was one more button in the first column labeled R. Next to this was a small, square panel the size of one of the buttons.

Dr. Jack reached toward the keypad, but Zoë stopped his hand.

"I'll get that if you don't mind, doc," she said and pushed the button labeled R. It lit up, but nothing happened. The elevator did not move. Zoë glared. "What gives?

"It needs a fingerprint," he said, reaching forward and pressing his thumb against the blank panel next to the R button. A thin green line flash from top to bottom, a chime sounded from above, and the elevator began to move slowly upward.

A few seconds later, the elevator stopped, chimed again, and the doors opened to a long, dim hallway. Zoë and Arthur exited first with the doctor, followed by Simon and Maggie. The group of five walked slowly, as cautiously as possible down the hallway toward a more well-lit area. Simon thought it odd, the shape of this top-most floor. He had to believe that there was a hallway of offices similar to the ones they had ascended from on the opposite side of the building as well. If that was the case, there was likely a second small elevator on the other side of the building, which meant another long hallway like the one they walked down now. In his mind, Simon imagined what this design must look like from above the building, two long hallways stretching from each side of the building and meeting up in the center where the head administrator's office and conference room were said to be. He pictured a small, elevated square set atop the center of the building, with two long lines leading out in opposite directions, like an unfastened wristwatch.

When they reached the well-lit space Simon had seen from the elevator, they saw two sets of doors on either side of the hall. To the left was a pair of dark brown, wooden doors. A small plaque on the wall told Simon that what lay inside was the conference room Dr. Jack had mentioned. To the right side of the hallway was a single door, again made of dark brown wood. There was no plaque of identification, but if what they'd been told was correct, this was the office of The Shepherd's Institute's head administrator

"Do you want to knock, or should I?" Dr. Jack said.

Zoë shot him a look that was part amusement, part annoyance.

"You've been in this office before?" she said.

"Once or twice, yes," the doctor said

"Do you know if there are any hidden weapons that would be easily accessible if we barged in?"

"Weapons? No. Why would Dr. Ellis need—"

"Are there or not?"

"I have no idea," the doctor said, shrugging.

A troubling scenario suddenly filled Simon's mind. One where they strolled into the office, believing they had the upper hand, only to find a man sitting behind a large, mahogany desk who pulled a shotgun or pistol out from some hidden slot and opened fire on them all, ending their quest in a bloody parade of falling, lifeless bodies. Simon shook the thought from his head and was about to ask the doctor some follow up questions himself when Zoë interrupted.

She reached forward and tried to twist the doorknob. It didn't budge. She tried turning it again, jiggling it, but still no movement. It was locked.

"Dr. Ellis may not even be in today," Dr. Jack said.

"Well, either way, we need to get into that office," Zoë said, looking toward Arthur. "Break it down."

It happened with such swiftness that Simon was positive this was not the first door Arthur had kicked in before. The hulking man lifted his leg as if preparing for a crane kick and then slammed his foot into the door just above the doorknob. There was a loud crunch as his foot impacted the door, then a cracking noise as the force of the kick ripped the door away from the frame. Splinters of wood exploded out as the door swung into the office beyond.

For a moment, everyone froze—the group of four intruders standing in the hallway, the doctor who had been taken hostage, and the woman seated behind a large desk near the back of the office that had just been broken into. The head administrator of The Shepherd's Institute looked to be of average size. She had a wiry frame and dark blond hair pulled up into a tight bun atop her head. Like every other member of the staff in the building, the youthful complexion of her face told them she'd gone through Rejuvenation. Simon suspected a woman in her role would have had to work her way up over the years and may even be as old as Lydia, but had no way of knowing for sure. Her straight-backed posture, wrinkled nose as if she was smelling something unpleasant—everything about her gave off an instant air of strict, bureaucratic professionalism. And as the last splinters of the door fell to the carpet, the woman stared back at them with large, incredulous eyes.

Simon thought she might be too shocked by their sudden intrusion to react at all. Surely, she must be frozen to her seat, unable to react, too frightened by the large man who'd just kicked in her office door.

But her eyes remained ahead, steady. She sat planted in her seat, with purpose. She didn't cower or scream for help. She hadn't moved at all. Hadn't even flinched at her imploding door.

She glared at them; not in fear, but in disbelief that anyone would have the audacity to enter her office without knocking, much less break in.

Time seemed to stop. She stared at them, and they stared right back, like two outlaw cowboys dueling in the center of Main Street at high noon.

26

───────

DR. ELLIS'S LEFT HAND SHOT OUT, GRABBING FOR THE PHONE ON the corner of her desk. At the same time, she yanked open a drawer, digging inside. Zoë pushed Arthur and the doctor aside, darting into the room. She sprinted toward the desk and reached it just as Ellis was about to speak. Zoë launched herself over the desk, knocking the phone out of Ellis's hand and tackling her back into her chair. Both women landed on the floor, wrestling for the upper hand.

Simon saw a glint of metal amidst the scuffle and knew what Ellis had pulled from the desk drawer. A gun—a subcompact 9mm, small enough to fit in her palm. Zoë saw it too. Ellis tried to aim, but Zoë held her wrist. The gun went off once with a loud clack! that reverberated off the walls. Zoë swatted at Ellis's hand, and the gun tumbled from her grasp.

All thoughts of Dr. Ellis as a frightened bureaucrat had been dismissed from Simon's mind. He watched as she planted her foot into Zoë's chest and kicked. Zoë flew back onto the floor, skidding to a stop against a small file cabinet that had moments before taken a stray bullet. Ellis climbed to her feet, scrambling for the gun.

"Hold him!" Arthur said, pushing Dr. Jack toward Simon and rushing into the room to help. Simon grabbed the doctor by the arm and gave him the fiercest stare he could muster, though he knew it probably didn't compare to the intimidating looks Zoë and Arthur could throw.

Ellis stumbled, eyes darting between a charging Arthur and the gun, which still lay a few feet away. She dove for the gun, wrapping her hand around it, pointing the barrel in Arthur's direction. But Ellis's eyes were fixed so much on Arthur's lumbering form that she didn't see Zoë until it was too late. Zoë tackled Ellis again. The gun fell to the floor, skidding across the room, coming to rest at the foot of a tall wardrobe, which stood against one wall

Zoë planted her knees into Dr. Ellis's thighs, pressing down hard, and grabbed the woman's wrists forcing them to the ground. Ellis flailed, jerking her head up to try to head-butt Zoë.

"Could use some help!" Zoë yelled as she struggled with the thrashing woman beneath her.

Arthur rounded the desk. He knelt and took over, pinning Ellis's arms to the ground. Zoë sat up, digging her knees harder into the woman's thighs. Ellis screamed in anguish.

With the commotion of the previous minutes settled, Simon pushed Dr. Jack into the room. Maggie followed. They walked forward cautiously until they could see the struggling trio behind the desk. Maggie took this opportunity to scoop up Ellis's gun from the floor.

"Quiet!" Zoë snapped, glaring down.

"Ah! Let me go!" Dr. Ellis spat back. Her eyes flicked to the side where she spotted the newcomers. "Dr. Wiley! What are— are you *with* these lunatics?"

"No, of course not!" Dr. Jack said. "They forced me up here. I'm sorry."

"Quiet! Both of you!" Zoë yelled. The room fell silent except for the ragged breathing of those on the floor and Ellis's distressed moans. Zoë looked down at her newest prisoner. "You're the head admin of this facility, correct?"

Ellis remained almost motionless for a few moments. Her eyes watered from the pain of Zoë's knees digging deeper into her thighs. She nodded.

"If we let you up, you're going to behave, right? No fighting, no trying to call security. *No shooting us.* We ask questions, you tell us what we want to know. No one gets hurt, everybody's happy."

Again, Ellis stayed quiet for a few seconds, squirming against Zoë and Arthur, but thinking, considering the proposal.

"Okay," Dr. Ellis said.

Zoë nodded to Arthur, who removed his hands from Ellis's wrists but held them close in case she tried anything. When she didn't, he climbed to his feet.

Next, Zoë rolled her knees off Ellis's legs and stood, watching the head of The Shepherd's Institute sit up and rub at her sore thighs.

"Take a seat," Zoë said, pointing to the chair she had tackled Ellis out of earlier, which now lay a few feet away. Zoë turned, motioned to Maggie for the gun. Maggie handed it over.

Ellis climbed to her feet slowly, eyeing Zoë. She righted the chair and plopped down onto it, looking up at Zoë again with a thin smirk.

"You think I don't know why you're here?" Ellis said.

"I know you do," Zoë said, inspecting the small gun in her hand, then looked up. "That's why we had Dr. Jack here bring us to you." Zoë motioned a thumb over her shoulder, but kept her eyes locked on the woman in the chair. "So spill it. Tell us where."

"Where what?" The smirk on Ellis's face grew more pronounced.

"You know damn well what I'm talking about!"

"I do?"

"Yes, you do," Zoë said, leaning in closer. "And I'm sure you know who I am as well."

"I do indeed."

"Then you know what I'm capable of. You can just tell us . . ." Zoë eyed the gun in her hand as if it were an insult. She pocketed the gun, cracked her knuckles in plain view, and finished, "or I can make it hurt. Up to you."

Dr. Ellis's smirk faded almost instantly. She swallowed and cleared her trembling throat.

"Well, if you put it that way," she said. "But let me ask you something first. Even if I tell you where to go, where the subject is being kept, it's not a place you can just walk into unannounced and expect to walk out."

"I'm sure we'll manage," Zoë said. "Now tell me where you're keeping her!"

The look on Ellis's face changed again, this time from fear of the pain Zoë might inflict upon her, to confusion. Her brow contracted.

"*Her?*"

"Yes!" Zoë said. "Lydia Darrow! Where is she?"

Ellis's brow relaxed, rose on her forehead as she tilted her head in question. It was astonishment; that and the look of someone who knew a secret others did not.

"Lydia Darrow?" Ellis said. "That's who . . . you're here for Darrow?"

"Of course we are, now tell us where she is!"

"My God, you . . ." Ellis shook her head slightly. "You don't know?"

"Know what?" Simon said, stepping forward, but keeping his lock on Dr. Jack.

Ellis gave Simon a reproachful look, her head jerking back, but kept her knowing smile all the time.

"What you're really looking for," she said. "You don't know what this, all this, is about."

"Sure we do. We're here to rescue Lydia and uncover whatever it is you and your EXLI pals are hiding."

Dr. Ellis laughed.

"But you don't *know*, do you? What you're really after."

"Then tell us!" Simon said. He felt his blood pumping, color rising in his face. He didn't like the feeling of this woman toying with them.

Ellis shook her head.

"No, no, no. I can't do that."

"Sure you can," Zoë said, stepping forward, showing her trademark intimidating look. "*Tell us.*"

But Ellis continued to shake her head and laughed again. "You wouldn't believe me if I tried. It's not something that can be explained, only witnessed—*experienced.*"

Simon eyed Ellis, now confused in his own right. What was this strange talk about not believing her? Why couldn't she just tell them what she meant?

Zoë, it seemed, was more frustrated and impatient than confused. She grabbed Ellis by the shirt collar, lifting her from the chair. "Take us to Lydia."

But Ellis stared back at her and in a soft, defiant voice, said "No."

"No?"

"You heard me," Ellis said. "You can demand whatever you want, but if you think I'll take you anywhere you're mistaken. Oh no. I'm going to sit right here. Call it a non-violent protest."

Zoë growled as her eyes squeezed together, squinting at Ellis, as if studying, trying to read her. She released Ellis's collar and for a moment, Simon thought Zoë would slap her. But he could see her thinking still, something happening behind her eyes.

Instead of attacking, Zoë reached into her pocket, pulled out the small gun, and pointed it at Ellis.

"Sure, you could refuse. Sit here, do nothing," Zoë said. "Of course, then we have no use for you and I'll just kill you now."

Ellis's defiant expression melted from her face. She swallowed, her eyes bulging as they danced from Zoë to the other occupants in the room. Zoë saw this change and went on.

"Then again, we *could* be merciful. Let's say we leave you here, tie you up. Then let's say we go back out there and get ourselves caught. Even if that happens, do you really think Sullivan will let you live after such a failure? After you allowed us to infiltrate this place, get up here, break into your office, and restrain you?" Zoë paused, staring Ellis in the eyes.

"Mr. Sullivan doesn't . . ." Ellis said, her voice shaky. "He would never—"

"Kill?" It was Zoë who laughed now. She shook her head. "He certainly has before and he will again. I *know* Sullivan. I know how that bastard operates, and he does *not* forgive."

Ellis's eyes scanned from Zoë to Arthur to Simon and Maggie. And finally, landed on Dr. Jack, a captor like herself.

"Do you really need to think about it, doc?" Zoë said. "Your only option—the only way you get out of this alive—is if you help us. Take us where we want to go. We save Lydia, take down Sullivan, and when the smoke clears . . . you may get to keep running the little husk house you got going here. At the very least, you'd be alive."

Ellis's gaze lingered on Dr. Jack the entire time Zoë spoke. When Zoë stopped, Ellis turned her eyes back, paused, then nodded.

"Okay," she said, her voice soft, calm. "I'll take you where you want to go."

"Good," Zoë said. She held the small gun up in front of Ellis's eyes. "But just to be safe, I'll keep this in my pocket, pointed at you. Just keep that in mind. No crazy ideas. Just do as I say and this'll all be over soon."

Zoë may have been satisfied enough with Ellis's apparent cooperation to move on, but Simon still wasn't sure. Not yet. He kept his eyes on Ellis, watching for a suspicious facial expression, or a twinkle in her eyes. Something that would confirm his lingering suspicions that she had ulterior motives for agreeing to help them. He knew there had to be something there, something brewing in Ellis's mind she wasn't saying outright. He'd watched her the whole time. He'd seen the way her eyes had lingered on Dr. Jack. There was something else there. A studying, scheming stare that unsettled Simon. A look that made him suspect they could be walking into a trap.

27

———

Despite Simon's lingering doubts about whether it was a good idea to trust Dr. Ellis, even a little, he realized they didn't have much of a choice. Trap or not, they needed her help. Without it, they'd have no way of locating Lydia, or the mysterious subject they knew was also hidden somewhere on the premises.

The subject, Simon thought. Why was Ellis so cagey about identifying this person?

You wouldn't believe me if I tried. It's not something that can be explained, only witnessed—experienced.

She'd refused to say anymore, even under threat of beating from Zoë. Why couldn't she just spit it out?

You wouldn't believe me if I tried.

Simon didn't believe a lot of what Ellis said, or did. Starting with her apparent willingness to help them and ending with the ambiguous language she used when referring to this subject. Whomever *he* was. Simon was sure of that one thing—that it was a he.

The he.

And he was the key.

"Lydia's being held in the same place as him, isn't she?"

Simon asked, trying to use what little knowledge they had to his advantage. "The subject. The man Sullivan's been keeping secret."

"What man?" Dr. Ellis said, feigning ignorance, not falling for it. Though her eyebrows rose ever so slightly.

"The *subject*." Simon's gaze burned at Ellis. "He's not some normal patient. He's a prisoner. Sullivan has him locked up here somewhere."

Ellis's eyebrows rose even higher.

"Does he?"

"We're wasting time," Zoë said. "We need to find Lydia and get the fuck outta here."

"No," Simon said, eyes still on Ellis.

"What?"

Simon turned to Zoë.

"I said no. Lydia can wait. We need to find this man, whoever he is."

Zoë blinked rapidly, shook her head as if she didn't hear Simon right.

"*Excuse me*, but we came here to get Lydia back and retrieve the information Max gave her. Not go chasing some ghost you think your friend told you about."

"Max?" Dr. Ellis asked, her ears perking up at the name, mind working. "Maxwell Lewis? He . . . ." Her eyes narrowed. She sneered. "Yes, I suppose he does seem like the rat type."

"Shut the fuck up," Zoë said, shooting a nasty glance at Ellis. She turned back to Simon. "You really want to just abandon Lydia?"

Simon considered Zoë's question, her chosen course of action, but he couldn't bring himself to agree. He didn't want to completely disregard the mission to save Lydia. He couldn't. He'd come along with the rest of them to save her, hadn't he? Because he'd grown to care for Lydia over the past two days, to recognize her importance in the struggle against EXLI. He knew her survival was paramount to the future of that fight and the entire human race . . . and yet, Simon couldn't shake the feeling that he had to go a different route. In that moment, everything for him led to this mystery man. This *subject.* That's where Sebastian's message was pointing them. That's where it would all end. And Ellis knew where he was, could lead them there. They needed to discover who the subject was and why he'd been locked up in this place. EXLI had been willing to kill to keep those secrets. Learning the truth would give them an advantage over EXLI, over Sullivan. It could be the key to everything.

"No. Not abandon her," Simon said. "I'm just saying once we find this man they're hiding, once we learn the truth, we'll have leverage. And leverage against Sullivan and EXLI is a powerful weapon, one we could use to bargain for Lydia's life, and our own, should it come to that. It's something we can use to get justice for Will and Maxwell and everyone we lost. And prevent EXLI from hurting anyone else ever again."

"You can't know that for sure. It's a big risk."

"True. But it's a risk I'm willing to take. To stake my life on. And I think, were our places switched, Lydia'd do the exact same thing. She'd understand the importance of all this. Of finally having a real chance to expose EXLI and Sullivan, and taking it."

"But if this man is as important as you say he is, then he's probably locked up tight." Zoë looked at Ellis. "Am I right?"

"Oh, yes," Dr. Ellis said. "We call it the vault, so . . ."

"And guards? How many?"

"A few. No idea about the exact number. They're stationed at various points around the floor."

Zoë turned back to Simon.

"You heard her," she said.

"Yeah, I did," Simon said, "But getting past guards is a problem we'll have no matter what we do. She said they're stationed everywhere. There's probably just as many around Lydia."

Silence fell in the room as Zoë stared at Simon for a few seconds more, studying his face. He could tell she was thinking, running things over in her mind. Her eyes darted around the room, to Arthur, Maggie, Ellis, and then back to Simon.

"No," Zoë said shaking her head. "I can't go along with this. We came here for Lydia. She's our mission."

A part of Simon knew that would be her answer. But he was prepared. He'd made up his mind and refused to budge.

"I get that," he said. "I don't want to see Lydia harmed anymore. I want her saved. I get that she's your mission, but I have a different one. I need to find this subject, figure out who he is and what they're doing to him. That's *my* mission. If I have to go alone, then so be it."

"Not alone," Maggie said with a confident nod at Simon. "I'll come with you." She stepped closer to him to show which side she was on, looking at Zoë and Arthur. "It's like Simon said, we have to uncover the truth. Finding this man, exposing his secret, that's the best option to hit Sullivan where it hurts most."

Simon felt a warmth inside him at Maggie's words, her support. Though he saw her look of confidence fade into a wrinkled expression, a disgust at the mention of Sullivan.

Zoë threw up her arms in disbelief. She shook her head again and said, "No. You two, by yourselves, with this one in tow." Zoë pointed at Ellis. "It'll never work. You'll be found out as soon as we split up down there and then we're all fucked. No. I can't allow it. I won't."

Simon had already been collecting his thoughts, forming his rebuttal as he listened to Zoë reject his idea to split from the group. He'd argue his case, tell Zoë she couldn't stop him. No matter what. She'd have to tie him up and lock him away to prevent him from seeking out the subject. But before he could say anything, another voice of reason spoke up.

"What if there's a way to do both?" Arthur said. Simon looked at him like an eager student waiting for a teacher's next word. Zoë, like a skeptical principal watching from the back of the classroom.

"You mean split up?" Simon said. "That's what I've been—"

"Yes, but not like you're saying," Arthur said, silencing Simon. "Whatever we do is bound to set off alarms eventually. If we all head off to save Lydia, then our chances of getting to this vault after are slim to none. Then again, if we go to the mystery man first, we could lose the chance to save Lydia. They might kill her as soon as they're alerted to our presence. So we split up. Divide and conquer. It makes the most strategic sense."

"But they can't go alone," Zoë said, motioning to Simon and Maggie.

"I know. That's why you're going with them."

"I'm . . ." Zoë looked confused, then what Arthur had said sank in. Her eyes grew large and she shook her head hard. "No fuckin' way!"

"You don't trust that I can save her on my own?"

"Of course I trust you! There's just no way in hell that I'm not going to be the one to go after Lydia. I won't allow it. I'm the leader here and I'm making the call! If anything, *I'll* go get Lydia. *You* go on the mystery man tour."

Arthur's face crumpled in concentration. He didn't like the thought of Zoë—his leader—going off alone. No support. Exposed. But what choice did they have? She was adamant about going, and Simon and Maggie couldn't go alone. He nodded at Zoë, acknowledging her command.

Zoë walked up close to Simon. She stared him directly in the face, her pointed brow and narrowed eyes an obvious attempt at intimidation. As if waiting for Simon to flinch and change his mind, to break and tell her he was wrong. That they should all just stick together.

But Simon stared right back, trying to show the confidence he felt in their new plan.

Zoë stared a moment longer, said, "Well then I guess that's it. No time to waste." She turned away. Her new focus, the cowering doctor they'd brought up from the 20th floor.

"Sorry, Dr. Jack," Zoë said, "but there's no room for tourists this time."

"Are you . . . going to kill me?" he said, eyes wide with fear.

Arthur and Maggie looked at Dr. Jack, then back at Zoë, waiting for her response. But Simon, his showdown with Zoë over, remembered what he'd seen minutes before and shifted his glance to Ellis. She hadn't looked at Dr. Jack like the rest. Her gaze was locked on Zoë. A focused, studying look. Expectant. Very much interested in Zoë's response to the question.

Zoë smirked but shook her head.

"No. We won't be killing you today," she said, stepping toward the frightened doctor. "Just gonna make sure you can't alert anyone to our presence. Nothing personal."

―――――――

EACH OF THEIR group (including their remaining hostage) had slipped on one of the white lab coats hanging in the wardrobe in Ellis's office. The coat Simon had put on turned out to be a little short and tight around the shoulders, but the others fit the three women well. Arthur had pulled the coat he would be wearing off Dr. Jack before tying the doctor's hands and legs together, placing a gag around his mouth, and stuffing him into the wardrobe. After that, they were on their way.

"Okay," Zoë said, once they'd all stuffed themselves into the small elevator at the end of the hall and the doors closed. "What floor?"

At Zoë's words, Simon's eyes moved to the elevator keypad. He stared at the columns of numbers, wondering which one it could be. What floor held the great mystery EXLI was trying to keep secret?

"One," Dr. Ellis said, staring forward, eyes unmoving.

Simon's gaze flashed from Ellis to the panel of floor buttons, and back to their hostage's unflinching face again. He watched her closely, waiting for some kind of tell, but she just kept looking forward.

"You sure?" Zoë said in a moment of hesitation as well, of careful thought. Zoë pushed the gun in her pocket outward, into Ellis's side. "You wouldn't be trying to play any tricks on us, would you? Heading to the main floor so the people there can catch us."

Ellis shook her head slowly.

"I wouldn't dream of it. Darrow and—" She stopped herself, and then said, "—the subject, are on the first floor."

Again, Simon's eyes darted between the panel of floor buttons and Ellis. But he was drawn back to the panel. The buttons. Why?

Zoë reached forward, her finger poised to press the circular button labeled with a black 1.

"Stop!" he shouted, his raised voice echoing in that confined space as his final realization sank in. Zoë's hand froze an inch away from the button.

"What is it?"

"She's lying. Lydia's not on the first floor."

Simon looked at Ellis, but her gaze remained forward on the closed doors.

"Then where is she?" Zoë said impatiently.

"I think . . ." Simon began, and then reached toward the elevator's keypad with both hands. He extended his pointer fingers and, at the same time, pressed the two buttons farthest apart on the keypad—floors 1 and 20. Both buttons lit up simultaneously, and for a second nothing else happened. In that moment, Simon thought his apparent epiphany had been incorrect. But a long second after that, a different, deeper chime sounded inside the elevator, and the small fingerprint reader next to the button labeled R pulsed with light. The thin line of light that had scanned Dr. Jack's thumbprint on their ride up started rising and falling. It'd been green before but now glowed a bright red.

Simon looked up at Maggie with a smile, then the others.

"How did you know?" Arthur said.

"Sebastian's message," Simon said. The number, he thought. 120. He'd been thinking about it wrong the whole time, as a single number. But Sebastian, in his hasty, garbled message, hadn't said it that way had he? He'd said 120. One twenty. Not one, two, zero. Not one hundred and twenty. *One twenty*. Somewhere in the back of Simon's mind, he'd realized the connection. He'd been looking curiously at the buttons in the elevators since they arrived at The Shepherd's Institute, but hadn't understood his preoccupation with them until just now.

"Well done," Zoë said before grabbing Ellis by the shoulder and turning her around. "No tricks, huh?"

"I had to try," Ellis said with a shrug.

Zoë's eyes narrowed. She tightened her grip on the woman's shoulder, drew out the gun in her pocket. Ellis's face crumpled in pain as she tried to shrink back from the pinch and the barrel of the gun, but Zoë's grasp was firm.

"*Don't* do anything like that again," Zoë said, pointing the gun at her, twisting her fingers deeper into Ellis's shoulder. The doctor yelped. "We just need your thumb. I could easily break it off and be done with you." She pocketed the gun again and thrust Ellis toward the elevator buttons, her grip unyielding. "Do it."

Dr. Ellis had gotten the message. She lifted a hand and

pressed her thumb to the glowing red fingerprint reader. The thin red light danced up and down. Another chime sounded and the elevator began to descend. Only then, did Zoë release her.

They watched the illuminated display above the elevator doors as the floor numbers ticked by, lower and lower. Simon felt a drop in his stomach, his heart rate growing higher as the elevator sank. From the looks on everyone else's faces, he knew he was not alone in his tense feelings. They thought they had discovered the secret means of getting to the level where Lydia was being held, but wouldn't know for sure until they reached the first floor. If they continued going, they were on the right track. If they stopped, well, then they'd been fooled by Ellis again.

They passed the fourth floor, then the third. The elevator did not slow. Simon felt more and more confident that they were headed on the right course. They passed the second with no signs of slowing down. The number on the display above the door changed to 1, then to 0, and the elevator continued to descend.

"Basement it is," Zoë said. "Get ready everyone. Try to stay calm, and let the doc here introduce us as needed. You got that?"

Ellis nodded but showed no signs of readying herself. This, as they soon discovered, was with good reason because after they passed the first floor, the elevator did not stop a single level below. Nor did it stop soon after that. The floor number on the display above the doors stayed at 0, but they continued to descend deeper and deeper below the building.

"How far down is this basement?" Simon asked.

"Oh, quite a ways," Dr. Ellis said.

No matter how deep it ended up being, they at least had a rudimentary idea of what to expect when they reached the subterranean floor—or as Ellis called it, *the lab*. Zoë's thorough questioning of Ellis minutes before in her office had made sure of that. Floor layout, normal guard positions, and security monitoring had all been discussed. Though, according to Ellis, the cameras hung throughout the laboratory floor were apparently only looked at in review, not monitored around the clock. And through all the questioning, Ellis had remained adamant that she didn't know where Lydia was being held.

But after Ellis's little stunt with the elevator buttons, Zoë remained less than convinced of her willingness to cooperate. Zoë grabbed their hostage, spun her around, and gave Ellis the same I'll-break-your-thumb-off look she'd shown moments before.

"How do we know you're not lying about what you told us before?" Zoë said.

Ellis shrugged. "We're headed to the lab, aren't we? He figured out the buttons."

"You didn't answer my question."

Ellis grinned and said, "No. I was not lying." Her eyes widened, eyebrows rising and falling, wordlessly asking whether Zoë was satisfied. Zoë remained still for a moment, searching Ellis's eyes, then spun her back around.

Silence fell once more.

They waited, watching the reflective elevator doors and the unchanging 0 on the floor display. As they moved deeper and deeper, Simon kept his eyes on Ellis. His suspicion of the woman seemed to grow with every second of their decent. Ellis had told them she'd help. She hadn't responded to Zoë's threats as well as their attempt to reason. The scenarios Zoë had laid out made sense. They all knew Sullivan was ruthless and he'd likely have Ellis killed for her failure. Helping them expose Sullivan and removing him from power at EXLI was the only way Ellis could avoid that death sentence . . . Or was it? Ellis certainly wasn't fully on board with their plan. She'd just tried to fool them with the elevator buttons. Simon's mind filled with questions, possibilities. Maybe she saw Zoë's reasoning at first, but had since changed her mind. He lingered on his memories of Ellis back in the office, the way she had looked at Dr. Jack—when he'd been their captive and they'd decided to tie him up. Why focus on him? What had she seen?

And then a new possibility struck Simon. What if they failed? What if Ellis led them to this secret, underground laboratory, and they did not find Lydia or the subject? What if they were found out and Ellis was the one to alert the authorities? Surely, she'd receive the benefit of the doubt for being the one to bring the intruders to justice. If she was the one responsible for their capture, if she showed her *loyalty* to Sullivan, even he might grant her some kind of reprieve from punishment, from death.

Simon stared at Ellis as though, if he tried hard enough, he would be able to penetrate her thoughts and discover what she was truly thinking. But, of course, it was no use. He couldn't read her mind. He could only watch her and hope that if she had plans to betray them, they would be able to spot her intentions before it was too late.

As Simon's mind worked, his thoughts spun faster and faster. The walls of the elevator seemed to grow closer. Simon had never been a claustrophobic type of person before, but was beginning to understand why some people were. He reached out and grasped Maggie's hand, felt instant comfort.

"Are you okay?" Maggie said.

"Yeah," he said. "I'll just be happy when all this is over."

"Me too."

He squeezed her hand and she squeezed back. If he could be certain about nothing else, Simon knew he'd be okay as long as he had Maggie by his side.

A few seconds later, the elevator finally began to slow.

"Ready," Zoë said, then added, "You better not fuck us, doc. I still haven't ruled out taking your thumb."

The floor display above the doors changed from 0 to B as the elevator came to a soft stop. A chime sounded.

As the doors slid open, Simon felt his prior sense of claustrophobia start to wash away, like releasing a long-held breath of air. His heart rate would slow, his nerves calm. Everything would be all right now that they were exiting that cramped elevator . . . that was, until he saw what was on the other side of the sliding silver doors.

It was another white hallway, this time without the blue streaks on the walls. It looked like it extended far into the distance, but Simon couldn't be sure because the view was obstructed. A few paces out from the elevator doors was a wall made of thick, metal bars like an interior gate in a prison. Cut into the middle, a door made of the same bars, a fingerprint scanner affixed to the side. And standing in the hallway on the other side of the door, a man in gray fatigues—a guard. His right hand sat against the butt of a pistol tucked in its holster on his hip. His left hand sat poised on his other hip. Dark crescents could be seen under his tired eyes, but he stared forward, locked on the group of new arrivals standing in the elevator.

"You said *unmanned* door!" Zoë hissed so only they could hear.

Dr. Ellis did not respond. She cleared her throat. Was there a tremble in her voice? She stepped out of the elevator and in a commanding, instructional tone, said, "Follow me, recruits."

Ca. No. 2432615184

Document 47, REDACTED. Filed 3/31.

Copy: Email correspondence from head of Subt.

Security, Shepherd's Institute.

———

XXXXXX, XXXAM

From: **XXXXXXX**@shepinst.exli.com

To: subt.sec.allteams@shepinst.exli.com

Attention:

ALL OFFICERS AND RESERVES REPORT FOR DUTY IMME-DIATELY.

Active duty guards currently on the clock, remain at your posts and your section leaders will be around soon to inform you of continued shifts and re-assignments as necessary.

All reserve and off-duty guards, report to the lab immediately for assignment.

LEVEL 7 ACCESS ENGAGED.

XX XXXX XXXXXX XXXXX XX being handled in the North Quadrant. Therefore, **the North Quad has been deemed restricted until further notice.** Only guards and select laboratory personnel will be allowed admittance. (List of allowed personnel is attached.)

Remaining personnel will still be allowed and active in South, West, and East Quadrants. They have been made aware of Level 7 Access and restriction of North Quad, but will still be using labs and moving about elsewhere.

All unmanned lab access points and the main elevator entrance will be assigned guards.

Guards will be posted at all fingerprint scanners. No access will be admitted without scans plus ID cards. The same goes for high-priority areas, such as **XXX XXXXX** and the retinal scan located there.

You **must** check in with your section leader upon arrival.

XXXXXXXX XXXXX

Head of Subterranean Security, Shepherd's Institute

28

SIMON, MAGGIE, ZOË, AND ARTHUR FOLLOWED AS ELLIS MADE her way up to the door in the wall of metal bars. They stopped and Ellis peered through the bars. Her face softened and she looked at the man standing on the other side like a friend, or at least a familiar work colleague.

"Identification, please," the guard said.

Up close now, Simon saw the tiredness of the guard more clearly, even on his youthful face. The dark shade under his eyes stood out more, the skin at his cheeks sagged. His short brown hair glistened under the harsh fluorescent glow of the overhead lights; it stuck out, looked almost frayed at the corners of his hairline.

"Identification hell, Bart. You know who *I* am."

"Yeah, I know, but, well—"

"And why do they have you posted here anyway?" Ellis said. "You're usually over in the eastern quad, right?"

Bart's shoulders sank a little as his posture relaxed. He gave a dismissive sweep with the hand he'd been resting on his gun and then dropped it to his side. "Yup. Until I was *volunteered* for this post last night. Double shift. I ain't been home in, ah, goin' on 26 hours now." He rubbed at his forehead, ruffling the hair there more.

"That's rough," Ellis said, her voice taking on a lighter, empathetic tone. "Well hopefully they let you free sometime soon, eh?"

"Yeah, *hopefully*." The corners of his mouth twitched, like he wanted to smile, but he couldn't pull off the muscle movement in his distracted, sleep-deprived state. "Anyway, gonna need to see your ID, doc."

Ellis started to pat at her coat pocket, searching.

"Not sure I have it," she said. "Everyone knows who *I* am. I've never needed it before down here."

Simon's ears perked up at Ellis's emphasis on the word I. What was that about? And had she done that before?

"Yeah, sorry about that. Temporary change of protocol."

Ellis pulled an ID card from her pocket, held it up to Bart the guard so he could see it through the metal bars. He eyed it, looked at Ellis's face, paused, then nodded. His gaze drifted back to the four other people standing behind her. He jerked his head in their direction.

"New recruits," Ellis said. "Transfers from downtown." She waved her ID to bring Bart's attention back to her. "Is my ID enough for them? I'm afraid they don't have theirs yet. Fingerprints aren't even in the system. They're *that* new. I just *really wanted* to show them around."

There it was again, Simon thought. That strange emphasis in Ellis's words. What was she doing? Whatever it was, Simon didn't like the sound of it.

Bart's gaze flicked between Ellis and the rest of the group again. Simon thought the guard's eyes seemed to linger on him longer than the rest. Was he just being paranoid?

Bart rubbed his tired, red eyes. He squinted, blinked as if they were dry, then brought his gaze back to Dr. Ellis. "More *Non-Rejuvenite* scientists, eh?"

"All but one, yes. She's the only *sensible* one, if you ask me," Ellis said, shooting the guard a wink. "But despite that, they *do* know their stuff. They know *a lot*, actually. That's why they're here."

Simon wanted to reach out and swat Ellis. Her odd speech patterns were clear to him now. He knew what she was up to and could only hope the tired guard wouldn't catch on.

Bart remained silent for a moment longer, struggling to think. He rubbed his stubbly chin and said, "Whatever you say, doc." He waved a hand, beckoning them to the gate.

Ellis's face sagged for the briefest of moments and then quickly shifted. She beamed up at Bart and thanked him. Ellis placed her thumb on the pad at the center of the small, black box attached to the wall. Red light scanned her fingerprint. The box beeped. A heavy click sounded from the locking mechanism on the door and it swung open.

"So you never told me, Bart. What's with the guard duty?" Ellis said, pulling the door open further and stepping through. Zoë followed close behind her, then the rest of the group.

"Temporary change of—"

"Protocol. Yes, you mentioned that. But *why*? There some kind of *trouble*?"

Bart shrugged. "No. Not that I know of. But they got our guys stationed all over now. Level 7 Access. Don't know specifics beyond that, except that the orders came down to my boss from Mr. Sullivan himself."

Simon froze when he heard the name. He looked away, up the hallway, as if expecting to see Sullivan standing there, watching them. But he only saw a few far-off walkers in lab coats. Simon tried to force his face into a more casual expression. When he looked back, he saw a narrow-eyed look on Maggie's face, as if she were both annoyed and deep in thought. Her cheeks throbbed as she clenched her jaw. She only relaxed her face again when she noticed Simon looking her way.

"Sullivan is here?" Ellis's tone held a slight quiver. As though the prospect of Sullivan's presence frightened her. "Why wasn't I notified?"

"Visit wasn't scheduled. Last minute arrival. I didn't actually see them come in. But the north quad's restricted until further notice."

"*Them*?"

"Yeah," Bart continued. "The big three, they're all here. First Mr. Sullivan and Purcell. Dr. Vapula came in shortly after."

"Any idea what they're up to?"

"Not really. Something about a high priority asset. If I had to guess, probably huddled in O-800. But who knows? Above my pay grade."

"Yeah, I understand. Thanks anyway." Ellis walked past the guard. "Well, see you around, Bart." She waved over her shoulder as she started down the hall, her recruits following in her wake. When they reached the first intersecting hallway, Ellis turned them down it.

Arthur scanned both directions. There were more guards armed with holstered pistols posted at either end of the hallway, but they were facing away. He seized the moment, grabbing Ellis by the arm and pushing her through a nearby door. The rest of the group followed into what appeared to be a vacant lounge, complete with a refrigerator, counter topped with a coffee machine, and small, round lunch tables surrounded by plastic chairs. Arthur's eyes burned down at Ellis.

"What are you playing at?" he said. "I heard the way you were talking to that guy, trying to give him signals."

"What? I don't—" Ellis hissed.

"Drop the act! I *heard* you."

"I heard her too," Simon said.

Ellis wrinkled her nose at Simon, then turned back to Arthur. Her lips formed a weak smile, her eyebrows rose, wordlessly asking what he was going to do. They needed Ellis to lead them where they wanted to go. They couldn't just tie her up and leave her there.

Arthur sneered but stepped away. Ellis's smile grew wider, basking in her small victory. Until Zoë took Arthur's place, glaring down at Ellis and giving her a quick elbow jab in the ribs. She doubled over and held up a hand to indicate she wanted no more.

"Now that *that's* out of the way," Zoë said, "Tell me which way I need to go. Sullivan and his cronies are to the north. Guessing Lydia's the asset your pal mentioned, that they're interrogating her there, correct?"

Ellis stood back up, rubbing her side, and nodded. "If Darrow is down here, yes, I think it's safe to assume Sullivan's with her."

Zoë shook her head, gave a frustrated sigh.

"I should have realized this would happen," she said. "They brought Lydia here on purpose. Of course Sullivan would be here." Zoë bit at her bottom lip.

Simon watched as Zoë started to pace the room and wondered if she was reconsidering their situation, their plan. They'd decided to split up when they thought they'd be facing a normal allotment of guards. But now, with Sullivan's presence and increased security forces, splitting up may not be the best idea. Was Zoë thinking the same thing? Would she suddenly change her mind and demand they all go together to try to save Lydia?

Simon was already preparing a rebuttal to that revised plan in his head. He looked to Maggie in hopes of support, but saw a faraway look on her face. She remained silent and appeared deep in thought. Simon assumed she was thinking the same thing he was.

"I don't like the idea of you going off on your own," Arthur said. "Not with Sullivan and the others in the mix now too."

Zoë stopped her pacing, gave Arthur a small nod, but looked back at Ellis.

"Your guard friend back there mentioned O-800," she said. "That's a room, right? In the north quadrant?"

"Yes," Ellis said, explaining in greater detail the layout of the entire subterranean floor. How the whole thing was a collection of small laboratories, offices, and examination rooms. She said there were a few free offices on the north side that they might use to interrogate Lydia, but she suspected that Sullivan, Purcell, and Vapula were more than likely in the room Bart had called out— the one designated O-800. Ellis said that that's where Sullivan normally spent his time at the facility. Though she made a point to say that Sullivan, Vapula, and Purcell had never all been there at the same time before.

"But that room isn't the same place the subject is being held, right?" Simon said.

"Correct. The vault's on the opposite end of the floor, in the south quad."

Simon's eyes flashed to Zoë again, still expecting her to declare the plan changed.

"Sullivan being here isn't ideal," Zoë said. "I agree with that." Her eyes danced between Arthur, Simon, and Maggie. "But I think we should stick to the plan. You three find the mystery man. I go get Lydia. And if Sullivan gets in my way, well, then too bad for him."

Simon couldn't speak. All thoughts of potential rebuttal evaporated from his mind. Zoë hadn't wanted to change their plan after all. They were over that hurdle and one step closer to finding the subject, to uncovering the truth, finally. Simon almost cracked a smile at the thought. He looked at Maggie, to share in the moment, but froze.

He saw a familiar expression on Maggie's face. Narrowed lips, brow creased in concentration. She was thinking, yes, but not about which decision to make. She'd already made up her mind. She was staring at Zoë, determined.

Simon's stomach sank. He knew what choice Maggie had made. It was as if he could sense it or see into her head, watch her thoughts coming together. And he knew he'd be unable to change her mind.

"We need to get going," Zoë said.

"Agreed," Arthur said, "We don't have—"

"I'm coming with you," Maggie said.

Simon closed his eyes, exhaled slowly, then opened them again and looked at Maggie.

"Yeah, of course. I—"

"No." Maggie did not shake her head. Her gaze moved from Arthur to Zoë. "Not you, Arthur. Her."

"Me?" Zoë said, pointing at herself.

"Yes. I'm going with you to save Lydia."

"Sorry, but that's not the plan. No way am I dragging *you* along."

Zoë screwed up her face at Maggie, but still looked baffled, shaking her head. She turned her gaze back and forth between Arthur and Maggie, then finally turned to Simon, hoping for some backup. But Simon did not say a word. He was staring at Maggie, a different kind of disbelief etched on his face.

"I'm *coming* with you," Maggie said, her face determined, unflinching as she stared down Zoë. "I know you don't like me. You don't like *what I am*. But none of that matters now. If you're going where Sullivan is, then I am too. He's the reason we're in this place. He's the reason Sebastian sent that message to Simon. *He's* the reason my brother is dead. And I'm going to be there to confront him, to make him answer for what he's done."

Maggie was standing in front of Zoë now, eyes forward, unmoving. No longer would Maggie be shielded by others, keep her head down in the backseat of the car, or get told to stay behind while everyone else set off on a mission. She was here. She was as much a part of the group as everyone else and she'd made up her mind. No one, not Arthur, Simon, or even the hardened Zoë could change her mind.

Zoë took a half-step back. There was a hint of a gleam in her eye as she stared back at Maggie, said, "Look, I admire your passion, but what if I still say no?"

"Then I'll go anyway," Maggie said. "You can't stop me."

As much as it pained Simon, he knew she was right. Even if Zoë refused to take her along, even if Simon begged her not to, Maggie would still go. She'd set out after Zoë and once they were outside, back in the open hallways, no one could argue or make any kind of scene without drawing the attention of the guards.

"Fine," Zoë said with a reluctant eye roll. "Have it your way then." She looked at Simon. "You two are meant for each other, you know that? So damn stubborn, the both of you."

Simon remained still, not even able to produce a weak smile in response to Zoë's comment. Maggie turned and stepped over to him. When she was close enough, she grabbed Simon's hands, squeezed them, and looked into his eyes.

"Simon, I—"

"I get it," he said before she could start what he suspected was to be an explanation for her decision. But he didn't need it. He understood. And Maggie didn't owe anyone an explanation. Her mouth hung open, wordless. Her eyes grew large, round. Those blue eyes of hers he loved so much. They weren't pleading or questioning, but resolute. "I don't like it, but I get it. If you're sure, then . . ."

"I just—he needs to pay for what he's done. And I need to be there when he does."

"I know," Simon said. "I understand. Even if I didn't, you'd still go anyway."

"I would," Maggie said. She started to look away, but Simon caught her chin, stopped her. He looked her in the eyes. "I'll be okay, really."

Simon nodded and gave her an encouraging smile. But in his heart, he doubted whether any of them would truly be okay. Not now. Not down here, in this place. Even if they were all to stick together, he doubted they'd make it out unscathed.

"Besides," Maggie said, motioning toward Zoë. "Zoë will be there with me."

"Oh, now *I'm* the one who's *with* you," Zoë said, scoffing. "Remember who's in charge here."

Maggie gave Zoë a casual salute that was not returned.

But Simon kept his eyes on Zoë. She stared back, then nodded. They understood each other. Despite not wanting the tagalong, Zoë would still look out for Maggie.

"We need to get going," Zoë said. She glared at Ellis. "Just head back the way we came, right?"

"Yes," Ellis said. "There are signs to guide your way once you reach the far end of the floor."

"Thanks, doc. While I'm gone . . ." Zoë gave Ellis another quick jab in the side. "*Behave.*"

Ellis backed away from Zoë, nodding and rubbing at her ribs again. She waved at the door to indicate her willingness to leave, though Simon assumed it was more an eagerness to be rid of Zoë than to lead them where they wanted to go.

"If she doesn't, use this," Zoë said, and handed the subcompact pistol they'd pulled off Ellis earlier to Arthur. "15 minutes." Zoë eyed Ellis, who nodded again. "That should give us each enough time to get where we need to go. After that, all bets are off. We'll probably be captured or killed by then. But if by some stretch of the imagination we both succeed without setting off any alarms, meet back at the elevator."

Zoë studied the faces around her, settling on Arthur. Despite the rough exterior and performance she put on as the commander of Life Liberation, Simon could tell Zoë felt more in that moment. Her bond with Arthur showed through as their group prepared to divide. It didn't appear to be one of romantic love. No, it seemed to be more a deep camaraderie, a kinship forged through their many years working together. He was sure Zoë and Arthur had split up like this plenty of times before, but down here, in this secret laboratory basement of The Shepherd's Institute, with so much on the line, this parting was different. This time, neither seemed confident that they'd ever see the other again.

Simon could relate. He pulled Maggie into a hug, squeezed her tight. They kissed. It was a hurried, casual peck on the lips. As they pulled apart, Simon wondered if he should have held her longer, made the kiss last. Would it be the last time he kissed her? The last time he held her? The last time he ever saw her alive, or her him?

They all shared a final look as Arthur checked the hallway for guards. No more words. No goodbyes. Just a shared, mixed look of concern for each other and determination for their separate missions. When the coast was clear, they exited the small room and stepped back into the hallway.

Their group split in two, then . . . they were off.

Simon watched as Zoë and Maggie headed in the opposite direction, walking casually, trying to seem as normal as possible. To blend in. Maggie looked back once, gave Simon a confident grin before turning back around.

"Simon, let's go," Arthur whispered, tugging on the sleeve of Simon's lab coat.

Simon turned his head and saw Arthur and Ellis standing

behind him, waiting. He nodded, but before he set off with them, Simon looked back again to catch one last glimpse of Maggie.

But there was no sign of the second group. They had already slipped down an intersecting hallway and were out of sight.

No Zoë.

No Maggie.

They were gone.

29

———

MAGGIE WISHED SHE'D TAKEN ONE LAST LOOK BACK BEFORE THEY turned the corner, seen Simon one more time. But that moment had passed. There was no going back now. She and Zoë were on their own, walking side by side down a new hallway, trying to blend in as much as possible and not draw attention to themselves as they passed another guard on patrol.

During that first minute, Maggie's mind raced. Was splitting off with Zoë the right course of action? She had thought so back in the room, and was still confident about her decision now but still . . . there was a tiny shred of doubt lingering in the back of Maggie's mind. One that she'd tried her best not to show Simon before they parted. Did she *really* think leaving the rest of the group behind was the right choice? Yes. Of course. Zoë was going to save Lydia, and chances were high Zoë'd run into Sullivan along the way. As soon as Maggie had learned that, she knew she had to go. Sullivan was to blame for all this, everything, for Will's death, and she would be there to confront him. To make him pay. But that doubt crept up again . . . could she—Maggie—be the one to hold him accountable? She was certainly confident in Zoë's ability to handle herself given a potential confrontation, but

Maggie wondered if she, herself, was strong enough. Would she be able to stand toe-to-toe with Sullivan, given the opportunity? She wasn't sure. She *wanted* to be, felt she was and yet . . . that lingering itch at the back of her mind endured.

Again, she wished she had seen Simon one more time. She wished he were there with her now, if only to offer a confident look, a reassuring nod. But they'd gone their separate ways, toward individual goals. What would come next, where all this would end, remained unknown. Would they all make it out of this alive? Maggie thought not, and it sent a shiver up her spine. Her skin prickled underneath her lab coat. Would she join her brother as one of the casualties? Would Simon? Another shiver. No. She tried to shake the thought from her mind, but it persisted. But so did her brother's words, from what seemed like so long ago, back in that car as they fled the assassin. *It can work.* She knew that was true now. Maggie realized that part of her knew it back then as well. *It can work.* Yes, it could. They could work, but only after all this. If they even had an after. If that last glance back at Simon weren't the last time she'd ever see him alive. Or at all. If they completed their missions. If they made it out of this place safely. Then, and only then, would they get the chance to make it work.

A chance. That was all she wanted, walking down the hallway beside Zoë, marching toward some unknown end.

Yes, just a chance. That would do. That was all she could hope for now.

Zoë turned them down another hallway and they passed a group of three people—lab techs—coming out of what looked like a small laboratory. They looked up at Zoë and Maggie as they walked by, most eyes drawn to Zoë's flaming red hair which, unfortunately, stuck out more than they would have liked. Particularly down here, against the sterile, white hallways of this place. But Zoë was prepared. She gave the group a tiny smile and a nod, then looked ahead as they continued on their way. No big deal.

Just acknowledging a colleague as she walked to her destination, something she did every day. The group seemed appeased by Zoë's reaction and started chatting about test results as they walked the opposite direction.

"Do you know where we're going?" Maggie whispered as soon as they were out of earshot of the group.

Zoë gave a playful laugh, putting on an act as she had earlier on the floors above. "Of course. Of course. Almost there." She finished her response with a sharp look that was gone almost as soon as it had appeared.

They continued walking . . . and walking. Maggie watched the signs on the walls; their numbers and arrows pointed to different blocks of rooms. It made sense, but even so, the surrounding hallways and doors they passed all looked so similar that Maggie wondered if the staff still got lost occasionally.

"Are you sure?" Maggie asked when the pair of guards ahead of them turned down another hallway. "Is this the plan? They said the room was O-800, but I don't—"

Zoë clamped a hand on Maggie's shoulder and stopped them both. Her fierce look was back. Her sharp voice. She wagged a finger at Maggie and said, "Yes. I'm sure. We're going north to find Lydia. We're going to save her. That's our plan. If you don't like it, then you shouldn't have come along."

Maggie got the message, but she'd known it already. Zoë had wanted to make this trip alone, not with a tag-along, much less a Rejuvenite one. But Maggie was having none of it. She was done taking grief from Zoë. She had made her decision. She was committed to helping find Lydia, to confronting Sullivan. She wasn't going back. Not now.

"I'm not going anywhere," Maggie spat back. "If *you* don't like that, if you don't like *me*, then stay the hell out of my way. I'm only trying to make sure we're going the right way."

Zoë straightened her back, stunned. That gleam in her eye

more apparent. She looked at Maggie with a studying stare, then cracked a small grin.

"You know what?" Zoë whispered. "I *do* like you. Now. You've got spirit."

It was Maggie's turn to look shocked, eyebrows shooting up, mouth falling open. An admission of fondness from Zoë, however minimal, was the last thing Maggie had ever expected to hear. The hardened LL commander had even smiled at her. Maggie could think of no words with which to respond and remained in stunned silence.

"Now let's just stay quiet and act natural," Zoë said. "Follow me."

They reached the end of their current hallway and Zoë banked left. Maggie, however, nodded forward at the sign ahead. It was labeled "North Q" and stated that rooms N-200 and higher were to the right. Zoë course-corrected and gave Maggie a quick nod as they turned right down the next hallway.

They passed several more guards and a diminishing number of laboratory personnel along the way. Most paid them no mind, others only gave a glance. One or two of the guards did lock eyes on Zoë, and Maggie had worried in those moments that they'd been found out. Maybe it was Zoë's Non-Rejuvenite appearance or her red hair again that had drawn their eyes. Whatever it was, Maggie feared it was enough to call attention. They'd been caught and were about to be led away in handcuffs. But the guards had only given Zoë leering grins and raised their eyebrows. One even called her *baby*. Maggie rolled her eyes each time and they moved on, closer and closer to their intended destination.

And then Maggie saw it. They'd reached it faster than she thought they would. A sign on the wall ahead told them rooms O-100 and higher were around the corner up ahead. They saw a guard walk past in the intersecting hallway. Zoë slowed their approach as another guard passed by. If the number of guards indicated anything, Maggie thought, they were definitely in the right place.

As they approached the next hallway, Maggie steeled herself for what they might find there. Of course, there were more guards. But what else? Would Sullivan himself be standing around the corner? Would she be able to control herself if she saw him, the man who'd caused all their strife?

They crept closer, glancing ahead and behind them repeatedly for any signs of personnel or guards. If anyone saw them creeping as they were, it was sure to raise an alarm. Closer and closer . . . up to the edge of the hallway. Zoë patted the air near her waist with a palm to signal Maggie to stop. They craned their necks around the corner and peeked into the hallway—the place where they needed to go.

It was crawling with guards. Stationed at intervals along the corridor as far as they could see stood pairs of guards, all dressed in gray fatigues, all with some kind of weapon. Most had simple pistols in holsters attached to their hips. A few held flattop semi-automatic rifles hanging from shoulder straps. Farther down was another interesting hallway. In front of it, talking to a small group of guards, were two faces Maggie recognized. She'd seen them on TV recently standing behind Sullivan during his announcement. Samar Vapula and Michael Purcell.

Zoë pulled away from the corner of the hallway, creeping back the way they'd just come. Maggie followed her. They moved in silence, saying nothing until they were a safe distance away.

"Walk," Zoë whispered.

"Walk?" Maggie asked. "Where—"

"We need to get out of here."

"But I thought . . ." Maggie looked around, confused. "Wasn't that the right place?"

Zoë nodded.

"Oh, it was the right place all right. Did you see Vapula and

Purcell? If they're there, then Sullivan and Lydia can't be too far away."

"But that's where we have to go then."

"Yup," Zoë said, her eyes dancing from side to side, up ahead, searching for something. She turned them down another hallway, leading them farther and farther away from where they'd just been. "But we can't just march right through that many people. It's suicide."

Maggie followed along, still confused. She understood they couldn't fight through that many guards, but they had to do *something*. "So, now what?"

Zoë looked at Maggie, her large green eyes sparkling again, and said, "I have an idea."

30

ELLIS WALKED AHEAD OF SIMON AND ARTHUR, THE POINT OF their triangle. She turned them down a hallway much less crowded than the last two they'd walked through since leaving Maggie and Zoë. A man and woman Rejuvenite, dressed in pale green scrubs, were talking near a door, going over whatever notes were on the clipboard one held. The only other inhabitants of the hallway were a single guard with a pistol holstered on his hip who patrolled the length of the corridor and another two who stood at attention by either end.

The trio kept walking, past doors that dotted the sides of the hallways, leading to small labs and offices. Through windows in the doors, they could see doctors, technicians, and other laboratory personnel in lab coats and scrubs working inside many of the rooms. Most of the people they'd passed in the hallways seemed to pay them no mind, busy with work. Though, one or two did glance up when they recognized Ellis, nodding, smiling, or saying hello. The rest, like Simon and Arthur, instead chose to keep their gazes down or to the side, avoiding eye contact altogether.

The person Simon kept his eyes on most, or tried to, was Ellis.

She had positioned herself in front to keep up the appearance that she was leading them, as new arrivals, around the floor. Simon tried to keep up with her as best he could, keep her face in clear view even as he kept a watchful eye on the personnel and guards they passed. He watched to see if Ellis would continue her duplicitous ways, try to signal any of the guards. She made no obvious gestures, said nothing. Simon did see her eyes twitch and bulge occasionally. He wondered if she was just nervous, or if those small tweaks to her expression were purposeful. He couldn't very well call her out under the vigilant stares of the passing guards.

Simon knew Arthur was watching her too, which was a welcome comfort. Despite Simon's efforts to focus on their mission, he found his thoughts drifting to Maggie. To Zoë. *Their* mission. Whether they'd be able to accomplish their goal, save Lydia. But most of all he wondered whether he'd see them again. He tried to reason it out, to convince himself, but the truth was, he just didn't know what would happen. Part of him did feel in control of their present situation, with Ellis in their grasp, on their way to the mysterious subject he'd been chasing for the last few days. But another, larger part of him felt helpless. Simon knew he could hope, that he *should* hope, but he just couldn't be certain of anything.

They were in the thick of it now. Moment to moment. He was sure Arthur and Zoë felt a sense of duty in what they were doing, were driven on by the idea of furthering their cause, or finally claiming victory over those they opposed. Simon could admire them for that, for believing in something.

But Zoë and Arthur had volunteered. He had not. Maggie had not. They'd been thrust into their situation and been trying to scramble out of it ever since. Simon felt no noble sense of purpose to a cause as he supposed his new Life Liberation friends did. He was just trying to give Sebastian some peace, to carry out his friend's last wishes. He wanted to give Will's sacrifice meaning and clear their names. He supposed those things, collectively, could be called a purpose, perhaps even a noble one, but Simon didn't think of it that way. It was all just instinct at that point. Survival. He'd done what he'd had to do, and it had led him here, to these sterile hallways, hands trembling with nervous panic at the prospect of what might happen to them all.

Above all the plans and purposes and possibilities . . . Simon thought of Maggie. Through everything, he'd wanted to protect her. He hated that Maggie'd been dragged into all this, that she'd suffered perhaps more than anyone had. And that she'd found no relief yet. A part of Simon—perhaps a deep down, selfish part—had been grateful to have Maggie by his side during the hardships of the last few days. Despite the discord their relationship had been through, her presence was the main reason Simon had been able to bear everything that had happened. She was his reason, above all else, to go on.

But now, Maggie was gone. She was out of his grasp. Simon couldn't protect her. He knew Maggie could take care of herself. Zoë was with her, could keep her safe. That at least provided Simon with some relief from his worries.

He knew that fear would never fully go away. Not here. Not now. Here there was no escape. They were trapped in an underground facility, Maggie and him heading in opposite directions toward . . . what? A goal? An end? Simon hoped they'd all see each other again. It was all he could do at that point. Each time the fear crept back up again, the worry; Simon tried to push it away. He told himself they would all get out of this alive. Arthur would see Zoë again. He'd see Maggie. He'd hold her again, kiss her. They'd do what they'd come here to do and then escape. Leave all this behind. *Live their lives.* Simon repeated this positive mantra again and again in his head as he walked on, closer to the vault, further away from Maggie.

How long had they been walking those underground halls? Five minutes? More? Turning here and there, passing fewer and fewer guards and other personnel. Even if he hadn't been lost in his thoughts, Simon thought that he would have been lost for real had he been on his own. The entire underground facility was a maze of hallways and doors. Everything looked so alike it was hard to distinguish one door or hallway from another, even with the gray nameplates and directional plaques tacked to the side of each door and at hallway intersections.

Ellis led them around another corner and they entered a corridor unlike any other they'd been in thus far underground. It was long, stretching out in front and behind them. Simon wondered if they were at the southernmost edge of the floor. The walls were painted the same sterile white, but the ceiling was much taller than the other hallways in which they'd been. Ellis's stride slowed, her legs stiffened, and Simon glanced ahead to see why. The corridor dead-ended at what looked to be a large, silver wall. It stretched from corner to corner, floor to ceiling, polished and shining even in the distance.

In front of that gleaming wall stood two guards dressed in the same gray fatigues as the rest of the guards. It wasn't clear whether these men were newly posted like the entrance guard or mainstays at the wall, but either way, they gripped their flattop, semi-automatic rifles as though they knew what they were doing. Each of the men stood at attention, backs straight, eyes forward, serious looks etched on their youthful faces.

Simon didn't need to see any more to know this place was different. This place was special.

That's it, he thought, staring forward, trying to stay calm. The vault. That's where they're holding him.

The subject.

They marched on. The strange, silver wall beckoning them forward like the final gateway to a long-sought treasure. Almost within their grasp. So close. But like most treasures, this one was protected. Not by flood tunnels or trap doors, but by a pair of heavily armed guards stationed in front of the silver wall like gargoyles, ever watchful, ready to eliminate potential threats.

Simon, Arthur, and Ellis headed straight for them.

31

MAGGIE KEPT WATCH OUT THE DOOR WINDOW OF THE SMALL laboratory, scanning the hallway outside for movement, any curious passersby who might chance a look through the window and see the two unknown people inside. She thought that if that were to happen, it would most likely be a member of the laboratory personnel entering the room. But Maggie knew it could just as easily be a guard, making his rounds, patrolling the hallway and sneaking a peek in each window. He'd go from door to door, looking inside, until he got to their door, and then . . . well, that'd be it. But so far, that had yet to happen.

While Maggie's eyes remained glued to the window, playing lookout, Zoë worked in the lab behind her. She knew what Zoë was doing, in theory. Or at least what Zoë was attempting to do. It seemed crazy to Maggie. Dangerous. But it had been their only option.

"A bomb?" Maggie had said minutes before, gasping at the idea. "You want to build and set off a bomb, down here? In this confined space? Are you mad?"

"Okay, maybe *bomb* is a poor word choice," Zoë had responded. "I don't mean bomb like a building-leveling, blow-everyone-to-kingdom-fucking-come type of bomb. Just, ya know, a small one."

"A *small bomb?*"

"Yeah." Zoë had said it so matter-of-factly, as if the differing degrees with which explosives were built was common knowledge and constructing *small bombs* was something everyone did regularly. Maybe it *was* normal for Zoë. "Something that won't kill us all but'll cause a nice size diversion, draw all those guards away from that hallway. Hell, if we're lucky, maybe it'll even draw guards away from where the guys are at."

Maggie's heart had throbbed at that mention of Simon. He was somewhere down here, still roaming the hallways, headed toward the mysterious prisoner. She hoped he was, anyway, and not caught like she and Zoë were about to be if they set off an explosion. But there was another aspect of Zoë's plan, outside of the ludicrous idea to detonate a homemade bomb, that had caught Maggie's attention.

"But if we set off an explosion, that's it," she'd said. "They'll know someone is down here."

"Yeah, I thought about that," Zoë had said, then shrugged. "But unless you know of a way to get by all those guards, Vapula, Purcell, and likely Sullivan, grab Lydia, and then get back through all of them again without being seen, I don't see a better option. They'll be alerted to our presence, but by then it'll be too late. We'll gain the upper hand. Cripple them. Draw the guards away, confuse them."

"What about the others?"

"What others?"

"Simon! Arthur!" Maggie's voice had grown louder, almost to a shout, but she caught herself and switched to an intense whisper as they moved along through the hallways. "You said it yourself. If we set off an explosion of any kind, everyone will know we're down here. We can't do that until we know Simon and Arthur have reached the vault."

Zoë had bit at her bottom lip as she pondered Maggie's words, then said, "I told them 15 minutes and we've just about reached it. For all we know they've already found their mystery man. There's just no way for us to know where they are. All I can give them is the time it'll take me to build the bomb. After that, we'll just have to hope they're where they need to be."

In the five or so minutes since, they'd traversed the hallways at as rapid a pace as they could without drawing attention. They passed a few more guards and personnel as they walked, Zoë peeking through doors along the way until she had found one she deemed suitable for their needs. They had slipped inside and Zoë went to work.

First, Zoë had gone through the cabinets, pulling various bottles full of different liquids out and setting them on the counter that ran along the back of the lab. Anything, it seemed, that might be of use to her in building explosives.

Maggie had been at a loss. She didn't have Zoë's knowledge, her apparent bomb-building expertise. She hadn't known what the scientific terms on the bottle labels meant and could barely pronounce half of them. But Maggie had helped where she could, digging through the other cabinets and pulling out anything she guessed might be of assistance.

There had been a lot of rooting in cupboards and shuffling around the room until Zoë exclaimed, "Here we go!" Maggie spun around and saw Zoë pulled a small, metal cylinder marked *Flammable* from a tall closet off to one side of the lab. She heaved it up onto the counter, her eyes round, eager.

"How can I help?" Maggie had asked, and Zoë pointed toward the door.

"Why don't you keep a lookout? I need a few minutes to sort this out."

And so Maggie had done as she'd been told, standing watch. She ducked out of view whenever someone in the hallway passed by, hoping they wouldn't look inside. Most people she saw moved past the door without so much as a glance. One or two guards eyed the door as they approached, but none looked through its window.

She felt her insides turning over and over with worry. About whether Simon and Arthur had reached their destination, about the *small bomb* Zoë was building behind her, and about their entire diversionary tactic. Nothing was certain. Not even their safety. Zoë seemed confident in her ability to construct a bomb, but who knew? For all Maggie knew she was seconds away from Zoë crossing a red wire with a blue wire or mixing the wrong chemicals. Boom. They'd be gone. And Simon and Arthur would be left alone with what seemed like a hundred guards barreling toward them.

Maggie heard a hollow clink behind her, flinched, and thought, "This is it." But Zoë's bomb did not go off. Maggie turned away from the door to see Zoë securing her makeshift bomb atop the center counter. She saw the metal cylinder with a mess of fluid-filled bottles and wires surrounding the nozzle at the top. Where did Zoë get wire? Maggie thought, looking around the room until she spotted a computer monitor tipped on its side on a nearby desk. The bomb looked crude, almost like a movie prop. Would it even work? Maggie didn't know. She was no bomb maker.

"How much time?" Maggie asked, approaching the table with tentative steps.

"A few minutes," Zoë said. "Enough for us to get some distance, be safe from the blast."

Maggie jumped back a step.

"Is it . . . *on*, now?"

Zoë rounded the table. She leaned over the bomb, attached one last wire, and said, "Now it is. Let's go."

Maggie turned as soon as she heard the words, striding toward the door, wrenching it open. She stepped out of the lab with haste, followed closely by Zoë, who closed the door behind her. They set off at a quickened pace and had just made it to the first intersecting hallway when—

"Oh!" Maggie said, stopping in her tracks. Zoë toppled into her from behind.

"What the hell?" Zoë barked, then looked up to see two Rejuvenite men, dressed in gray fatigues.

Both guards had one hand on the butts of the pistols on their hips, the other, palm up, held out in front of them.

Stop.

"Hold it," one of the guards said. "Where you ladies off to in such a big damn hurry?"

32

———

BEFORE THEY WERE WITHIN CLEAR EARSHOT OF THE GUARDS, Arthur stepped next to Ellis, who whispered something into his ear. Simon couldn't make out what was said, but Arthur gave the tiniest of nods in response.

As they moved closer, Simon got a better look at the large silver wall he'd first seen moments before. The more he saw, the more its moniker of *the vault* fit. It was a door. A huge, metal door that stood so tall it only looked like a wall from afar. Upon closer inspection, Simon saw lines cut into the metal façade where, he assumed, the door could open. His first thought was of a bank vault, though this one was unlike any vault Simon had ever seen. It was much larger in scale, more imposing. There were no windows, hinges, or handles on the door, just a flat silver surface and a black box affixed to the wall on the right.

"Identification," the tall guard on the left said, looking down on the small group that had just stopped in front of him.

"Anyone working inside today?" Ellis asked. She waved a hand at the pair of men with her. "Showing the new recruits around. Wouldn't want to interrupt though." She pulled her ID card from the pocket of her coat, held it up for the guard to see.

"No, Ma'am. Everyone's in the north quad." The guard turned to Arthur next. "Identification."

Arthur mimicked Ellis, reaching his hand inside the side pocket of the borrowed coat he wore, feigning a search for the facility ID card he knew wasn't there. He reached into the pockets on the breast and inside of the coat, digging deep. Then he pulled his hands out again, scratching the point of his chin, giving a perplexed huff.

"Well, damn," Arthur said, looking at the guard who'd asked for his ID. "I just had it at the elevator."

Ellis hooked her thumb at Arthur and said, "He always does this." She gave a weak, forced laugh. "Can't trust him."

Simon groaned in his head, sighed silently. Ellis was back to her old games again. Why had they trusted her? His eyes darted between the guards, looking for any sign they'd caught on, but saw their gazes fixed on Arthur as he continued his fruitless search.

In that moment, Simon wished Zoë was still with them, or had come in place of Arthur. She'd be able to flash her green eyes, flit her lashes at the guards, just as she'd done earlier to distract Dr. Jack. Though Simon questioned whether that sort of trick would even work on the two men standing in front of them. They looked much tougher and unwavering than any of the guards they'd passed so far, much less the doctor they'd left tied up on the 21st floor. These men seemed to have a familiarity with Ellis, but Arthur and Simon were unknowns.

The guard on the right flashed his eyes from Arthur to Ellis, to Simon, then back to Arthur, examining them all. The left guard kept his eyes locked on Arthur, but tightened his grip on the bullpup rifle in his hands ever so slightly.

"Sir, we need identification. No ID, no admittance. We'll also need to detain you for—"

Arthur cut the guard's words off with his own. "No, no," he

said. "I have it here. I just—" Arthur snapped his fingers. The sound was sharp and echoed off the walls and tall ceiling. "Ah! Now I remember!" And with that, he reached into the right side pocket of his coat.

Maybe it was Arthur's whole act that did it. His seemingly frustrated attempt to find a missing identification card. He was very believable, Simon thought. Maybe his casual demeanor had indeed worked, lulled the serious guards into a false sense of security, if only for a moment. Whatever it was, when Arthur acted out his eureka moment, the shoulders of both guards sagged and they seemed to relax.

Arthur saw this too, because that's when he made his move. He yanked his fist from the pocket of his coat, only this time it held the subcompact pistol Zoë had given him before they parted. He lifted the gun toward the closest guard. The guard spotted it immediately and swung his rifle up, hitting Arthur's hand and knocking the gun away. The pistol went skidding across the hallway. Arthur launched himself forward, pushing the guard's rifle higher and striking him in the side of the face. The guard stumbled back, dazed from the hit, confused by the actions of who he had thought was just another doctor, but had now turned into an imposing fighter.

The second guard looked equally puzzled in that first second, but Simon knew that wouldn't last long. Arthur had thrown the first punch and while Simon didn't doubt his toughness, he was sure Arthur wouldn't be able to overpower both guards at the same time. Not with their brutish strength and the semi-automatic weapons they carried.

Simon pushed past Ellis, charging toward the second guard and the rising rifle pointed his way.

33

———

They'd been caught.

It was all Maggie thought at first as she stood frozen with Zoë in front of the two guards they'd just run into. This was it. The guards would start asking questions they couldn't answer. They'd demand identification they couldn't provide. After that, they'd be found out. Maggie didn't know what would happen next, but she suspected it wasn't good. Detainment and questioning for sure. Just like Lydia. Then, probably death. Sullivan wouldn't want any loose ends.

"Excuse us. We really need to be on our way," Zoë said, trying to sound as professional as possible. "Urgent lab business."

The guards traded smirks and then looked back at Zoë.

"Don't think I've seen you down here before," the fatter of the guards said, his eyes looking Zoë up and down.

She tried to hide her disgust of the man, forced a smile, and said, "Yes, well, we're transfers from downtown. Been here a few days. But we must be—"

"Why the hurry?" the second, shorter guard said, taking a step closer. His beady eyes flitting between Zoë and Maggie, less

403

interested in the redheaded female as his partner was. He kept his hand on the butt of his holstered pistol as he studied them.

"There's been an accident," Maggie said, the lie popping into her head. Well, she thought, maybe it wasn't a complete lie. There *would* be an accident. Very soon, in fact. In the lab, behind them. The clock was ticking. How much time did they have left? A couple of minutes? Maybe three? Four? They'd all know well enough if they weren't allowed to move on.

Both guards shifted their eyes to Maggie now. Out the corner of her eye, she saw Zoë give her a momentary quizzical look as well, then straighten her face.

"An accident?" the short guard said, his tone concerned at first. Then he relaxed and tapped the small, two-way radio attached to his front coat pocket. "We didn't hear anything about no accident."

"Well I don't know what sort of information *you're* privy to," Maggie said, the lies rolling off her tongue with ease now, "but we just received an urgent call from Dr. Ellis, the *head adminis-trator* of this facility, saying our help is needed in the south quad-rant. *That's* why we are in such a hurry. Now if you wouldn't mind, we need to—"

The fat guard nodded and started to step to the side, his eyes back on Zoë, leering. But the short guard wasn't buying Maggie's story. Not completely. Not yet. He gave her a round-cheeked grin, but held up his hand when Maggie tried to move forward.

"All right then," he said. "Show us your identification and you can be on your way."

Damn it, Maggie thought. For a moment, it'd seemed like the guards had bought it. But now this. How much time did they have left before Zoë's diversionary bomb went off? They had to be cutting it close now.

"Really!" Maggie exclaimed, throwing up her hands. "This is preposterous. We don't have time for this! If you want to explain to Dr. Ellis why the containment of a laboratory accident was compromised, today, of all days, with Mr. Sullivan on the premises, then you go right ahead!"

The name felt acidic on her tongue. She'd hated saying it out loud, but the face of the short guard dropped at the mention of Sullivan. Maggie knew he wouldn't want to be the one responsible for any sort of problem when the big boss man was here. The guard paused for a second, thinking, eyeing Maggie.

How much time did they have left now? Maggie tried to work it out. A minute? Two, if they were lucky.

"You know what I think," the short guard said. "I don't think you were in a hurry to get somewhere. I think you two were running *from* something."

"Oh, this is—"

But Maggie's protest was cut short by the flash of a pistol, pulled from the short guard's holster—a black and silver gun, just like Bart the entrance guard had carried. He kept the barrel pointed at the ground, his eyes on Maggie and Zoë.

"Woah!" the fat guard said. "Do we really need to—"

"Quiet." The short guard glared at them. "Maybe they're not lying, but maybe they are. And we're gonna find out. It's like she said, we can't have any slip-ups. Not today. Now move." He waved his pistol, motioning for Maggie and Zoë to back away. They reversed a few steps into the hallway they'd just come from. "Keep going. Back to that door there. Let's see what you're running from, eh?"

Maggie and Zoë turned around slowly, shooting each other matching side-glances of concern. The dread from moments before, of being caught and possibly killed started to build into something more as Maggie approached the door to the lab. The door they'd just fled from, behind which she knew was an explosive set to go off at any moment. Whether the guards found them out and killed them, or the forthcoming blast did, Maggie realized their chances of surviving the next few minutes were dropping with every step closer to the door. All she could do was keep her ruse going in the hope they could find a way out of this.

"I want your names," Maggie demanded. "I'll be reporting you both to Dr. Ellis!"

She stepped past the door and Zoë followed, positioned in the center of the hallway. Maggie hoped, if nothing else, they might be able to make a run for it the other way.

"Ah, ah, stop right there," the short guard said, wagging his pistol at them. He then nodded toward the door in front of which he'd just stopped. He glared at Maggie. "You, open the door and let's see what you two were so eager to leave behind."

Maggie remained standing, unmoving. She looked at Zoë, hoping she would take the lead, say something, or tell her what to do. But Maggie found Zoë looking at the floor, bobbing her head minutely in time with something. What was she doing?

"Go on then. Open—"

But the guard's words were cut short by the shriek of an alarm splitting the air. The hallway around them filled with flashing red light.

The short guard gritted his teeth and raised the pistol in his hand. He shouted over the pulsing sound of the alarm. "Both of you! On your knees! Now!"

34

SIMON SLAPPED AT THE GUARD'S RIFLE, PUSHING IT TO THE SIDE just as the trigger was pulled. The tall expanse of the hallway suddenly filled with the loud CRACK-CRACK-CRACK of semi-automatic gunfire. Shells ejected from the opposite side of the rifle, clattering to the ground as bullets sprayed the floor and nearby wall. Simon gave the gun a harder push, jarring it loose from the guard's hands where it swung down, caught by the shoulder strap. He threw one fist into the jaw of the guard. Then another into the side of the guard's face. Simon was anything but a prizefighter, but he knew how to throw a punch. Simon recalled every schoolyard scrap he'd been part of in his youth and continued to swing away.

A pulsing, blaring alarm split the air. Red lights set at intervals along the ceiling lit up and started spinning. Flashes of red light swept the hallway, streaking across the brawl happening in front of the massive silver door.

Simon's opponent stumbled back against the vault and looked up in response to the alarm and lights. The guard realized his mistake the next second, raising his arms in an attempt to block Simon's blows, to get a grip on the situation. But he'd been caught off guard. Simon had him against the ropes, pushing him into the corner.

On the other side of the hallway, Arthur was landing more expertly thrown punches, seemingly unaffected by the continued flashing red lights, well on the way to victory.

Despite the rain of blows being laid upon him, the second guard still wore a look of confusion on his face, unsure of how he'd found himself in this position when only a few moments earlier he'd been the one in charge, standing watch in front of the door. When Arthur tugged at the strap of his rifle, the guard clamped his arm down tight, holding the weapon in place, refusing to let it go. Arthur reared an arm back, ready to dish out a few more punches to convince the guard to let go—but the arm remained behind the hulking man, caught in the grasp of Ellis, who'd suddenly appeared, attacking from behind. The guard acted fast, grabbing his opponent's other arm, holding Arthur so his chest was open, exposed. The guard unclamped his other arm from around the rifle, freeing himself up to punch Arthur in the stomach. Once, twice, a third time. Arthur expelled sharp gasps of air each time the guard's fist made contact. Another hard-knuckled blow, this time to the side of his face.

Arthur's bottom lip split with this last punch. Blood started to ooze out, the stinging taste of copper filling his mouth. His torso growing tender as the guard brought up a knee to Arthur's chest this time. He'd been caught by surprise, just as the guard had been. Arthur had thought Ellis would run as soon as she could, not join the fray. But she was there, holding onto his left arm with all her might to allow the guard room to fight back. But she underestimated Arthur's strength, and as soon as he overcame the surprise of her sudden participation and the guard's ensuing attack, it was his turn. Arthur flexed, muscles bulging underneath the stolen lab coat he wore, as he used all his strength to pull his arms together. The guard had a firm hold on his right arm, but still had to hold on tight to prevent Arthur from breaking free. But Ellis could not stop his left arm, and so Arthur gripped Ellis tight, pulling her along, using her as a human club to strike the guard.

Ellis toppled into the guard and they both fell back against the wall, stumbling as they tried to untangle themselves from one another. They launched at him again, but this time, Arthur was ready. He grabbed the guard's arms, preventing any attack or reach for a gun. At the same time, he kicked Ellis square in the chest. A crunch of broken ribs. Ellis yelped in pain and sailed back against the wall where she fell to the floor, clutching at her chest. Arthur pulled the guard's hands down, returning the favor of a knee to the chest. With the guard doubled over, Arthur yanked the weapon strap, unclipping the bullpup rifle from its owner. It dropped to the ground and he kicked it away, behind him.

With the guard still bent at the waist, Arthur brought a knee up again, this time into the guard's face. His nose gave a nauseating crunch. The guard was knocked back up into a standing position, dazed, stumbling for a brief moment. Blood oozed from his broken nose. Arthur swept a leg against him, and the guard fell. His head snapped back against the vault door and he crumpled to the ground, unconscious.

Simon continued his wild, boxing-style barrage of punches on the second guard, landing quite a few of them. But the guard fought back, pushing Simon hard in the chest, creating enough space to launch a few reciprocating blows. One hit Simon's right cheek, sending an electric spike of pain down his jawline. The next struck Simon's neck, the next his ear. Simon could feel the stinging power behind each blow, but was thankful the guard hadn't connected with his jaw again. His blood boiling, senses piqued, Simon closed the distance between them.

The guard went for his rifle again but wasn't quick enough. He'd left his head exposed and Simon exploited it, clocking him hard in the temple. Once. Twice. An uppercut for good measure. The guard's head whipped back. His eyes rolled. The hands at his rifle fell away, and he crumpled into the corner.

Simon stood over the guard, breathing rapidly. His chest heaved under his lab coat, which had been torn at one shoulder during the struggle. His mind was hazy. Simon thought he heard Arthur shout something, but he couldn't make out the words over the blaring sirens. No matter. He knew what Arthur had said. Simon stepped forward, removing the guard's weapon.

"Simon!" Arthur barked, stepping closer to shout over the alarm. "We're going to have a big problem any second."

"Going to?" Simon shouted back, pointing up to signal the siren and red flashing lights.

"I mean more guards! We need to get this door open now!"

35

Maggie and Zoë were on their knees, hands on their heads, staring into the muzzles of two pistols. The alarm continued to blare overhead, red lights flashing. And in a nearby room, just a few paces away, was the bomb they'd set, ready to go off at any moment.

Maggie didn't know if the alarm had sounded because of them, or something else. Perhaps it'd been triggered by Simon and Arthur. Did that mean they'd been captured? Or killed? Whatever the case, she and Zoë were about to join them. There was no way out now.

"Don't move!" the short guard yelled, though his voice was faint, drowned out by the shriek of the alarm. He stabbed at them with his gun each time he spoke. "What are you doing here? Tell me! Who are you?"

Maggie looked to her side. Zoë's eyes, like they'd been before the alarm started, were still looking at the floor. Her head rocked in small, measured increments. Up . . . down . . . up . . . down . . .

What was she doing? Maggie wondered if the fearless leader of Life Liberation had cracked. After everything they'd been through, had Zoë finally hit her breaking point? Maggie watched her closely, even as the guards kept yelling at them. Zoë's lips were moving, but Maggie couldn't make out what she was saying. It was as if Zoë was whispering. But that made no sense under the blare of the alarm. And why wasn't she looking at anyone?

The guards noticed as well and shouted for Zoë to speak up. But she just kept on rocking her head, up and down, and moving her lips.

Maggie leaned in closer, trying to catch what Zoë was saying. The guards yelled for Maggie to halt, but she kept moving. Why stop now? They'd all be dead soon anyway. Closer now, she heard Zoë's voice but it only sounded like mumbling. What did it matter anyway? They were caught. They'd be shot by the guards at any moment or—

Maggie's eyes bulged as it clicked. Under the blare of the alarm, she finally understood what Zoë was doing. The rocking, back and forth like a metronome. The whispering. She leaned in closer to confirm her suspicion and could just make out Zoë's voice.

"Eight . . . seven . . . six . . . five . . ."

The lab.

The bomb.

Maggie looked up at the guards as though they'd realized what Zoë was doing too. Of course, they had not, but they were clearly affected by the strenuous situation, the blare of the alarms and flash of lights. Drops of nervous sweat had formed on their foreheads. Their eyes danced with panic. Their hands trembling around the guns they pointed at their hostages. The fat guard stood a few paces back, but the short one was closer, standing directly in front of the door to the laboratory. He yelled again, but Maggie couldn't hear it over the alarm.

". . . four . . . three . . . two . . ."

Maggie looked back to see Zoë had lifted her head. She was

staring now, her green eyes mixing with the flashing red lights from above, now a strange shade of gleaming yellow.

"One!" Zoë shouted and dove at Maggie, tackling her back into the hallway.

A roaring boom split the air, drowning out the shriek of the alarm. The laboratory next to them exploded from within. A burst of bright white and yellow and orange light filled the hallway. Flames climbed up the walls, across the ceiling, spreading down the corridor in both directions.

The force of the blast ripped the room's door off its hinges, breaking it in two, flying outward. It struck the short guard, half of it slicing into his knees, the other half hitting him square in the shoulders and head. A wound opened on his head, gushing blood as he flew back against the wall and slid to the floor. The fat guard was lucky enough to avoid the door's wrath, but was thrown back just the same. The force of the explosion propelling him into the wall as his gray fatigues caught fire. He shrieked and crumbled to the floor as the fire consumed him.

Maggie's ears filled with the deep rumble of the blast. The floor beneath her shook even as she felt pushed backward by the blast. The heat of the explosion licked at her arms and legs as she slid across the hallway floor and slammed into a nearby wall. She heard a sickening crack and crunch, a quick, agonizing yelp, but did not feel the pain in her body. The brunt of the collision and the intense heat of the flames around Maggie had been absorbed by something on top of her.

As the roar of the explosion abated, the sound of the alarm returned to Maggie's ears, though it sounded faint, far away. She opened her eyes and saw flashes of darkness, dust, flames all around her. Her breath was ragged, choking on the hot air. She struggled to free herself, but couldn't move. What was pinning her there? It wasn't rubble, it was—

Zoë. Unmoving. Unspeaking.

Zoë's body flopped above her as Maggie tried to free herself, to crawl out from under the woman who'd covered her, protected her from the blast.

"Z-Zoë!' Maggie croaked out amidst the swirling dust and debris. She couldn't get a good, full breath without choking. She felt lightheaded. She tried to open her eyes again, but the burning hallway swam in front of her. She closed her eyes, tried to crawl away, but Zoë's weight was holding her back. Maggie felt weak, dizzy. The weight of Zoë on top of her was too much—that dead weight.

Maggie tried to move once more, to crawl, but the effort made her head swim even worse. What little she could see of her surroundings were spinning. Consciousness faded. And then, darkness took her.

36

Simon looked up at the large, metal door. Its imposing form stood before him, appearing even taller now with the prospect of needing to open it. Its attractive, silver gleam all but gone under the harsh red lights.

"How do we get it open?" Simon said. He shifted the rifle in his hands awkwardly, unsure what to do with it, but not wanting to drop it.

"We need to wake her up." Arthur reached down, pulling Ellis to her feet. She wobbled, clutched at her chest. She would have fallen to the ground again had Arthur not caught and stood her up straight. He slapped her across the face.

Ellis's eyes sprang open. She clutched at the side of her face where the imprint of a hand might have shown on her skin had she not already been bathed in red alarm light.

"Ow! What the hell are you . . ." she mumbled, her legs still wobbling slightly.

"What's the code for the door?" Arthur said.

"The door . . . wha . . . that noise? . . . What door?"

Arthur slapped Ellis again, harder this time.

"Hey! Stop that!" Ellis screamed. Her eyes were now open a

415

little wider. She reached up, touched her face where she'd been slapped. But her eyes rolled again, mind still hazy. She winced and clutched at her chest.

"Listen! There are numbers. On the panel. By the vault door. What's the code—"

A distant, but still quite loud boom and rumble of an explosion sounded, breaking Arthur's words. The hallway around them shook, as did the entire underground facility. Arthur and Simon staggered for a second before the rumbling died completely under the sound of the siren, and they regained their balance.

Arthur turned to Simon.

"I'm gonna guess that was Zoë," he said.

"Do you think—" Simon began.

"Don't know. Nothing we can do about it now."

Arthur was right. They were at the vault. Maggie and Zoë were somewhere else, likely on the other side of the floor. Simon could only hope they were all right and deal with his situation. Ellis. The door. Whether EXLI figured the intruders in their facility were headed toward Lydia or where Simon was now, it didn't matter. They'd be sending more guards to both locations.

With any luck, the explosion they'd just heard had been on purpose. And if so, it might be enough to divide the guards into separate groups, and possibly buy them all some time.

Arthur shook Ellis hard again.

"What's the code? Tell me now!"

"7-1-5," Ellis began, her head rolling from side to side. "Oh, my chest hur—" Arthur gave her another hard shake and she refocused. "7-1-5-9-4-2."

"Is that it?" Arthur yelled through the alarms. Ellis nodded her head limply.

Simon stepped over one of the unconscious guards to the black keypad mounted on the wall by the door. He swung the rifle strap over his shoulder, letting it hang, and punched in the numbers of the code. A yellow light lit up on top of the box. A small, circular screen came to life with a thin, green light in the center of the box. A single line of text flashed at the top of the screen: *Retinal Scan Required.*

"Arthur!" Simon yelled, waving. "Bring her over here! This thing needs to scan her eye!"

Arthur dragged the stumbling Ellis over to the keypad, holding her under the arms in front of the scanner. Simon steadied her head and pried open one of Ellis's eyelids. The bright, green line streaked up and down on the screen. Once. Twice. The box buzzed. The light on top changed from yellow to green. Simon heard a faint hiss come from the heavy metal door, muffled by the ringing of the alarm. The door began to move, opening outward.

"Go! Go! Inside!" Arthur yelled as he pushed Ellis away into the center of the hallway. The woman stumbled, then fell to the ground. Arthur crouched to pick up the remaining rifle. He held that position for a moment, re-clipping the rifle strap before swinging it around his shoulder. As he did, a group of five guards came sprinting around the corner of an intersecting hallway about fifty feet away—all of them holding similar bullpup SARs.

When Simon saw this, he yelled for Arthur to come with him and then sprinted into the open vault.

Arthur held his position, the rifle planted firmly against his shoulder, and began to fire. CRACK-CRACK-CRACK! CRACK-CRACK-CRACK! The rifle fire shot out in quick bursts, ejected shells bouncing off the nearby wall, rolling as they hit the floor. The guards scattered, diving to the ground. Arthur used this chance to spin around and head toward the open door. As he did, two things happened in almost complete synchronization. Three of the new guards stood, raised their guns, and began firing. And Ellis suddenly sprang to her feet, waving the small pistol that'd been knocked from Arthur's hands minutes before. The same pistol that had been taken from Ellis earlier, used to threaten her into leading a group of intruders to the most secret level of The Shepherd's Institute. A pistol she intended to use on those intruders, but which now appeared she was raising toward the oncoming guards.

Ellis saw the guards, the gun in her hand, and realized what would come next.

"Don't shoot! Don't shoot! I'm on your—" she yelled, but it was too late. Bullets exploded from the rifles of the guards, ripping through Ellis's body. Splatters of blood hit the nearest wall, the floor behind her. She tumbled back, crumpling to the ground with a wet thud. Her shiny pistol still clutched in her dead hand, just as Arthur slipped through the door behind her.

Spurts of gunfire continued for a moment longer, pelting the vault door. The guards advanced, kept their rifles aimed forward.

But Arthur was gone, joining Simon in the vault. Inside, a button was pushed with urgency, and the heavy, metal door swung quietly shut, sealing them inside.

37

———————

THEODORE SULLIVAN SAT, LEGS CROSSED, WATCHING THE ROW OF small video monitors hanging on the wall. His suit coat was folded neatly over another nearby chair, his white shirtsleeves meticulously folded up to his elbows. He pinched his strong, pointed chin between his fingers as he studied one monitor in particular, his brow furrowed. But Sullivan's concentration was more curiosity than worry. He was confident in the eventual outcome of what he was watching. Still, he enjoyed playing with his food. He liked to watch it wriggle and squirm, fight to survive, until the last moment when he would show mercy and put it out of its misery.

One monitor showed a laboratory that had, minutes before, been empty, quiet, but now raged with fire following an explosion that'd shaken the entire underground facility. Flames licked the walls; glass was shattered everywhere, plastic containers from broken shelves melted from the heat, oozing their contents onto the floor. Guards could be seen at the door holding fire extinguishers, blasting white foam at the flames, attempting to keep them from spreading into the hallway while the remaining operational sprinklers inside the room rained down quenching waters.

And yet, Sullivan's dry, red eyes weren't focused on that chaotic room, nor the firefighting efforts. He wasn't switching the feed to try to track down the arsonists. His security forces had that handled. Those responsible would be dealt with properly.

The corner of his left eye twitched at the thought of the two women he'd seen on the recording minutes before. His mind focusing on the woman with red hair; ever-present thorn in his side. Her entire organization—a menace. He gritted his teeth so hard his jaw ached. His nostrils flared and his lips trembled back like a rabid dog, ready to attack.

Yes, he thought, his forces would handle them. And then he would have his guards punished for allowing the intruders in. They'd all pay for their mistakes. But at that moment, Sullivan's attention was locked on another monitor.

It showed a second lab. Though, this one was different. Primarily, because it was not on fire. But on a normal day, it would still be dissimilar from the rest because of the large, silver door set into one of its walls. A door that had just closed, locking the room's newest occupants inside. Two men. Both dressed in lab coats that were not their own.

Intruders.

Terrorists.

Sullivan knew who they were.

The larger man was a cohort of the red-haired woman. Just like—

Sullivan cranked his head away from the monitors, toward the corner of the room. He sneered, then looked back, refocusing on the activity on the monitor.

The other man—he was a tag-along. A nuisance in his own right, at least he had been over the last few days. He'd escaped Sullivan's forces before. They all had. But no longer. He had them now, both of their groups. Despite them somehow managing to sneak into this facility. Despite their apparent thought that they'd uncovered his deepest, darkest secret. None of that mattered now. He had them. They were trapped, within his grasp.

Sullivan grinned like a hungry tiger as he stared at the intruders standing in the vault, hands on their knees, panting after the confrontation in the hallway. *Yes*, Sullivan thought. *Catch your breath now, while I still allow you to breathe.*

There was a whimper from the corner. Sullivan's eyes twitched again. He shook his head erratically, ignored the sound. Then a muffled voice. Another whimper. He tore his eyes away from the monitors, glared into the corner again.

"Quiet!" he spat, pointing at the screens. "We'll talk more after this is done."

The muffled voice continued. Sullivan sighed, stood from his chair. He stepped over to the corner, straightening his folded shirt-sleeves as he went, pushing them a little higher above his elbows. He stopped, looking down at Lydia Darrow, tied to a chair, face bloodied, mouth gagged with a thin towel tied around her head. He considered her for a moment, eyebrows raised in question, but not saying a word.

Lydia tried to speak, but her voice was once again muffled by the gag. Sullivan shook his head, then slapped Lydia across the face. He stared at her with wide, wild eyes, waiting. Lydia whimpered, but did not attempt to speak. Sullivan returned to his chair, sat, and looked upon the monitors once more.

Silly girl, Sullivan thought, but kept his eyes on the screen. Darrow was just a silly girl with foolish ideals. But she was his prisoner now. *He* had the upper hand. The minor distraction caused by her friends was meaningless. It wouldn't stop him from getting the information he wanted from her. He would know what she knew and EXLI would remain strong. Sure, it'd be easier if the little bitch just gave him the access code for the data in the lockbox. His scientists would break the encryption eventually. Still, part of Sullivan preferred it this way. He wanted to *break* her. And when he did, whatever kind of revolution she and her friends thought they were starting would officially be squashed. It would end here. It would end today, before it even began.

Sullivan watched the intruders on screen, could see them talking but couldn't hear the audio. *Why the hell couldn't he hear them?* He was sitting in one of the most advanced laboratories on the entire planet and couldn't get simple audio to go with a video feed? He'd talk to Purcell and Vapula about it, make them upgrade the monitoring systems. Tomorrow. No, today goddamn it. As soon as Darrow and her friends were dealt with. No sense in waiting.

It was all but over now anyway. His eyes peered up at the monitor. What more could these intruders do? Two of them had caused an explosion. The others had made it to the vault. So what? No farther. Even if they realized where they truly were, even if they—

No, they wouldn't be that foolish, would they? They wouldn't dare free—

A jolt of pain hit Sullivan, an ache deep inside his head. It was gone almost as soon as it had appeared.

No. They wouldn't. Not that it mattered, Sullivan thought. The subject wouldn't even be able to—no. Sullivan doubted the man would be able to help them, even if they found out. Not in the state he's in. Such a waste. He—

Another spike of pain throbbed inside his head. Sullivan squeezed his temples, felt sweat collecting there. He closed his eyes for a moment. Then, the pain was gone.

None of it mattered, Sullivan reminded himself, shaking his head to dispel his questions. Even if they—they still wouldn't be able to get to him. Not here. Not in this place. Here, he was safe, Sullivan thought. Here, he was *invincible*.

It's all be over soon anyway.

Sullivan dragged his eyes over to the third monitor. Onscreen, he saw the hallway leading up to the large vault door. A growing cluster of guards was now present, huddling around the door while two men worked on the keypad, punching in a code and then looking around confused. Sullivan rolled his eyes. *The retinal scan! The door needs a retinal scan!* He searched the corner of the screen, saw the two guards who'd been knocked out by the intruders, now awake but hazy, sitting, backs against the wall. Next to them, the body of Dr. Ellis lay pushed to the side. *She's right there. Just—*

Sullivan turned away from the monitors, stomped over to the only door in the small room, and opened it. But he did not step out; only called from the open doorway to the two suited men standing a few paces away.

"Radio the guards at the vault," Sullivan spat. "Tell them to use Ellis for the secondary scan. Cut the bitch's eye out if they have to."

The redheaded man nodded. His associate with the black hair reached for the radio on his hip. Sullivan saw none of this. He was already closing the door. He assumed the task would be completed. He'd commanded it, and whatever he said was done. That was the way of the world.

Sullivan walked back toward his seat, glancing at the examination bed pushed up against one wall, bunches of wires where a pillow should have been. He dragged his gaze over the small table in the center of the room where the bank lockbox had been set. Next to it, a compact 9mm. He eyed both items, then shot another nasty sneer at his hostage in the corner before turning back to the monitors.

The ruined laboratory, now a wet mess of charred equipment, cabinetry, and lingering smoke. But the fire was out, at least.

The vault door, where more guards had just arrived, stationing themselves along the long expanse of the hallway.

And the room, the interior of the vault itself, where a sudden flash of light pulled Sullivan's attention. *What was that?* He only saw the two terrorists, still standing, talking silently on screen. One of them gripped a stolen weapon as if he was preparing to make a stand.

Futile efforts, Sullivan thought. Everything they'd done to get into that vault was pointless. They were in a room with a single exit they could not use. Whatever ammunition was left in that rifle would not be enough to break through the swelling ranks of guards outside. They could not save themselves. No one was coming to help them. Soon enough, the door would be breached. Soon, they would all be dead.

38

Simon and Arthur collapsed onto the floor of the vault, panting after their battle in the hallway. The alert sirens still blared outside, though strangely not inside the room. The flashing red lights were absent as well. The muffled gunfire of the guards in the hallway continued for a few seconds more, then stopped. There was no use. The door had closed and no bullets could pierce that thick metal.

They sat for a few moments, then climbed to their feet. They said nothing at first, only remained hunched over, hands on their knees, breathing deep to calm themselves. They could hear muffled shouts and stomping footsteps of guard boots outside, but knew they were safe, at least for the moment, behind the protection of the massive locked door. When they stood upright, both men shed the restrictive lab coats they had worn as disguises. There was no need for them anymore; their presence was known.

"Shouldn't we . . ." Simon said, breaking the silence, looking toward the door. "I mean, those guards might not know the code, but I'm sure they can get it. And I'm sure someone else can provide a retinal scan. Is there a way to keep them from getting inside?"

Arthur spun around, aimed his flattop rifle at the black box on the wall to the left of the metal door. He squeezed the trigger, sending a few short bursts of gunfire at the box. Each rapid burst reverberated off the walls, sounding even louder in the tiny confines of the room. The box blew apart, sparked in a quick flash of light. Shards of the sleek black exterior showered the floor and nearby countertop. Arthur tried pulling the trigger again, but the gun did not fire.

"Does that actually work?" Simon asked, eyeing the frayed wires sticking out of the destroyed box. Fragments of the green circuit board and other electronic innards continued to trickle out.

Arthur shrugged. He checked the magazine of the gun, saw that it was out of ammunition, and discarded both to the floor. "Let's hope so. If not, our stay here is going to be pretty damn short." He swept the room with his eyes, frowned, and looked back at Simon. "Then again, even if it does work, our hopes of escaping are slim to none. Unless your mystery man can help us out like you think he can."

What Arthur said was true. It only took Simon a quick look around the room to realize there was no other exit. The only other doors in the room led to a storage closet and a small lab supply fridge. The heavy, metal door was the only way out and that was suicide. They were trapped, Simon thought, because *he* wanted to split up, to go after the man being held prisoner while the others went for Lydia. Though, in his current pessimistic state, Simon doubted very much that going after Lydia as a complete group first would have ended up much different.

His eyes lingered on the small room. Stainless steel counter-tops ran around almost every wall. Above these were rows of cabinets with doors made of frosted glass. Simon could see shadows of items behind the glass, but couldn't tell what any of them were. It looked like some sort of lab/operating theater hybrid—nothing remarkably out of the ordinary, except for what lay in the middle.

A row of soft, fluorescent lights hung like a pendulum from the center ceiling of the room. Below this was what looked like a hospital bed, though it was unlike any Simon had ever seen before. Its base was a single metal column that rose up from the floor to a flat, cushioned table. On top of this was a large bubble made of some sort of delicate plastic, frosted in the same way as the doors of the surrounding cabinets. The bubble covered the entire table; a soft, blue light glowed somewhere inside, revealing the shadowy outline of a man lying on his back.

"Is that . . . *him*?" Arthur asked.

"Yeah," Simon said, swallowing a hard gulp of air. "It has to be."

"Is he conscious?"

"I don't know. By the look of this place, who knows what kind of things they have running through his system?"

"Well, let's hope we can wake him up," Arthur said, his tone harder. "He's no use to us if he's a vegetable."

Simon stepped closer, squinting his eyes, trying to peer through the thin bubble that encased the man on the table. The lines of the man's shadow became more distinctive as Simon approached, outlined by that eerie blue light. He could make out arms and legs, feet sticking up. And the man's head, which was oddly larger than it should be, out of proportion to the body. Even still, Simon didn't see any other specific features that might tell him who the man was.

He stepped to the side of the table and saw the bubble that covered it looked different up close, like a series of oversized vertebra. Thin ribs of stiff wire or plastic ran through the material of the bubble forming supportive arches that spanned from one side of the table to the other. Running down the center was a long zipper.

The faint sound of the alarm ringing in the hallway outside suddenly stopped, breaking Simon and Arthur from their trance of fascination on the central table. They heard footsteps and yelling more clearly outside. The guards were still hard at work on the door. Arthur's destruction of the black box had apparently worked. It had bought them a few more minutes at least.

"If you're going to do something, now's the time," Arthur said, stepping up to the other side of the table. His eyes moved up and down, as if searching for some kind of answer between Simon and the figure under the bubble.

Simon stared back, felt a pressure in his chest, like a weight had been placed there. Felt his heart thumping back in response to the phantom pressure. He wished Maggie were there to give him an encouraging nod or squeeze of the hand.

Simon swallowed hard again. He took a deep breath, then reached toward the table.

39

———————

Footsteps.

Shuffling.

Radio static.

Despite a faint ringing in her ears, Maggie heard a mix of what seemed like random noises as she awoke, her senses coming back to her one by one.

First the sound of—where was she? There were more footsteps, closer, the heavy clomp of boots on hard vinyl flooring. Unintelligible voices. And again, radio static in short bursts following the voices.

Maggie tried to open her eyes, but her eyelids were heavy, felt stuck together.

She smelled burning. The scent of singed cotton, the earthiness of charred wood, the nauseating odor of melted plastic. And something else, sulfurous . . . was that, burnt hair? Maggie tried to take a deep breath through her nose. One nostril was clogged, the other prickled as the air passed through it, and she started to cough.

A rush of footsteps coming toward her. A kick to her stomach. Maggie lost her breath completely. She choked and gasped for air.

"Awake, huh? Time for some answers!" an unknown voice shouted at her.

She was kicked in the stomach again. Maggie curled into a ball after. She lifted her hands to signal she could take no more. Her hands felt odd, stuck together. Tied. She wiggled her body and realized her ankles were tied as well.

"Who are you? Tell me!"

Maggie forced her heavy eyelids open. All she could see at first was a brightness, shining down on her from above. Fluorescent light that stung her eyes and intensified the throbbing ache inside her head. Maggie could tell she was in a room of some kind. There were several figures—people—standing in front of her. But everything was blurred. She blinked. Then again, trying to acclimate to the bright light. After a few seconds, she was able to focus. She saw her surroundings more clearly and wondered just how long she'd been unconscious.

She was lying in another lab, larger but almost identical in every other way to the one she and Zoë had blown up. There were counters running along white walls. Frosted-paned cabinets filled with what looked like bottles of liquid and glassware. There were several tables in the center of the room topped with beakers, computers, and other lab equipment. The floor beneath her was a pale blue, reflecting its coolness against Maggie's cheek.

Standing and sitting at various spots throughout the room were five guards, all dressed in gray fatigues, all holding some sort of weapon. Mostly pistols, but the two guards nearest the door held flattop semi-automatic rifles. The guard looming over her was an average-sized man, black hair, the smooth skin of his face red with anger as he barked questions and commands down at Maggie.

But she ignored him as best she could, instead looking down at herself, assessing her condition. Her hands and ankles bound with thick, black cable ties. Her pant legs singed. Cuts and red marks could be seen through the holes in the arms of the white lab coat she wore, though that too was blackened and ripped, falling off her. She felt a deep cut near the hairline on her forehead, already stiff with dried blood. The throbbing in her head continued, as did the faint ringing in her ears. Her body ached. But aside from those few things, she felt okay.

What little breath Maggie was able to gather caught in her chest as she looked down, past her feet, and spotted the crumpled figure in the corner of the room.

Zoë lay on her side, arms and legs at strange angles. Her eyes were closed, though it was hard to tell at first because her entire face was covered in thin, black dust. Her once long, red hair had been burnt, singed into an uneven, shorter cut. Hairstyling by fire. Her lab coat was gone. Her clothes underneath burned in various spots as well. The skin that showed in these holes was purple, bruised, and burnt. Her left calf and side of her torso were wet with blood.

She's dead, Maggie thought. Any breath that remained in Maggie's lungs seemed to disappear. Zoë was dead. Zoë had died protecting her from the blast. Maggie felt a strange mixture of grief and intense gratitude for her fallen protector. She remembered the feel of Zoë on top of her when the blast hit. And moments after—that dead weight pressing down on her as Maggie lost consciousness.

But . . . what was that?

Movement.

Zoë's chest, moving. Pushing out. Was it just a trick of her hampered vision? No. The movement was almost imperceptible, but the more Maggie stared, the more she saw it. Zoë's chest, rising and falling beneath her tattered, blood-soaked shirt. She was breathing. They looked like short, ragged breaths, but they were breaths nonetheless. She was badly injured, but Zoë was breathing. *She was alive.*

The guard barking commands at Maggie reared back and kicked her in the stomach again.

She gasped for air once more, struggling against her bonds.

"Who are you?" the guard spat down at her. "Tell me now!"

Maggie's face went red in anger. She scowled up at the guard, gritting her teeth as she regained her breath.

"No!" she spat right back. She tasted wet copper in her mouth. Blood.

The guard froze, stunned for a moment. He waved his pistol at Maggie. "What did you say?" he said.

"I said fuck off!"

As the guard reared back to kick Maggie again, she questioned whether she and Zoë could get out of this situation. Even if they found a way, would Zoë survive that long? She wished Zoë would wake up soon, give her some kind of direction. But most of all, Maggie thought of Simon. She wondered if he and Arthur had fared better. She hoped so. Watching the guard's boot come down on her again, tensing her bruised stomach for the impact, Maggie had little hope for anything else. This seemed like the end.

40

———

SIMON GRABBED THE SMALL TAB AT THE END OF THE BUBBLE'S
zipper and slowly began to pull it back. The light fabric of the
bubble peeled away down the middle, the stiff ribs under it
retracting. He saw a bundle of multicolored electrical wires first.
The wires climbed up from the end of the table into a cap affixed
to the man's head, like a futuristic motorcycle helmet. So that's
why the head seemed so large in shadow, Simon thought. He saw
the source of the blue light, a rectangular display near the top of
the cap, which glowed with numbers and various medical read-
outs. Simon recognized the jagged line of the EKG, but nothing
else. He'd hoped to get a clear look at the man's face, but a visor
attached to the cap extended down to just above the man's chin.
Simon pulled the remaining length of the zipper, all the way to the
other end of the table, and the rest of the bubble fabric fell to the
side.

The man on the table was naked and incredibly gaunt. His
arms and legs were skeletal, his entire body atrophied to the point
where bones bulged through in places they would normally not,
even in the skinniest or sickest of living people. Despite his
emaciated appearance, the man, or at least his body, was still

youthful. The skin bore no blemishes, no wrinkles. The only defect, an indentation in the skin of his chest where a clear tube had been inserted, feeding his lungs with oxygen. Like those running into the cap on his head, more wires were coming out of the table at sporadic intervals. These electrodes ended in small, circular patches stuck to various parts of the man's frail body.

"What the hell is this?" Arthur said, his top lip curling back in disgust. His frantic eyes had stopped moving, fixed on the grotesque figure on the table. "What are they doing to him?"

Simon couldn't speak. He just shook his head in response to Arthur's questions, his eyes never leaving the prisoner. He studied the wires all over the man's body, traced them back and forth. Finally, he looked up toward the covered face again.

"Wonder who he is," Arthur said, reaching toward the cap on the man's head.

"Hold it!" Simon said. "Are we sure that's safe?"

"I don't know. Maybe. Maybe not."

"Then we shouldn't do it."

Arthur's expression turned stony again, though exasperation could be seen creeping into the twitching corners of his eyes. He jabbed a meaty finger at the table. "We split off from the group to come here, to find this man. If you didn't want to free him, then what the *hell* are we doing here? You said he could help us." His gaze swept over the man for a moment, then lifted back to Simon. "From the look of him, he probably can't even stand on his own. And if he can't help us, then we're as good as dead. So before I die, I want to know who the hell this guy is and why he's so damn important!"

Arthur's chest heaved rapidly under his shirt. Simon stared at Arthur, but said nothing, trying to impart some calm in the room with silence. A moment later, Arthur's face softened a little. He raised his eyebrows in question.

"Okay," Simon said. "But let me do it."

Arthur took a step back from the table and nodded at Simon. Simon leaned in, inspected the visor covering the man's face and discovered small hinges near the edges, where the visor met the cap. He reached his trembling hands forward and touched the visor's edge with one hand, applying slight pressure upward. The visor clicked and flipped up, revealing the man's face.

Though still mostly covered by the wired cap on his head, thin, scraggly brown hair cut at uneven lengths peeked down over the man's ears. His eyes were a bright shade of blue-green, his face hollow and gaunt like the rest of his body. It was a face they both knew, but it took a few moments for them to realize who the man was. His thin face looked so different from the round one they were familiar with seeing in history books. But the largest factor of their delayed recognition of the man was that he was the last person they thought they would find here, or anywhere. How could they have expected him to be there, alive? After all, he was thought to have died many years ago.

"Is that—"

"It can't be."

"But it is."

"How?"

"I don't know, but it's him," Simon said, the skin on his neck and arms prickling. He stared down at the man on the table, shaking his head in disbelief. "It's Rodderick Price."

"But how can he be here?" Arthur said. "He can't. He's been dead for . . . ages, hasn't he?"

"Apparently not."

They stared down, silent for a few seconds, considering the man that couldn't be there. It was impossible. Wasn't it?

"What is he doing here? Why are they keeping him locked up like this?" Arthur said.

"It looks like they're studying him," Simon said.

"But why?"

"Maybe on his request."

Arthur shot Simon a tilted-head, quizzical look.

"Rodderick Price is the father of Rejuvenation," he said. "He was a scientist. It doesn't seem strange to me that he would donate his body to science."

"But it's not just his body, Simon," Arthur said. "He's not dead. This man is *alive*."

"His brain then," Simon said. "He's got to be one of the oldest living people to undergo the Rejuvenation procedure, maybe even the first. They're probably studying the lasting effects on his brain."

"But it's been *years*," Arthur said. "*Hundreds* of years. Even the brains of Rejuvenites deteriorate and die eventually. Long before they reach anything close to this man's age."

Simon went silent for a second, thinking. He turned, gazing at the room, the sterile countertops, the cabinets full of medical equipment and supplies.

"Then they're doing something else," he said. "Something to keep him alive somehow. Keep his brain alive. I don't know. The question is, *why*?"

"One way to find out," Arthur said, and before Simon could stop him, he pulled the cap of wires off Rodderick Price's head.

"Wait! Stop!" Simon said, jumping back toward the table. "You could kill him!"

But it was too late. The cap had been removed and now hung by its wires off the edge of the table. They froze, watching the man on the table. Wondering what would happen. Would his eyes shoot open? Would he suddenly sit up? Gasp for breath? Say something? Simon and Arthur stared, looking for any sign of life.

But Price remained still, eyes closed.

Yelling from the other side of the metal door broke their concentration. The words were muffled, indecipherable. But they came in short bursts as if someone was barking orders. Then, more shuffling feet.

"Whatever they're doing to this guy," Arthur said, "whatever messed up experiments they've been running on him all these years, it doesn't matter now."

"What do you—"

"I mean this guy's a damn lab rat! That's it! He can't help us. You led us into a dead-end, Simon!"

Simon lowered his head. He knew Arthur was right. He *had* led them into a dead end. They were trapped. The man lying on the table in front of them couldn't help. There were men with guns outside the door waiting to kill them. There was no way out. They were doomed, Simon thought, and it was all his fault.

"I'm sorry," he said, looking down at the motionless face of the naked man on the table. "I just thought—I don't know why, but I thought he could help us."

I can *help you.*

Simon and Arthur froze.

The voice was not one either of them recognized. It sounded as if it was all around them, surrounding them on every side.

They looked at each other and then to the metal door, expecting to hear the voice coming from outside. A guard standing by the open door. Or perhaps even Theodore Sullivan himself. What they found, however, was the large, metal door, still shut and locked.

"Who said that?" Arthur said. He looked up, searching for a speaker above, somewhere from which the voice might have been emanating, but found nothing. Only a flat, pale ceiling that ran the expanse of the room but for a large exhaust fan to one side. Arthur stepped under the fan and squinted his eyes up, trying to peer inside it. "Are you up there, in the air ducts?"

No, the voice said.

"Then where are you?"

Right here, on the table.

Arthur turned around slowly and looked at Simon. Their eyes met, equally large, and then looked down at the motionless form of Rodderick Price lying on the table as they both realized what was happening. The voice they heard was not coming from someone outside the door. It wasn't coming from a hidden speaker in the room or from the ducts beyond the exhaust fan in the ceiling. The voice was coming from everywhere and from nowhere. The reason it seemed to surround them, encompass the whole of each one of them, was because the voice was sounding inside their minds.

41

"How can this be happening?" Simon said, stumbling back from the table. He whipped his head around, looking to the side, behind him, back to the table. "I mean, this *can't* be happening."

I'm afraid it is, though I understand that it takes some getting used to, Rodderick Price said inside their heads.

Simon's mind was swimming. Was he actually having a conversation with the man on the table? *Yes.* Could this man really speak using his mind? *Yes.* It was impossible. *Not impossible.* Simon's head began to throb with confusion, but was strangely soothed a moment later. If this man could speak to him using his mind, did that mean he could also read his mind? *Yes, but it is a practice I will try to avoid because I find it very rude.*

My God, Simon thought. The man was doing it right now. Price was inside his head. He felt almost violated, bare to the world. The invasive feeling suddenly diminished.

I apologize if I was intrusive. I can't help it. Not after all this time.

Can you hear this, Simon thought. *What I'm thinking right now?*

Yes, but your friend, Arthur, cannot. I can speak to each of you

439

individually just as we are speaking now, but he cannot hear your thoughts as I do.

And you can speak to both of us together as well? Simon thought.

Yes.

"Yes, what?" Arthur asked. His eyes were wide, round, darting around the room again.

"He was talking to me," Simon said aloud. Vocalizing his words felt like a great effort after the ease of speaking with his mind.

"Son of a bitch. What'd he say to you?"

Just that I can think to you both individually if needed, however, I would like to speak to you as a group.

"But . . . how are you d-doing this?" Arthur stuttered out. His voice was trembling. His usual hardened exterior cracking, a surprise to Simon.

Do not feel alone in your astonishment, for the ability was a great shock to me when I first discovered it. I do not know exactly how it happened, but I have had a great many years to think about it.

"How . . . how long have they kept you here?" Simon said in a low voice as he watched Rodderick's motionless lips.

Oh, I think one immense shock is enough at this moment, so let's just say I've been here quite a long time. Although, I differentiate the time between when I was here of my own free will and when they started keeping me here against it.

"What do you mean?"

I mean that it is almost entirely my fault that I came to be in this place. You see, many years ago, before I became like one of the tired old souls lying side by side in the building above us, I made arrangements to keep myself at the center of Rejuvenation research. When my brain finally succumbed to the ravages of age and could no longer support my body, which was long before this place was built, I was transported to a special retirement facility and kept for study. I became, as Arthur put it, nothing more than a lab rat.

Arthur's eyes bulged again at the mention of his name by Price. How could he know? But Price was in his head. He was in both their heads, could sift through their thoughts, find any information he wanted or needed. Arthur shrank back, still shaking his head at the whole situation.

"Sorry about that," he said.

Don't be. It's true. That's what I have become.

"But you volunteered for all this?" Simon said.

No. I volunteered for medical research, not for this.

"What do you mean?"

I mean that I volunteered myself to be studied not just for the average effects of Rejuvenation, but for something more. An extended research period where, through methods I devised earlier in life, my doctors would be able to keep my brain stimulated and functioning at a certain capacity for well beyond the expected years of a normal Rejuvenite. I lost the ability to use my body, but my mind remained functioning. My study was not meant to be permanent. I figured I would live out the remainder of my days under observation like was planned for all Rejuvenite retirees, albeit under higher scrutiny in accordance with the specific research for which I submitted myself. But I never thought they would take it this far.

Simon was amazed at how fast Price's words made sense in his mind. It was as if Price's thoughts, whether a small idea or a lengthy explanation, were told in a fraction of a second as opposed to the amount of time it would have taken to physically speak the words aloud. It was as if all the words, Price's complete thoughts, simply popped into Simon's head and he instantly understood what they meant. Judging by the shocked expression on Arthur's face, he was experiencing the same thing.

"This is what they used to keep you alive all this time, isn't it?" Arthur asked, gaining composure of himself again, pointing to the electrodes still attached to Price's body and the ones attached to the cap dangling off the table.

Not at first. As I said, in the beginning they used methods of my own invention and design. It has only been in the last hundred years or so that they have used the methods you see now.

"So they just decided to keep you alive to study this . . . *ability* of yours?" Arthur said.

Abilities, yes. At first I was in a specialized facility, but under very much the same care as other old Rejuvenites. That all changed one day when one of the nurses came in and, to my surprise, I found myself engaging in my first dialogue in over 80 years.

"So just like that?" Simon said. "It just happened one day?"

Yes. I'm not sure if it was simply the advanced age of my brain suddenly unlocking something hidden in every mind, something that was catalyzed by the methods being used to keep my brain functioning, or a combination of both. I lean toward the last explanation, but it is impossible to know for sure. So what you said is the best explanation I can give—one day, it just happened.

"And once they discovered what you could do, then what? They just—"

Did everything in their power to keep me alive, yes. You can understand what they thought, because you are thinking the same thing right now, as I did then. It seems so impossible—the ability to communicate with another through just the mind. Telepathy. Impossible though it seemed, it happened, and I have been their prisoner ever since.

"They just kept you locked up all these years, not allowing you to die?" Simon said.

At first it was for the sake of science, which I understood. I was just as curious as my caregivers to discover what had led to my newfound telepathy. Everything was handled scientifically and, though I was indeed a lab rat, I was still treated like a human. That is, until someone new came to power within EXLI and subsequently, the research being done on me.

"Sullivan," Arthur said.

Yes.

"That son of a bitch!"

When Sullivan took over and learned what I could do, my analysis changed drastically. He had this place built. This vault, to keep me quarantined, hidden. When he took over, there were a great many people who knew about me within the company, the majority of which have since met their ends. He limited access to me, put new scientists and doctors on the team researching me. Started running his own private experiments. I was able to see into his mind even then, and in times since. See, but not influence it. I saw his plans, his ambition for my special abilities.

"What was it?" Simon said, knowing he would not like the answer.

What does any great evil want to do when presented with a new, powerful ability that his opponents do not have? Use it against them. What Sullivan saw in me was not the possibility to expand what it means to be human. He didn't, or couldn't, see what abilities such as mine could mean for humanity as a species. He didn't see the potential for greatness, for enlightenment. All Sullivan saw was a way to increase his power, and that is exactly what he set out to do—to become like me or to somehow weaponize my abilities for his own gain.

"Has he?"

Unfortunately for him, no.

"But he's still trying, isn't he?" Simon said. "That's what's going on down here. This underground laboratory isn't just to study you, is it? He's got other people, subjects, down here to study. He's trying to do it again, what happened to you."

Correct. Though his attempts at replicating what's happening in my brain have only led to disrupted neurogenesis, and misplaced and malformed neurons in his own. An irreversible deterioration of the mind that's made him all the more desperate.

Simon went silent for a moment, as did Arthur and the thoughts coming from Price. The only faint sounds on the air were those of the guards and whomever else was outside, continuing their work on getting the door open. Though even that noise seemed distant in comparison to the thoughts running through Simon's mind.

"What I don't understand," Simon said, then stopped himself. "Well, I don't really understand any of this, to be honest, but something else I can't figure out is what all this has to do with Sebastian."

He was your friend.

"Yes, and he's dead because of all this. He's the reason we got wrapped up in this from the beginning."

Your friend Sebastian's involvement and your own, I'm afraid, are purely coincidental.

"What do you mean?"

Please. Forgive me. I was desperate. A few weeks ago, they were transporting me from one of the other labs on this floor and I was able to break free for just a moment. It was only a second or two, but to someone who spends the entirety of his time inside his own head, it felt like a deep, cool breath of air after ages of suffocation. Like I was discovering a whole new world. I had planned for years what I would do if such a moment presented itself, so I acted.

I used all the strength of mind that I could muster and reached out my thoughts, outside this facility, searching for someone that could help me. I scanned through the minds of countless people in the city—everyday people, educators, scientists, religious leaders, politicians . . . so many people. I even encountered several Reju-

venation resistance group members, which is how I learned of the secret name of this place—Hillbrook. I scanned until I found a person who seemed ready. It was your friend, Sebastian. I was hesitant at first, because he worked for EXLI, but as I delved deeper into his mind I realized he was different. He was pure in a way no one else I had scanned was. I also knew his mind could understand the implications of what was happening should I try to speak with him. Most people would go mad if they heard a voice in their head that was not their own, but Sebastian was different. He was ready and open to believe it, so I reached out to him.

I tried to protect him, set him on the right path to the proper people. Only those who would know the name Hillbrook. Those who would believe him, who would lead him here. I had no idea the series of events it would set in motion, and I am sorry to anyone those events impacted negatively. But I beg of you, to please understand that it was a necessity. It was a required risk to stop Sullivan and free me from this prison.

Simon thought of Maggie. Always of Maggie. But in this instance, it was because of what Price had just said. *I had no idea the series of events it would set in motion, and I am sorry to anyone those events impacted in a negative way.* If she were here, Simon wondered how she'd react to hearing those words. Would she be crying? Perhaps scowling down at Price? If nothing else, he knew Maggie would have been thinking of her brother, because Simon was thinking of Will too. How Price's actions, however inadvertent, had led to Will's death. He wondered if Maggie would have had a private think with Price. Perhaps a calm discussion about the role he played in her brother's death. Then again, perhaps she would have screamed at Price inside her mind, or aloud with the full force of her voice. But Simon didn't know what would have really happened, because Maggie wasn't here. He wished more than ever that she was, if only so he could feel the soothing comfort of her hand in his.

There was a thundering boom against the metal door that shook the inside of the vault. Simon and Arthur snapped out of their thoughts. They grabbed the table to steady themselves, looked to the door, and then back at each other.

"We don't have long," Arthur said.

They are working on the door's electronics right now. I can see it in their minds.

Arthur looked down at Price.

"Can you do anything to stop them?" he said. "Can you, ya know, mess with their heads?"

I can do much more than that.

Something about that statement sent a shiver through Simon. He hoped Price hadn't sensed that feeling in him, read his questioning thoughts. If Price had, he made no mention of it.

I will help you get out of here. I will help you find your friends and rescue Lydia. And I will use whatever strength I have left to help you escape with the information you need to bring Sullivan and EXLI to justice.

"Thank you," Simon said. "Is there anything we can do for you? Do you want us to take you with us?"

No. Leave me here. You have already done that which I could never repay. You have set me free.

"But . . . won't you die? I mean, if we just leave you like this?"

Yes. I will die. The process has already begun and I believe I have but a few hours left. This, I am grateful for, more than you will ever know. I have been alive for longer than any human in recorded history, longer than I ever dreamed or wished to live. Long enough to learn and appreciate the value of life lived over time. Long enough to realize that whatever death may bring, I am ready for it, anxious even. By freeing me, you have given me the one ability I was denied for many, many years—the ability to move on.

They looked down on the motionless body of Rodderick Price and although what they saw was the gaunt, yet youthful body of a man, they knew it was nothing more than a lie. Simon was sure of it. He looked at Price's face—such a young face, for such an old soul. It wasn't right. The man lying on that table was much more. He deserved more.

More shouts echoed from the hallway outside.

They are close.

"If you're going to do something to help us, Mr. Price," Arthur said, "now would be a damn good time."

"How do you plan on stopping them?" Simon asked.

When I told you that my moment of freedom a few weeks ago was like discovering a whole new world, I meant both figuratively and literally. When I broke free, not only was I able to contact your friend Sebastian, but I also discovered the unfounded abilities my mind had developed throughout the years of my captivity. And now, set completely free, I am . . . struggling to fully understand some of what I may be able to accomplish. Others, I may never comprehend. These abilities are . . . powerful.

"What abilities?"

Let me show you.

42

STAND AWAY FROM THE DOOR, PLEASE.

Simon and Arthur stepped away from the table on which Rodderick Price lay and made their way to the opposite corner of the room.

Be ready to move when I say so.

Simon could still hear the muffled sound of shuffling footsteps and barking orders from the other side of the door. He wasn't sure how many guards were now outside, but it sounded like a great deal more than the five who had fired on them as they entered the vault.

In the moment they waited, Simon wondered what Price had planned. Was he simply waiting for the vault to be breached before invading the minds of the guards? Did he need some kind of specific proximity to influence someone's mind? That couldn't be it, Simon thought. After all, Price had been able to reach out into the hallway and learn that the guards were working on the door. Price had reached out to Sebastian too, who had been many miles away at the time. So what was Price planning now? And what did he mean when he said that his abilities had developed?

Then, Simon got his answer.

The heavy, metal door suddenly ripped off its hinges and flew outward into the hallway. Based on the sheer size of the door, it must have weighed at least five tons, if not more, but it had soared from its fixed spot in the wall as if it were a tiny scrap of paper caught in a strong gust of wind. The enormous door burst forth into the hallway, taking along with it those guards who had the misfortune of being nearest. The door tumbled on, smashing into the walls and other armed guards who screamed in shock and fear. Many of the guards attempted to drop to the floor, but never made it before being struck by the heavy door as it continued plowing forward. There was another loud crash as the door finally came to rest, lodged inside the corner of a wall near one of the intersecting hallways.

Simon and Arthur jumped back at the sight of the massive door tearing away from the wall.

"Did you just—" Simon began to say out of instinct, but he knew. Before he could think about it anymore, the voice of Rodderick Price sounded inside his head.

Go! Now!

Simon knew Arthur had heard Rodderick's command as well, because he pushed out from the corner at the same time, both men bolting for what was now a gigantic hole in the front of the room.

When they crossed through, Simon got his first clear look at the carnage in the corridor outside. Guards lay everywhere, some unconscious on the floor still holding their guns in a tight grip while others moaned in pain as they tried to pull themselves along with broken limbs. There were spots along the hallway with large craters in the walls where the door had bounded off, a few arms and legs sticking out of these holes—the unfortunate ones who had been forced through the wall when the door struck them. But even as Simon witnessed the many injured and subdued guards who lay throughout the hallway, there were still others who had avoided the wrath of the door. These men were getting to their feet and some were already closing in on Arthur and him with guns aimed directly at them.

Help! Simon screamed inside his mind, hoping that Rodderick could still hear him and that he had a plan for dealing with the surviving guards.

What they saw next stopped them both dead in their tracks.

It was otherworldly, as if some giant, invisible hand was thrusting the guards back. In one moment stopping their charge and the next throwing them in the air away from Simon and Arthur. As the fleeing pair started running forward again, they watched as the guards who had been able to get to their feet were tossed around. Some of the guards flew back, doubling over as if pulled from behind at the waist. Others were hurled into the air, spinning and slamming into the walls or landing 10 or 20 yards away on their backs. Those guards who'd been holding automatic rifles had them ripped from their grasps, clattering to the floor.

Arthur instinctively reached down and grabbed one of the rifles. Perhaps it made him feel safer, Simon thought. Maybe he did it out of instinct. Or perhaps Arthur simply didn't register that with Price's unnatural influence, none of them would need guns.

Turn at the hallway ahead.

The voice sounded inside their heads while guard after guard continued to fly into the air around them. Arthur reached the next intersection first and turned the corner, followed by Simon. When they entered the new hallway, Simon saw a mix of people. There was another large force of guards headed their way in the distance, but there was also a smattering of doctors and scientists in lab coats and scrubs whom, whether they had witnessed what happened in the other hallway or not, were diving into rooms and under tables for cover.

The approaching group of guards was closer now, their guns aimed ahead. They stopped and began firing toward Simon and Arthur through the still scattering crowd in the hallway. Several lab coat wearers fell to the floor as the guards' gunfire ripped through them, however, none of the bullets reached Simon and Arthur. Simon didn't know if this was Price's doing or not, but he was grateful nonetheless.

Suddenly the entire group of firing guards launched backward, broken apart like a set of bowling pins. They flew in the air, slamming into the walls and landing on the floor. When Simon reached the guards, he saw that most appeared to have been knocked out, while others were simply lying on the floor with open, hazy eyes.

They continued running, following Price's directions, always waiting for the next. The people in the hallways they traversed had thinned out considerably. Simon assumed word of Price's abilities had spread and the floor's inhabitants were all staying out of sight on purpose.

"Do you know where Lydia is?" Arthur yelled.

I cannot reach into her thoughts, but I know where they are keeping her from the information I've gathered in the minds of other personnel down here.

"Why can't you reach her?"

She is . . . It's as though there's a barrier between her thoughts and mine.

"What about Maggie? And Zoë?" Simon yelled as they continued to run, laboratory personnel scattering away from them as they passed. "They're with us, but we were separated."

I've found them.

Simon felt his stomach sink as he prepared to ask his next question.

"Are they . . . are they alive?"

Yes, Maggie is okay.

The sick feeling in Simon's stomach disappeared. He wondered if Price had read his mind, sensed Simon's connection to Maggie, and started with her wellbeing first.

However, Zoë was very badly injured by an explosion in the northern quadrant.

"How bad? Arthur asked.

"Debris from the explosion has punctured one of her lungs. The force of the blast sent her crashing into a wall. She has fractured the fibula in her left leg, broken several ribs, and has internal bleeding in multiple areas. I do not know how long she may have."

"Can you take us to them?"

Yes. They are being held by a group of guards in a location that is on the way to Lydia.

"Is there . . . anything, ya know, you can do for them, or, for Zoë? To help her out until we arrive?"

I will try.

43

———

THERE WAS A QUIET MUMBLING COMING FROM SOMEWHERE nearby. The voice was small, pained. Maggie lifted her head from her curled position on the floor to listen.

"Wha . . . wha's goin' on?"

It wasn't the guard who'd spent the last few minutes beating her. He was standing on the other side of the nearest lab station, talking to another guard. Maggie tilted her head, looked toward the corner, the only other place the voice might be coming from.

Zoë was awake and sitting up on an elbow. Her opened eyes showed a mix of bloodshot red and her usual green irises, somehow paler. The thin layer of black char from the explosion fell off her cheeks and forehead in small clouds as she moved her face, trying to speak.

"Wha happen?" Zoë mumbled out. Her face clenched up in obvious pain. Her eyes drifted from Maggie to the guards and back again.

Maggie raised a finger to her lips, trying to signal to Zoë to remain quiet. She then put her thumb and pointer finger together, fanning her remaining fingers, asking if Zoë was okay.

Zoë looked down at her body, her eyes contracting with

453

concern. The burned clothing, the singed skin, the blood. She tried to sit up, then sank back down to the floor as another wave of pain hit her. But ever the soldier, Zoë looked up at Maggie with a grimace and gave her own okay sign.

Maggie knew it was a lie. Zoë was far from okay. She'd be even worse if the guards saw that she was awake. Maggie didn't think Zoë could take much kicking from the guards, if any at all. Not in the state she was in.

Zoë gritted her teeth as she propped herself up with her one good arm. The pain in her shoulder from the gunshot of the night before had returned along with the other injuries she'd sustained. Another grimace and then, relief, as she pushed her body into a sitting position against the wall. Maggie thought that doing so would draw the guards' attention, but they seemed to be too preoccupied to notice, discussing something amongst themselves. Zoë waved a hand at Maggie, pointed, and mouthed the word *coat*. Maggie ripped the remains of her tattered lab coat off as best she could with her bound hands and slid it over to Zoë, who proceeded to wrap and tie it around her bloodied leg. She expelled a low grumble when she pulled the coat tight, then leaned back against the wall, sighing with exhaustion.

The radios clipped to the guards' vests squawked, echoing around the room, but Maggie couldn't quite make out what was said. The guards nearest the front of the lab leaned out the open doorway, looked up and down the hall outside. When they spun back into the room again, Maggie saw their eyes had narrowed, brows pointed and wrinkled. They re-gripped the flattop SARs in their hands, as if to make sure they were indeed holding weapons that would keep them safe. They looked at the other guards in the room, then at each other.

They're *worried*, Maggie thought. Worried about what? She didn't understand. She and Zoë had set off their diversionary bomb in hopes of drawing the guards away, but instead, they'd been caught in the explosion, taken prisoner. She assumed the guards standing in the room, the ones beating her, had been responsible for capturing them. Shouldn't they be proud of their efforts? Shouldn't they be high-fiving and gloating about their accomplishments? Not afraid.

Maggie felt a surge of hope well up inside her as she considered a possible answer. *Simon. Arthur.* Could they actually be alive? And if so, had they somehow gained the upper hand? So much so, that these guards who had taken her and Zoë hostage were fearful of retribution. Were Simon and Arthur coming to save them?

The group of three guards standing near the center of the room stopped talking as their radios crackled again. Maggie still couldn't make out the entirety of what was said through the radio, but she thought she heard the words "breach" and "south quadrant." It *was* Simon and Arthur, she thought. It had to be. Though she couldn't be certain, the panicked expressions on all the guards' faces at least told her something unexpected was happening.

One of the door guards saw Maggie staring. *Shit.* He pointed at her and yelled, drawing the attention of the others. The black-haired guard who'd beaten her earlier stomped around the laboratory table, his slanted gaze on Maggie. When he spotted Zoë awake and sitting up, his eyes grew wider, hungrier.

The radios on the guards' vests crackled again. This time, Maggie heard the words coming through clear as day. The voice was shouting, terrified.

"South quadrant compromised! We need . . . backup! I don't know what the hell is—"

The radio cut out.

The room went quiet.

The black-haired guard had stopped, his feet planted to the floor. He looked back at his fellow guards, who did not move, did not speak. Fear etched on their faces as they processed what they'd just heard on the radio.

Maggie and Zoë remained as they were, both sitting on the floor, backs against the walls. They'd heard the same frightened words from the radio, were just as confused.

The black-haired guard was the first to break the silence. He turned on Maggie and Zoë again, striding toward them. The heavy clomp of his boots on the floor seemed even louder now. He glared at Maggie, but spoke to his fellow guards. "We're staying here. These bitches are gonna talk or else—"

Maggie saw the look in his eyes, that mix of fear and anger. She knew that even if Simon and Arthur were on their way to save them, they wouldn't get here in time. By the time they arrived, she and Zoë would be long dead.

But then, in the farthest depths of her mind, Maggie heard a whisper. No, it was more like a feeling, a sensation. It told her that everything would be all right. They were safe now. The guards would no longer hurt them. She didn't know where the feeling had come from, or why it was there. The black-haired guard was still marching toward her. He was barking. And yet . . . his voice seemed far away, faint, as if he were talking underwater. His glare no longer looked threatening. Yes, Maggie thought. They'd be fine. There was no need to worry. Not anymore.

Maggie looked to the corner and saw a small smile on Zoë's face, a softness in her eyes. She knew that Zoë felt the same calmness. No need to worry. Everything would be fine.

The black-haired guard was mid-stride when he was jerked backward into the air by . . . by what? It was as though he'd been falling toward Maggie and his parachute had been pulled, sucking him back into the room where he collided with the rest of the guards who'd been lifted into the air as well. They crashed into each other, then exploded outward in different directions. Each guard struck a different part of the room, some slamming into cabinets, shattering the frosted glass doors. Others were dragged across the countertops before being thrown into the walls. The black-haired guard was lifted to the ceiling, his head crashing into a fluorescent light, then tossed back down hard onto the center table where his right arm and leg gave a grotesque crack of busted bones and his head lolled to the side. By the end of the thrashing, all five guards were beaten, broken, and unconscious.

Despite their sudden and unexpected calmness, the sight of five grown men being picked up by unseen forces and tossed around the room left Maggie and Zoë in a state of shock. What had just happened was impossible, Maggie thought. What *had* happened? It didn't make sense. One moment the guards were in control, the black-haired man bounding toward her for yet another beating . . . the next, all five men were flying around the room, pulled by hidden strings, beaten against the walls and cabinets and countertops until they were all knocked out.

Maggie's eyes locked on Zoë and she saw the same look of fear and confusion on her face. Maggie's heart started to race. Were they next? Whatever was happening, whatever mysterious force had taken out the guards, would it send Maggie and Zoë flying too? They both scanned the room, a mess of busted cabinets, glass shards, and broken bottles oozing liquids that gave off pungent, sulfurous smells. They looked at the floor around them, their arms and legs, as if expecting to see warning signs the guards had not. Something that would tell Maggie and Zoë it was their turn to fly.

But just as quickly as her fears had risen, Maggie felt the return of that peculiar sensation in the back of her mind. That whisper that told her everything would be okay. She felt her heart rate slow, her nerves calm. They wouldn't be flying through the air. They were good and didn't require punishment. They were safe.

And yet, there was something different to the strange calming sensation this time. Something more. Something just for her. An image of Will flashed in her mind. She didn't know why. Of all the times to think of her deceased brother, why now? In this place. At this exact moment. But his memory was there, his smiling face. And with it, the pain of mourning, that regret that she wasn't able to do more for Will. But then . . . relief washed over her like a cool wind. Not the kind of relief one feels when resting after a long journey or hard day's work. It felt different, as if someone had severely wronged her and then given an earnest apology. Just like the sudden calmness, Maggie didn't know where this new feeling had come from, but it soothed her heart.

"I think . . . I think we're safe now," Maggie said, scooping up a nearby, large piece of glass from a busted cabinet, using it to cut the cable ties around her wrists and ankles.

Zoë gave a slow nod and said, "Yeah, I think so too." She looked out at the room, the unconscious guards, and then back at Maggie. "I don't know why, but I *feel* like we're gonna be okay."

"We should get out of here," Maggie said, getting to her feet. The words had come to her without even thinking. This was their opportunity to escape. To go . . . and she knew where they needed to go. How could that be? She didn't even know where they were now, what room they'd been dragged into after the explosion, but . . . somehow, she knew. She saw the hallway outside in her mind, saw the one after that, and after that. She saw the path they needed to take to get back to their true destination. O-800. The room where Lydia was being held. "Can you walk?"

Zoë braced herself against the wall, started to slide her legs underneath her, but crumpled to the floor in pain, shaking her head and gritting her teeth. "Ah, I don't think—"

Zoë's words were cut short by her own sudden gasp. She planted her hands on the floor, arms straight, and arched her back as if her chest was being pulled outward.

"Zoë? What's happening? Are you okay?" Maggie said.

They'd been mistaken, she thought. They weren't safe and Zoë was about to start flying around the room, just like the guards.

But Zoë's chest relaxed and she exhaled a long, deep breath. Her body sank back against the floor and the wall, and she looked up at Maggie, her green eyes large, round, and bright again. There were tears there as well.

"Zoë?" Maggie said, stepping over to her, crouching. "Are you—"

"I'm . . . fine," Zoë said, her open-mouthed look of astonishment matching Maggie's.

"What do you mean you're fine? What just happened?"

"I . . . I don't know what it was but . . . I was just sitting here. I could feel the broken bones scraping together in my leg when I tried to stand, that *burning* all over my skin, like there were knives shredding my insides . . . and then I . . . I got this warm sensation in my chest, almost like . . ." Zoë went silent. Another tear rolled from her eye. "I felt it spread out, to my shoulder, my leg, my side and then I . . . then the warmth was gone and I could breathe again. I . . . felt better. A *lot* better."

A warmth in her chest? And now she felt better? Just like that. None of what Zoë was saying made any sense to Maggie. At first, she worried that Zoë's injuries might be far worse than she feared, that the pain was causing Zoë to lose her mind. Maggie stared at Zoë, searched her eyes for madness. But she saw only those bright green irises staring back, round and bewildered, but *alive*.

"I know it doesn't make sense," Zoë said, "but it's like something fixed me. *Healed* me."

"Can you get up?" Maggie asked, standing again. She offered her hands to help, but Zoë shook her head.

Zoë pushed up on her hands, cautiously at first, as if she thought whatever cure she'd just been given wouldn't last and the pain all over her body would return. But after that moment's hesitation, Zoë stood with ease. She patted her side, her stomach, but did not wince. She rotated her shoulder and flexed her bloodied leg, even put all her weight on it, but it remained strong. She untied the coat from around her leg and let it drop to the floor.

As Maggie watched all this, she marveled at Zoë's sudden change in health. One minute she'd been a broken, bloody mess on the floor, a few breaths away from death . . . and now, she looked back to normal, strong. Zoë's leg, shirt, and face were still smeared with drying blood. Her arms still showed the redness of burns. But her spirit seemed to have returned. She stood tall, eager to continue the fight.

"Good?" Maggie asked.

Zoë took a few steps, kicked her legs out a few times to test their strength, and nodded. She walked over to the crumpled form of the nearest guard, laying near the back wall, unconscious, his right arm jutting off at an odd angle. It was one of the door guards, who'd been flown across the entire length of the room. Zoë crouched, unstrapped the flattop rifle from his shoulders, and swung it over her own. She ejected the magazine, checked it, replaced it, and then looked up at Maggie.

"Let's get the fuck outta here," Zoë said.

Maggie marched through the room, past debris scattered across the floor, stepping over more unconscious guards. Zoë grabbed a pistol off one of the other guards, performed a quick brass check, and offered it to Maggie. But Maggie shook her head. She didn't know why, but she knew she wouldn't need it. Just like she knew the hallways outside, their path to Lydia.

Zoë shrugged and slid the pistol into the back waistband of her pants. She followed Maggie to the door.

"Which way ya think?"

"Follow me," Maggie said, stepping outside, leading the way.

44

*T*URN LEFT HERE.

They followed Price's command and found themselves in a quiet hallway. Two unconscious guards lay on the ground by a nearby door. Simon assumed this was Price's doing. He'd taken care of the obstacles in their way before they could even be a threat to them.

Your friends are close. Zoë is . . . restored now.

Neither Simon nor Arthur were quite sure what Price meant, but they had no time to get into specifics. If Price said Zoë was better, they would just take his word for it, no matter the strange word choice.

They continued, passing the unconscious guards and following Price's directions inside their heads.

Turn right at the next hallway.

They turned and headed down the next corridor. The underground facility truly was a maze, Simon thought. Now that he was daring to hope that they might see Maggie and Zoë again, be able to save Lydia, he wondered if they would still be able to find their way back to the elevator. With Price, no doubt. But if their omniscient guide didn't last that long . . . He shook all thoughts of a potential after away and instead focused his hope on whether Price would live long enough to continue to protect them all. At least that long. They just needed his help to—

Simon quieted his mind, sure that Price had just heard his wonders, his hopes. But if Price had, he didn't say a word about it.

They marched on, turning once or twice more down other hallways, encountering mostly subdued guards along the way. Though, on occasion a few active guards surprised them. But they never got close. Price took care of these men with ease, sending them flying back into the walls, knocked out cold.

You are almost there.

Simon and Arthur turned another corner and saw a long hallway stretch out before them. There was one guard splayed out on the floor far ahead. No other personnel. Just a few vacant hospital carts pushed up against one wall and a rack full of medical equipment. Almost as soon as Simon and Arthur had turned into the hallway, Maggie and Zoë stepped into view from a smaller intersecting hallway a few doors down.

Simon skidded to a halt, unsure if his eyes were playing a trick on him. Was it really her? Clothes blackened, singed. Her face was bloodied, bruises already forming in some spots. Any other day he might have mistaken her for someone else. But no, his eyes weren't fooling him. It was Maggie.

Simon rushed to Maggie's side, wrapped his arms around her, and squeezed tight. She hugged back, despite giving a soft, pained moan from the pressure of his arms on her injuries. Simon kissed her and then pulled back to look at her closer. He felt tears welling up in his eyes as they looked at each other, grinning. Each of them had thought—but here they were. Together again.

"Are you okay?" Simon asked, his hands clutching Maggie's shoulders.

"Yeah I . . . I'm good," she said. "You?"

Simon nodded, then embraced her again. When they broke apart a second time, they noticed Arthur had been sharing a reunion with Zoë, who Simon now saw looked in far worse condition than Maggie.

"—explain later. You're covered in blood and burns," Arthur said. "Do you need help? I can—"

"Arthur. I'm . . ." Zoë rubbed at her side again, looked down at her leg, almost out of instinct. She then raised her eyes back up at Arthur and said, "I'm fine."

"Are you sure? He said you were hurt, dying even."

"Yeah, but—wait, who said I was hurt?" Zoë asked.

"Well . . . it's . . ." But Arthur couldn't find the words. Simon knew what must have been going through Arthur's head. As far as they knew, Price had yet to speak to Zoë or Maggie. How could Simon and Arthur explain Price's abilities to them without sounding like madmen? Arthur looked up at the ceiling, as he'd taken to doing whenever he considered Price, but no response came. "It's, hard to explain. But you were hurt?"

"I *was*," Zoë said. She shared an intense, yet confused look with Maggie, and then looked back at Arthur. "But now I'm not."

Arthur didn't seem to understand it any better than Zoë did, but at that exact moment, the how didn't seem to matter. He hugged Zoë, with some hesitation at first, then stronger when she squeezed him back. "You're really okay?" he asked.

"I could use a drink, but yeah, I'll survive."

Simon watched as the two Life Liberation members embraced. His eyes lingered on Zoë. Then it hit him. *Restored.* Simon made an effort to keep his eyes forward and thought: *You did this, didn't you?*

He asked for help, Price answered in a matter-of-fact tone, and only to Simon. *I did what was needed. What I could.*

Any further discussion was tabled as Simon's thoughts were interrupted by Zoë.

"*Lots* of weird shit's been happening," she said. "What going on? Did you two find your guy?"

Arthur locked eyes on Simon. Simon knew what he was thinking. *Weird shit*. It seemed that Zoë and Maggie *had* witnessed some of Price's actions along their journey, though they did not know the true source of the incredible acts. Guards flying through the air, knocked unconscious. Some kind of miraculous healing. Weird shit, indeed.

"Oh yeah, we found him," Arthur said.

"And?" Zoë's face turned back and forth between them, waiting for them to speak.

They remained silent for another second. Simon took a deep breath and said, "It's Rodderick Price."

Zoë and Maggie did not say a word. Not at first. They shared another look of confusion, eyebrows pointed, faces squinted. Maggie's mouth fell open like she was about to speak, but it was Zoë who talked first.

"*Rodderick Price?*" Zoë said, shaking her head. "I don't—you mean they got his body down here somewhere?"

"Yes, but . . ." Simon said, talking slowly, thinking, trying to find the right words. "Well, it's not just his body. Price *isn't* dead."

"Of course he is!" Zoë said. "The guy died, what, a hundred years ago. More than that. He can't be—"

"He is," Arthur said. "He's the one doing . . ." Arthur pointed at the unconscious guard lying on the floor down the hallway.

Zoë's eyes lit up. Something had clicked. She looked at Maggie. At the guard on the floor. Zoë patted a hand to her left side again, and then looked back at Arthur and Simon.

"But, how?" Zoë said. "Did he say how—"

"We don't really understand it either," Simon said, tapping the side of his head. "But he can speak to us and . . . he can *do* things."

"This is unbelievable," Maggie said, staring off down the hallway, as if deep in thought.

"Well I'm just glad he's on our fuckin' side," Zoë said, shaking her head again. "We need to get moving. Lydia's close."

Maggie came out of whatever thoughts she'd been lost in, looked at Zoë, nodded. She stepped forward.

"This way," Maggie said, pulling Simon along by the hand.

Simon watched Maggie lead the way, their reunited group marching down the long corridor. Maggie kept her eyes forward, determined, and Simon eyed her with curiosity.

"You know where Lydia is?" he asked and Maggie nodded. "How?"

She looked at Simon. Her brow was pointed, confident, chin high, and said, "I just know."

Simon didn't question Maggie further, but realized what she must have been pondering moments before. He gave her a reassuring nod and thought to Price. *You're doing this, aren't you? You're guiding her.*

Just a little push.

Why not just talk to her? Simon thought.

They have not seen me as you have. I did not want to shock them. Not too much, without context.

Maggie led them to the end of the corridor and turned right into a new hallway. More unconscious guards were scatted across the floor, their weapons piled in one corner. She pointed ahead at the opening of another intersection to the left.

They turned the corner and found themselves in a short hallway that dead-ended with a single door set in the center of the wall. In front of the door stood two men whom Simon and the rest recognized instantly as Sullivan's closest confidants, Purcell and Vapula.

Though they'd seen these men countless times on television over the years and knew their faces well, seeing Michael Purcell and Samar Vapula in the flesh brought with it an instant pause of hesitant recognition, like spotting a movie star walking down the street. They were both tall and had clear, youthful faces. Vapula's skin was a light shade of brown. His thick shock of black, wavy hair, usually groomed to perfection, was disheveled, as if combed hastily. Purcell, on the other hand, was almost sickly pale by comparison. A look of contempt plastered on his pointed face, set beneath a blaze of short, red hair that stood up straight on his head.

As soon as Simon and the rest of the group rounded the corner, Purcell and Vapula raised pistols at them in unsteady hands.

"S-stop," Purcell stuttered out, his high voice cracking. "Drop y-your g-guns. Now!"

They all skidded to a halt, Simon not before stepping in front of Maggie to shield her. Zoë started to raise the rifle in her hands. Purcell stabbed his pistol out at her, and Zoë stopped.

"You heard him. Drop the weapons," Vapula said. His words were an unconfident command, his accented voice just as shaky as his counterpart's. Brown eyes dancing side to side.

"Give us Lydia," Zoë barked, still holding on to her rifle.

Purcell shook his head. His eyes darted to Vapula, then back at the group. "We c-can't do that. He said y-you'd come. S-supposed to s-stay here."

Zoë sneered.

"Boss making you do his dirty work, huh? Why don't you tell Sullivan to come on out of that room? Face us himself instead of cowering inside."

"We do what w-we want!"

You've done enough. Both of you.

In an instant, Purcell and Vapula's faces dropped. Their mouths agape in fearful astonishment. Sweat rolled down Purcell's red temples as he jerked his eyes to the door again, then back. The hand Vapula used to hold his gun trembled harder, sank.

"You f-fools," Vapula said. His gaze was frozen, but far off with thought. "You d-don't know . . . oh, no no . . . you d-don't *realize* what y-you've done."

They've granted me a long-overdue release, nothing more.

Purcell's eyes bulged. "Why? *Why* would you free him?" he pleaded. He shook his head as if confused. "You've doomed us all!"

I've come to confront my captors. No one else.

Purcell locked eyes on Vapula, whose face was still blank, deep in thought. Both men acting as if they'd forgotten everyone else in the hallway. Purcell turned, throwing himself at the door they'd been guarding. He pounded and kicked at it. Shouted in a strained voice, pleading for entry. But the door did not budge. Nor did Vapula, who'd dropped his gun to his side and stood expressionless, resigned.

Zoë and Arthur took the opportunity to raise their rifles, but—
That will not be necessary.

Arthur lowered his rifle. When Zoë shot him a questioning look, he patted the air, signaling for her to follow suit. That it'd be all right. Zoë lowered her weapon slowly, though the odd expression on her face remained. Of course she was confused. She hadn't heard Price as Arthur had.

At Price's words, Purcell stopped his pounding on the door and turned around. He knew what was coming and stabbed his gun out again, readying it to fire, but his finger held firm on the half-squeezed trigger. His entire body was frozen, as was Vapula's.

Do you not regret what you have done?

"It w-was all in the name of y-your work," Purcell said, pushing the words out with extra effort through rigid lips.

My work was intended to save people, not subjugate them.

The guns in Purcell and Vapula's hands suddenly fell to the floor. Their bodies appeared to unfreeze, relax. A look of relief grew on their faces, replaced a moment later by a wide-eyed expression as they realized something was still very, very wrong. They started choking, gasping for air, but they could not breathe. Oxygen all around them, but they could not inhale. They clawed at their throats and started to stagger forward toward Simon and the rest of the group, motioning with their hands, begging for help. But just as suddenly as their breath was taken from them, they stopped. Their bodies lifted into the air, feet stretching down, trying in futile effort to remain connected to the ground.

Zoë and Maggie each jumped back. Mouths agape. Though they'd been told about Price's abilities, had seen guards launched into the air, the sight of two men floating before them was still jarring.

Purcell and Vapula hovered in mid-air, faces turning blue as they continued to fight for even a single breath, as if trapped underwater. A moment later, their struggling ceased. Their bodies went limp. They hung suspended in the air for a few, long seconds, like forgotten puppets, and then flew back down the hall-way, crumpling together in a heap on the floor.

Simon could barely watch the scene as it happened, and was glad when it was finally over. He looked at Maggie, whose face showed just as much shock as his did. Perhaps more. Zoë and Arthur bore similar expressions, though less pronounced. All four of them had seen people die in recent days, and that had been difficult enough. But none of them had ever witnessed something like this. Men suffocated by invisible means. By nothing. Simon wondered how Price had done it. Had he physically blocked the airways of Purcell and Vapula, or simply forced them to hold their breaths? Either way, the deed was done.

Simon doubted he'd ever get the image out of his head. How afraid Purcell had looked, how Vapula seemed to have accepted his fate, even before their breath had been stolen from them. The fear they'd shown at the mere prospect of freeing someone like Price, someone with his abilities. Despite their evils of imprisoning Price, Simon could relate to that dread. He thought of the vault door being ripped from the wall. The guards flying backward through the air. What had happened to Zoë. And then, Purcell and Vapula, hanging there in the air before them, dead puppets on strings. Simon felt a sudden panic inside him, a nervous energy course through his veins. For the first time since they'd done it, he questioned if freeing Price had been the right thing to do. He was certainly glad Price was on their side . . . then he wondered if someone with those kinds of abilities—*that kind of power*—could really be on anyone's side but their own. And what danger waited for them all if Price decided they *weren't* on his side anymore?

Shit, Simon thought, realizing his error. Had Price heard everything he'd just thought about? Had he seen into Simon's head, heard his questioning ideas? There was no way to know, and that scared Simon even more.

If Price had heard Simon, he did not make it known. Instead, he remained focused on the task at hand.

Lydia is in there. I saw it in their minds.

"And you still can't reach her?" Arthur asked.

No. That room is something different. Some kind of barrier.

"Can you do something with the room itself?" Simon said. "Break down the walls or, I don't know, throw a table at Sullivan?"

No. I see nothing beyond the door. I cannot influence anything inside. That room is a dark space to me—a void.

Simon looked at the group, searching for signs of willingness. Then he realized Zoë and Maggie hadn't heard what Price had said, and explained.

"We need to be careful," Zoë said, and pointed to the crumpled bodies of Purcell and Vapula. "Those two were Sullivan's last line of defense. That means he's inside that room with Lydia, with his back against the wall. No telling what he'll do now. And if we don't have your friend Price the great and powerful to help us . . ."

Arthur nodded, shared a look with his commander. He needed no further instruction and moved toward the door. Zoë, Simon, and Maggie joined him, and the entire group approached together. Arthur reared a leg back to kick in the door.

Stop.

Arthur refrained, holding his cocked leg in the air for a moment longer as he looked quizzically up at the ceiling.

They heard a soft click come from the door. The lock, undone. Thanks to Price.

Simon reached forward, turned the doorknob, and pushed the door open.

The door swung inward revealing a small, gray room. In the center was Theodore Sullivan, standing near a table topped with the silver lockbox from the Regency Bank. Sullivan's tie was loose around his neck, the top button of his dress shirt undone. Under one arm, he held the small body of Lydia Darrow. Her hands tied together, legs hanging limply, face bruised and perspiring, her hair a scraggly mess. In Sullivan's other hand, a 9mm pistol, the muzzle of which he pressed to the side of Lydia's head.

Zoë and Arthur rushed inside the room after Lydia, stolen security rifles held high.

Still nothing? Simon thought to Price. *Even with the door open.*

No. I am sorry.

Maggie tugged at Simon's hand, meaning for them to follow. He did, but before stepping over the threshold of the doorway, Simon thought: *You won't be able to talk to us in there, right?*

Correct, Price responded in Simon's mind. *Be careful.*

Simon and Maggie entered the room. The group of four fanned out, making to advance on the man in front of them. Instead, they were forced to stop just as quickly as they'd entered when met with the barrel of the pistol in Sullivan's hand, suddenly pulled away from Lydia and waved in their direction.

Rodderick? Simon thought, but received no answer. He glared at Sullivan and tried once more. *Rodderick?*

Again, no response.

Nothing.

They were on their own.

45

"THAT'S FAR ENOUGH," SULLIVAN SAID, SLOWLY WAVING HIS GUN from side to side. The newly arrived foursome rooted themselves to the floor, though now only a few paces away. "Good. That's good."

"You can't shoot us all," Zoë said, a snarl on her lips.

"Maybe. Maybe not. I may not be as adept with a firearm as you and your terrorist friends, Drake, but I have fired a gun or two in my day, be sure of that."

"I bet you have," Arthur said.

Sullivan's gaze flashed to Arthur. The corners of his eyes twitched. He grinned and said, "Indeed. With people like you and your misguided cohorts out there—oh yes, I know who you are, very well in fact—a businessman like me can never be too care-ful. But I stand by what I said. If you try anything, I shoot without hesitation. Maybe you get to me before I can get everyone, but I highly doubt it." Sullivan motioned his pistol at Zoë and Arthur as he said, "Besides, you two would be first on the list. These others . . ." he nodded toward Simon and Maggie this time, "well, I doubt they are much of a threat. It seems they have enough trouble on their own, chased by the police, faces plastered all over the news—"

"You bastard!" Maggie yelled. "You killed my brother!" Color rose in her face as Maggie took a hurried step forward. Simon grabbed her arm. Sullivan waved his gun in her direction. She stopped, chest heaving, eyes shooting an infuriated stare at Sullivan.

"Did I?" Sullivan said. He blinked rapidly, raised his brow, and looked uncaringly at Maggie. He shrugged. "Hm, I don't recall—"

Maggie jerked forward, but Simon held her back. She struggled against his arms, trying to free herself, to rush Sullivan with all her anger, all her rage. For her brother, for *Will*. But in her struggle to escape Simon's grasp, Maggie looked back at him. Simon expected a questioning, angry look, but saw red, pleading eyes brimmed with tears. The tension in her body faded and she fell back into Simon's arms before steadying herself on her feet again.

Despite his continued erratic facial tics, Sullivan looked almost bored. He swung his gun back to Zoë and Arthur again. "Now that that's settled. You two. Drop your weapons."

Zoë and Arthur did not move an inch. The demand from Sullivan was heard, but the stocks of their rifles remained planted firmly against their shoulders, sights trained on him.

"No." The relentless snarl on Zoë's lips could almost be heard in her growling tone now, even in that single word.

"No? If that's the case, then I suppose one of you will have to suffice." Sullivan turned his gun back on Lydia, digging the muzzle into the side of her head hard, producing an anguished moan from beneath her mess of dark hair.

In that brief second when Sullivan pulled the gun away from them and moved it to Lydia, Simon thought that Zoë and Arthur could have acted. There had been enough time to fire if they were good enough marksmen and he had no doubt they were; enough time to possibly end all of this . . . but they had not moved, had not done anything. Perhaps they saw something Simon did not and chose not to act. More likely, he thought, in that instant they had felt something similar to what he had, and become distracted, if only for that briefest of moments. If that was the case, Simon couldn't blame them. He'd fallen victim to the same reaction countless times since meeting Lydia in the flesh. Seeing one of their closest confidants captured, bruised, and battered, hanging under the arm of a man who could not be reasoned with was one thing. But seeing that same person in the form of a young, seemingly helpless girl—even though they all *knew* Lydia was anything but—produced an instinctually different reaction altogether.

Sullivan pressed the gun against Lydia's head harder and her painful moan filled the room again. That did it. Zoë's hands relaxed, she let the rifle drop from her shoulder, and held it out in front of her. Arthur followed suit.

Sullivan grinned. "Now we're getting somewhere. Place them on the floor." Zoë and Arthur both crouched low, never taking their eyes off Sullivan, and laid their rifles on the ground in front of them. When they stood back up, Sullivan added, "Take a step back." They obeyed, each shuffling a single small step back from their guns. Sullivan pulled the gun he'd been digging into Lydia's head away, hefted her up so his arm wrapped tightly around her waist, and then repositioned the muzzle of his pistol against the center of her back, right between her shoulder blades, floating above her heart on the other side.

"Now then," Sullivan said with a wicked grin. "You've caused me a lot of trouble today. All for your little friend here." He squeezed Lydia under his arm.

"Why don't you come out into the hallway with us? So we can apologize," Zoë said. "We feel kinda cornered in here."

Sullivan sneered. "Do you think I'm that gullible?"

Zoë gave a flippant shrug in response.

"You can't trick me. I've been watching you," Sullivan said, motioning his head to the row of monitors on the wall behind him. An image of a hallway strewn with the bodies of guards filled one screen, the heavy, metal door from Price's room still lodged in the wall. Another image showed Price himself, still lying motionless on the table where they had left him. Behind him, the large hole where the massive metal door had been ripped from the wall. "I've seen what's been happening in this facility. What you've unleashed. I'm not leaving this room. Oh no. In here I'm safe, from *him*."

Sullivan squinted his eyes, his face squeezed together in apparent pain. Simon thought Sullivan looked like he had suddenly come down with an intense headache of some kind. But the next second, Sullivan's sneer returned.

But what Sullivan had said was right, Simon thought. Still, he wondered. *Rodderick?* He waited.

Nothing. No response.

They would need to find a way to lure Sullivan out, if they could. Otherwise, they'd have to take care of him on their own.

"I designed it myself," Sullivan continued, his eyes sweeping the room, stopping briefly on the examination bed against the wall. "For my personal experiments. It keeps *him*," Sullivan nodded beyond Simon and the rest of the group, back into the hallway, where Price's influence was free to roam, "from messing around in here." He ended by raising the gun from Lydia's back, tapping the side of his head with the barrel, and then quickly replacing it between her shoulder blades.

"Are we supposed to praise you for your cleverness?" Zoë said, unimpressed. "Sorry to disappoint, Teddy."

Sullivan sneered and dug the pistol's muzzle harder into Lydia's back. She moaned in pain. "Go on. Keep talking and you know what'll happen."

Zoë fell silent and Sullivan grinned.

"That's more—"

"Do it." The voice sounded odd, yet still familiar. It was Lydia, who'd managed to remove the gag over her mouth with her tied hands. She'd found her voice again while Sullivan had been chatting on. "Shoot him," Lydia croaked from under her adversary's arm. "Forget about me, just do—"

Sullivan shook her again, squeezed her tighter, rougher.

"Quiet!" Sullivan said. "They wouldn't dare pick up their guns against me if it means losing their precious leader. What would they do without you?"

"Shoot him," Lydia croaked again, her voice weakened from interrogation. "I'm ready to die if it means stopping this bastard."

"I told you to be quiet!" Sullivan quickly snapped the gun up and struck Lydia on the back of the head. She screamed as a fresh wound opened on the spot, warm blood leaking out. Her head lolled momentarily, and Simon wondered if she had lost consciousness. A second later, Lydia moaned and picked her head up again in a dazed sort of way. Her groaning ceased when Sullivan returned the gun to its previous position, muzzle pressed deep into her back.

"You won't get away with this." The words surprised Simon, even as they came from his mouth. Mainly because the sentence sounded so . . . cheesy, like dialogue from an old action movie or something he'd heard in one of the police procedurals Will had liked to watch. He looked sideways at the group for strength, but found Zoë and Arthur's gazes locked forward on Sullivan. Maggie was the only one who looked back and she gave him a reaffirming nod.

"I won't?" Sullivan said incredulously. "I won't get away with what? Securing my company? Keeping my investment safe?"

"*Your investment*? Is that all you see him as now? He's a *human being*, Sullivan. You can't—"

Sullivan squinted in pain again but pushed through it.

"Yes I can! I will do whatever it takes to keep this company running and at the forefront of advancement! The service we provide is saving humanity. The whole world needs it."

"Do they though?"

Sullivan shook his head at Simon, confused. He looked at the rest of the room's occupants, as if appealing for support. "Of course they do! They need it! And we provide that service. *I* do! I'm taking Rejuvenation beyond anything *he* ever thought possible. I am advancing the human race beyond anything we ever imagined. You've seen what is possible with your own eyes."

"What are you—" Lydia moaned from under Sullivan's arm, but was silenced by another rough shake.

"I'm doing the talking!" Sullivan screeched down at her. "I'm in control!" When he looked back up at Simon, Sullivan's eyes seemed to have grown larger, wilder. "You . . . You people just don't understand what's at stake. And you two," he jerked his head at Zoë and Arthur while squeezing his captor again, "you're as misguided as this little bitch here."

"You'll never have complete control," Zoë said.

Sullivan smiled a slanted, wicked grin. His eyes darted between them all, the corners twitching. "You still don't get it, do you?" he said, growling in pain and frustration. "None of you do. I've already won. You think because you found your way in here and caused some trouble that you have an advantage now? You think *he's* on your side. You freed him and in doing so, doomed him. He'll be dead in a matter of hours. His freakish power gone. No, no, no. You have no advantage. I can outlast you, in here. You and all your like-minded friends of the world. The Deniers, Abstainers, whatever you call them. All those foolish enough to refuse Rejuvenation, they'll all die eventually. I can wait. Then there'll be nobody left but us Rejuvenites and the true power will shift back to *me*. Because *I* know the secret. *I* know the power that lies buried in the human mind, the power *he* was able to tap into. And soon, I will tap into it too. While the rest of the world is damning themselves with a farce of eternal life, *I* will have control."

"You're fucking mad!" Simon said.

"I think not," Sullivan said. His voice was calm again, but his eyes continued to twitch. "Every person in this world thinks stopping their death makes them all-powerful. As if their tiny, insignificant lives matter. But I've discovered the true secret. Becoming a god doesn't mean living forever; it means controlling those who do."

"You've lost it, Sullivan," Zoë said.

"I'm not the one taking orders from a child."

Sullivan shook Lydia roughly again and gave a hardy, confident laugh.

A moment later, the faint sound of crying broke the air. It was Lydia. Her body trembled in Sullivan's grasp and she began to sob.

"Stop crying!" Sullivan said, looking down at Lydia, taking his eyes off Simon and company for a split second.

And this time, Zoë did not hesitate. This time, she made a move. Zoë didn't reach for her gun, but instead, launched herself at Sullivan. A second later, his eyes were back up, catching sight of Zoë hurtling toward him. Sullivan turned, putting his shoulder into Zoë, using his weight and strength to match hers. Leverage was not Zoë's ally. Just as quickly as she had lurched forward, her momentum was stopped and Zoë tumbled backward onto the floor at Sullivan's feet.

"I told you not to move, Drake," Sullivan said, and with that, pulled the pistol from Lydia's back, and fired a single round into Zoë's leg. The bullet pierced her calf, sending a bolt of fire up her body as the shot tore through her flesh. The group screamed. Arthur advanced a step, but stopped in his tracks when Sullivan raised his pistol at them all once more.

"I'm going to fucking kill you, Sullivan," Zoë growled through gritted teeth as she clutched at her second gunshot wound of the last 24 hours. She held her calf tightly, applying pressure, as she seethed up at Sullivan with fiery eyes. "You think you can wait us out, but you can't stop us forever. Kill us now and others will take our place. We'll never stop. Out there, or in here. Bullets or no."

Sullivan looked down on Zoë with his icy stare, and moved the muscles of his chin up into his lips in a considering gesture. "You won't stop, will you?"

"*Never.*"

"I believe you. I truly do."

The contemplative facial expression suddenly dropped from Sullivan's face. One corner of his mouth twitched, matching his eyes where that wild madness had returned. And yet, there was a resolute nature to his face. He'd made up his mind.

For a split second, Simon wondered if Sullivan was actually going to give up. Had he resigned himself to defeat? To capture? Had Sullivan realized he was no match for the four of them, or the man with the powers he'd held captive for so many years? But that second of hope dissolved from Simon's mind as quickly as it had entered. Had it ever really been there? He thought not.

Sullivan planted the muzzle of his pistol between Lydia's shoulder blades and squeezed the trigger.

The gun fired, and although Simon was sure he heard the shot, in that moment all sound in the room seemed to drain from his ears. The scene before him swam in slow motion as Lydia shook violently from the sudden blast of the gun against her back. Lydia Darrow's tiny body trembled as if in seizure as the bullet ripped into her back and through her body, exiting out her chest. The bullet buried itself into the floor, covered quickly by a spray of blood.

Arthur shouted "No!" as he vaulted forward. Zoë yelled the same from the floor, attempting to get up, but falling back on her injured leg. Maggie screamed in horror and Simon felt his insides turn, sick, even as his stomach dropped. All emotion drained from them, save for pain and anger.

Sullivan lifted his pistol again, pointed it at the group, mainly to halt the advancing form of Arthur and shouted, "Stop!"

Arthur froze. Zoë seethed. Maggie and Simon stood planted on wobbly legs.

"That's it," Sullivan said. "Stop right there, or you'll be next." With his gun held straight out, Sullivan bent his knees and lowered Lydia with an odd sense of care to the floor. As soon as her small feet touched the ground, he let go.

To the surprise of everyone, including Sullivan, Lydia did not fall. She did not crumple to the floor from the weakness of whatever beating she had taken earlier, or even the pain of the gunshot that had moments before ripped through her body. Though her legs trembled with her minimal weight, she remained standing, even as blood leaked from the wounds in her back and chest. Lydia raised her head, looking at her rescuers directly for the first time since she'd been taken from the bank. Her left eye was blackened, swollen closed, the color even more prominent in contrast to her pale face. Lydia's right eyelid flickered up and down, struggling to see. Her forehead had collected a thin layer of dirty sweat where strands of her dark hair clung in messy bunches. She tried to speak, but when she opened her mouth, only blood dribbled from the corners of her lips.

Lydia extended her bound hands and took a single step forward. Then another. Each one more of a stumble, as if she was lost in a dark wood, trying to find her way amidst fallen trees and roots strewn across the ground. She didn't appear to know where she was going, only away from the man who'd just shot her. She continued to stumble her way forward, and with her last step before finally succumbing to the stress on her body, Lydia reached Simon and fell into his outstretched arms.

Simon scooped Lydia's small frame into his arms. He looked down at her bruised and swollen face, red around her strained eyes. An even deeper crimson continued to leak from the corners of her mouth as she coughed and choked on her blood. He could feel the wound in her back, felt the warm blood leaking out, soaking into his shirtsleeves. He saw the mirrored exit point in her chest, blood spilling from it as well, and wondered, even amazed, at the amount of blood held within her. And even in that instant, Simon felt the familiar sensation he'd had so many times over the last few days, of seeing Lydia not as the wizened woman she was, but as a child. A child, shot in the back, dying in his arms.

Simon looked over at Zoë, up at Arthur, as if for help. Pleadingly, as if they could do anything to save Lydia, even though he knew they couldn't. No one could. Simon's gaze then fell on Maggie, who looked at him, tears streaming down her face. It was then that Simon noticed he had tears of his own falling across his cheeks. The sight of Maggie crying, the sinking pit of his stomach, the feeling of a friend bleeding out before him; it was all too familiar. Simon's mind flashed to Will, his laughing face, his lame jokes, and then, the sight of him bleeding in the passenger seat of a car. Will leaning up against a bright white birch tree. Will still smiling up at them, even as life left him.

And then, the hole in the forest where they had attempted a burial, the makeshift mausoleum where they had been forced to leave him.

First Sebastian. Then Will. So many others. All victims of the person standing in front of them now. Theodore Sullivan. The one who captured and tortured Lydia Darrow for information. The coward who shot her in the back. The man who thought himself a god. But Sullivan was no god, Simon thought. He was barely a man. No, if anyone was close to godly it was—

Simon's mind sudden broke from his anguish. It sprang to life, as if a fire had been lit in his thoughts, a blaze doused in gasoline. His eyes turned to Zoë as he considered the possibility.

Maybe.

Simon secured Lydia in his arms, even as she continued to tremble and choke. He lifted her as he stood tall and made to turn, to rush from the room.

"Stop!" Sullivan said. "Stay where you are."

Simon stopped, but turned his face to Sullivan and shouted, "We have to—"

"I told you there would be consequences if you didn't do as I say."

"But we—"

"Quiet! Just shut up. You're not going anywhere. You can't—"

"But there's still time to save her!" Simon barked back, overpowering Sullivan's words.

Sullivan's face went blank for a moment, dumbstruck by the interruption. "And why would I want to do that?"

"You don't understand," Simon said, turning to the door again, but hearing Sullivan tap the side of the gun he held pointed at them.

"Stop or you'll get the next one!" Simon halted again, looked back at Sullivan, glared at him. Sullivan went on, "Even if you hadn't chased away my staff or had that freak murder my guards, no one out there would help you. And she'll be long dead before you reach the surface. So you might as well—"

"But that's just it. I don't want your help, Sullivan. You, or your people. Jesus! All this time and you still don't understand anything. You've only wanted to take for yourself, never listen. You don't understand what he can *do*." And with that, Simon turned on his heels again, and stepped resolutely toward the door. One step. Another. In his mind, Simon felt like he moved in slow motion, as if the door was a mile away. He wondered what was taking Sullivan so long to yell for him to stop again. But with each step he took, Simon felt more and more confident that maybe, just maybe, Sullivan would simply let him go.

Simon was a step away from the doorway when he heard the gunshot. He felt it before that. The bullet. It ripped into his left shoulder and he felt his muscles go loose there. He struggled to hold Lydia up as he stumbled forward, propelled the last few feet by the momentum of a bullet from a coward's gun.

Maggie's scream sounded far away, dull in his ears. As did the other commotion Simon heard behind him. Had he turned around, in addition to seeing Maggie reaching for him, Simon would have seen Zoë kick her injured leg out at Sullivan. He would have seen Sullivan lose his balance, falling first forward, stumbling, and firing off another round, this time into Arthur's arm, before falling back. Had Simon been watching, he would have seen Sullivan tumble onto his back, lose his grip on the pistol even as Arthur kicked it away, while Zoë pinned Sullivan to the ground.

Simon would have seen it all, had his eyes not been locked on Lydia's. Despite the growing pain in his shoulder, despite the activity in the room behind him, Simon only saw Lydia. He saw her pain, her gasping for breath again and again, each one shorter and more choked. As Simon saw and heard what he knew was Lydia's last breath, he stumbled across the threshold of the room, falling through the open door, and collapsed onto his knees in the hallway outside.

46

———

SIMON WASN'T SURE IF RODDERICK PRICE WOULD EVEN STILL BE alive. While they were under the impression that Price still had a few hours to live after being freed, who really knew? It was all speculation. There was no way to accurately predict just how long Price would last once he was detached from the machines that had been keeping him alive for so many years. But it was all Simon had at that point. It was all he could think to do.

And so he fell into the hallway, landing hard on his knees with a cracking thud. Simon finally felt the full weight of Lydia in his arms. Not just her tiny child's body, but the weight of her person. Who she was and what she meant, not just to the movement, or to him alone, but to the world. He felt it pull at his arms, drag him down lower as he bent over her, staring down into her face. What little activity there had been in her eyes moments before was gone. She had stopped choking, stopped struggling to breathe. The sight of that eerie stillness made her feel cold in his arms, even as the warm blood continued to stain her clothes and his, dripping onto the floor beneath. He clutched her tighter, and as the muscles flexed he felt searing pain shoot across his back and down his left arm.

You are hurt.

Simon started, shaken from his thoughts and the pain in his shoulder by the sudden sound of Price's voice in his head once again.

Let me help you.

Simon shook his head, and inside it, thought: *Help her first. Help Lydia.*

I'm afraid she's too far gone, Simon. I can't.

But, you healed Zoë! Heal her!

My powers are not . . . It doesn't work like that. At least, I don't think it does. She is—

No! She can't be! Just try!

Simon. I'm sorry. She's gone.

"JUST TRY!" Simon screamed these words aloud in anguish. He didn't even realize he was switching from thoughts in his head to his actual voice until he heard the strained yell break his lips.

His voice reverberated off the hallway walls, then faded, replaced by far off sounds of commotion coming from inside the room behind him. He heard the click of footsteps approaching, felt a presence beside him, but did not turn to see who it was. He already knew. Who else would run to his side? Simon's focus stayed on the small figure lying motionless in his arms.

A second later, all was silence. No movement from the room. No voices. Not even breathing—his own, the person next to him, or that of Lydia.

Of course Lydia was not breathing. She was dead.

Simon slumped over her more, crying. He felt the burning sensation in his shoulder intensify, the blood pouring down his back and arm. He tried to push it all away as he spoke again in a weaker, frail voice, "Just . . . *try*."

A moment passed.

Nothing.

Another moment.

And then, there was a gasp from under Simon's slumped form. But it did not issue from his lips.

Lydia began to stir. One second, she had been dead in Simon's arms. He blinked, and when his eyes opened again, he saw her chest rising and falling. First in ragged breaths, then in more steady intakes . . . in and out . . . in and out . . . until she was breathing again with considerable ease. Her left eye, still swollen, and bruised, struggled to move, but her right eye fluttered, then opened. The gaze of that solitary eye locked on Simon's eyes once again.

At first, the look on Lydia Darrow's face was confusion. About her surroundings, what had happened, who this crying man was hovering over her. And then, in an instant, all the pieces of the puzzle snapped into place. Simon saw thoughts churning behind her one good eye, and all confusion disappeared from her face. Her new gaze held recognition and . . . something more. A *knowing*. Perhaps about what had just happened, but it seemed like there was more to it. As if she knew a secret, had learned something else in those brief seconds between when her breath had stopped and started again.

Simon smiled down at Lydia, his tears of anguish now of joy. He laid her down softly on the floor of the hallway and untied her hands. He was instantly thankful for the release of even her small weight. He felt relief come to both his arms, but more so his left shoulder, where the bullet from Sullivan's gun remained lodged. It tore into him more with every move he made, accompanied by an intense burning, like fire under his flesh.

It was then that Simon finally turned his gaze and saw Maggie at his side. She clutched at him, asked if he was all right, all while flipping her gaze between him and Lydia. He saw confusion in Maggie's eyes and knew she was questioning what she had just witnessed. Simon was about to speak when—

He felt it. Something . . . strange. It was different than the fire he felt moments before in his shoulder. It burned just as intensely, more even, but it wasn't actual burning. It was more like . . . a *warmth* inside him. At first, he thought it was unlike any other sensation he had ever felt in his life. It was a calming, soothing warmth that seemed to come from the very core of him. He felt it spread from the top of his chest, radiating through his body, surging to every cut and bruise he had sustained over the last few days, but specifically targeting the gunshot in his shoulder. That warmth pulsed there for a few moments. It was all he could feel, not the ache of his body, fatigue, or the rip in his skin from the bullet. And just like that, the sensation—that warmth—was gone. He no longer felt the bullet moving under his skin or the tickle of warm blood pouring from his wound. He felt whole again and knew the tear in his shoulder was gone without looking at it. Just like he knew the wounds in Lydia's back and chest were now gone as well.

That warmth. It had saved them.

Simon turned his gaze to Maggie again, locked eyes with her, and smiled. "Don't worry, Maggie," he said. "Everything is going to be okay now."

Maggie grinned back in relief, hugged him tightly.

Simon looked down at Lydia, who stared up at him with an inquisitive eye. Simon looked up, at nothing in particular, and said, "Thank you, Mr. Price."

"Price?" Lydia said, finally climbing to her feet on wobbly legs. "What—"

"It's . . . hard to explain," Simon said. "He's here."

"Who? *Rodderick Price?* But I don't underst—"

"Rodderick?" Simon said aloud. "Are you still with us?"

Yes.

"My God!" Lydia exclaimed, clutching her chest.

Simon grinned wide. He couldn't help it, even though it felt odd to smile at all after the last few minutes. In the short time he'd known Lydia, he could recall her mentioning God, in this way, only once. And even then it'd been with a mocking attitude. He understood Lydia to be a deeply scientific woman, with ideals based on proven facts, with no room for mere belief. In this respect, to hear her call upon the name of God sounded strange to Simon, even if she had, herself, been resurrected mere moments before. He figured the exclamation was in no way a sign of religious conversion, but simply a colloquial reflex. Even still, the words sounded strange coming from the lips of someone like Lydia.

Hello, Lydia.

"You . . . how am I hearing you?" she said, gazing searchingly around the hall.

In your mind, my dear woman.

"How do I know it's you? How is this even possible?"

"I know it's hard to understand," Simon said. "I don't fully understand it. No one does. It's a long story."

But still one I wish to discuss with you before I go.

"Go?" Lydia said. "You're leaving?"

In a way.

Lydia understood.

"You . . . You're dying?" she said.

Yes, but of my own free will. Thanks to your friends releasing me. Though, given my recent . . . actions to help you, and its draining effects on me, I fear I have much less time than I initially anticipated.

"But how—"

Lydia, as I said I do wish to speak with you about everything, but given my predicament and judging from the thoughts of Simon, there is something else that needs to be taken care of first. Before we talk. Before I move on.

"Oh . . . of course. You mean Sullivan."

I do.

"Sullivan's the one who kept Price here all these years," Simon said. "He kept him alive to try and use Price's abilities for his own gain. You heard Sullivan in there."

"I did, but I guess I didn't understand what he was really talking about. I thought he was just referring to the new procedure."

"They were both part of Sullivan's plan. The new procedure was so Sullivan could stop people from developing their minds. He wanted to find a way of using Price's abilities to control them all and hoped to become like him, only with the ability to truly live forever."

I believe you are right, Simon.

"Do you . . . do you want to deal with Sullivan yourself?"

If you allow me to, I will. Though if you wish for him to be tried for his crimes, then I am fine with that as well. I leave the choice to you.

Silence fell, in the hallway and inside their minds. Lydia stood still for a moment, her eyes on the floor. She stared at a dark red smear there, her drying blood, where minutes before Simon had held her lifeless body. Her brow was furrowed in thought. She opened her mouth to speak, then closed it, not uttering a word. Instead, she looked up, turned her eyes to Simon and Maggie.

Simon saw her gaze at once as he'd already been watching her. He knew that she'd been considering the options presented by Price. And now, she was looking at Simon, at Maggie. She was asking for silent guidance. At first, Simon didn't know if he could give any. How was he qualified to pass judgment on Sullivan? What gave him the right? But then an image of Sebastian flashed in his mind. An image of Will. And in that moment, Simon knew what he'd decided. But he did not say a word, only looked to Maggie.

It was clear that she too was deep in thought, about their situation, about Sullivan, about their entire ordeal. Simon knew she was likely thinking of Will. He wondered if Maggie had started talking to Price in her head, asking for guidance of her own or demanding Price give Will the justice he deserved. Simon wished he could see inside Maggie's mind, to know what she was thinking, what she was feeling, so that he could be sure they were in agreement. But he was not Price. He couldn't do such things. Instead, he relied on the information Maggie gave him—her confident eyes, the resolute expression on her face.

Simon, Maggie, and Lydia did not say a word to each other. It was as if they were all telepathic. No discussion. No debating. The looks they shared were enough. They agreed.

"Sullivan needs to pay for what he's done," Lydia said, "and for what he's tried to do. With the evidence we have on him and EXLI now, they'll have no choice but to shut him down. But . . ." She looked around as if searching for Price's disembodied voice. "He's kept you here all this time. He tried to use you. You deserve to deal with him in any way you see fit."

As you wish.

Simon turned and looked back through the doorway into the room. He saw Zoë standing, Sullivan's tie wrapped tightly around the wound in her leg. Arthur stood with her as well, ignoring the fresh gunshot wound in his arm. They flanked Sullivan, who sat on his knees, hands on his head. Zoë and Arthur held their rifles again, both trained on the cowering man at their feet.

"Bring him out," Simon said.

There was an ear-splitting scream from inside the room. Sullivan thrashed on the ground and tried to crawl away. Simon watched as Zoë and Arthur grabbed Sullivan and started dragging him toward the doorway.

"Do it!" Sullivan screamed, echoing Lydia's own words from earlier as he flailed his legs and arms. "Just shoot me now!"

"Nope, you're going outside," Arthur said.

"No! Don't give me to him! Please, no!" Sullivan cried out, kicking and screaming all the way.

They reached the doorway and pushed Sullivan through. As soon as he was outside, his protesting stopped as if someone had clapped an invisible hand over his mouth. Zoë and Arthur stepped into the hall as well, keeping their weapons pointed at him just in case.

Sullivan fell to his knees, his back bent and eyes on the ground. Though he was no longer protesting, he sobbed quietly.

As he watched Sullivan weep, Simon had to fight back a feeling of what he first thought was empathy for the man. He reminded himself of the atrocities Sullivan had orchestrated, the murders Sullivan had ordered all for the sake of keeping a secret. Sebastian. Will. Maxwell. So many others. No, Simon realized, he didn't empathize with Sullivan. He pitied him.

"What are you going to do to him?" Simon asked.

I have strength left for one more gift. I'm going to give Sullivan what he's always wanted.

Hearing the unrestricted words of Rodderick Price in his head had a frightening effect on Sullivan. He trembled uncontrollably on his knees and his skin went an instant ghostly pale. He flipped his head up, looking to the ceiling with bulging eyes.

"I was only trying to finish what you started!" Sullivan pleaded. "I was just trying to make us all better. To improve Rejuvenation to a level that you never dreamed! My intentions were good!"

It has been said many times before that some of the worst things imaginable have been done with the best of intentions, and that statement still holds true today. You may have started with admirable intentions, Sullivan, but it did not take long for them to become corrupt. Your mind has fractured. Make no mistake. The blame is yours. Your intentions turned sour long before you began tinkering around inside your own brain, trying to replicate my abilities. Oh yes, I have seen into your mind. I know the terrible things you have done to validate your intentions. All for the sake of your secret. What's worse, you began to enjoy it. I know you were there, Sullivan, the night Sebastian Martin was murdered. You may not have done the poisoning, but you were there. You sat there and watched that poor man die.

"It was your fault!" Sullivan cried. "Martin didn't have to die. *You* were the one who reached out to him. It was your fault!"

It is true that we are all to blame for a great many things, but some are more to blame than others. Some play a much greater role, Sullivan. I reached out to that man out of desperation, but it was you who decided to have him murdered. It was you who locked me away in the first place.

"But you created Rejuvenation! It's all your fault. Everything! It all comes back to you!"

I created Rejuvenation to save humanity, not enslave it. It was you who took that gift to the human race and twisted it into an abomination. It was you who took it too far.

So far in fact that you were about to unleash the worst plague yet on the world. To strip away the very essence of humanity.

Thankfully, there is still time to stop this last evil, and the first way of doing that is to stop you, Sullivan. You want complete control over your mind? You want everlasting youth?

So be it.

Sullivan released an even louder, piercing scream. He grabbed the sides of his head as he wailed in agony. A moment later, he collapsed to the ground, curling up into the fetal position. He raised a single hand, inserted a thumb into his mouth, and sucked it gently.

"Sullivan?" Zoë said, lowering her gun and looking down at him. She took a step toward him.

Sullivan shrunk back like a frightened child who'd just seen shadows move near his closet—the boogeyman come to claim him. He looked up at Zoë with large, watery eyes and continued to suck his thumb, mumbling nonsensical words in a trembling voice.

"What's he done to him?" Simon said.

Lydia stepped forward, looking down at Sullivan.

"Exactly what he said he would do," Lydia said. She crouched down, looked Sullivan right in the eyes, and tapped a finger to her temple. "Eternal youth. Just not the sort he was expecting."

MORE EXLI REJ. CTRS. CLOSE AMIDST INVESTIGATION

by Ellie Franks
City Globe, Sr. Corr.

The Kingsley Centre of Birmingham, UK and The Adriatic Conservatory of Zagreb, Croatia are the latest retirement facilities to announce they will be closing their doors as the investigation into EXLI Corp.'s private practices continues following shocking developments revealed nearly three months ago.

"We are saddened to announce the closing of these two great institutions," Henry Croft, acting head of EXLI Corp., said on Thursday afternoon. "Both were long-standing landmarks in their host cities and the surrounding communities. They will be sorely missed by the Rejuvenite families who frequented these facilities to visit retired friends and family."

When asked what would happen to the thousands of Rejuvenites housed at both locations once they are officially closed, Croft gave no comment. EXLI Corp. spokespersons have yet to provide any direction on this topic, leaving many families to speculate how retirees from all of the numerous closing retirement communities will be handled.

The City Globe reached out to the personal estate of former EXLI Corp. head, Theodore Sullivan, for comment, but received no reply. Sullivan, under stringent police cust-ody for an ever-increasing number of criminal charges, continues to be treated for what doctors have called "abnormal brain damage" suffered when a laboratory explosion occurred at The Shepherd's Institute, though they fear the condition irreversible. Readers may recall earlier coverage of Sullivan's condition, noting the degradation of his mental and speech faculties to that of infantile levels.

Sullivan's unchanging condition and the continued closure of EXLI Corp. retirement facilities trail the worldwide ban on the latest Rejuvenation procedure announced by Sullivan just a few short months ago. A ban resulting from critical statements made by leading Anti-Rejuvenation spokeswoman, Lydia Darrow.

Darrow's prior and continued interviews (see pgs. 6-8 for more) are based on personal accounts of what occurred in late September at the now-closed Shepherd's Institute as well as explosive evidence provided by the late Dr. Maxwell Lewis, former Senior Scientific Advisor at EXLI Corp.

"The closing of the Kingsley and Adriatic retirement facilities is a victory for humanity," Darrow said at a recent press conference. "It proves the world is listening. We must keep listening and learning if we are to right the ship that (contd. on pg. 2.)

EPILOGUE

Simon removed the thin, plastic bag from around the newspaper, unfurled the paper, and saw a familiar headline splashed across the front page. He thumbed through the pages, pulled out the sports section, and then dumped the rest of the newspaper into the recycle bin against the wall. Simon sat at his dining room table and smoothed out what remained. He had just started to read when Maggie strolled into the room.

"Good paper?" she asked, eyeing the recycle bin.

"This part is," Simon said, tapping the paper as he looked up, shooting Maggie a smile.

"Sure you're not missing out on anything?"

"Positive."

And he was. He knew Maggie was sure as well. She was only teasing.

He and Maggie had been there, months ago, at the first news conference held by Lydia Darrow. Thankfully, credit for the destruction left in their wake had been taken by the faceless entity known as Life Liberation. While Simon and Maggie escaped that blame, they still had to explain their role in the whole mess—albeit slightly fictionalized—and did so willingly. Simon quickly learned that speaking into cameras, addressing the entire world, was not on his list of favorite things. But it was necessary to clear their names for the murders he and Maggie had been accused of, so he did what he had to do. Maggie as well. After, they did their best to retreat from the spotlight, allowing it instead to shine on Lydia.

And Lydia gladly seized the role of champion, telling all who'd listen the lies and secrets of Theodore Sullivan and the EXLI Corporation. Almost every dirty little detail.

Everything.

The truth.

Most of it, anyway. While Lydia had been more than willing to share their story again and again, she had, after all these months, still left out one aspect. She had not told anyone yet about Rodderick Price.

Simon hadn't been present when Lydia talked to Price for the final time. Following her miraculous resurrection, and after Sullivan had been dealt with, she'd rushed away to the room where Price had been kept—held prisoner—for so many years. From the little Lydia had told them after, she proceeded to have a lengthy conversation with the Father of Rejuvenation, mind to mind. When Lydia met back up with them near the elevator, she had been lost in thought, her eyes entranced with a faraway look. She told them Price had gone. Simon still found her language at that moment peculiar, for a scientist. Not died. *Gone*. Lydia had told them that Price requested they keep his presence and unusual powers a secret, or at least try. So far, months into the investigation, they'd all succeeded.

Even the scientists and guards who'd worked in the underground lab seemed to be keeping their mouths shut. Whether Price had warned them, or they were all simply too afraid of EXLI reprisal, no one knew. Lydia seemed to think their experiences might start to leak out eventually. Whether the public believed them would be a different story.

At first, Simon had no qualms whatsoever lying for Price, or rather, omitting certain information when questioned. The bulk of the job lay with Lydia anyway. But as the days wore on, he'd begun to rethink the decision. Had they made the correct choice, keeping such a monumental discovery a secret? When he crossed paths with Lydia a few weeks later, Simon voiced his concerns.

Forever steadfast in her decisions and thorough in her justification, Lydia explained her reasoning to Simon and put his mind at ease. They should continue to keep the secret, she said, because it was a dying man's final wish. Just as everything Simon had gone through was to honor and follow through with Sebastian's final message. Just as he and Maggie had pushed on to find justice for Will. Lydia wished to maintain the same integrity for Price.

Her second reason took only three words to explain—words that Simon recalled hearing from Price himself, in one form or another. *We're not ready*, Lydia had said. Somewhere down the line, maybe far into the future, perhaps humanity would be ready then. For *some* of what Price could do, that is. But Sullivan and Price had shown them all that such a time was still a long way out. No one was ready to wield such power, Price had told her. It was too dangerous.

Simon agreed.

And so, the knowledge remained unspoken. The power, unmentioned. Zoë and Arthur also vowed to keep the secret, though their job was much easier as they didn't have to suffer the questioning of federal agents and journalists. With the exception of their efforts to exonerate Simon and Maggie, Life Lib had extracted itself from the aftermath of the story, kept to the shadows as any good underground group did. Simon told Zoë that with EXLI in shambles, there was no longer a need for such secrecy. Zoë had waved Simon off, told him it wasn't over, not by a long shot.

He knew what Zoë meant, but couldn't agree with her. For Simon, the battle was over. But for Zoë, it wouldn't be enough until all forms of Rejuvenation had ceased completely. A goal that Simon knew was impossible. Even if EXLI and the other, smaller companies performing the procedure were to stop, there would still be black-market doctors out there more than willing to administer Rejuvenation to paying customers. But Simon knew the total repeal of Rejuvenation would never happen. It would be closely scrutinized from here on out, but never gone for good.

And to his surprise, Simon realized he was fine with Rejuvenation's persistence. In proper circumstances, and with strict adherence and understanding of its consequences, he thought Rejuvenation could still be beneficial to the people of the world—a humanity with a renewed perspective.

Ultimately, that was the gift he hoped they had given the world—a new outlook on life. What he, Maggie, and the rest of them had been through, the secrets they'd uncovered, had rippled throughout the world. He hoped it echoed in the minds of every kind of person—supporters and adversaries of Rejuvenation alike. He hoped they'd forced humanity to take a step back and look at itself. Reevaluate the way lives were being spent. Question whether or not more time on the earth meant a better life. Or was the quality of that time what really mattered? After so many years, Rodderick Price had certainly made his decision. Simon knew *his* answer as well. The rest of the world would need to make up their own damn minds. He hoped they would choose wisely.

Simon looked up from the article he was reading on the front page of the sports section (SENTINELS DRAFT DYLAN!), his attention pulled away by Maggie. She was now standing in the kitchen and had just pulled a bottle of orange juice from the refrigerator. She noticed him looking her way and gave the bottle a gentle shake.

"Want some?" she said.

Simon smiled, but shook his head. Maggie pulled a glass out of a nearby cupboard, filled it, and then returned the bottle of OJ to the fridge.

Simon watched Maggie as she performed this routine task. He wondered how many more times she'd do this same thing day after day. How many times would she ask him if he wanted a glass of orange juice? How many times would he read the paper, listening to Maggie hum a tune down the hall as she dressed? How many times would she kiss him goodbye as they left for work? How many more times would they be together like this in the morning? How many nights? Days? How many times . . . But the real question was, how many *years*? They'd made their decisions; their road together had been laid out before them. Maggie told him, flat out, "*It can work.*" She said she would stay. Always, she would stay. No matter what. But Simon admitted to himself, and her, that he would understand if she didn't. When the future arrived, he'd understand. Because no matter what happened, no matter what else changed, one fact would remain the same. He would grow old and she would not. He would die and she would live on—not eternally, but for a long time after him. That was what lay ahead at the end of their road together.

"What is it?" Maggie said.

Simon came out of his thoughts. His eyes focused again on Maggie, who was looking directly at him.

"Huh?"

"You're sitting there staring at me and grinning like an idiot."

Maggie sauntered out of the kitchen over to the table where she placed her glass on top of the sports section and sat in Simon's lap. She wrapped her arms around his neck and looked right into his eyes.

"I suppose I'm just a fool for you," he said with a sly grin.

Maggie laughed, shaking her head at the horrible joke. She leaned in and kissed him.

"You mean that?" she said.

He nodded.

"Even tomorrow? And the next day?"

"*Forever*."

Simon kissed her again and in that moment, whatever uncertain thoughts he'd had about their future together melted away. It could work. It *would*. Yes, he knew what lay ahead on their road together, but he also knew they had plenty of miles to go before they reached that end. He loved her, and she loved him. He didn't need the ability to read minds to know that.

ACKNOWLEDGMENTS

Writing a novel is easy if you've got the inclination and at least a little discipline. You sit your ass down in a chair and type for hours and days and months and years until you end up with a fat stack of pages. It's at that point when things get difficult. Going from a first draft to the finished product you're holding in your hands is the real journey. It's long, arduous, and one that no author makes alone. *Apotheosis* is no exception and would never have been possible without the following wonderful people.

To my parents, Bob and Linda: there's a reason this book is dedicated to you. Thank you for being the best parents and always encouraging your baby boy's crazy writing dreams.

To Eleanor: thank you for being an amazing wife, for your unending support, and for putting up with me while I spent so many hours, weeknights, and weekends putting the finishing touches on this book. Love you moo.

To Laura Callison, Jill Harrell, and Tricia Crivac: thank you for being my first readers, of this novel and drafts of others. I appreciate your constant willingness to read my work, especially on this one, way back when it was just a meandering, incoherent manuscript. Your feedback and support then and since have been instrumental in making this novel what it is today.

To Keri Brooks, Chris Corbat, Andy Dixon, Sara Iverson, Nicole Milkovich, and Kim Wineman: thank you for volunteering as beta readers. Your honest, insightful feedback helped put the final polish on this novel.

To Kristin Cronkright: thank you for lending your exceptional artistic talents to this project and for your patience as I bombarded you with countless requests. The cover art is a real beaut!

To Kate Grace: thank you for your willingness to help out a complete stranger with his writing all those years ago, for your feedback, writerly insights, and continual support.

To Hannah Sikorski: thank you for your expert editing services that helped break this novel down and build it back up into something much stronger.

And finally, to all the other family, friends, acquaintances, and hey, even the strangers—anyone who ever expressed interest or support for my writing over the years. Every little encouraging comment and go get 'em helped keep the dream alive. So thanks.

RESEARCH

This novel is entirely fictional, including the Rejuvenation procedure which I initially conceived of in the winter of 2009. I knew what I wanted Rejuvenation to do for the sake of the story, but in developing the mechanics of the procedure mentioned in this text, I have drawn on and been inspired by actual scientific research. Most notably the article cited below. Do I understand everything in this article? Not even close. Was I able to grasp rudimentary concepts from it and then pick and choose the details that served my story? You betcha. At least, I think so?

So while the fascinating research outlined in that article is very much real, the fantastical manner in which I've depicted aspects of it in this novel is not. The views expressed are my own, as are the extrapolations I've made in interpreting that research. Still, I want to give credit where credit is due. Thanks for sharing your work with the world.

Fahy GM, Brooke RT, Watson JP, et al. Reversal of epigenetic aging and immunosenescent trends in humans. *Aging Cell*. 2019;18:e13028. https://doi.org/10.1111/acel.13028

ABOUT THE AUTHOR

Nicholas Crivac was born in Michigan, where he still resides. He studied English at Central Michigan University. When he's not writing, Nicholas can be found somewhere comfortable reading, listening to Bob Seger's *Live Bullet* on repeat, making pasta for his beloved Eleanor, or further exploring the true meaning of suffering via his unending loyalty to the Detroit Lions.

To learn more visit:
www.NicholasCrivac.com

Follow him at:

facebook.com/NicholasCrivac

twitter.com/NicholasCrivac

instagram.com/NicholasCrivac